FOR A FEW CREDITS MORE

MORE STORIES FROM THE
FOUR HORSEMEN UNIVERSE

Edited by
Chris Kennedy and Mark Wandrey

Seventh Seal Press
Virginia Beach, VA

Chris Kennedy/Seventh Seal Press
2052 Bierce Dr.
Virginia Beach, VA 23454
http://chriskennedypublishing.com/

Publisher's Note: This is a work of fiction. Names, characters, places, and incidents are a product of the author's imagination. Locales and public names are sometimes used for atmospheric purposes. Any resemblance to actual people, living or dead, or to businesses, companies, events, institutions, or locales is completely coincidental.

Editor: Chris Kennedy; Co-Editor: Mark Wandrey

The stories and articles contained herein have never been previously published. They are copyrighted as follows:

For a Few Credits More/Chris Kennedy. -- 1st ed.
ISBN 978-1942936848

This book is dedicated to CPL Shawn Thomas Lasswell, Jr., who was killed in Iraq on April 23, 2006, and to all the other men and women who have given their lives defending our freedom. This book is for you.

"And when He had opened the fifth seal, I saw under the altar the souls of them that were slain for the Word of God, and for the testimony which they held. And they cried with a loud voice, saying, "How long, O Lord, holy and true, dost Thou not judge and avenge our blood on them that dwell on the earth?" And white robes were given unto every one of them, and it was said unto them that they should rest yet for a little while, until it was fulfilled that their fellow servants and brethren were killed, as they had been."

— Revelation 6:9-11

Preface by Chris Kennedy

This book was born in the same place as the rest of the Four Horsemen Universe—in a bar. Mark and I were talking about the universe, and where we wanted to go with it, and we realized the galaxy was a *lot* bigger than we were going to be able to flesh out on our own any time soon.

We needed help.

So we asked some authors we knew, and some we just sort of knew *of*, if they'd like to help us expand our universe by writing a short story set in the universe. We were overwhelmed at the response—it will take us several books to accommodate all of the authors who immediately said "Yes!" when we asked them to participate. Like us, they found the universe a lot of fun and couldn't wait to jump in.

We gave them a short primer on the universe and sent them on their way with only two points of guidance: it had to be set in the Four Horsemen Universe, and it had to be good. As such, these 16 tales describe the highs and lows of life on the battlefield, as well as in the streets and alleys of the Four Horsemen Universe. While some deal with mercenaries, others introduce readers to members of the other guilds, organizations, and races. There's even a new form of life to get acquainted with and a look at alien interaction at its youngest level.

Like its predecessor, "A Fistful of Credits," "For a Few Credits More" includes all-new stories by a variety of bestselling authors—and some you may not have heard of…yet. Edited by universe creators Mark Wandrey and Chris Kennedy, authors Peter Cawdron, Rob Howell, Josh Hayes, Scott Moon, JR Handley, Corey Truax, Tim C. Taylor, Terry Mixon, Thomas A. Mays, Ian J. Malone, Troy Carrol

Bucher, Chris Winder, James Young, Nick Cole, Jake Bible, Kacey Ezell, Mark Wandrey, and Chris Kennedy take on various aspects of the universe, giving you additional insight into a galaxy where people will do almost anything for a few credits more.

Mark and I are indebted to the authors who participated in this project for their time and talents, and to David Weber for the foreword.

What makes David Weber worthy of kicking off this book? A New York Times bestselling author, he is one of the military scifi masters, having written a number of bestselling series, including the Honor Harrington science fiction series. If you don't recognize his name and body of work, you're not a scifi reader (and you'll want to fix that soonest—it's awesome!) He's also probably the best person I know—just being around him makes me want to be a better person.

Take a look at what David Weber has to say. He knows science fiction.

Chris Kennedy
Virginia Beach, VA

Foreword by David Weber

The great thing about electronic publishing, is that a ton of stuff that would never have made it into print with traditional publishing houses is available to be read.

The *terrible* thing about electronic publishing, is that a ton of stuff that would never have made it into print with traditional publishing houses is now available to be read.

This creates a quandary. What rules do you use when you're trying to figure out whether what you're looking at is likely to be the *great* stuff that *wouldn't* have made it into print or the *terrible* stuff that *shouldn't* have made it into print? How do you pick and choose, short of simply diving in and starting to read? And if you aren't one of those fortunate souls with unlimited time to spend spelunking through the labyrinthine bowels of electronic publishing, who *can't* afford to sample everything, how do you prioritize the effort? It's worth figuring out a set of rules rather than just deciding to let the traditional publishing houses decide for you, because there really is a lot of good stuff out there. But as the King of Siam says in "The King and I," when it comes to finding it, "Is a puzzlement."

Enter Chris Kennedy and Mark Wandrey.

Now, Chris is a friend of mine, so you might want to take this with a certain grain of salt, but, having issued that fig leaf in the name of truth in advertising, I have enormous respect for what he has accomplished, both in his life before science fiction (as a pusher, not an addict) and since he and Mark joined forces to explore the potentials of electronic publishing. And, I might add, that the two of them understand what a completely natural fit science fiction and electronic publishing truly are. They understand that they are dealing with a format here which is particularly suited to the sorts of minds and interests that create science fiction *readers*. Moreover, they understand that the realities of electronic publishing mean that if they don't consistently produce good stories, their patrons have any number of other places they can go to find them. Which makes it a good thing — for all of us — that they have demonstrated the judgment to pick the good ones for inclusion under their imprint.

Both of them do pretty darned good work as writers themselves, which also helps immensely, and they also have a grasp of something I think may be even more important — from the editorial/publisher's perspective — given the nature of electronic publishing in general. They understand the value of unifying themes.

There are no word count limits in electronic publishing, because photons are cheap and the supply of pages is unlimited. I'm sure all of us have encountered stories with too many words in them — some of us have even written them (although I have no intention of going there) — and that can happen even more frequently in an electronic format. Mind you, I'm not saying that it always does; I'm saying that it *sometimes* does and that it is something of which both writers and publishers need to be aware. My personal feeling is that, despite the potentially unlimited word count, electronic publishing is the twenty-first century version of the 1930s and 1940s pulp magazines. There's a constant need for new content, production costs are low, and it's an ideal format for *short* fiction. For stories that get up and move and deliver in a relatively tight word count. And for anthologies of short fiction or for shared universes.

And that, finally (I did mention that electronic publishing allows for unlimited word counts, didn't I?), brings me to *For A Few Credits More*.

Chris and Mark have created something that plays to what I consider to be the strengths of electronic publishing. Shared universes have been around for a long time, but as someone who's done quite a few collaborations in his time, I can tell you that the Internet makes collaborating incredibly easier than it used to be. I know, because I've done it both ways. Yes, I've been around *that* long.

Before the Internet, collaborators basically had to live in the same town — the same *house* was even better — or else accept interruptions in the writing process while mail moved back and forth. When Steve White and I were working on *Insurrection*, our first novel, I discovered that for some reason known only to the US Postal Service, it took three days for a letter from Charlottesville, Virginia, to reach Greenville, South Carolina, but it took ten days (on average) for a letter to go from Greenville to Virginia. We never did figure out why that was, aside from some pretty bad jokes. But it was a definite factor in the speed and flow of what we were doing.

Today, I can be working with John Ringo or Eric Flint or Tim Zahn and the chapter I've written, or the review comments they've inserted, can be emailed back and forth in seconds. That's an advantage that would be almost impossible to overestimate. And what is true for collaborative novels, is also true for collaborative universes — for *shared* universes.

That's what Chris and Mark have done here. They have provided a well laid out literary universe in which their contributors can labor, and they've taken full and intelligent advantage of that ease of communication *as well as* the availability of electronic publication.

The universe they've created is guaranteed to generate tons of action, it's also one that offers an enormous spectrum for the types of stories to be placed within it.

The Four Horsemen Universe is one in which humanity is the new kid on the block, very much at the bottom of the interstellar totem pole, with only one real asset: our willingness to fight. We're not the only species that *has* it, we're just the only species that doesn't have anything *else* to offer, and so, inevitably, we become some of the most proficient bounty hunters and mercenaries in a galactic "community" that makes China's Warring States or the condottieri's Italy look effetely civilized. There *are* rules, enforced by the various guilds, but just about anything goes *within* those rules and for those more enlightened races which don't like to do their own fighting (but don't much care who gets killed in the pursuit of their goals), humans become a valuable commodity. It creates a situation that is a natural setting for storylines ranging from "Rio Bravo" to "The Dirty Dozen" to "The Good, the Bad, and the Ugly," but with the addition of starships, nanotech, combat mechs that could give Optimus Prime a run for his money, genetic engineering, and good, intelligent speculative fiction that goes well beyond a simple "shoot up the bad guys" mentality. That delves beneath the surface of the action to examine why it's happening . . . and what it can cost.

Which is what brings us to the stories in this volume.

They cover a wide range of "other peoples' conflicts" from the human's-eye perspective, and Chris and Mark have chosen them with their usual discerning eye. I think you'll not only enjoy them but quickly discover why they've given this volume its title after naming its predecessor *A Fistful of Credits*. I'm not saying Sergio Leone and Clint Eastwood would have been right at home in *all* of them, but Colonel Mortimer and Manco could certainly sit down to a beer with the characters in most of them.

Some are stronger than others; none are weak, and which ones you'll like best ultimately comes down, as always, to your own taste as a reader. I can say only that Chris and Mark have done their best — successfully, in my opinion — to give you a varied selection.

You'll find something for every palate in this smorgasbord, and I look forward to book number three.

David Weber

August 28, 2017

Contents

Butch and Sundance
by Peter Cawdron

Moscow

I hate myself.

Standing in the darkness, with the barrel of my gun inches from the old man's head, I'm not sure quite how I ended up here in Moscow. Physically, it's pretty damn obvious. I boarded a sub in Chicago—strapped into the commercial suborbital flight along with forty other people—sardines in a can, and blasted into the mesosphere. At apogee, the skin of the orbiter went from negative two hundred to over five thousand degrees Fahrenheit in roughly a minute. Russia might be a shit hole, but I'll never tire watching the fireworks on reentry. Ballistic drops are always worth the hefty ticket price, even if some of the older launchers are repurposed ICBMs.

We glided into Sheremetyevo Starport, on the outskirts of the Russian capital. Glide is an exaggeration. Sub-flights are bricks with wings. There are no second chances at approach, no fuel for go-around if we're coming in long. Coming in short is worse. Like the shuttles of old, subs fall rather than fly. The pilot dropped that tin can like she was headed for the junkyard instead of refueling and returning the next day.

The mark lying before me is a scientist born in Kyrgyzstan, a former soviet state—a country that might as well still be in the Cold War. Aliens may have made contact, linking us with the Galactic Union and over 30 different interstellar species, but they still drive teams of horses to plough the fields in Kyrgyzstan. This poor bastard pissed off someone in some guild, and he's gonna pay.

Me? How did I get here, inside this shitty apartment off Gorky Park? Thirty years ago, I thought hunting for bounties would be cool—adventurous. I guess everyone starts out that way, but eventually it's about one thing—the money.

Most hunters like a public takedown. Perps tend to get flustered, taken off guard when they're out and about. If they run, it's a taser in the back. There's something immensely satisfying about watching someone writhe and spasm in pain beneath fifty thousand volts. Zeus never had it so good.

Me? I don't like to fight. I'm no coward, but bounties can be set for anything from fraud to rape—no one ever tells us. Frying someone's heart or blowing their leg off when they're being collared for the equivalent of a shitty parking ticket sucks. I'm too old, too soft. I need to harden the fuck up and stop being a Care Bear.

I flick the charge cycle and the gun hums. A tiny red LED glows in the darkness. My perp stirs. He may only just have been roused from sleep, but he knows. He's dreaded this moment for months. I doubt he's slept soundly since his contract was released. He had to know this was coming, but he probably didn't think it would go down quite like this. No doors being kicked in. No yelling. No pounding of boots. Just fifty thousand volts crackling beside his ear.

The woman beside him stirs but doesn't wake. Our eyes meet, and I gesture to the door. Slowly, he gets out of bed, grabbing a pair of jeans and a shirt. I keep my distance, holding the gun close by my side so there's no temptation for him to lunge at me. He seems resigned to his fate. No words are exchanged. He picks up a pair of sand shoes and sneaks out the bedroom door. I follow, closing the door quietly behind me. I'm expecting him to make a run for it, to bolt for the front door or try something stupid, like throw some furniture at me, but he understands that's futile and only going to end in considerable pain.

I turn on a small lamp by the television as he sits and puts on his shoes.

"Please," he whispers. "A note for my family. So they know."

I nod, and he grabs a scrap of paper and hurriedly writes something. I'll read what he's written before deciding whether to leave it, but I'm aware this could be a ploy. Reading is a distraction. Even if I keep my distance, it's time I lose eyes-on and he could grab a knife, or a gun, hidden under the pillows on the couch, or taped to the bottom of a drawer. He's been expecting this night. Surely, he's got some kind of contingency planned. I don't buy the note as anything other than a distraction.

Tears fall as he writes.

You're getting soft, Manning. Should have dragged his ass out of here. The prospect of avoiding a scene, though, has me second guess my instincts.

"Papa?"

Oh, shit. A kid stands in the hallway, rubbing her eyes.

"Go back to bed, honey."

The kid stands there. My finger's getting itchy. The job is to bring him back alive, but alive can be broadly defined. Generally speaking, a heartbeat is enough. As for collateral damage, that tends to be ignored. Fifty thousand volts is going to French fry a kid. Is this you, Manning? Really? You'd do that? You sick bastard.

"Get rid of her," I whisper.

"Go," he says. The girl is probably six or seven, too young to know what's happening, but old enough to remember. This is the kind of shit that messes people up for life. She yawns, turns, and shuffles back down the hallway. I gesture with my gun. Time to go.

He gets up and walks to the front door, leaving the note on the coffee table. I shift it with the barrel of my gun, turning it around, glancing briefly at it.

I'm sorry. I love you. Goodbye.

No code, not that I can tell. No rambling. No signals. Just honesty. Fuck, I hate this job. Bringing in scumbags is one thing. Suckers like this is another.

The perp opens the door. Floorboards creak softly. Outside, several police officers mill around. One of them's smoking. Old world habits die hard. The crackle of a radio sounds. Muffled voices. I close the door.

"No trouble?"

"None," I reply, pulling an envelope stuffed full of rubles. It's monopoly money given their crazy economy, but a couple of million rubles buys protection. The police here are a heartbeat away from the Mafia. I get a nod and a sneer. Job's done. The law has been enforced, apparently. They're gone.

"Down here," I say, leading my perp to the landing at the far end of the corridor. I should cuff him, rough him up a bit, let him know who's boss, establish dominance. Perps need to learn to be helpless, so if ever an opening arises, they second guess themselves. A fat lip and a bruise under the eye doesn't count as damaged goods, but his stooped shoulders and hung head suggest he's resigned to his fate.

What will happen to him? What happens to any of them? Don't know. Don't care. Stop thinking about it, Manning.

He stops by the window at the end of the hallway. I shove my arm in his back, pushing him up against the wall with the butt of my gun firmly against his spine.

"Stay." I'm peering out into the darkness. Not watching him. It's important to rely on haptics. My implants will warn of any muscle impulses if he starts to flex. "Jessie, we're ready for extract."

In my earpiece, the response is, "On my way boss."

I relax slightly and then shove him roughly back into the wall as though I'm trying to stop him from escaping, only he's like putty. He's not putting up any kind of fight.

With one hand, I open the window, hoisting it high. The wind curls past. Sirens sound in the distance. A flyer drops down the alley, kicking up a storm. Jessie opens the gull-wing door and brings the craft up to the windowsill.

"Move," I say. The perp climbs up, pauses for a second, probably to take one last look at freedom, however perverse that may be in Russia, steps on the running board, and then into the craft. The flyer sways slightly with the shift in weight, its gyros automatically compensating for the change.

Jessie looks at me without saying anything. I can see he's not exactly thrilled about our perp not being cuffed and sitting directly behind him.

I climb in, sitting next to the perp, digging the barrel of my gun into his ribs as a gentle reminder not to move. Firing a taser this close, though, would fry us both, but he doesn't know that. For all he knows, I'm on projectiles. No thermic barbs, but he must figure I'm carrying armor piercing rounds at least.

The door closes and we rise into the night, leaving bewildered neighbors staring out their windows, wondering if we're in a police cruiser.

"Starport, boss?"

Normally, I'm keen to skip the country as soon as possible, as the prospect of local law enforcement leaning toward someone with a bigger check book is always a possibility. The guild want this guy delivered to Argus-4, which means we need to get into orbit and jump on a freighter bound for the stargate. It's at least three hops to Argus, but—

"You don't like it, do you?" the perp says. "Too easy, wasn't it?"

I ignore him.

"How much are they paying you?"

"Shut it." This guy wouldn't be the first one to offer to double my fee. Problem is, then I'm on the hunt list. Money. It'll be the death of me.

Jessie pulls up into a sky lane, merging with other flyers and heading toward Sheremetyevo.

"Much chatter?" I ask. I can't put my finger on why, but the perp is right. This went down a little too easy. The Russians are touchy about bounty hunters operating on their turf. The GRU is normally quite intrusive, but there's no sign of Russian Intelligence monitoring our op. Either they're damn good, or absent. Both prospects seem equally troubling, as both raise the same question—why? Why throw tier one surveillance at a standard bounty pick up? Or conversely, why ignore it?

"Real quiet," Jessie replies, reaching down and checking the police scanner.

"Too quiet?"

"You tell me, boss."

Russia isn't lawless—it's that its laws are a racket. Even before the Galactic Union turned up on our doorstep, Russia was a blight. Justice is for chumps. Money is the only real law in this country. Rubles will get you anything from a flight to Antares to a sex slave—only slavery in this patch is willful. It's a ticket out of purgatory. There should be chatter. Deals going down. Cops monitoring merchandise being offloaded by shady traders.

"Inbound drops? Ballistic flights?"

"There's been a few, but for a Friday night, this place is like a ghost town."

"You're being played for a fool," the perp says.

"I'm no one's fool," I say, my finger tightening on the trigger. "Especially not yours."

"Sheremetyevo's coming up," Jessie says.

"Keep flying," I say. "What else lies along this corridor?"

"Not much. A few small towns. It's mainly forest and farmland to the north. St. Petersburg is about 500 klicks on this heading."

"And Finland," the perp says. "Smart."

It's as though he's reading my mind. If we're being set up, I want the authorities to think we're making a run to Finland. It's too far to reach, but if we're being tracked, it'll make someone nervous as hell as the flight time is only half an hour. If they panic, they'll show their hand, and we'll know what we're up against.

The other flyers in the air corridor bank, veering on approach for Sheremetyevo. Jessie follows normal protocol, gliding beneath the turn. I've got my gun buried in the ribs of the perp, but I'm up on my knees, leaning over the back of the seat, watching the airport.

Air traffic control says, "RF155, this is Sheremetyevo. Comms check. Over." It's a not-so-subtle attempt at subtly asking if everything is okay. They're watching us like a hawk.

Jessie says, "Sheremetyevo, this is RF155. Confirm comms check. Over."

"RF155, what is your flight plan? Over."

I hope Jessie isn't on transmit as I say, "Since when does an international starport care about a rental being flown into the country? Tell them we're heading for St. Petersburg."

Behind us, two flyers race into the air, avoiding the corridor and cutting across country toward us. The lack of navigation lights suggest they're military. I lose sight of them as they move away from the brightly lit port. Jessie relays our intentions and Sheremetyevo signs off rather too casually.

"You're a pawn," the perp says.

"I'm not liking this, boss," Jessie says.

"Go dark," I say. "Take us to the deck."

"You got it."

My stomach rises in my throat as Jessie dives for the ground. His fingers ripple over the flight controls. The first thing we did when we hired this bird was to bypass the regular GPS tracking circuits and transponder unit—not so much out of paranoia as good OpSec. Most of my habits are poor. Too much booze. Loose lips. Overweight. But if there's one thing I never cut corners on, it's operational security. Today, it's paying off.

"Volga River is 50 klicks out. We could make a run for there and slip below radar, hugging the rapids."

"No, those birds are going to have FLIR—they'll pick us up on infrared."

There are city lights ahead. I point. "We've got to disappear. Fast."

"On it," Jessie says as we plummet through 500 feet.

The sun is just starting to peek over the horizon, lighting the sky in a blaze of orange and yellow. I can see a couple of dark smudges, our pursuers. If I can see them, they're not more than a klick or two behind us. Too close for comfort.

"Heavy traffic?" Jessie asks.

"Yeah," I say, noticing our guest is as interested in our followers as I am. He's ignoring me and is more concerned about how quickly the military craft are closing on us.

"You think they're mercs?" Jessie asks, swerving between buildings, well below the safety limit for flyers, which causes some alarm from those down on the street. Like most cities following the advent of hovering vehicles, the streets have become malls, often evolving into sprawling markets.

"Nah, these guys are straight. No mercs. Not yet."

I'm dying to grill our perp. To bring down this kind of heat takes a special type of asshole. What was supposed to be a simple snatch-and-grab is looking decidedly political, and I'm wondering which factions are involved.

21st century politics got a damn sight more complex with countries being superseded by the world government and the guilds. Like the multinational companies of yesteryear, the guilds sway entire continents. For the most part, they're content to leave countries alone, but when conflicts of interest arise, the guilds outmuscle everyone else.

"You thinking GalNet has something on this guy?" Jessie says, pulling up and racing between local traffic. Our perp is deceptively quiet.

"Nope."

"Trade? Merchants? Mercenary Guild?"

"Fly," I say, not answering and not wanting to guess. I'm sure the perp knows.

This bounty was raised by the Peacemakers, although their name can be somewhat of a contradiction. In theory, they maintain peace throughout the galaxy. In practice, corruption, backroom deals, greed, ideology, and sometimes down-and-out stupidity rule the day. I'm not a conspiracy theorist, but I don't buy the party line either. Loyalty is a tool to manipulate people. Why ascribe cunning and deception when plain old coincidence and folly work just as well? People aren't half as smart as they think they are, and perhaps that's the biggest weakness within the Peacemakers. They're boy scouts. Three finger salute, honor badges, craft skills and fundraising drives and all. Problem is, that makes them predictable, and if you're predictable, you can be manipulated. Speaking of predictable, I'm kicking myself for jumping at a high-paying easy job. Nothing with big bucks is ever easy. I should have sat back and taken a good look at this mark. Should have done more background research before jumping in. Stupid.

Without an active transponder, we throw the air corridor into chaos. Computer nav units on the other craft switch to active radar to calculate our speed, trajectory and probable path, which has them swerving to maintain separation. Jessie's using their safety margins to hide us. By swooping close, racing up behind various craft, or peeling off behind them, we throw their computers into avoidance mode.

It's a bit like running among a flock of seagulls walking over the sand at the beach.

Jessie knows the drill. We've practiced evasion techniques enough, and he executes a dog's leg perfectly, working the angles, and finally cutting back and slipping into a parking garage as the troubled flock races on. We hover a few feet from the ground with our windows down and guns leaning out. Jessie's got a portable rocket launcher. I've switched to thermal barbs. Seconds pass. Nothing.

"Keep us on the move," I say.

Jessie stows his rocket on the front passenger's seat as I take one last look around. Sooner or later, they'll backtrack, so we can't stay here.

"Where to, boss?"

"Moscow."

* * * * *

Science

We join a civilian air corridor and fly at regulation speed back toward Moscow. Hundreds of military craft race past the other way, swarming into the region. Fighters, troop transports, a couple of gunships, even a heavy bomber. As I watch, a cruiser begins deploying mercs. Dozens of armored mercenaries begin falling from the open sides of the drop-ships. They're using rockets to control their descent. It's as though the knights of old, with their polished armor and chainmail have swapped lances and horses for machine-guns and jet engines. They fan out, landing by one of the markets. They think we've gone to ground and are looking to flush us out like dogs hunting pheasant.

"Keep her slow," I say. "Let's not draw any attention."

"No shit," Jessie says, sitting behind a fuel tanker in the slow lane.

I lose sight of the mercs, but they've got me worried. Mercs aren't supposed to be operating on Earth. They're supposed to be out on the frontier, clearing out hostile planets. Running a merc regiment in Russia is illegal, if the Peacemakers are to be believed. That's some serious heat for running down a bounty hunter and a mark.

"Just who the hell are you?" I say, turning my attention to our passenger. The name I was given was Alexei Popov, but I'm guessing that's fake. The wife and kids, though, I'm not so sure. Looks like he assumed a false identity and was trying to fly under the radar. I push the gun up under his chin, knowing the thermal barb loaded in the chamber will make the barrel uncomfortably hot.

"Ebenezer Scrooge."

"Fuck with me, and I will throw you out of this flyer and let them scrape you off the sidewalk."

"Jonathan Harker."

I pistol whip him, smacking the butt of my gun in the middle of his forehead.

"Doctor Moreau."

"Head for Khodinka," I say, slipping the gun into its holster and grabbing some cuffs. "Wanna play cute, huh?" I slap the metal rings over his wrists, locking them tight. A second set of cuffs hooked over the link on the first secure him to the rear door handle. If Jessie pops the door, it'll lift him off his feet, and I smile, almost willing that to happen.

"This is bigger than you can imagine," he says. "You're disposable."

"And you're not?" I ask. "Remember, you're the one with a price on his head."

"You're being used."

"Any more shit from you, and we'll deliver you at room temperature." That shuts him up. Although I've been commissioned to deliver a pulse, a corpse will still get at least 10 percent to cover costs. Right now, I'd settle for getting out of Russia alive.

"What are you thinking, boss?" Jessie asks.

"Dimitri Belgoff is deputy head of Signals Intelligence. If there are mercs on the ground, he would have swung the rubber stamp."

"You know him?"

"Only by cold-blooded reputation."

"And you're just going to waltz in there?"

"Something like that."

We descend into Khodinka airport, well within the ring corridor surrounding Moscow. The Kremlin is less than a minute's flight time from here, in the heart of the city, but the real action happens in the Aquarium—the headquarters for the GRU, the Russian Secret Service. Aliens may have integrated with human society, but rather than changing, some of our worst habits have flourished. Paranoia. Control. Manipulation. Greed. It takes more than a hyper jump to change our core nature. Just as the KGB never really dissolved with the fall of communism, the GRU is stronger rather than weaker these days. The Russians feel threatened by the guilds, so seeing them side with mercs is alarming. As a relationship, I imagine it's a bit like two porcupines fucking.

"We're going to have to ditch this thing," Jessie says, and I know what he means. It's a matter of time before someone runs a physical check against a flyer with a faulty transponder.

"Do what you have to," I say, climbing out through the open gull wing and dropping to the tarmac. "But keep him quiet and out of sight."

A light rain falls. I wrap my trench coat around me and walk calmly into the terminal. Domestic flights aren't subject to screening, although there are the ever present security cameras and facial recognition software, so I sit my hat firmly, angling it slightly across my brow. Computer algorithms are smart—too smart. But like most smart people, that also means they're easily fooled if you stray outside the norm. I'm five foot eleven and a bit, easily clearing six foot when wearing boots. Computers know that. They take those kind of details into account, so bounty hunters like me lower our profile. It doesn't take much, but when I'm on a job, I wear flats—hollowed out boots with an almost nonexistent heel to throw off at least one metric. Padded shoulders in my jacket, and a shorter, quicker stride, and the algorithms already got three mismatches that will help undermine any correlation.

I slip a few cotton rolls into my mouth, pushing them up above my gums. To the untrained eye, they look like cigarette filters, and I'm sure the NSA has wondered more than once why I keep ordering dental supplies, but positioning them high or low will change my cheek structure enough to throw the algorithms off the scent. To a human, it looks like I've got a swollen face, but computers aren't that smart. All they measure is numbers. Beat the numbers. Beat detection. Simple tradecraft like this has kept me alive more than once, and it'll help me get into GRU undetected.

A couple of Mendorian critters walk ahead of me. They're brute beasts from a star system 57 light years away and not known for their patience. I stay close, knowing eyes on them means eyes not on me. Mendorians are ugly by human standards, but then, aren't all aliens? Fluorescent blue tentacles, fishbowl eyes, teeth like a piranha—razor sharp and resembling a wood saw. Yeah, I'd be nervous if one of those guys smiled at me too.

I paid a small fortune for a fake ID before coming to Russia and almost didn't bother. Now, my paranoia is paying off. I take the tunnel beneath the river, jumping on the metro for one stop, and get off beneath the Aquarium. Security is tight, which is good. If it was lax, I'd be worried. I'm always happy when the other guy's nervous.

A set of escalators takes me up to ground level. Armed guards carry machine guns. Amateurs. The Russian obsession with control means they're slow adopters of alien tech. To be fair, bullets and MAC rounds are both equally effective at perforating a body. With aliens from at least five different star systems wandering around Moscow these days, I'm guessing the guards are skittish as hell.

I present my ID at the security desk and ask for Colonel Dimitri Belgoff. Movies always get this shit wrong. Sneaking in through air vents is dumb. They're a lot smaller than Hollywood suggests, and they're noisy as hell. Sheet metal flexing back and forth beneath two hundred and twenty pounds of alpha male is just plain dumb. As for waltzing in without building security, that's another surefire way to have your ass handed to you on a stretcher. Nah, nothing beats knocking on the door and being polite. Suspicion melts away.

The guard reads out the name on the ID, and I hear the colonel replying, sounding surprised. Why break in when asking nicely will bring him down? Curiosity—it's not just effective against cats. That's the thing about humans. We're as tough as nails when we're prepared and in control. Catch anyone off guard, and they're as weak as a baby.

Dimitri walks out of the elevators and through security, looking around for someone he might recognize. As there are three security desks in the lobby, spaced between the elevator towers, with seven guards wandering around, he's confused. He talks to one guard, who shrugs, pointing at one of the other desks. That's when I make my move.

"Good morning, comrade," I say, slipping one arm over his shoulder, and digging my pistol into his ribs with the other, carefully hiding it from view beneath my trench coat. '*Comrade*' is a nice touch. It's cliche, but tells him something important. I'm not Russian, therefore, I'm not predictable, so don't fuck with me. "Coffee?" I smile, pretending to laugh at something he said, as his face is as white as a sheet. There are so many people passing through the lobby, no one notices as we walk out into the rain.

"Tell me about Alexei Popov," I say, removing my arm as we walk through what the Russians consider a park in front of the Aquarium. Concrete seats line a gravel path. The focal point of the square is a hideous concrete sculpture that could be the remains of reactor four at Chernobyl. I can't imagine anything more depressing than working in a building called the Aquarium, looking out floor-to-ceiling glass windows at this monstrosity. Dimitri is tight-lipped. The initial shock has worn off and his professionalism is coming through. I respect that.

"Does the name Ian James Manning mean anything to you?"

He looks at me as the realization hits. He'd have a short list of bounty hunters operating on Earth.

"I'm a dead man, right? You wanna join me? Plenty of room in this grave."

"Popov is from Naukograd," he says. "And this conversation never happened."

"Understood."

Naukograd is one of the old Soviet-era closed cities, cities that never existed on maps until Google started publishing satellite photography. My Russian is a little rusty, but Naukograd means 'science city,' although science is a somewhat convenient term. Shit holes where Russians enslaved their scientists, experimented on smallpox, developed thermonuclear weapons, and generally plotted the destruction of the planet. Best I understand it, Naukograd isn't one city, but rather a general term for dozens of closed research centers. It's probably as much as Dimitri knows, even though he's SigInt.

"There was an experiment."

Here it comes.

"The results were inconclusive."

Bullshit. If they were, there wouldn't be a manhunt being waged by proxy. Whatever's going down, it's not being fought at my level. Popov is no fool. He knows Jessie and I are UPS. We're bit players, delivery boys. The Peacemaker Guild, the Science Guild, and probably the Merc Guild are locked in an arm wrestle over whatever Popov was working on, but this is a high stakes poker game—lots of bluffing, with no one willing to show their hand. I'll see you and raise you, now turn over another card.

Given these three guilds are ostensibly all on the same side, no one can be seen to be fighting the other. As for the Russians, it sounds like they were hiding Popov in plain sight. My police escort last night must have been a plant. Whatever I gave them was a bonus, a bit of icing on top of the cake. They were being paid by someone else, probably one of the guilds, as their allegiance to Mother Russia seemed dubious at best.

Dimitri says, "You'll never make it out of Russia." It's not a threat. He's stating the facts. We were supposed to play nicely. Dump Popov on a flight to one of the space stations and take a paycheck. How the fuck did I screw that up? The number one rule for bounty hunters is don't ask questions, and yet my gut still churns. There's something horribly wrong about all this. They wanted this to be a simple retrieval. The history books would show a valid contract issued and enforced. Popov would be brought in to stand trial and then disappear. History is an illusion of convenience. But the Russians teamed up with mercs to secure his passage off-world; why would the Russians sell out one of their own?

Gravel crunches under our feet as we walk around the statue. At the moment, the only card in my hand is that Dimitri would like to make it home for borsch. Sometimes, silence is the best interrogation technique.

"Popov was in the biological warfare unit," he says. "He's a geneticist. That's all I know. I swear."

"Keep walking," I say, coming to a halt by the entrance to the subway. Dimitri pauses. He's expecting a KGB special—a bullet in the back of the head. "Go." He walks on with his hands slightly away from his sides, his fingers spread, wanting to indicate he's not going to do anything stupid like reach for a gun, while not drawing too much attention to himself. He's not dumb. He knows his history. To avoid a scene, the KGB would walk a convicted man out to the courtyard, but before they got to the firing squad, they'd put nine grams in the back of his head, often just a few feet from the poor sap's cell. Messy, but it avoided theatrics. No staring down your killer.

I suspect Dimitri's done his homework on me. He knows I'm not a killer—or he hopes I'm not. The remote control taser badge still stuck to his shoulder, from when I first nabbed him in the lobby says I'm not, but he doesn't know that. Fifty thousand volts ought to numb his tongue for a good hour. As he reaches the automatic doors I hit the control, dropping him in the entrance and forcing a bottleneck. That'll cause maximum chaos, and throw the building into lockdown.

Back at the airport, I hail Jessie. A bright red Lamborghini glides down from the clouds with its fins extended beneath its fuselage. The hover jet kicks in at the last minute, and the sports flyer pulls up, flaring as it touches down. The gull wing opens, and I climb in.

"Good to see you're keeping a low profile."

"It belongs to Luzhkov." The blank look on my face speaks volumes. "Oligarch. He's the Speaker of the Duma."

"And he won't miss a red Lamborghini?"

"He's got dozens of them. It'll be a month before he realizes this baby never made it back from the shop. Besides, this bad boy will pull close to MACH 1, which could prove handy. "

Popov is sitting in the back with cuffs on and duct tape over his mouth. I reach back and rip it away in a single motion. Tiny red dots of blood appear where facial hair once grew. He won't need to shave for a month.

"What did you learn?" Jessie asks, maneuvering the Lamborghini to one side and resting it over a charging station.

"Pretty boy, here, is a scientist. Geneticist. Weapons grade. Peacemakers want him, only he'll never make it there. The Russians want to look compliant, but they're in league with the Mercs. It's all an act." I reach in and undo his cuffs. "Get out."

Jessie looks at me surprised. I back up, gesturing with my pistol. "I said, get."

Popov asks, "What are you doing?"

"Going off-script," I say. "Dumping your ass here at GRU."

"You can't."

"Why?" I climb back in the front of the Lamborghini, making as though I'm ready to leave him standing on the tarmac.

"They'll kill me."

"Why?" Same question, and yet entirely different now the context has shifted. He looks at his shoes.

"Your family is already being exfiltrated, aren't they?"

He nods.

"You're a traitor to the Russians, a liability to the Peacemakers, a weapon to the Mercs, and a paycheck to the oligarchs. Is that about it?"

Again, he nods.

"Did I leave anyone out?"

He shakes his head.

"Why should I care?"

"The Canavar."

"The Canavar are a myth," I snap. "At best, they're a legend. They're extinct if they ever actually existed. There's no more Godzilla, or King Kong, or whatever the fuck they were supposed to be."

"That's what they want you to think," he says as the rain mats down his hair, rolling down his face like tears.

"Who?"

"The Science Guild."

"Now, we're getting somewhere," I say. The Science Guild is supposed to be the gatekeepers. They're the glue that holds the Union together. Without them, everything falls apart—the cartographers, the traders, the Peacemakers, the mercs—none of it works without the boffins. I rest my boot on the side of the door, getting comfortable, knowing he feels horribly exposed standing in the open with security cameras on all the terminal buildings. If anyone looks too closely at some old guy standing in the rain, facial recognition is going to go ballistic. Us? We'll simply fly away. He'll be surrounded in less than a minute. I want him to feel particularly uncomfortable.

"There are limits to what the mercs can do, even with their powered armor."

"So they'll make bigger mercs," I say. "Something like the Raknar. Big nasty robots."

"Don't you think that if they could, they would have done that already?" he asks. "They can't. Material strength doesn't scale. An ant can lift a thousand times its own weight. We can't. There are physical limits."

"And that's where you come in?" I ask.

"Yes. Yes."

"So how does a geneticist overcome the physical limitations of a machine?"

"CRISPR but not on the germ-line. Somatic manipulation. Your cells."

That's meaningless to me. I turn to Jessie, winding my hand in the air, indicating it's time to leave.

"No, wait. Please."

I raise two fingers, and Jessie lowers the revs.

"Imagine if you could engineer your warriors. Not from birth. But on each specific mission. Giving them features adapted to a specific goal. Imagine if you could give someone the burst speed of a cheetah, the muscle density of a gorilla, or the crush resistance of a blue whale, allowing them to operate in a high-gravity environment without a power suit. Or the ability to see polarized light. Or increase their offensive capability. They could have the strike power of a Mantis shrimp, hitting with ten thousand times the force of gravity. Canavar wouldn't stand a chance."

"Neither would mercs," I say, suddenly understanding their interest in intercepting Popov.

"Holy shit," Jessie says.

"And this is possible?" I ask. "This isn't just theory?"

"I've engineered a virus to impart genetic sequences. We have had success—applying and reversing. Catch a cold and two weeks later body adaptations begin kicking in."

It's no wonder the Peacemakers want this guy. They want to secure his research, but without alarming too many people on Earth.

"Who knows about this? Your research, I mean. How widespread is it?"

Popov stammers, "My—My team."

"You're team's dead, right?"

He nods.

"And your records?"

Popov points at his head.

"Oh, that's bad," Jessie says.

"Get in."

Popov climbs in, slumping on the backseat. Jessie lifts off, taking us up into the dark clouds.

"I don't understand," Popov says. "Why isn't this a good thing? We can protect ourselves from the resurgence of the Canavar."

"For a smart guy, you sure are dumb," I say. "An arms race is predicated on gradual change. You make a better missile, the other guys beef up their defense. They make their missiles smarter, you counter. It's a seesaw, rocking one way, then another, but you..."

"You've changed the rules of the game," Jessie says.

I say, "What was well understood..."

"Is now meaningless," Jessie says, completing my thought.

"Whoever ends up with this tech is going to have a massive advantage over everyone else. They're going to get to dictate the rules. Other factions will try to reverse engineer it, but having a head start could mean winning the war."

"What war?" Popov asks.

"The civil war you just started. It's cold today. Hot tomorrow."

The gravity of what's happening seems to finally hit home for Popov. He stares at his hands as though they're stained with blood. They might as well be.

"Who took your family?"

"They—They were going to flee with the help of the Science Guild."

"Help?" I say, trying not to laugh. "In my line of business, that's not help. It's leverage."

"What have I done," he mumbles. His hands are shaking.

Jessie looks at me. Without speaking aloud, he mouths the words, "Should've left him down there."

I know.

"Wh—What am I going to do?" Popov asks, but he's not asking us. He's still staring at his trembling fingers.

"Where to, boss?"

I'm looking at a map. "Southeast. Join the air corridor to Kazakhstan. If we make the border, we'll run on silent down across the Caspian, over Azerbaijan and Armenia, until we can hit international waters in the Black Sea."

"And from there?"

I love this kid. Optimist. We probably won't make it out of Moscow airspace once they realize we backtracked and hit Dimitri.

"If we make the Straits of Bosporus, we cut down toward Greece, and Popov here claims political asylum. Hell, I'd settle for asylum in Turkey, but they're liable to turn us over to the Russians."

"The Peacemakers are going to come after us," Jessie says. I really do love this kid. He could jump ship if he wants to, make his way out of Russia on the next suborbital, but he's in for the long haul.

"They won't give up," I say. "You know that, right?"

He grins. Dumb bastard will die with that grin on his face, and I'll die with him, squeezing off one more round. Butch Cassidy never had it so good with Sundance.

"It's me, isn't it? Dump me and your problems are gone."

"Oh, it's not that simple," I say to Popov. "Cross the Peacemakers, and they'll ensure you have peace with your maker."

"There's got to be another way," he says.

"Spoken like a true scientist," I say as Jessie banks, joining a flight around the capital. Tourists are busy snapping shots of the Kremlin. We join them, faking our interest by tilting the Lamborghini, blending in, trying to avoid the attention of a mobile air block setup by the police.

"Science," he mumbles. "Publish or perish."

"What?"

"Publish or perish," he repeats. "It's the mantra among scientists. If you want to stay relevant, you've got to publish research papers."

"Or you perish?" I ask, not getting his point.

"In academia, yes."

I laugh. I know what he's thinking. "Jessie, make for the public library."

"Huh?"

"You understand, right?" Popov says.

"Publish or perish," I say. "Yes. You're only a threat until you publish. While it's all on you, everyone's after you."

"But publish," he says.

"And the genie's out of the bottle. The playing field is level."

"Exactly."

Lights flash behind us. A siren sounds.

"How long do you need on GalNet?" I ask.

"For a basic paper—couple of paragraphs outlining background, theory, technique, highlighting dead ends, documenting chemical pathways and splicing—an hour or two. It'll be rushed, but that would give other scientists enough clues. They'd be able to replicate my work and piece together the next steps."

"Do it," I say, "We'll run interference."

Jessie brings the craft down, swinging around the side of the central library across from the Kremlin, opening both gull wing doors. Popov slips over the side wing, rolling to the ground on the opposite side from the police cruiser tailing us. A Russian police officer walks over. He seems rather casual, but I can see his partner running our plates. Right about now, he's probably wondering if he's pulled over the son or brother of an oligarch. He'll be polite initially, not wanting to ruffle feathers.

"Your papers?"

"Right here," I say, leaning across in front of Jessie and pulling my pistol from my jacket. I hit him in the chest with the taser and his body shakes. He falls to the pavement convulsing.

Jessie floors the Lamborghini as I buckle in for a rough ride. The police cruiser gives pursuit. Several other cruisers swoop down from the clouds, joining the chase. We lead them away from the library.

"Let's see what this bad boy can do."

As we lift into the air, I can't help but feel both a sense of trepidation and excitement. There's only one way this can end. It's going to be ugly—messy—but if we can buy Popov time to get the word out, we'll get the guild off our back. I'm not sure how many laws we've broken, or if we'll end up rotting in a Russian jail, but the next hour is going to be epic. Knowing how well the skies of Moscow are covered, we're going to be front page vid for the next day, and that should spread public awareness at least. Who knows, maybe we'll shake them. Not likely, but sure beats running like a dog with its tail between its legs. Yeah, Jessie and I are just like Butch Cassidy and the Sundance Kid.

"Yeeehaw!" Jessie yells, pushing the flyer into a barrel roll as he races headlong through the air corridor.

# # # # #

Where Enemies Sit
by Rob Howell

“ “This beast and his assassins slaughtered an entire colony of Sidar! Why haven’t they been executed yet?” The voice screeched like a hawk celebrating its catch, the cry echoing in the empty hall appropriated for the tribunal. The speaker stretched his wings over me.

I grinned back at his attempt to intimidate me. After all, he was right. My platoon *had* murdered scores of his race on a little moon in a boring system. *What was one more? At least this time, I’d have good cause.* *Besides…*

“By Ch’kal’a’s blue bile, close those wings.” Still glaring at me, the Sidar folded himself so I could see the Cochkala Peacemaker adjudicating our tribunal flipping his prehensile tail irritably at us.

“And you.” The giant badger-like creature pointed his tail at me. “If I understand the mannerisms of your species aright, you bare your teeth when you find something humorous. Despite Anathiola’s rudeness, his question is pertinent. We see no reason for humor when innocents are murdered.”

“That’s certainly one reason we bare our teeth, Peacemaker. We also do so when we despise someone.”

“And you despise Anathiola?”

“I’ve not yet met a Sidar worthy of anything but.”

"Is that why you killed them?"

"No, but it sure made it easier."

Anathiola started to open his wings again but the enforcer flicked his tail at him dismissively, and I started laughing.

"Enough." The Peacemaker pointed at me again. "You are Lieutenant Frasier MacKenzie of the human mercenary company Queen Elizabeth's Own Foresters?"

"Yes."

"And you were in command of the unit employed by the Karalukluk Mining Consortium at Cimaron-283133-6A during the time in question?"

"I was." I grinned at Anathiola, showing every tooth I could.

The Peacemaker snapped his tail at me. "Do you not take these proceedings seriously? It is within my power to eliminate you and all of your soldiers."

"Might as well. There aren't many of them now, anyway. Besides, as I understand it, that's what you're going to do no matter what I say."

"Lieutenant," he snapped.

"Yes, Peacemaker, I take these proceedings with all the seriousness they deserve."

He regarded me for a moment, tail circling occasionally. Finally, he turned to the last creature in the room. "Kukuluki, do you have something to add to your hireling's rudeness?"

The Zuparti's eyes shifted from the badger to me and back. "We-we-we did not order this to happen, no we d-didn't, and we think a c-c-close look at the sensor logs would show that my, yes m-my company is blameless. Blameless. Blameless."

Kukuluki looked like a giant, overfed weasel, just like every other corporate lawyer I'd ever met, only here the likeness wasn't simply metaphorical. The race's chittering, stuttering speech pattern had seemed merely odd when I first arrived on station, but after several months, it grated on my nerves.

The Cochkala seemed to share my annoyance at the Zuparti. "Your people are often blameless in their own mind, Kukuluki. Yet your mercenaries murdered a colony of Sidar. Does anyone dispute that fact?"

The Zuparti did his weird hind paw twitch, like a cat covering its shit, which the species used instead of shaking its head. I glanced at my hands, which had never actually touched Sidar blood. CASPer gauntlets were easily cleaned, after all.

* * *

I jumped past the forklift as far as my CASPer would allow. As I flew across the garage, I rolled three light grenades towards the line firing at us. We avoided using the heavier K bombs on our CASPers when we could if civilians might be around. Even though the Zuul would easily withstand the small explosions, as would the Sidar in mining suits, it would make them all turn away long enough for me to reach my desired firing point among the far line of mining vehicles.

The plan worked to perfection, at least in the sense I achieved my goal. Some Sidar might have had a different opinion, however. I hadn't realized that they weren't all in mining suits. Part of a wing, smaller than normal, landed in front of my new position and splattered my gauntlet with blood spray. I ignored it and sent a burst of three rounds back at the line.

* * *

"Lieutenant, I asked if you disputed the fact." The tail of the Cochkala stretched like a spear at me.

I looked up. "Not at all, Peacemaker. By the end of that day, the remains of my platoon and a few Zuparti were the only ones living on Cimaron-283133-6A."

"See, even this beast admits he's guilty! As precedent dictates, you should summarily bestow clear title to the moon to the Sidar and assess a fine to the KMC." The Sidar tried to loom again, but the Cochkala would have none of it.

"Anathiola, sit down! I will not ask again."

The wings folded, and the Sidar leaned back.

"What would you have me do with the humans, Anathiola? If I decide to do what you ask, surely they deserve some punishment as well."

Anathiola's wings twitched, but he controlled the motion. "Punishment, Peacemaker? How can you punish them? They should be eliminated. As should all mercenaries who become murderers."

"As you say." The Cochkala's tail flitted in a circle. "This is foolish. Anathiola and Kukuluki, leave us. I want to hear the Lieutenant's version of the events without your interruptions."

"But—" Anathiola repeated.

"I said, 'be silent.' I've heard nothing but your complaints as we traveled here to resolve this. From both you and Kukuluki. I _will_ make sure this situation is resolved peacefully. If I do not hear the human's version—without interruption—the most peaceful result might be to drop *all* of you into one of this system's stars."

Grumbling, the Sidar and Zuparti left, leaving the two of us alone in the cavernous amphitheater. The Cochkala regarded me.

"Lieutenant. Why did you kill the Sidar?"

"You really don't want to know."

"No?" His tail stopped at a cocked angle. "And why not?"

"You just said you want a peaceful resolution. I'd happily get pushed out of an airlock if Anathiola and Kukuluki are in it with me. That's the closest thing to 'peaceful' you'll find in this clusterfuck."

"Clusterfuck." He turned his tail slowly. "If I understand the translation properly, that's an apt description."

"As I said, you really don't want to know."

He leaned back and rotated his tail for a while. Then the tail drooped. "I am sure you're right. I do not even want to be here at all." He smacked his tail solidly against the table. "I should never have let Anathiola talk me into coming."

"Let me guess, Anathiola convinced you when Kukuluki not only didn't argue, but instead also pushed for your involvement."

"How did you know that?"

I took a deep breath. "Just kill us all, including Anathiola and Kukuluki, and be done with it. You'll be happier in the long run."

"Ch'kal'a cover me in bile if I don't agree I would be, but I think I must hear it all." His tail drooped. "Just tell it to me. All of it."

* * *

"Uh, lieutenant, there's something strange going on here."

Before I could answer the voice on my comm, another voice snarled back, "Sunray Minor to trooper, you better make a proper report, or I'll do something strange up your ass!"

"Yes, Master Warrant Officer! 31b to Sunray, we have Sidar miners running out of their tunnels."

"Sunray to 31b, why do you think they are doing that?"

"Not sure, sir."

"And what are the Zuul doing?"

"The doggies look as confused as—"

The transmission broke off.

"Sunray to 31b, continue report."

No answer.

"Sunray to Sunray Minor, get all dets CASPered up."

"Sunray Minor to Sunray, already on it."

"Good, then get your section out to the mining shafts as soon as your CASPers are fully operational."

"Roger."

"Sunray to 31b, continue report!"

A breathless voice came back, "31b to Sunray—" an explosion sounded in the background.

"31b, say again."

"We're taking fire. The Zuul have us pinned down." A CASPer's 12.7mm gun loosed a three-round burst in the background.

"Sunray to 31b, Sunray Minor is coming with the reaction section."

"Tell him to fucking hurry."

That wasn't necessarily the last thing I would ever say to my Master Warrant Officer, but it was damn close. I turned my attention to the other active det.

"Sunray to 31a, report."

"31a to Sunray, we've got movement down the corridor in our side's seating area."

"Are you being attacked?"

"No, sir."

"What *are* they doing?"

"Hold one, sir." After a moment. "They're setting up a barricade." The echoes of an explosion sounded along with the report. "They opened fire when we approached."

"Be prepared to support Sunray Minor with the reaction section, but stay in place until the rest of the platoon is a go."

"Wilco."

"Sunray to Sunray Minor, 31a reports the Zuul setting up a barricade in the common area. They'll support your breakout."

"Roger, we're there now."

I cursed myself. *Of course they're there now.* The reaction section needed about 50 seconds to get their CASPers fully live and another 20 or so to reach the pressure door between the Zuparti living quarters and the common areas of the mining station. It's why we *had* a reaction section prepped in the first place. Over the months since we arrived here, the Master Warrant Officer had not-so-subtly ensured I created four watches, one active section, one reaction, and two off-duty to serve as a reserve. Now, his tone told me to keep my head in the game.

Which I hadn't done, as I had yet to reach my own CASPer. Our MK 6s took about five minutes to boot up and complete diagnostics *after* its wearer suited up. I sprinted down the hall to the armory.

The two off-duty sections waited for their suits to go live. A Coffee Crisp wrapper lay on the floor. Corporal Leeman always had one before suiting up and liked to twist his platoon warrant officer's tail by just tossing the wrapper onto the ground. He never argued about the extra pushups or miles running with his pack that the habit had earned him over the years. It wasn't the strangest superstition I'd seen in the regiment.

Even the support section was mostly suited, despite first preparing their other equipment. I hastened to get everything plugged in correctly while listening to the Master WO's running commentary of the breakout, which he accomplished smoothly.

It must have seemed easy to him, given that Master Warrant Officer Graham Russell had done and seen everything in his decades in uniform. He shouldn't have been here on Cimaron-283133-6A, but with the whole regiment deployed on various contracts, he needed to be somewhere. He and the colonel surely thought it best that he be with the idiot lieutenant on his first deployment, even if this was only a boring security assignment on a not-terribly-valuable mining moon.

I pondered my options as I waited for my CASPer to boot up. The mining station had three large corridors carved into the rock. Mainpath, the long axis, led down into the mines, where it branched out into a labyrinth of passages that followed veins of platinum, palladium, and rhodium. There were two crosspaths: Nearpath, which was closest to the surface of the moon, and Farpath. The quarters of the races were at the end of these two crosspaths, and the common areas like the shuttle bay, fusion plant, water extraction plant, gymnasium, and storage bunkers lay in the middle ground.

"11a to Sunray, we're a go." The two sections rose and moved to the door.

"Reserve sections rally to Zuparti area checkpoint when ready. Support section hold for me." My first and fourth sections shuffled off in the skating steps of a powered armor in light gravity.

"Sunray Minor to Sunray, checkpoint cleared. On our way to the mining section."

"Sunray to Sunray Minor, take 31a with you. The reserve sections are up and will be there in a moment."

"Wilco."

An eternity later, my HUD showed live, and I led the support section to the checkpoint.

Three wounded troopers met us on the way. Two were ambulatory, and they carried a heavily-damaged CASPer. My medic guided them to the room designated as an infirmary, and the rest of us moved on.

At the checkpoint area, Sections 11 and 41 had moved to cover all the exiting corridors, and the situation was stable. Troopers had shoved three Zuul corpses to the side to clear the way, and the doggies' copper-based blood left blue trails on the smooth stone. The blue blood seemed especially sticky under my booted feet, which was surely an illusion, but one I felt nonetheless.

* * *

"That was the first time I walked in another creature's blood, Peacemaker. I knew it would happen sooner rather than later in this trade, but I guess I expected my first blood to be red. Why should the color matter?"

He looked at me for a long moment and then twitched his tail. "Continue."

* * *

"Sunray to Sunray Minor, report."

"Sunray Minor to Sunray, slow going toward the mining section. We've found and disabled several booby traps, but we're proceeding slowly."

"Roger. I've got the other two sections, plus the support sections here at the Zuparti checkpoint. I'll have the support section get its weapons set up to hold here and take 11 and 41 in a sweep through the common areas."

"Roger. Will report when we get to the mining area."

The support section unlimbered the two heavier weapons I'd been assigned by the regiment, a MAC and a 120mm rocket launcher. The sappers armed several claymores and a couple of stunner fields we'd put in place, at the Master Warrant's direction of course, the first day we were here.

But I realized I'd been an idiot, green, cherry lieutenant again when I saw my long-range comms guy waiting for something to do.

"Sparks, set up a link. Send everything from all the CASPers, both comms and camera. Set up batch bursts to the regiment every minute."

"That's a lot of bandwidth, sir. And I can't guarantee it won't be intercepted sending bursts at that rate."

"Yes, but someone's going to have to clean up this mess, and it sure as hell won't be a lieutenant. Use the full regimental encryption and do what you can to make it as secure as possible, but let's make sure the colonel isn't surprised. I may not know much, but I damn well know he wouldn't like that."

"Yes, sir."

* * *

"Anathiola picked through all of that raw footage for evidence throughout the entire trip."

"Of course he did. I knew someone would when I figured out what happened to our suits."

The Cochkala rotated his tail slowly as he pondered my words.

* * *

"Sunray to 11 and 41, we're going to sweep through the common areas. Section 11 down Nearpath. 11a, you get close to Mainpath and set up a covering position to keep anyone from going in and out of the shuttle bay. 11b, you sweep in this order the fusion plant, water plant, and the refined ore bunkers. 41a, get out in Farpath and cover all the doors. 41b, when 41a has coverage, hustle down to Mainpath and make sure the Master Warrant Officer has a clear path to retreat. 11 and 41, Contingency Plan Gamma. I say again, Gamma."

"Sunray Minor to Sunray, CP Gamma? Over."

"Sunray to Sunray Minor, I know we'll take fire, and maybe casualties, but there'll be a bunch of Sidar civvies in here. The Zuul might use them to hide behind. We can't fire at every bit of movement."

"Sir, this is technically a battle zone not initiated by us. According to the rules of the Mercenary Guild, civilian casualties are expected."

"We're the Foresters, Master Warrant. We're going to avoid civilian casualties even if the law says we aren't at fault."

"I get that sir, but we don't have all that many casualties to take."

"I know. That's why your sections are CP Alpha. Take it to them in the mining area. They already fired on 31b. Also, the mining suits should reduce civilian casualties out there."

"Roger."

* * *

"To clarify, Lieutenant, you instructed your troops to fire only when fired upon?"

"Yes, Peacemaker. Contingency Plan Gamma anticipated a conflict where civilians were present or likely to be. Our instructions were to hold fire until a target shot at us, set our rifles to single-shot, not three-round bursts or full-auto, and to limit use of powerful lethal area-effect weapons like K bombs to situations where multiple targets presented a clear threat to our troopers. I think it's also important to note that we are a poor unit."

"So?"

"I wanted you to be aware that what most of our suits were firing were 12.7mm cannon rounds, usually loaded with high-explosive anti-tank rounds. We couldn't afford MACs for our suits, so we relied on the HEAT rounds."

"Ah. Then what happened in the Sidar quarters?"

"I'll get to that soon enough."

"Very well."

"The sweep through the common areas was a grim and slow process. You've got the raw footage. Initially, we thought we were only fighting the Zuul, but as you can see, the Sidar fought hard..."

* * *

"4 1b to Sunray, we're taking heavy fire!"

"Sunray to 41b, location?"

"Mainpa—"

My ears rang from an explosion and brief, sharp screech.

"Sunray to 41b, say again!"

"41b to Sunray, still taking fire. The corporal just bought it."

"How many Zuul?"

"None, sir."

"None?"

"Sidar in mining suits. Their lasers don't kill immediately, but they've got us pinned down. The corporal hid behind a corner, but a Sidar just bored through it, and he didn't realize until it overloaded his CASPer."

"Sunray to all sections. Contingency Plan Beta on all Sidar in mining suits. I say again, CP Beta on Sidar in mining suits."

"Sunray to Sunray Minor—"

"I heard, el-tee. Good call on changed CP. We're now facing suited Sidar here too. Looks like low-powered lasers; we've got 20-25 seconds to get them off us before they burn through. It's fucking with our cameras, though."

"Roger. And the Zuul?"

"Their rockets penetrate about half the time. In these tunnels, though, we're often too close to the Zuul for their rounds to even arm. We're taking it to them since they don't have armor. And to be honest, they are not near as organized as I expected."

"OK. Let's use that. Hit them fast, then, and keep moving."

"Right in one, sir."

"Sunray to all sections. Rush them. Use your CASPer's speed. Fire according to your CP, but you are free to push 'em down with your armor."

I led 41a into the large shared gym. A Zuul det waited for us, but our rush took them by surprise. A rocket hit me, but it glanced off to send its tungsten rod into a rock wall. I shot a doggie, and the half-inch HEAT round provided me with a satisfying blue spray when it exploded.

Two of my troopers had followed in fast. They also left blue patterns on the rock wall with their shots, but the third hesitated at the door and let a Zuul get a good shot with his rocket launcher. The trooper was blasted back into Farpath. I fired at the doggie before he could aim again. One of his paw-feet landed on a treadmill standing up, as if exercising without the rest of its body.

Something about this small firefight bothered me, but I didn't have time to realize what.

"Sunray to Sections 11 and 41, status report."

"41b to Sunray. Stable now. Just killed four Sidar. Mainpath covered, but there's only two of us. One down, one headed back to the medic."

"Hold in position as long as you can, but retreat at a serious push. We'll be there soon." Out of the corner of my eye, I saw the damaged trooper staggering past, his gun arm truncated and clearly suffering from shock.

"Sunray to medic. If you got a walking wounded with a clear head, send him down Farpath to help another one back."

"Wilco."

"11b to Sunray, plants and bunkers clear."

"Casualties?"

"Two CASPers damaged by lasers, but more pissed off than hurt."

"Sunray to 11a. Casualties?"

"One gone to a rocket. Another headed back. His cameras took some laser hits, and he can't see."

"Roger. 11a and 11b, leapfrog forward. I want the rest of Nearpath clear. Hold at the shuttle bay."

"Wilco."

Sections 11 and 41 had started with fifteen troopers, down one from the TOE. I'd lost three dead, two more out of the fight, and at least two others wounded. *Was rushing them the right plan?* I shook away the doubt. Time for that later.

"Sunray to 41a, let's finish clearing Farpath."

No Zuul or Sidar were in the first long-term storage bunker we got to. Not surprising, given its long layout with shelves on either side but no good ambush spot. The same was true for the auditorium, but the next room, the vehicle garage, would be a bitch if Zuul occupied it.

"41a, there's only three of us, so let's be smart. We'll each toss in a flash-bang, go to the left, and get behind the best cover we find. Remember, the Zuul visors won't be dampened for but a second so hustle."

"Roger," they chorused.

I pulled the door open, and I took the tail end spot as we went in under cover of the flash. One of the Zuul was quick on the trigger, and a rocket caromed off my ass. It'd probably hurt to sit later, but at least I still had my ass.

As I had guessed, several forklifts and pallet movers sat in that corner, giving us decent cover. A Sidar miner lay crumpled in the corner, his suit's chest crushed where a CASPer fist had punched it in the rush. He had hoped to enfilade us with his laser, I guessed, but I would never get to ask him as deep as that dent in his breastplate was.

A quick succession of Zuul rockets impacted on the heavy vehicles. Several lasers flashed above us. We had about two seconds before the Zuul flushed us with grenades.

"Sunray to 41a, on my count, toss concussion grenades and flashbangs then advance along the wall. I'll cross to the other side and see if we can create some angles."

* * *

"Again, to clarify, you used grenades, not knowing if there were unarmored Sidar civilians in the room?"

"Yes, Peacemaker. To be honest, I never really thought about it at the moment. We were taking significant fire. There was at least a Zuul section and several Sidar miners. Our tactical advantages were speed and coordination. The light grenades we used wouldn't really do much damage, not like K bombs, but would give us time to maneuver. If I'd have waited to check, we'd have been dead before I could have used them."

"Yet your suits were resistant to the lasers and small grenades available to the Zuul. Would that have given you the time to look?"

"I couldn't take the chance. You're right; Zuul grenades needed to hit us directly to do much damage, but we were crowded in a tiny spot, and their odds were too good. And frankly, I assumed with all the lasers passing over us, all the Sidar were in their suits."

"And were they?"

"No. My grenade landed among three without armor, an adult and two immature apprentices."

The Cochkala contemplated the moment with his slow tail movements, before snapping it to me in a gesture to continue.

* * *

The quick rush got the three of us to decent firing positions giving us crossfire. The other two had reached their spot first, so several of the Sidar had focused their fire in that direction. I switched the selector to three-rounds and fired several bursts at their exposed flank. All three went down. Another Sidar had an angle on me, though, and hit my canopy with a laser I was barely able to turn away from. It stopped when a HEAT round from the other side went through its head.

I looked up again. Another CASPer was down, but the remaining member of 41a was pumping out rounds on full auto. They must have thought I was dead because the Zuul and Sidar had all turned towards him. I went down the line like it was a shooting range.

The other trooper on that side went down as I killed the last Zuul.

"11a to Sunray. The observatory is clear. Killed a Zuul det and two Sidar. No casualties for us, but there are four Zuparti and two Pendal dead."

"Sunray to 11a, confirm the Pendal are dead."

"Caught in the crossfire, I guess. Lasers clean through 'em."

"Roger."

* * *

"What were Pendal doing there? According to my records there were only supposed to be Sidar and Zuparti, along with such guards as they hired."

"Your records don't show the Cartography Guild sent someone, Peacemaker?"

The Cochkala waved his tail back and forth in a gesture of negation not unlike a human shaking its head. "The Cartography Guild?"

"The mining station was the only habitation in the Cimaron-283133 system, so the Sidar and Zuparti put an observatory out there. About a month ago, the Pendal arrived flashing all the credentials and arrogance of the Cartographers. The four dead Zuparti in the observatory were the scientists assigned to the station."

"Ah. If it has only been 30 Earth-days since arrival, then they would not be in my records."

"Let me guess, Peacemaker. None of the guilds share their records promptly with each other."

"You are correct."

* * *

"**S**unray Minor to Sunray, the mining section is clear."

"Sunray to Sunray Minor, how many Zuul did you face?"

"Eight."

"Confirm one eight-man doggie section, Master Warrant!"

"Confirmed. Eight doggies total. And about twenty Sidar miners."

"Damn it! No wonder we're facing so much fire. Get back here on the bounce."

"Can do. Out."

I skated over to the two troopers. Corporal Leeman would never again eat a Coffee Crisp wrapper, what with the laser hole in his breastplate, but Private Manning had crawled up the wall to lean in a mostly vertical position. A Zuul rocket had crushed her shoulder.

"Manning, what's your status?"

"Fine, sir."

"Bullshit. Can you get back to the medic?"

"I'm tenacious and versatile, sir. I can do it," she gritted out. If there was ever a time for the regimental motto, this was it.

"Right. Let me clear the hall, and you get back to the infirmary."

A huge, sharp crack sounded near the Sidar section.

"Sunray to 11. What was that?"

No response.

"Sunray to 11, I say again, what was that noise?"

Again, nothing but static.

"Sunray Minor to Sunray, it sounded like one of our K bombs."

"That's what I thought too."

"El-tee, if everything is that fucked up, don't rush to find out. That'd fuck things up even more. Be there in two mikes."

"Roger that. I'll send 41b up to get eyes on the situation and wait on you to advance."

"Yes, sir."

"Sunray to 41b. Get to a spot where you can see the Sidar checkpoint. Do not, I repeat, do not go any farther."

"Roger, Sunray. Advance to observe, but no farther."

I covered them as they went past my position down Farpath. Up ahead, they settled in place, with Sergeant Mueller leaning past the corner to take a peek.

"41b to Sunray. In position. The Sidar checkpoint is blasted apart. One CASPer down in front of it. I can't see the identifier from here. Shall we advance?"

"Negative, 41b. Hold there. Be there with sections two and three in a mike."

"Roger."

* * *

"This was the first you knew about your soldiers going into the Sidar spaces?"

"Yes, Peacemaker."

"And you did not order it?"

"No. I did not."

* * *

When Russell and the other sections arrived, we advanced to where I could lean past the corner to see the damage myself.

"Sir, we've seen nothing move since we got here, but I'm pretty sure 11's been involved in a firefight. I heard HEAT rounds exploding. Lots of HEAT rounds," said Mueller.

"Thank you, Sergeant." No time to curse. "21a and 41b, on my mark put a flash bang into the doorway. Russell, you take 21b and cross to the far corner. Try to get eyes down the corridor past the checkpoint."

"Roger."

Once Russell had gotten into position, he waved us forward.

"41b, remain here. Cover our tail. 21a, stay with me." When I got to the checkpoint doorway, Russell was pointing at all the impact spots where HEAT rounds had shattered the doorframe. "They blasted the hell out of this, sir."

"Gotta keep going, Master Warrant."

"That we do."

* * *

"You led your remaining soldiers into the Sidar section?"

"Yes, Peacemaker. We advanced with my remaining detachments leapfrogging to give us cover, but there was little need. It was only in the last part of the Sidar quarters that we found anyone living."

"And you killed them?"

"They gave us no choice. We tried to get them to surrender, but they just kept firing."

The Cochkala waved his tail back and forth. "That makes no sense. I suppose I can see why the Sidar might continue to fire on you, but the Zuul should have surrendered. Mercenaries don't fight to the death."

"That wasn't the only thing that didn't make sense."

"Oh?"

* * *

Russell and I stared down at the bodies of four different races in front of us.

"Well, I think we know why 11 came in here," he said.

"Yes." Six Zuparti bodies lay shredded by rocket fire, lasers, and HEAT rounds. I'd have minded that much less if four of them weren't Zuparti wardlings. The blood of the weasel children mixed in a purplish kaleidoscope with the blood of the two doggies laying on top of the pile, almost as if they had died to protect them. Three of my troopers and four Sidar encircled them.

"Master Warrant."

"Yes, Lieutenant?"

"Before we go any farther, I think we need to take time and think."

He cocked his head, clearly listening for more fire. "And the rest of 11?"

"Dead already. This was a trap, and I let them fall into it."

"No, sir. I heard you try to keep them out."

"Why didn't they hear me?"

"I don't know, sir."

"And that's why I—" My comms cut out.

His CASPer tilted, then he popped open his canopy. "Our comms are gone."

I opened my canopy in response. "Yes. Just like Section 11's."

"Our systems are compromised."

I nodded and looked at the rest of my troops. "Shut your comm systems down completely. Hand signals from now on." I looked by at Russell. "Warrant Officer, you lost two members of 21 in the mines, right?"

"Yes, sir."

"We'll retrieve them in utilities. No armor. As soon as we're secure, I want the CASPers off and into storage."

He tilted his head again. "A virus."

"I'd guess. Something that can't penetrate the walls here."

* * *

"Y ou say it was a virus?"

"Yes."

"That's extremely far-fetched Lieutenant."

"I know. I would show you the data…"

"But there *is* none." He rapped his tail on the table. "I find this lack of records most inconvenient."

"I thought so too at the time." I chuckled grimly.

"What happened?"

"Believe me, both Master Warrant Russell and I wanted to know at least as much as you do and we had time to figure things out. We first tried to pull the footage from Section 11's CASPers. The data cores are tiny and hardened. Even if our CASPers get destroyed, the cores have a good chance of surviving."

"But there's no data, Lieutenant. Almost like you erased it."

"It's harder to erase than you think, Peacemaker. The Regiment relies on that data. Before you ask, for that same reason, it's impossible for a trooper to halt the recording."

"And yet, there's no data," the Cochkala repeated. "I must say, Lieutenant, this does not look good for you."

I laughed. It was a long laugh. Harsh and bitter. "I was a dead man the moment you arrived here."

"Lieutenant, I can indeed make that happen!"

"And you will." I laughed again as his tail wavered in confusion. "Anyway, we then looked at the arrangement of all the bodies and their wounds. Since we realized almost immediately all of our CASPer's were compromised, we hand drew sketches of the bodies. We gave copies of those sketches to your forensic team."

He glanced at his slate. "Ah, yes, I do have them."

"Good. As you can see, the Sidar civilians were in the middle of the firefights. Most were killed by HEAT rounds, but many died to lasers and Zuul rockets."

"That, too, is in the examination."

"I mentioned a while ago that something about some of the firefights bothered me."

"Yes, what was it?"

* * *

"**S**unray?"

"Yes, Warrant Officer?" I had had nothing to do but watch as my remaining troopers gathered what evidence they could.

"Been thinking about the booby traps some."

"Booby traps?"

"The ones that slowed us in the mines."

"Right. What about them."

"They were all IEDs using mining plastique."

"None of them military designs?"

"Not that we found."

"What does that mean?"

"Well, there's another thing I've been thinking on. I read all the reports about the Zuul before coming here."

"Me too."

"They're smart and skilled, but here they fought dumb."

"So did we."

"We were surprised…"

"You think they were just as surprised. And that means all of this was done by the Sidar."

"Yes."

* * *

"**H**e was wrong, though I didn't realize it until after your forensic team arrived, and we were taken into custody. Or rather, he was half-right."

"You think the Zuul knew more than he thought?"

"No. They were even more blind-sided than we were. He was right on that. Had they had the time, they would have barricaded us in the Zuparti quarters."

"But they did."

"Not really. That barricade only had a detachment. They called them 'paws.' One paw to hold us down, that's it. If they were serious, they'd have had more in front of us. During the battle, I thought they had simply tried to get us to overcommit to the mines and therefore outnumber us in the common areas, but what really happened was the events surprised them. We beat them in detail. Their tactics rely on numbers and surrounding the foe, but they never had the chance to do it."

He rotated his tail around as he considered that.

"No matter how surprised they were, though, when the firing started, they fulfilled their contract. Whatever else you decide, I wish that to be reported to the Mercenary Guild."

"Why does that matter to you? And how can you say they fulfilled their contract? The creatures they were to defend all died."

"They're victims as much as we are. They fulfilled the contract the Sidar actually wanted, not the one they thought they were fighting for."

"I don't understand."

"Let me ask you a few questions."

"Very well."

"First, your forensic team has our data cubes, right?"

"Yes."

"And you have found most have no data at all. Only a few of them kept their records."

"That is so."

"The most obvious conclusion to arrive at is we went berserk and deleted the data in an attempt to cover up the massacre, right? Although the Mercenary Guild informs all units that the Peacemakers enact draconian penalties when a unit goes rogue, it does happen."

"On occasion."

"And if that's what you conclude, then how likely is Anathiola's request that the station be ceded to the Sidar."

"Likely, actually. There's precedent for such a decision. In fact, there's almost no other ruling I could make at this time."

"That's what I thought. Now, in this instance, what would that mean?"

"I do not understand the question."

"There are no other habitations in Cimaron-283133 currently, right?"

"Ah, yes, I see. If the Sidar are the sole owners of all habitations in the system, then they can claim it entirely for their own."

"However, if two races hold the system jointly, they cannot exclude other races, correct?"

"Correct."

It took a long moment for the Peacemaker to process the ramifications. "You are suggesting the Sidar sacrificed an entire colony in order to lay claim to this system? Preposterous. There's nothing in this system that valuable."

"Not exactly, and I think you could be wrong."

"Not exactly? And what do you mean, I could be wrong."

"You made the same mistake Master Warrant Russell made. The Sidar want control of this system, it's true, but I don't think the Sidar arranged this whole incident alone. At the same time the virus shut off our communications, our data cores were erased."

He circled his tail. "If, indeed, a virus eliminated all of your communications and your data core, it would seem more likely that you yourselves introduced the virus in order to protect yourselves than for the Sidar to have introduced one that helped you kill their own people."

"You're right. The Sidar never had a chance to insert a virus because we paid for protection from Sidar code. Nor was it the Zuul. We protected ourselves from their code, too."

"Those are standard precautions."

"Exactly. That leaves three possibilities. Ourselves, the Pendal Cartographers, and the Zuparti. Of these, we can exclude the Pendal, unless they are likely to volunteer for suicide missions where their species or guild gain no advantage."

"Logical. That would make me suspect you."

"Yes, and I don't blame you. However, I will point something out."

"Oh?"

"Were our data cubes the only data that was wiped clean?"

He swiped through his pad, looking at the forensic report.

"Yes. All of the Sidar and Zuparti computers seem to have all their data. The personal slates of all those in the station had varying damage, but they were not erased. In fact, many recorded parts of the firefight."

"Does that footage match what I described?"

"Yes."

"Thought so. Well, there's one other computer."

"Oh?

"The astrographical one in the observatory. And all its data is gone, right?"

He consulted his slate. "Yes. That is interesting."

"For two reasons."

"Oh?"

"That computer was by far the most powerful one at the station. It's the only one with the processing power to possibly bypass our security."

"Perhaps. And the second thing?"

"What's the only valuable data on an astrographical computer?"

"Processing from the telescopes, I suppose."

"Exactly so."

"You're suggesting the Sidar saw something that made the system valuable enough for this?"

"Not the Sidar alone."

"Oh?"

"The astrographical computer *could* bypass our security, but not quickly."

"So?"

"So, the only time any of our troops was in range of communications with that computer, which was shielded for data protection, was when Section 11 went into the observatory."

"That's hardly conclusive."

"True, but when did Section 11 stop communicating?"

He looked through the recording of my testimony on the slate. "Right after going into the observatory."

"Exactly. And it was only after the rest of us proceeded into the Sidar quarters that our CASPer data cores and communications became corrupted. When we were in close range of 11's corrupted CASPers."

"How could they anticipate you would enter the observatory to let the virus attack?"

"We had to clear the common area, meaning we'd *have* to visit the observatory at some point. Then the virus would spread."

"I suppose."

"All of the surviving data is from CASPers that were never in range of the virus. Nor did we ever communicate to the troopers in those CASPers."

"How can you know that?"

"Because it's all from CASPers of dead troopers. Even the wounded and special section CASPers were corrupted before we realized what was happening. Check the data yourself."

Again, he consulted his slate and his tail drooped. "It's completely circumstantial."

"But it's plausible."

"Not really. You yourself said the astrographical computer would need time, and it never had it."

"Yes. It would need time *if* it didn't have a vulnerability to exploit."

"Your systems have a vulnerability?"

"I think one was introduced."

"Introduced?"

"Yes. I think the Zuparti opened a back door into our CASPers."

"Again with the Zuparti. I don't see any advantage here for them."

"They're the only ones with the resources and opportunity to create the back door."

"Not your own troopers?"

"Nope. The handshaking with the astrographical computer had to happen too quickly, and we never had access to the observatory. In fact, only about 10 creatures had access to the observatory: the Zuparti and Sidar scientists and the Cartography Guild."

"That would not be uncommon for such observatories, in my experience."

"Exactly. The Sidar could not have introduced the opening. Nor could the Zuul. The Pendal had no reason. None of my troops ever had access. Only the Zuparti had access to both the astrographical computer and our systems."

He moved his tail back and forth rapidly. "It still makes no sense."

"It does if they saw something that's valuable enough. Something conveniently erased from the astrographical computer."

"F11 or red diamonds would be the only things."

"Exactly."

"But there are no sources of either anywhere around there."

"None that we know of. But I'll bet there's one only the Sidar and Zuul know about. And that's why Sidar lasers 'accidentally' killed the Pendal. Otherwise, they report this find to their guild."

"Assuming this tale bears any relation to the truth, I *still* don't see how the Zuparti gain."

"With shared control of Cimaron-283133-6A, what's to stop other races from following up when the Sidar and Zuparti start mining whatever this prize might be."

"Nothing."

"But if only one of the two races holds clear title?"

"Then that race would hold title to that prize. Yes, I see how the Sidar benefit."

"I think that the Zuparti and Sidar negotiated a deal where the Sidar give them a share, which they could do without ceding sovereignty."

"Yes, they could."

"And it's why we were the killers," I spat out.

"Explain."

"We're new. We've no real track record. There's no long history, like with the Zuul, of successful contracts. You'd have no reason not to believe we went rogue, right?"

"I still have no real reason."

"Why did you come here?"

"What?"

"Why did you come here? You told me earlier."

"Because Anathiola requested it."

"And so did Kukuluki."

"Yes. Which was odd."

"If you hadn't come here what would have happened?"

"Nothing."

"Right. The Sidar and Zuparti would share the system and the bodies would be spaced, but nothing else would change. The only punishment might be the Cartographers slapping some fines for their dead Pendal. The Peacemakers don't really care about things this small."

"That's true." His tail drooped. "My superiors suggested I just ignore the request."

"But you wanted to prove yourself."

The drooped tail twitched. "Yes," he said softly.

"By coming here you *have* to make a decision. Every precedent I know of says you have to execute me and my platoon, fine the rest of my company, and give the Sidar title to the system because it was the Zuparti's mercs that went rogue."

I paused.

"And now you know why I'd as soon you threw me, Anathiola, and Kukuluki out of an airlock. Those two surely know what's going on, and I surely deserve it, after getting more than half of my platoon killed. My only hope is you don't kill the rest of my platoon. And I will fucking *hate* to see Anathiola and Kukuluki profit."

His tail twitched, but mostly remained drooping. "I don't know why, Lieutenant, but I believe you. About all of it."

"The truth can sometimes be convincing. But it doesn't matter because no one else will. We've had too much time to create whatever evidence we want to fool your investigators. Our data cores are slag, and the precedents are too clear."

"Yes. And if I dramatically change the precedent..."

"That might encourage other mercenary groups to turn rogue."

"Yes."

He pondered things as his tail lashed about, getting more violent as he worked through things. Finally, it stopped and for the first time, I saw him bare his teeth. "Anathiola, Kukuluki, please return. I have made my judgement," he growled into a communicator.

They returned almost immediately. They radiated anticipation.

"First," the Cochkala began, "I will judge on the Zuul. It is a tad unusual, but I will report to the Mercenary Guild that they have fulfilled this contract." His tail waved away the Sidar's incipient protest. "Yes, I know that will cost your people a bonus, and I know they did not actually protect all of your species. However, I find no fault in their actions, and they fought until completely eliminated. For the record, I specify this as a unique change from precedent intended in no way to influence future decisions."

Anathiola folded his wings. He was not happy, but he still anticipated the great prize.

"Precedent dictates the Sidar should receive full and complete title to the moon Cimaron-283133-6A. This precedent exists for good and important reasons. No race should hire a mercenary unit and then use that unit to eliminate another race's presence in a situation where covenants between the races dictate shared exploitation of resources. Therefore, I judge in favor of the Sidar."

Anathiola and Kukuluki both quivered in excitement. The prize was theirs. I shrunk into myself.

Then the Peacemaker continued.

"However, Cimaron-283133-6A is a special case. The conflict here spread to members of the Cartography Guild. I find no evidence supporting the fault of one race or another in the deaths of the two Pendal assigned here. Therefore, I choose to assess no penalty at this time, though should new evidence arise, I leave this decision open to future Peacemakers."

Suddenly, hope filled me and I could breathe again.

"I also find that the Cartography Guild has a legitimate and important interest in the Cimaron-283133 system. I am sympathetic to the death of its members and wish their research be continued. Since Cimaron-283133-6A now belongs to the Sidar, I assign to the Pendal any moon, planet, or asteroid of their choosing to set up a new research station, and that station is to include open and free access to the Cartography Guild."

Anathiola and Kukuluki looked stunned. The Cochkala's tail twitched as their expressions confirmed my allegations more than anything I could have ever said. The look on their faces made what was coming completely worthwhile.

He forestalled any protest they might have had by continuing remorselessly. "Now I turn to the Human mercenary company…

* * *

"Thank you, Peacemaker."

The Peacemaker wrapped itself with its tail. "I do not deserve your thanks. You were right. I regret knowing what happened, and what I must do."

"You have no choice. You cannot open the door, even a little, for mercenaries to overstep their bounds. Even so, you saved my platoon. And at least neither the Sidar nor Zuparti will benefit."

"It was the best I could do."

"I know. And I did get one message from my Colonel."

"Yes," the Peacemaker responded. "It said, 'tenacious and versatile.' Nothing else."

"Nothing else was needed."

"I don't understand."

"It's our company motto. The Queen Elizabeth's Own Foresters never stops, and it always figures out a way. In this case, to get justice."

"Ah."

He paused.

"I understand your species clasps forepaws at certain times."

"Yes, we do."

"I think this is one of those times." He stretched out his paw before me until I shook it. He then turned around and left the airlock. When the hatch closed he turned back to look through the window before gesturing.

The outer door opened…

# # # # #

Boss
by Scott Moon

ULTRA MAX STATION

J ohnny Boss looked across the interior of the rented assault ship. The broker had spent an hour describing how reliable it was for a planetary assault, and Johnny hadn't argued. The fewer people who knew about this highly illegal insanity the better. Infiltrating an Ultra Max Prison had nothing to do with a planet in the traditional sense.

He wasn't sure if he had talked his XO, Gabriel Davenport, into the scheme, or if it had been the other way around.

The last three contracts he'd secured for the Ogre Fist Company (OFC, LLC) had made 10% profit. Problem was, he needed 75% to pay back money he'd borrowed to repair and upgrade the CASPer mechas in his unit. He needed everyone functioning at full capacity on every mission. Davenport had disagreed, as always, and claimed it'd be smarter to get special upgrades for the best performers in the OFC.

"Everyone wins or everyone dies in this unit," Johnny said.

Davenport snorted. "Idealists die first, Boss."

"Tacticians lead from the rear," Johnny retorted, holding the XO's gaze.

A moment passed. "Not this tactician." He shifted his weight, then tightened something on the cuirass of his armor.

Johnny settled against the bulkhead, his armor already tuned and synced.

He needed money; that was the first fact.

The second was that Jessup Moran, one of his better mercs, had been arrested for murder. Some of his Ogres thought it was a frame job, and some thought Jessup had always been too quiet and had been storing up rage that had come out at the wrong time. The thing was, Jessup wasn't the type to go rogue.

He was responsible.

Level-headed.

Idealistic.

So why had he run off to Calista at exactly the same time this mysterious, worth-more-money-than-a-battleship slate went missing? Johnny'd never seen a contract with this type of bounty attached to it—not for equipment recovery.

"This would've been easier if Jessup'd come to us in the first place," Davenport said. "You need better control of the men."

Johnny looked at him. "You're my executive officer."

"And you don't let me do things the way they need to be done. We're all killers, Johnny. If one of our mercs disrespects either of us, we need to land on them with both feet. You know I'm right."

Johnny stared at the wall, concentrating on all the things that had to go right if they were to survive an assault on a space station.

"You let Jessup off the leash. He stole a slate worth all our lives plus the price of a new house back on Earth, then got arrested for murder. Now you and me and the rest of the OFC have to break him out. Don't get me wrong, it's gonna be a good time, but some of us are gonna die," Davenport said.

"Says the Tactician," Johnny drawled, then counted to 10 in his head. "Give the mission brief, XO."

"All right, listen up Ogre Fist," Davenport said as he stood gripping a hand ring on the ceiling of the transport. "Everyone but New Guy over there has done this, but let's review. We must have surprise. That means no shooting until I tell you to start killing people."

"That's *no* shooting on this one," Johnny said without standing or raising his voice. "Snatch and go. Like a hostage rescue except from a prison."

"Peacemakers call that a breakout," Marney said, her voice scratchy from a nicotine lozenge.

"That's why we're not going to make any noise," Davenport said, winking so hard he dropped his shoulder and leaned forward.

The Ogre Fist Company mercs laughed and closed up their CASPers. Davenport continued the briefing in a rough voice. The only non-human in the group licked his chops, sealed his clear wolf-head helmet, and slammed a chemical laser magazine into his back-up weapon.

"Not so hard, Nightmare," Marney said.

The Besquith warrior growled but otherwise ignored her. Other members of the OFC jumped on the opportunity.

"That's what you say to Nightmare every night," Lamart, the OFC engineer and mechanic, said.

"That's gross," Marney said. "And true."

Chaos exploded on every radio link as Lamart stared as though he'd been hit on the helmet with a pneumatic hammer.

"Settle down," Johnny said. He leaned closer to Marney. "Really? Are you trying to make everyone lose focus?"

"Sorry, Boss."

"Get ready, Ogres," Davenport said. "Deploying in five, four, three, two, go…"

The hatch opened.

Johnny, despite knowing every detail of the plan he'd designed with Davenport and the senior team members, was surprised to see the inside of a landing bay. Even knowing the plan, he'd imagined jumping to the surface of the ultra-max station and cutting his way in with lasers.

His feet remembered the drill from dozens of previous ship assaults, a rare skill few of the OFC possessed. Johnny Boss had learned his skills in some high-speed merc units prior to purchasing the OFC charter. Moving toward the primary objective, he led Lamart, Marney, and Nightmare at a run—which could injure a novice in the zero-gravity environment. Ultra Max Station had spin to give the illusion of weight, but no thrust as a starship might use.

Without gravity, every magnetic step had to be perfectly timed. Too soft and you missed. Too hard, and you might give yourself a concussion from the kinetic force transfer releasing into your armor and your bones. A poorly-timed step could feel like landing flatfooted on concrete.

"Marney, don't forget the self-destruct timers on those relays," Johnny said.

She grunted.

Nightmare growled.

The hallway remained as vacant as his sources had promised. "Davenport, what's your status?"

"We're standing guard. No one's coming into your section. It would've been cheaper to clear this level the old fashioned way."

"Bribes have less consequence afterward," Johnny said.

Marney and Nightmare looked at him.

"You'll get paid. Don't worry about it," Johnny said, teeth clenched inside his armor. Keeping his battle lust under control was wearing him out. Worrying about money gave him a constant headache. "Stay cool. We get Jessup, we get the slate, and we collect the contract fee."

Marney and Nightmare smiled, her face invisible in the suit, and his mouthful of teeth disturbingly obvious through his clear helmet.

Johnny moved ahead of his team in search of Jessup Moran, who was supposed to be in an exercise room with a single guard. None of his OFC mercs knew what he'd paid to make this happen, and he prayed they never would. Some currency meant more than credits. He wouldn't have paid this price, not even for Jessup, if there was another way to save the OFC.

"Contact! Contact! Contact!" Davenport shouted over the radio relays. "Forget the knee shots, hit 'em in the torso. They can take it. Don't worry about killing them; they ain't worried about killing us!"

Johnny cursed and rushed forward, muting his speaker so he could think. First into the room, he saw three guards with environmental suits on standing around Jessup. The prisoner didn't have a suit on, though, and that was supposed to have been part of the deal.

"Team One, stick to the plan. Kinetic weapons. Keep the engagement less lethal if possible," he said, then fired 15 millimeter rounds at reduced velocities from his left arm gun as he moved. Three strides and three shots later he grabbed Jessup.

"Nightmare, I need one of those suits."

The Besquith merc jumped on a guard and convinced him to shed his gear. Johnny tried not to watch.

He prayed the low tech slugs he'd fired hadn't penetrated and ruined the suit Jessup would need if prison controllers vented the atmosphere. He knew they shouldn't, but things never worked according to plan in the heat of a fight. "Hurry up. We've got to go!"

New guards responded in teams of two.

Johnny pointed at the doorway to his right. "Marney, that's yours."

He faced his own zone and fired at each new threat, conserving ammunition. "Headshots," Johnny called out, stomach churning. Killing wasn't new to him, but shooting from the wrong side of the law pressed inward on his ability to think clearly.

"This sucks," Marney said as she dragged a body clear of her position.

Flash bang grenades tumbled into the room. Five guards in MK 8 armor rushed in followed by five more who went for Nightmare and Jessup like they had bounties on their heads.

Johnny clicked the firearm to his leg plate and pulled his laser carbine from his back, firing before he finished aiming. Instinct served him well. The prison Special Weapons and Tactics team scattered.

Marney staggered from an injury that pierced her left thigh plate. She fired her laser with one hand while trying to use a medkit with the other. Johnny ran across the room, posted in front of her to absorb and return fire, and grunted orders. "Secure your weapon and see to your injuries and armor."

Nightmare flanked the SWAT team and enfiladed them with laser blasts.

Johnny switched out the chemical laser magazine and dropped the partially used mag in a large pouch on the opposite side of his armor.

"Team Two, we have the principal. Rendezvous at the ship," Johnny said.

Marney finished spraying nanite gel into her leg, and gave Johnny a thumbs up.

"Nightmare, carry Jessup. I don't care if he can walk on his own. Let's move!"

He bounded to the front of their formation at each intersection, then allowed Marney to do the same, although she was limping badly.

"Is your CASPer damaged or are you hurt?" Johnny said.

"Little of both," she said.

Davenport and the rest of Team Two burst into the hallway from a smoking intersection.

Johnny cursed as someone bumped him hard enough to slam his MK 7 CASPer into the wall. "We're bunched up. Get into the launch bay and get on the shuttle. Best possible speed."

Ten feet into the room, with the shuttle already hovering for launch, the prison guards made a massive assault...platoon strength or greater.

Cheeto Briggs, the youngest of the Ogre Fist Company and part of Team Two, charged the guards with lasers in both hands. He drove them back but Johnny understood the effect would last only seconds.

Ballistic rounds and lasers slammed and cut and chopped into Cheeto's CASPer, knocking him off his feet three times. He rolled back to a fighting stance, twisted this way and that, and fought like an alley cat.

"Crazy ass kid," Davenport said as he stood on the assault ship ramp next to Johnny. "Get in here, Cheeto!"

In response to the order, Cheeto fell flat on his face as his CAS-Per went into death throes.

Johnny and Davenport ran to him, shooting guards and screaming the OFC war cry as they moved, then dragged the ruined mecha back to the escape ship.

"Cheeto," Johnny said as the ship fled the Ultra Max Prison.

"Boss?"

"You need to work on your technique. Having huge balls isn't enough in the Ogre Fist Company."

UNGRATEFUL

The ship dumped them on the first smuggler's world they came to with both pilots cursing Johnny Boss and the Ogre Fist Company in three or four languages.

It was hard to say what they said for sure. One pilot had foamed at the mouth, thick white goo flying on the wings of his profanity.

"They can have the environmental suit, or what's left of it after Nightmare ripped the guard out of it."

"I don't think they want it," Davenport said in a low voice. "It's evidence."

"Make it work. I don't have anything else to pay their extra fees." Johnny left Davenport to deal with them and slept the rest of the trip.

Later, when he'd paid the final bill and sent the pilots on their way, he parked his mecha in the first secure storage area he could find with an attached boarding house. He took a shower with real water and spent a considerable amount of time shaving. After that he ate two meals in one setting and went to check his wounded at the local clinic. Even a run-down smuggler's hole like this had certain amenities available to mercenary units in good standing.

Which he was, if not for much longer.

Marney smiled from where she sat with nanite IV bags plugged into both of her legs and her neck. "Good to see you, Boss. I'll be up and running in no time."

He patted her on the shoulder. "I know you will, Marney. That's what I like about you and the rest of the OFC. You never quit, never surrender, and never use one bullet when two will do."

He stepped into the hallway to find Davenport waiting. The man chewed his fingernails like they were the only protein source left in the galaxy. "Give me the bad news, Davenport."

His XO stared at him and exhaled slowly. "I have to admit I'm surprised we lived through that debacle. I'd do it again, though; don't get me wrong."

"Don't dance around it, just tell me what you want to say."

Davenport looked at his boots, then stood, and stepped closer. "That punk kid we rescued has ditched us again. I don't know what he's so afraid of, but he's on the run like no one I've ever seen."

Johnny slammed his fist into the clinic wall, and several people emerged from their rooms in search of the cause of the noise. The next several moments were a blur as Davenport, in a weird reversal of roles, tried to calm him and escort him from the facility.

STARPORT

Heat defined the disembarkment quarter of Nemis City, the second largest starport on Calista. The temperature was bad enough, but the constant roar of engines coming down on the landing pads could drive a person crazy. Johnny Boss and the OFC moved away from the pad as quickly as possible.

Sweat weighed down the haptic uniform inside Johnny's CASPer, causing him to wish he had his helmet on and suit sealed against the environment. One of Lamart's biggest modifications to the Ogre Fist mechas was making them work with their canopies open—a jury-rigged power-saving mode.

Johnny squinted through the glare of the late afternoon. The dry air made him thirsty, and the smog from the industry of a half million residents scratched at his throat. Sunburn cracked the exposed flesh where his scarf didn't cover his face and his gloves didn't cover his finger at the first knuckle.

"I know we're tired and beat up," he said. "Just keep moving. I don't want to stop here. Not until we find Jessup."

Johnny wanted to close his suit and turn on the internal climate control but didn't have the extra fuel for such luxuries. Hauling his passenger was already draining his MK 7 CASPer, all the more annoying as he considered the six lane, elevated highway not far off, where ground cars raced away from the city. *Probably heading to a nightclub or a cozy little baby factory in the suburbs while I drive this mecha toward the next contract.*

Down here on the ground, life felt primitive. Mercs like Johnny Boss and his company of hot-blooded fighters didn't do sports bars or tract homes.

Graffiti covered the support pillars. And nearby buildings. And ground cars that lingered too long in one place. Johnny smiled at an image of fictional street kids painting his company logo as they limped toward their objective.

I need to sleep. Take in some calories. Forget about this mess for a day or three or twenty.

"Where is the Merc Pit?" Cheeto Briggs said, his feet dangling from the back of Johnny's MK 7.

Cheeto had lost his entire CASPer after the Ultra Max battle and wasn't too proud to ride. Facing backward seemed to bother him; Johnny felt the scrappy kid twisting this way and that to look around as the battered remnants of the Ogre Company marched toward the merc quarter.

Everything was old and raw in this part of Nemis City.

The first buildings had been carved from red rock with yellow veins of worthless minerals scribbling everything like the graffiti of a lunatic god. Walls were thick enough to withstand biannual dust storms that had been worse prior to terraforming attempts. There were prefabricated structures converted from temporary outposts to permanent facilities. Designed to last three years...why not use them for 100?

He longed for the early days in Bartertown on Karma, much closer to Earth than this hellhole. The farther a merc went from Bartertown, the less likely he or she was to return.

Everyone understood this fact.

A fortress strong enough to withstand the assault of monsters who would never come and orbital bombardments that would never be allowed dominated the heights of each Nemis City quarter. Johnny Boss, Commanding Officer of the Ogre Fist Company, paused in the street. The shadow of Fort Mocarani should have offered a waft of cool air, but didn't. Beyond what the natives called the First City, and everyone else called the Merc Ghetto, were highways reaching across the barren landscape to connect cities and mining towns and desperate farms. Mechas weren't allowed on high speed thoroughfares. Calista wasn't Earth, where human mercenaries were high rollers or rock stars.

Traveling the planet at will in full battle regalia wasn't allowed, which probably made sense. Johnny Boss wasn't in a pro-cop mood right now. Jessup Moran, one of his quietest, but best, fighters had been beaten within an inch of his life not far from here and sent to the Ultra Max for murder. One rogue cop had set this doomed odyssey in motion.

Dirt stuck to his sweat. Copiously-applied grease leaked from the suits and the cheap wheeled conveyances he'd won in a bet three contracts ago. Which was good because a third of his people had their partial mechas loaded on the primitive flatbed trucks.

His mechanic loved and hated the hunks of junk.

"Everything sticks to this crap," Lamart said.

The man was a caricature of humanity. Balding—except where hair grew from his ears and nostrils—he sported one lazy eye, breath a man didn't get without rotting teeth, and a laugh that could shiver paint from a mecha. His sun-damaged freckles made children cry, or laugh and call him a freak.

He was strong as an ox, a solid fighter who took orders, and was good with a wrench. Ground vehicles were his responsibility.

"Luck'in speed restrictions," Lamart snort-grumbled.

Johnny shook his head.

The freckle-faced old man had been a kid like Cheeto once…a long time ago. He complained like a Giamidaq and could fix a power converter with spit and gum—or so he was fond of saying.

"Dirt and grease, grease and dirt. Luck'in, duck'in, flim-flarin-filth." Lamart dragged a stained rag over his gauntlets as though it might get them clean. He shuffled sideways, then forward, then sideways to keep up with the moving vehicle he was working on.

That was the OFC way; never quit, never surrender, never use one bullet when two would do, and never stop moving.

"Gotta lube the gears," Davenport said, earning a laugh from the rest of the company.

Same joke, different planet. Johnny Boss's knees ached, even with his suit running at 93 percent efficiency. His ears wouldn't stop ringing even with his canopy open. He didn't look at his executive officer. The man wore him the hell out with his sleazy politics and self-aggrandizement.

Gabriel Davenport was bandaged to his elbows—somehow able to act tough and show off his wounds at the same time. A less-seasoned performer would come across as a self-pitying whiner.

Johnny swept his vision over the growing crowd of mercs and mechas, then checked his slate for news of Jessup Moran and his escape from the Ultra Max Prison Station 39. News feeds still showed the accomplices as an undisclosed merc group whose contract was under Peacemaker review. The credits he'd spent to keep the information from smaller law enforcement agencies—like the

Calista Marshals—weren't showing a good return on investment. If they didn't know the OFC was under investigation, they would soon.

"News?" Davenport asked.

"The Contract Defense is still holding up."

"I always liked lawyers," Davenport said, looking at Johnny as though saying *no one was supposed to hear about that yet.*

Lamart and several other OFC mercs within earshot laughed.

"Anything on Rylin Tobias?" Davenport asked. "That Lumar should've tried to arrest me and seen what would have happened."

"One vendetta at a time, Tactician," Johnny said. "We don't have time for drama with the Peacemakers."

Johnny put away his slate and moved ahead of his company. Their last contract, a real war-of-wars fight, had taken a toll on the already depleted members of the OFC even before the prison breakout mission. Lamart, who also did the books with Jessup out of the picture, estimated the financial expenditure of the last contract as "in the piss-mouthed red," which he claimed was an actual accounting term. Either way, it sounded bad.

"I need a vacation," Johnny said.

Grumbling and laughter came right on cue, but not as enthusiastically as it had come for Davenport with his stupid gear lubing joke.

Johnny looked around as the sun set.

The city, where it wasn't set up to serve mercs and their mechas, seemed like a decent place to live. He imagined Peacemaker Rylin Tobias shooting up the place, cutting cars in half with his weapons just to get Jessup to stop.

Then pounding his face like…well, like Jessup was a cop killer. *Accused cop killer.*

"Hey, Cheeto," Johnny said over his shoulder.

"Yeah, Boss?" the kid said as he pulled an earbud free to listen.

"You think Jessup is a cop killer?"

"Ah, no way, Boss. That's some bullshit," Cheeto said. He pushed in the earbud and bobbed his head to the beat. "Show me fire, fire, *fire!*"

The kid sang like his throat was a bandsaw.

"His idea of melody is a toilet flushing," Lamart said.

Johnny Boss laughed for real. "Thanks, Lamart."

The guards at the gate of the Merc Quarter opened massive blast panels without asking who Johnny was. They knew him.

He was in his prime.

Everyone knew Johnny Boss and the Ogre Fist Company.

Johnny joined Cheeto Briggs' rendition of Space Dirge. "Right now! Battledogs! Ahhhhhh!" For once, he stole the spotlight from Davenport. "Show me fire, fire, *fire!*"

THE EX WIFE

"**B**oss!" the woman shouted.

Johnny turned, forcing his heart rate down and his stomach back into place.

She marched across the square, parting the sea of soldiers, mercenaries, and contract killers with womanly fury.

"Cindy," Johnny said.

One more stride, then up on her tiptoes with a right hook—she showed her perfect teeth under the narrowed eyes of a committed street fighter.

Johnny jerked his head back, bracing for impact. Last time she'd knocked him out cold.

"Johnny Boss, you son-of-a-bitch," she said, then threw her arms around him, squeezing until he wished he was still in his MK 7.

"Are we making up then?"

"Not like you mean," she said.

"Damn you're beautiful."

"Stop, Johnny Boss. No touching. No sweet talking. That's what leads to marriage and divorce and marriage and divorce," she said, then smiled at what must have been an intimate memory. "And marriage and divorce."

Johnny laughed. "True."

"What are you doing here?" she asked in a lower voice. "I have good information you and the rest of these losers should be taking a vacay on a contractually-protected world."

"I need to find Jessup Moran," he said.

"I fucking knew it! You broke that ungrateful little turd out. I should have collared him when I had the chance," she said.

"I can neither confirm nor deny any details about my association, past or present, with the Ultra Max prison," Johnny said, sweeping his eyes over her form. She was sweaty and dirty, like she'd been during most of their relationships.

"You're too smart, lucky, and good-looking for your own good, Johnny Boss, but there are limits. Take the OFC and lie low for a while."

"Not going to happen. I'm financially up against the wall," he said.

"You're here for the slate contract? Shit, Johnny, if I find it I'll pay off your debt and hire you as a subcontractor," she said.

"Whatever," he said. "I need to find Jessup. Where'd you see him?"

"Who says I've seen him?" she stepped back.

"You did," Johnny said. "You said you should have collared him when you had a chance."

She narrowed her eyes.

"What? No snappy comeback? This is serious, Cindy."

She clenched her jaw and shook her head. "Not my problem anymore. It just isn't."

"I thought you liked Jessup. You don't want me to help him?" Johnny felt his voice rising.

"You're a real piece of shit, Boss!"

"Oh, it's Boss now? What happened to Johnny? I need to find Jessup before he gets himself killed," Johnny said. "He's been nearly as destructive to my life as an ex-wife since he went AWOL on the Protness contract."

Her nostrils flared, and her eyes unfocused for a second.

"He's a good kid, but you were a bad influence—putting ideals and morals into his head like he wasn't a merc."

Nightmare grabbed her and held her back.

"You haven't changed, Boss. Always blaming everyone else for your problems. I told you going after Protness was a bad idea. Did you listen?" She jerked one arm free of Nightmare's grip. "You left us there to die!"

"You refused to exfiltrate when I gave the order!" He shouted manufactured insults to distract the gathering crowd which seemed to include a couple of Calista Marshals. Then he leaned close enough to whisper in her ear. "We can't keep this up. What do you want to tell me?"

"I was trying to give you the signal, but you were staring at my tits. For the love of God and explosives, you never change. Two guys just snatched Jessup from under your nose. Took him in an air car."

Johnny leaned down and punched the ground with his bare knuckles. Tears of pain and rage exploded in his eyes.

Cindy laughed sweet venom. "Maybe I do still love you, you big ape. I know where they are taking him, or I have a good idea at least."

He stood slower than he intended. "Cindy, I'm too old for this shit."

"The guys who nabbed Jessup are regulars at the Twelve Gage Laser," she said.

Johnny grunted. "Stupid name for a bar."

"I didn't fucking name it," she said.

"Calm down, no need to keep the act going," he said.

"That's why I divorced you last time, Johnny Boss!" she yanked free of Nightmare and stormed away with her own merc company surrounding her.

"What the hell was that?" Davenport asked as he swaggered forward with what looked like a barbequed turkey leg in one hand.

"We're going to the Twelve Gage Laser," Johnny said. "I can never tell when we're really arguing or putting on a show. She exhausts me, and now I have to go to the TGL."

"Stupid name for a bar," Davenport said, then flung the turkey leg toward a trash bin. Landing shuttles flared their engines on their approach to the merc starport they'd recently left. In the other direction, Nemis City rush hour was getting underway for both ground and airways.

BAR FIGHT

The Twelve Gage Laser satisfied all the local codes. Fire proof, bullet proof, and coated with antimicrobial paint, the place still felt like a dive bar. A passed out merc lay at the corner of the establishment where the first alley presented itself. From beyond the seemingly sleeping man came the sounds of a dice game and a prostitute's sales pitch.

Johnny looked up at the sign. "Marney, Davenport, and Nightmare will go in with me. Everyone else wait at your designated rally points."

"Are we on a war contract or looking for a slate?" Lamart asked.

"Do your job, Wrench," Davenport said. "Johnny and I are going inside to kick some ass."

Johnny wanted to punch his XO, but didn't have time. He talked as they strode into the dimly lit room. "Cindy says a couple of mercs drug him off and were taking him here. If we see him, he doesn't get away. No Jessup, no slate."

"Gotcha, Boss," Davenport said. "You're speaking my language."

Marney and Nightmare followed close but moved to the left and right as soon as they crossed the threshold.

"Is that him?" Marney asked.

Johnny looked at the innocent-faced kid, less so now that his nose had been broken and set a dozen times and none of his teeth were real. Incarceration hadn't been kind to the former OFC member. "He doesn't see us but he will. Marney, let Lamart and the others know."

She made a call, keeping her eyes on the dangerous crowd of power drunks, mercs, and locals.

"We have a problem," Nightmare said.

Johnny looked up at the bipedal wolf giant, having almost forgotten the Besquith could speak. The monstrous alien claimed he was brain damaged at birth and shunned by his people who were not only a merc race, but shrewd and devious traders. This was an act, of course, but the only way humans would trust the highly skilled and extremely loyal Ogre Fist member.

"Golden Feet," Nightmare said. "Still angry at XO, I think."

The Golden Feet Company had plenty of reasons to hate the OFC, high among them Davenport's propensity to make fun of their name and logo.

"Forget about the GFC. We need to get to Jessup before he looks this direction, which will be in about five seconds if I trained him right. Which I did," Johnny said, already moving across the center of the room.

"Well, well, well, it's Johnny Boss and his Ogre *Face* Company," a tall, one-eyed albino said.

"I don't have time, Elfrick. Stand aside," Johnny said, barely looking at his rival.

Elfrick, lean-muscled and covered with scars, put a hand on Johnny's chest to stop his forward progress. "That…"

Davenport punched Elfrick on the left side of his face, driving forward as the GFC leader went down. "Come and get some you Golden Toes!"

"Damn it!" Johnny shouldered his way through the melee, keeping his eyes on Jessup who was heading for the back door.

Nightmare hurled a Golden Feet merc across the room, then leapt after him, teeth flashing as he roared his Besquith war cry. Davenport went down under the rush of three men. Marney jumped on a table and kicked someone in the face. Chairs and bottles flew. The music and video screens stopped playing, and the public address system announced the cops were on the way.

Lamart and the other OFC mercs he'd brought for back-up swarmed into the bar shoving their rivals backward like a Roman shield phalanx. Today, sober trumped drunk.

Johnny pulled Davenport out of the scrum. "No one is covering the back. Come with me."

He'd lost sight of Jessup and knew the kid was too smart to stay and gawk. Part of him had hoped unit loyalty would prompt the fugitive to stay and fight alongside his brothers-in-arms. "If wishes were fishes beggars would eat."

"What?" Davenport asked.

Johnny ran through the kitchen, guessing Jessup would have scouted a better escape route than the back door. Sure enough, there was access to several rooms with small beds and a multi-stall toilet. Beyond the delightful suite of essential rooms was a fire escape.

Johnny ducked through the open hatch and clattered down the metal ladder. Davenport followed.

"We've got him now," Davenport grunted as his feet hit the ground.

But Jessup was fast, and he had a head start.

Johnny Boss ran like the survival of his friends depended on his speed. Shadows flashed by as he ducked under pipes and low fire escapes jutting across the alleyway. Water dripped from air conditioner units and leaky pipes. Davenport followed. His ragged breathing made Johnny smile.

Whenever he looked up, he saw a sliver of the Calista sky and caught glimpses of freighters and merc transports circling toward the starport landing areas. City sounds echoed strangely here.

"Jessup," he shouted. "Stop right there. I need to talk to you."

At the next corner, Jessup hesitated long enough to look back. Davenport put on a final burst of speed to catch and tackle the young fugitive. Johnny, who had been three strides ahead of his XO, arrived as the beating began.

"You little shit," Davenport said as he straddled Jessup's chest and punched him in the face. He slapped him right and left hard enough to draw blood.

Johnny snaked his forearm around his XO's neck and dragged him back.

"What the hell, Boss?" Davenport grunted.

Johnny punched him in the gut, dropping him to his knees, then rushed toward Jessup as he tried to stand. "Stay down, kid. I'm not pulling him off you a second time."

INTERROGATION

Johnny hadn't been to the farmhouse since he was a green merc in his first unit. He sat on a crude bench in the front yard, reading from his slate—wishing it was the slate Jessup was supposed to have—and thinking about Cindy. This had been her childhood home. He thought her family still owned the lease, which was unfortunate for them, or would be once the shit hit the automated planters and harvesters.

Better she isn't here, he thought.

Marney sat beside him and nudged him with her shoulder.

"You're not Cindy," he said.

"No one's Cindy," she said. "Not sure what all the fuss is about. She's not that cute."

Johnny put away the slate.

Marney nodded at it. "Bad news?"

"Swear not to tell anyone, and I'll explain what I gave up to get the Ultra Max breakout covered up," he said.

"You trying to turn me on, Johnny Boss? Secrets get me wet," she said.

He laughed, then looked at a spot between his feet. "I had an exclusive pre-order on a MK 9 package."

"What the hell? And you let it go? Have you heard what they can do? That would have put us in the big leagues. How many were we going to get?"

"The sales rep, if you can call him that, didn't say." Johnny popped his knuckles and ignored the sound of Davenport yelling at Jessup inside the barn.

"Oh," Marney said. "Probably just one or two then. That'd cause some problems with Davenport and his circle. Speaking of which, are you sure about…that?" she asked, cocking her head toward the barn.

"No. I'm not," he said.

A dangerous silence grew. He refused to look at the barn.

"Why haven't you ever come on to me?" Marney asked.

"You'd hurt me."

She shoulder bumped him. "You are a smooth talker, Johnny Boss."

"You only want one of those MK 9s," he said.

"Are you still getting them?"

"Not without the slate contract." He stood and faced the barn. "Take the team on a patrol. They don't need to be here for a while. Leave a couple veterans for security. You can tell them the bounty for the slate tripled again. Then mention they should stay alert until I can deal with the Peacemaker warrants they just issued for all of us."

She nodded and looked down as Jessup screamed.

Johnny slipped inside and leaned against the wall, arms and ankles crossed. It was a terrible way to stand and a guilty pleasure he rarely indulged. Dust motes twisted in sunlight streaming down from a vent near the apex of the ceiling. Several of Davenport's cronies lounged in the hayloft. For a second, their shadowed faces reminded Johnny of Nightmare—which was unfair to the Besquith.

Blood puddled under Jessup's chair.

Johnny thought about his last argument with Cindy. *I thought you liked Jessup*, he'd said.

Davenport walked around the chair, patting the young man on his left shoulder, then his right. He stopped just out of sight, forcing Jessup to look around for him—not an easy thing to do the way he was tied up. He barely moved his eyes.

Johnny looked at his feet.

Davenport arrived in front of Jessup and stopped, then gently slapped his victim. The other men and women in the room, Davenport's inner circle, watched without a word. A few of the hayloft spectators moved close enough to the edge to dangle their feet.

Another gentle slap, then another, and another until Jessup cursed.

Davenport stomped on Jessup's toes and Johnny almost went outside. Tears filled the corner of his eyes. He moved forward.

"Don't do it, Boss. You gave this job to me," Davenport said.

Johnny stood close enough to get spattered with blood, but remained silent for as long as he could. "Take a break, XO."

Davenport stepped back and toweled blood from his knuckles.

"We're all going to hell, Jessup," Johnny said.

Jessup nodded. His eyes were swelling shut. He wouldn't look up. "You taught me to do the right thing."

Johnny pinched the bridge of his nose as hard as he could and closed his eyes so he wouldn't have to see the young merc. "I never taught you that."

"Aren't you going to tell me you need the slate to save the OFC? That it's for the good of the Company? You'll forgive me, get me a new identity. Put me back in my old job?" Jessup asked, crying each time he tried to draw a breath.

Davenport injected healing nanites into Jessup's arm.

"Is that what you told him?" Johnny asked.

Davenport looked at him and smiled. "I told him a lot of things."

Johnny pushed down his battle rage, locked his jaw tight, clenched his fists, and counted to ten in his head. "Get this over with. We've all got warrants and the Golden Feet Company is making noise on the Galnet about being the ones to collect it."

"They're weak," Davenport said.

"They're not the only merc unit on Calista right now. If they find out we're close to getting the slate it will be us against every merc on the planet. Are you ready for that, Davenport? Make him talk. Get it done," Johnny said.

He stormed out of the barn, went around back, and puked until he stopped crying.

OGRES VERSUS GOLDEN FEET

E xplosions echoed from the perimeter of the 380-acre cornfield. Columns of fire mushroomed on the horizon—one, two, three. Johnny stared, recognizing not only the type of explosion but who had fired them. He didn't know why, but Lamart's rockets sent up a debris cloud tinted red and green like something from a holiday parade.

He snatched binoculars from his belt, zoomed in, and saw kinetic projectiles ripping through an automated harvester. A missile struck the combine causing an explosion of yellow kernels. Lamart and the others crouched 50 meters apart in the two-meter-tall corn rows. The attacking Golden Feet squads moved forward, seeking the same concealment but sending waves through neat, dense rows as they picked up speed.

Ogre Fists and Golden Feet exchanged heavy weapons fire, including rockets and then grenades as the distance closed.

A few seconds later, Johnny felt a pulse of air from a distant shockwave. No one in his unit was certified for nukes or nearly nuclear armaments. That didn't mean they lacked some big bangs.

He sprinted to his MK 7 and clambered in, shouting orders on the OFC communication band even as he was gearing up. Nightmare and the rest of the rear guard Marney had left at the farmhouse moved with practiced efficiency to reinforce the inner perimeter. They made two rings of gear and improvised barriers; one of them was 100 meters from the house, and the other was 300 meters out. His Ogres never defended fixed positions for long; he preferred to shoot and move. Defenses just had to be strong enough to make whoever was coming work for it.

"Put the first ring farther out, Nightmare," Johnny ordered. "Davenport, do you copy?"

No response.

Nightmare growled over the comm band. "Perimeter out this far. Do it now you dog Ogre Fists!"

"Do it now you Ogre Fist dogs," Johnny corrected.

"That is what I say," Nightmare said. "You must tell what a dog is."

"You're a dog, Nightmare," Johnny said on cue. Laughter rippled through the company radios.

Johnny marched his MK 7 to the barn and yanked open the door.

Davenport and the others were scrambling for their CASPer units. "We got it! Jessup gave it up like a little punk kid," Davenport said.

"Fine. Right now we have at least one merc unit coming to cash in on our warrants," Johnny said. "Probably the Golden Feet."

"This day just keeps getting better!" Davenport shouted, then high-fived several of his team. "Someone get this piece of shit out of that chair. Dose him with healing nanites and tie him up. Put him on a flatbed."

Johnny watched until Jessup was lifted from the chair by Davenport's personal medic, who was a decent guy despite his choice of friends. Never talked much unless it was about horses or the latest medical journal publication.

One laser after another punched holes in the top of the barn.

Johnny moved out, taking three of his Team One and one of Davenport's Team Two to face the main thrust of the GFC assault. "Marney, are you back yet?"

Static crackled through the communication link as she answered. "Back at the farmhouse. Setting up inner defenses. Nightmare has it all fucked up."

"Roger that," Johnny said. "Lay down mortar fire. We will sally with a five-mecha sortie."

"Good luck, Boss. Thanks for the invite, you asshole," Marney said.

"You'll get your turn," Johnny said, then raced toward the Golden Feet MK 6 mechas rushing forward as they launched rockets from shoulder mounts.

The GFC mechas charged three by three—just as Elfrick and his dumbass squad leaders always did. Little trios of inverted V icons moved down Johnny's heads-up display. *Vs of Vs*, he thought without laughing. Humor died a little each time he faced Elfrick's nutjobs. Thoughts of the one-eyed albino in the Twelve Gage Laser invoked a stream of curses Johnny didn't share with his mercs. Maybe Cindy was right. Maybe he did blame all of his problems on other people.

For starters, there was Jessup, who should've known better than to steal a slate, and especially should've known better than to steal a slate without asking Johnny first. Then there was Rylin Tobias, the Lumar Peacemaker who'd spit on the honor of all the Ogre Fist Company members by beating Jessup half to death in front of God and everyone. No matter that Jessup was on the run from the law. No one gave an OFC, past or present, that kind of beat down.

Then there was Cindy, playing games instead of just grabbing Jessup and bringing the kid to Johnny.

Worst of all was Gabriel Davenport, his Executive Officer and rival. He needed to get the man his own company soon or there was going to be a mutiny. Or he could kill the hot-headed jerk. Maybe in battle, or in a duel, or however it had to be done.

Without the OFC, Johnny Boss was nothing. His life lacked purpose without the ability to take contracts and go to war for someone who couldn't or wouldn't do it themselves.

"Mortars!" Johnny called to Marney. "Use 'em all. Bonus for ending this fight with empty mortar tubes."

"You heard the boss!" Marney shouted to her fire team. "Mortars away!"

Whump. Whump. Whump.

The sound of mortars leaving their tubes brought a smile to Johnny's face. He laughed as he picked up speed. Dirt and organic debris blasted into the air just in front of him. He smashed through the smoke and flying cornstalks to hit the first of the Golden Feet losers hard.

"Is that you, Elfrick?" he shouted.

The nameless, faceless man in the CASPer mecha shouted something in the GFC Cant Elfrick had bought years ago from a second rate linguist on Therman's World. Johnny had learned a few phrases the last time they worked on the same side of a large contract.

"Ver dis Elfrick Dingl-dikl-dac?" Johnny said. Instead of waiting for an answer he closed to melee distance, something he told his less seasoned mercs never to try. Aiming by instinct, he shot the mecha in its feet, then slammed into its armor frame, tumbling it to the ground.

The battle raged above and on all sides.

Whump. Whump. Whump.

Whump. Whump. Whump.

Marney and her mortar team worked the field indiscriminately since there were far more enemies than friendlies at this point.

In the distance, five or six thousand meters at least, Elfrick's famous battle tanks responded with hard hitting sabot rounds. Right on schedule, a second squadron of tanks shed their camouflage and pushed in closer with lasers and energy weapons. Mercs in CASPer units rushed around the right flank only to face Nightmare and two of Johnny's best Ogres.

"Marney! Bury those tanks! This soil is soft. The armor units will sink if you give 'em some encouragement," Johnny ordered.

The battle lost cohesion and resembled the bar fight from the night before.

Enthusiasm for violence led to individual victories here and there.

"Rally in five, four, three, two, go!" Johnny ordered. He watched to be sure his order was being carried out, then turned and raced toward the prearranged location.

"Lamart, have you contacted that air support?" Johnny asked.

"There is an on-call wing of freelancers, but they say the price is double because the Golden Feet smuck-jobs paid to keep them on stand-by," Lamart said, barely audible above the weapons fire around him...wherever he was in this smoke.

"Then they should be ready," Johnny said. "Being on stand-by and all. They just didn't realize they were on stand-by for us."

"I took the liberty of having our credit pre-approved. The interest rate we're getting charged should be illegal, but I figured this is all or nothing for us," Lamart said.

"It is," Johnny replied. He spent the next fifteen minutes on the move with Marney and one of Davenport's bodyguards whose name he forgot. "Cover me, I need to switch magazines on my main laser."

"Covering," Marney said.

Davenport's goon sprayed a burning cornfield with suppressive ballistic fire.

Johnny moved to his side, beeping him on the radio link rather than touching him on the shoulder as he would if they were out of their CASPers. "Got it. Go reload and take a piss if you need to."

The new guy laughed and fell back to attend to his gear.

He wasn't that new, Johnny realized. None of them were.

Red V-carets regrouped and thrust downward at the blue upside down V-carets. "No rest for the likes of us," Johnny said.

Davenport emerged from the barn. "I left four solid men to guard Jessup until we get back. He's in no shape to travel."

"Just leave him here," Johnny said, immediately realizing how stupid that decision was.

"Got to keep him here in case he is sending us on a wild goose chase," Davenport said. "Are you about done with these Golden Toes jerkoffs?"

"Get in the fight, XO," Johnny said.

"Don't have to ask me twice," Davenport said. "Team Two, break from whatever you are doing and rally on me. We've got the left 50 of this sector."

Johnny moved, expecting Team One to do the same without being told. He didn't want to echo the orders of his XO.

"Did you get a location?" he asked Davenport on their semi-private channel, the one they agreed to use but that almost anyone could eavesdrop if they knew the arrangement.

"He was taking it to sell to a Zuul trader, but got caught trying to go around the Cathedral," Davenport said.

Johnny cursed. "We need to get there before they can call in their muscle and synchronize their autocannons. That place should be called the Fortress."

"Well, at least it ain't a real Cathedral. We shouldn't go to hell if we die smashing our way in," Davenport said.

Johnny was too tired and pissed off to laugh.

Team One pressed hard, drawing most of Elfrick's wrath. The one-eyed albino hated anyone who'd ever dated Cindy, and since Johnny had married her three times, the GFC versus OFC vendetta was practically codified in merc law.

"Reload," Johnny's CASPer computer advised.

He stared at his gauntlets and shook off fatigue. It had been years since he heard the reminder. Training and experience taught him to bump his mags frequently, always keeping a full one in his primary weapon and the partially used mags close at hand in an emergency pouch.

He needed to focus. Moving and firing at GFC CASPers, he worked through his priorities.

The facts of his situation hadn't changed much since the Ultra Max Prison breakout. He still needed money to keep the OFC viable. Jessup was still an outlaw and was likely to remain wanted until the Peacemakers brought him in, with or without the slate that was worth so many credits.

A casual observer might say the current battle was his biggest problem, and it was, to an extent. But fighting was what he and his Ogres did. He found it relaxing at times. Routine.

A game-changing revelation dawned on him as smoke cleared from the scorched and cratered cornfield. He needed money and wanted Jessup safe, but his real problem was his Executive Officer.

Gabriel Davenport began the mop up operation, disarming Golden Feet who were smart enough to know they were beaten and punching the rest with directed laser fire. Most of Johnny's Ogre Fist Company followed him and cheered each time a Golden Feet CAS-Per merc was humiliated and disarmed.

I only have one real problem, and its name is Gabriel Davenport.

"Marney," Boss said when no one else was paying attention.

"Yeah, Boss?"

"Status?"

"Little banged up. What'd you need?"

"Stay here and make sure Davenport's men don't kill Jessup. Once we have the slate, we need to turn him over to the Calista Marshals. I can't bear to give him directly to the Peacemakers."

"Davenport is in rare form," Marney said. "When this is over, we need to talk. I have some concerns."

"Those concerns are about to be addressed."

THE CATHEDRAL

Like the automated farm, the Cathedral was located well beyond the influence of Nemis City. The thick-walled structure stood at one end of a massive plateau. Veins of red and yellow minerals streaked the rock where it had been carved and shaped on an industrial scale. Corrosion-resistant alloys and carbon-bonded concrete linked manufactured structures that were not part of the raw stone.

Nimbus clouds arrayed themselves on the horizon like an armada touched by the dying day. This part of Calista was harsh, and the changes of a landscaped abrupt. The desert gave way to robust cornfields and other staple crops. Networks of arterial canals nurtured the plants with snow melted from distant mountains.

At the center of the fortress was a gothic church with elaborate stained glass windows glowing in the harsh sunset of Calista. Johnny saw the colorful spire from kilometers away.

"That's close enough," Johnny said.

Davenport, canopy open, carried out the order.

The Ogre Fist Company settled down for the night to observe the fortress town around the Cathedral. Over the years, a warlord known as Bloody Ambrose had built a system of modern defenses.

"I see fixed energy and kinetic weapons on every tower of the wall. I assume no man's land is a minefield," Davenport said as he lay prone with binoculars next to Johnny on a hilltop.

Johnny made his own assessment. "Don't sound so dire. What are a couple of high intensity laser batteries, heavy machine guns, and missile racks to guys like us?"

Davenport shifted uncomfortably.

CHALLENGE AND RESOLUTION

Johnny spent much of the night watching regular patrols around the edge of the plateau. He rested when he could and made sure his Ogres did the same. In the morning he rejoined Davenport near the observation post.

It was time to make a decision.

"Just you and me on this one. The rest of the OFC will remain here as a quick reaction force," Johnny said.

"Are you showing off, Boss? This is a tough nut. We need numbers. I'm tempted to send for everyone we left at the farm," Davenport said.

"It would take a full division plus air support to storm those walls. You and I can fight our way across the Challenge Bridge," Johnny said.

"Are you trying to get me killed? Bloody Ambrose leaves that causeway partially defended to entice green units with more guts than sense," Davenport said.

"He honors the victory of anyone who can run his gauntlet. We get past that, we have a chance at seizing the tablet," Johnny said, then turned the conversation without warning or hesitation. "Do you really think it's in there, or does it make more sense that Jessup tricked you?"

"Tricked us, maybe," Davenport said. "Not just me."

Johnny stared him down.

"The OFC is broke, Boss. You've run it into the ground with your idealistic bullshit. I'm about to take half the company and start over someplace new," Davenport said. "Why the hell are we here if you think I screwed up?"

"Jessup always got along with Marney. She's like an aunt to him," Johnny said, examining his gauntlets one at a time.

Davenport snorted a laugh but looked worried.

"You've got two options, XO, go through the crucible that Bloody Ambrose set up and maybe come out worthy of your own company charter—one that I'll endorse—or go back and admit Jessup pulled the wool over your eyes. Then you can leave with whoever will go with you."

"There's no way that kid is tough enough to have lied to me," Davenport snarled.

"Torture taints the answers. You know how stubborn Jessup is. You think that's the worst beating he ever had? I know that's wrong because he would never surrender the slate to Ambrose. But now we have to fight our way inside and prove it, or the men will lose faith in both of us."

"I'll kill that little punk," Davenport said.

"Marney has probably already turned him over to the Calista Marshals. The only thing I'm gambling on is that he tells her where the slate is before he gets locked up a second time," Johnny said.

Davenport fumed wordlessly for several minutes, then headed back to camp. "Let's get this over with. I've got your back so long as you've got mine. As much as I'd like to frag you right now, neither of us will survive Ambrose's funhouse alone."

Johnny nodded.

"You're a psychopath, Johnny Boss," Davenport said.

"I've been called worse." He ran a fresh diagnostics check on his MK 7's armor and weapons. Information scrolled down the heads-up display in his helmet. Ignoring most of it, he watched Davenport.

His XO hefted a partial laser shield. Johnny remembered ordering the damaged, arm-deployable shield trimmed down rather than repaired. Davenport had hated the idea but learned to use it for defense and offense—creating one of his signature decapitation moves that struck fear into his enemies on the battlefield.

Cold dread filled Johnny as he realized Davenport's pinplant links were functioning. The man must have made a detour in Nemis City and had them re-synced. Replaying the battle at the farmhouse he understood why Team Two responded as though reading his mind. He could communicate without overt radio traffic and process information fast. The man had performed well during the fight, rarely missing a target and avoiding damage with an agility few CASPer drivers could match.

Two of Davenport's men, Victor Cambridge and Elliot Mao, checked his systems then donned their upgraded and heavily modified MK 6 CASPers. At nine feet tall and 1,800 pounds, the Team Two veterans looked like bodyguards beside Davenport's sleeker MK 7. Cambridge and Mao had worked for years to improve the laser resistance of their mechas. As MK 6 units went, they were well set up.

Johnny stared for several seconds.

"What?" Davenport said over the radio. His canopy was already sealed. "I didn't ask them. If Nightmare and Cheeto are shadowing you, then I get my boys here to keep things even."

"We're on the same side, Tactician," Johnny said.

"Sure. Ogres into the fight and all that," Davenport said.

Johnny finished his setup, casually turning to see Lamart inspecting the gear of the Besquith and the kid.

Nightmare wore a MK 6 of such variety that only its basic shape identified its model. His natural size caused the unit to stand head and shoulders above anyone else in the OFC. His strength allowed him to carry a rocket launcher on his left shoulder—the slightly curved magazine jutting two feet above his head—and a MAC (Magnetic Accelerator Cannon) on his right shoulder, belt fed from an ammunition vault bolted to his back. Members of the OFC joked that his smaller arm-mounted weapons were only there to swat his fleas.

Cheeto Briggs wore a MK 5 that was covered with dried blood and seemed to give Lamart fits. The mecha unit was the approximate size of the improved MK 6 design, but the similarities ended there.

Davenport and his bodyguards laughed and shook their helmeted heads.

"I told you to polish off that rust," Lamart said.

"I did, but I woke up and it was like this again," Cheeto said. "Swear to God!"

"You two don't have to do this," Johnny said.

"The hell we don't," Lamart, Nightmare, and Cheeto said in unison.

Lamart locked his judgment-filled eyes on Johnny. "When the hell did you stop doing pre-combat checks?"

"No time for that when you're going solo or trying to frag your XO," Cheeto said as he bobbed his head to music playing inside the MK 5. "This hunk of junk has a great sound system. Wanna hear it?"

"No," Johnny said. "Where did you get that thing?"

"Farmhouse. The cellar, actually," Briggs said.

Johnny led them to the Ambrose causeway when the sun was full up. That was one of the rules. A large sign of welded iron bore the words, "Challenge Bridge." It wasn't really a bridge, but a portion of roadway that weaved through several gatehouses. The paved surface of the road was wide enough to allow several mega tanks to drive side by side. There were ditches to the right and left full of razor wire and deep pits. Walls contained the entire "bridge" so that once an intruder ventured into the trap it was impossible to get out without retreating.

"On my left, XO. Everyone else hang back a bit. Don't group up," Johnny said.

"Jumpjets?" Davenport asked.

"Save 'em," Johnny said. He looked back at the four Ogre Fist mercs who didn't have jump jets. "And save the fuel. We may need it for something else."

"Roger that," Davenport said.

"Contact!" Johnny shouted as he charged the first machine gun battery (MGB). "I expected a little bit of parley at least." His words tangled with the noise of running in full gear.

The MGBs were triangulated to cover the roadway leading to the first set of towers. Johnny wished he could jump on one and tear apart the remote controlled killing machines but had already decided against using his MK 7's jump ability.

"Speed, Boss. Speed!" Davenport grunted.

The two of them separated and ran faster than any of their men could follow. Johnny angled away from a marching line of green tracers. Closer and closer they came. Davenport, he saw, was pulling ahead of his threats and would reach the first MGB easily. Johnny veered toward the second part of the triangle.

All four of the support Ogres lobbed rockets over and around him, blasting the second set of machine guns to hell. He charged through flying debris at the final part of the defensive triangle. On the run, he aimed his laser rifle, stopped for what felt like a long second, and fired a laser pulse down the barrels of the guns swinging toward him. A heartbeat later he was on the move, even though this threat was over.

The smoke cleared.

"Who are you and why do you challenge Bloody Ambrose?" a dry voice broadcast into their radios.

Johnny looked at the first gate. "One of my men left something here. I want it back."

Silence.

Johnny checked on his companions and breathed a sigh of relief.

"No Ogres have entered my fortress since the contract five years ago," Ambrose said.

"Hey, Boss, I think I believe him," Cheeto said.

"You wanna go back?" Davenport snapped.

"Shut it, XO," Johnny said, then stepped in front of the others. "He may have been in disguise. He's on the run and desperate."

Ambrose laughed but it was so dry it took a second to reach recognizable volume. "So he broke my rules, if he did in fact shelter in the Cathedral. There is a fine for that, Johnny Boss, and you're responsible for payment."

Johnny cracked the knuckles of his gauntlets. "This miserable odyssey is getting expensive."

Davenport laughed. "You sure know how to spend money, Boss. I'll give you that."

"I would have appreciated a call about a fugitive from Peacemaker justice trespassing within my walls. I could have seized the tablet and only taken a small commission," Ambrose said.

"Ah, man," Cheeto Briggs groaned.

Lamart, Cambridge, and Mao swore expansively.

The ground fell away under Johnny and his Ogres. He landed flat on his back and spent several seconds getting to his feet. "That was new."

Davenport sounded like he was choking. Nightmare roared defiance in his native language. Cheeto Briggs sang, "Show me fire, fire, *fire!*"

Coming out of the hole was like taking a hill under fire. Johnny trusted his heads-up display, shooting at targets he couldn't actually see through the smoke and anti-missile chaff raining down from the first gate house. Davenport jumped to the catwalk and dropped grenades inside the towers. From Johnny's viewpoint the explosions looked and sounded muted, but the gate opened, and the countermeasures stopped.

"Good work, Tactician," Johnny said.

"Thanks, Idealist," Davenport replied.

Johnny gathered the six-mecha assault team in the next section of the Challenge Bridge, ordering an injury and equipment check. "Buddy system. Don't do it yourself."

He went over Davenport's gear remembering why he'd once trusted and respected the man. "Looks good. You've spent some money on this gear."

"Your CASPer is tight, Boss," Davenport said.

"You're good to go, Tactician."

Side by side, they led the way through MGBs, mine fields, and trip wires leading to nasty traps. At the next gatehouse, Johnny and Davenport charged together, jumped, and annihilated the defenses.

Each section of the Challenge Bridge grew harder, the explosions larger and hotter, and the number of live defenders greater.

"Ambrose has his CASPers falling back when we push hard," Davenport said, ducking behind a bunker Johnny and Nightmare had just cleared out.

"For all his savage reputation, he cares about his troops. They fight and fall back knowing we can only keep this up for so long. If Bloody Ambrose is the merc I remember hearing stories about when I was a kid, he has calculated our ammunition capacity and fuel range. He isn't worried."

Davenport nodded. "Cambridge and Mao, work your way around on the left flank of this roadway but don't get pinned against the left wall."

"Nightmare, do you have rockets to cover them?" Johnny asked.

"Many rockets. I am strong to carry," Nightmare said. "Wuff, Wuff."

"It's woof, woof," Davenport grunted. "I hate it when he does that. Stick to being the straight man, you stupid mutt."

"Nightmare angry," Nightmare said. "Tactician insensitive."

"Use the rockets, Nightmare," Johnny said. He worked his way closer to the next gate—the final gate he hoped—and vented his remaining jumpjet fuel on the armored hinges.

Davenport watched but did nothing. "I see what you're about, but I'm not sure it will burn hot enough."

"Just need to soften the hinges and let gravity do the rest," Johnny said, watching his XO covertly with one of his CASPer camera feeds on his heads-up display. The merc hesitated, then approached.

"I want you to know how much this pains me, Boss. I really love my jumpjets," he said.

Johnny talked without facing him. "Like you love your pin-plants?"

Silence.

"That's a huge investment you can't afford on your own," Johnny said.

Davenport vented jumpjet fuel on the hinges as Nightmare, Cheeto, Cambridge, and Mao fought for their lives against a rocket and laser barrage from the wall turrets.

"How many Ogres in Team Two have upgraded to pinplants without you telling me?" Johnny asked.

"Three," Davenport said.

"We could have upgraded the rest of our people who are still in MK 5s or bought two additional MK 7s, maybe even an MK 8 if we could find one," Johnny said.

"I told you we should reward high performers," Davenport said.

Johnny backed away from the work. "Let's move before Ambrose and his defenders realize what we did."

Davenport joined him behind a pile of debris in no man's land. The rest of the attackers rallied behind a similar position on the opposite side of the roadway.

"We can't continue as a divided company," Johnny said to Davenport.

"I'll take a dozen men and women and start my own merc unit," Davenport said.

"No," Johnny said. "The OFC is small enough already. One of us is going to lead the Ogres, and it won't be you."

"Damn it, Boss. Be reasonable," Davenport said.

"I could push you into the inferno we are about to send up and shoot you in the face. No one would say a word. You betrayed your commanding officer," Johnny said.

"I wasn't betraying you, I was saving the OFC," Davenport said.

Johnny stared him down and said nothing.

A guard reloaded a MAC with depleted uranium rounds and sprayed the area between this gatehouse and the one they had recently broken through. Nightmare and the others backed into a crater for shelter and were pinned in place.

"Keep your head down," Johnny said. "And follow me." He rushed into position and aimed his laser rifle at the fuel-soaked gate hinges. It was an easy shot and soon the hinges were softening to slag as the fire raged hot and quick. "Nightmare! We attack!"

Johnny and his Ogres charged through the gate, shooting defensive emplacements and sidestepping a maze of mines and other traps. A squad of mercs in MK 8s covered each other as they retreated by the numbers.

The final gate opened, and Bloody Ambrose walked forward without so much as a helmet. Long white side-whiskers hung down to his barrel chest. The padded undershirt favored by CASPer drivers from an earlier age stretched over his massive gut and hung down over his muscular legs.

"You see me?" he asked as he spread his arms wide. "Would you stand there in full CASPer regalia while I'm unarmed in the face of your unreasonable aggression?"

Johnny opened his canopy and signaled Davenport and the others to fall back to the last point of cover. "Do I call you Bloody Ambrose?"

The big man laughed. "Call me old and wise. Right? That's what you need to remember."

Johnny waited.

"No one has come this far across the Challenge Bridge," Ambrose said.

"Not really a bridge. You should rename it the Challenge Road, or No Man's Land," Johnny said.

Ambrose laughed. "I'll take it to my board of directors. You and I have business first."

"I'm listening."

"Do you have any choice but to listen?" Ambrose asked.

"No."

Ambrose studied him with narrowed eyes. "You seem to match your reputation. I bet you're mad as hell on the inside."

"It's been a tough day," Johnny said, resisting the urge to look back at Davenport.

"Then keep your mouth shut and listen," Ambrose said. "Jessup Moran has a slate that some people think will rock the foundation of the Peacemakers. You are flat broke, and your team is feeling the strain. If you walk out of here alive, it will probably be as a solo contractor looking to join another company."

Johnny tilted his head to one side. "But you have a better offer, I assume. Why would you get involved now?"

"I don't want any part of the slate contract. Take my advice and stay clear of that. Convince Jessup to turn himself in and visit him in prison—without breaking him out of course." Ambrose stopped to control his amusement, then began again slightly short of breath. "Oh, Johnny, I like your style, but if you're going to work for me I need you to show greater caution."

"You're offering me a job?"

"Of course! What do you think the purpose of the Challenge Bridge is?" Ambrose put his fists on his hips. "What's the motto of the Ogre Fist Company? I heard it once and found it amusing."

"Never quit, never surrender, and never use one bullet when two will do," Johnny said.

Ambrose smiled and nodded. "I'll have my snipers take out Davenport."

"No."

"No?"

Johnny turned and looked at his companions. "He's still useful to me. I think I can bring him around to my way of thinking, remind him of why he joined the OFC in the first place."

Ambrose abandoned his good humor and stood like an old warrior ready to fight for the rest of his life. "War is serious business, Boss. I'm not looking for someone to guard my keep. I want someone I can mentor. Are you that person?"

"I have a lot of debt," Johnny said.

"Not a problem."

"Every member of the OFC needs equipment upgrades."

"Done."

"Jessup needs a good lawyer for whatever he is about to face with the Peacemakers."

Ambrose darkened. "I'll spend the price of one CASPer for his legal defense, but will not be associated with the case and neither will my employees."

"Okay," Johnny said. "You just hired the OFC. I will bring my officers to review the contract once I set a few things in order."

"I can recommend a new XO," Ambrose said.

"I've already invested a lot of time and energy in this one," Johnny said.

"It's your company, but remember who you work for," Ambrose said.

Johnny saluted and returned to his assault team.

"What the hell was all that?" Davenport asked.

"We have a new long-term contract. Everyone is getting equipment upgrades, but most importantly, Bloody Ambrose has agreed not to murder us where we stand," Johnny said.

"This isn't how I thought it would be," Davenport said.

"It never is XO. Send your people back to base. You and I need to go for a walk."

"Are we both coming back?"

"I'm not sure. What you did to Jessup crossed the line."

The color drained from Davenport's face.

Johnny smiled. "Now you remember why *I'm* running the OFC."

# # # # #

Leverage
by Josh Hayes

Chapter One

Macintosh Sacobi pressed a hand against the roof of the flyer, groaning as the sleek aircraft twisted through Nemis' skyline. He glared at the pilot to his left, and the senior Peacemaker grinned as he pushed the flyer's throttle forward.

"I said I believed you," Mac said through gritted teeth.

Rylin Tobias grinned, and the Lumar leveled the flyer with his lower set of hands.

Mac relaxed slightly, taking his hand from the ceiling. Even after a year, his Peacemaker Training Officer still treated him like a rookie.

"He's got a pretty big head start," Rylin said. "If we can cut him off before he makes the starport we can avoid a week in hyper."

"I still don't understand why we just don't call the Marshals," Mac said, forcing down another groan as the flyer dipped suddenly to the right. "I can have a team there in ten minutes and lock down the whole place."

"And let some backwater-nobody cop take credit for bringing in Jenkin's killer? Not going to happen. No offense."

Mac gritted his teeth against the jibe. He'd left the Calista Marshal Service to join the guild. Fortunately, there had been an opening in the local Peacemaker office for Mac to train here and not have to travel halfway across the galaxy to chase his dream. Unfortunately, his training officer had made it a point to remind him of his roots at every opportunity.

Rylin leaned over, checking the street below them. "Besides, catching this asshole is bound to earn me some favor among the guild leadership. Hell, it could be the leverage I need to push right into the Regional Director's office. I'll be damned if anyone gets to Jessup Moran before me."

Mac resisted the urge to roll his eyes. A Regional position had been the only thing on Rylin's mind for months now. Knowing how competitive it had been just to get into the guild, Mac had no illusions about how difficult it would be to move through the ranks, especially for a Lumar who wasn't anywhere near as bright as he was brutal. Worse, within the guild hierarchy, who you were and what you'd done wasn't nearly as important as who you knew.

In an effort to steer off another "the whole system is flawed" tirade, Mac said, "I'd really like to know what he was doing all the way out here in the first place."

"Gotta hide somewhere," Rylin said. "Can't spend too much time in one place, especially someone in Moran's position. Calista is just as good as any other rock. There's the bastard."

Ahead, six lanes of traffic flowed in and out of Calista's only starport. It wasn't quite bumper-to-bumper, but the roads were far from empty. Nemis, Calista's capital, was home to three-quarters of a million people, not to mention tourists and hyperspace layovers, making travel around the city decidedly slow during rush hour. For a moment Mac didn't see their target, then a compact car abruptly changed lanes twice, passing cars in three lanes without slowing.

"Not very subtle, is he?"

Rylin grunted. "Would you be?"

Mac considered for a moment. "I guess not."

Rylin grunted again. "Hold on."

The flyer dipped, descending toward the stream of traffic below. Even with his Peacemaker body armor keeping him snug and secure in his seat, Mac pressed a hand against the ceiling again, praying the flyer wouldn't come apart under the stresses of Rylin's piloting.

If I never have to fly with this maniac again, it'll be too soon, Mac thought.

"Okay," Rylin said, leveling the flyer out. He centered them over the starport's inbound lanes. "Don't let that son of a bitch pass the outer marker."

A reticle appeared on the heads-up-display in front of Mac, flashing orange and red. He turned to his trainer, unable to hide his shock. "You want me to *fire* while he's in traffic?"

"You have another way of stopping him?"

"Don't you think that's a bit risky? He's surrounded by civilians."

"Our charge is to bring him in. You wanted to be a Peacemaker; here's where you earn your tree."

Mac flexed his fingers around the fire controls, eyes focused on the traffic below. Jessup Moran's car continued its reckless slalom, narrowly missing cars in his bid for freedom. Mac was a decent shot with the cannons, but what if he missed? How many civilians were down there? How many of his people?

He released the controls. "I—"

"Oh, for the love of…" Rylin flipped a switch, bringing the flyer's weapons under his control, aimed with his upper hands, and fired.

The cannons barked underneath the flyer, spewing bright beams of energy, and the pavement directly behind Moran's car exploded, sending a plume of debris into the air. Lines of cars behind the explosion slid sideways, crashing into each other, trying to avoid the destruction.

"Son of a bitch!" Rylin adjusted his arm and fired again.

This time, the two beams cut into Moran's car, ripping through the rear of the vehicle, sending it spinning.

"Got 'em!"

Rylin brought the flyer around, making a wide circle around the smoking wreck. A lone figure crawled from what was left of the car and looked up as they touched down on an open space in the road. Mac locked eyes with Jessup Moran for the briefest of moments before the murderer turned and ran.

The flyer's glass canopy slid open as they neared the ground.

"You waiting for an invitation?" Rylin asked, unbuckling his harness.

Mac cursed, unclasping his harness, and jumped to the pavement. He caught a glimpse of their quarry disappearing through a cloud of smoke and started after him.

"Stop!" Mac yelled. "*Peacemakers!* You're under arrest!"

Citizens backed out of his way, and he zig-zagged through the maze of stopped cars. Moran checked over his shoulder once, then seemed to push harder, opening the distance between them. Mac gritted his teeth and pressed on.

A blast of warm air hit him from above as Rylin's flyer shot past. It flew over Moran and banked hard, bring the bottom of its turbofans to bear. The powerful downwash knocked him off his feet, sending him sprawling. He rolled to a stop just as Mac rounded a car between them and charged.

Mac dropped his shoulder and plowed straight into Moran, knocking him back. They hit the pavement and rolled, a single mass of arms and legs. Mac ended up on his back, fending off a series of quick blows. He bucked his hips, throwing Moran sideways off of him, then spun, coming up behind him on his knees. He pulled his stunner from his belt, clicked it on and brought it up.

"Don't mov—"

Something crashed into him, knocking the wind from his lungs. He fell back, his head smacking against the pavement. Pain shot through him as stars danced in his vision. He brought up the stunner and he squeezed the trigger, firing blind.

A scream ripped through the air and Mac forced himself to ignore the nauseating pain, pushing himself upright. Moran had fallen to his side, his entire body locked in convulsion as 50,000 volts pulsed through his body.

Mac got to one knee, keeping the stunner aimed on Moran, ready to fire again. "Roll to your chest!"

Moran groaned. A second later the charge subsided, and his body stopped twitching. He rolled over, but instead of laying down, he got to his hands and knees.

"Stay down!" Mac yelled, getting to his feet.

Moran rose to his knees, glaring at Mac, anger and hatred filling his eyes. "Peacemakers." He spat. "Bunch of crooks with badges."

"I'll hit you again," Mac told him, emphasizing the stunner.

Slowly, Moran started to raise his hands. "Fucking pig—"

Something connected hard with Moran's head, knocking him sideways. He cried out, landing hard against the pavement. Out of nowhere, Rylin was on top of him, slamming gloved fists into Moran's face.

"You son of a bitch!" Rylin yelled between blows, his four fists punching like pistons.

Stunned, Mac lowered his weapon and watched as blow after blow landed, turning Moran's face into a bloody mess. Rylan held him up with his lower set of hands, while the upper set continued to pummel him. The sheer brutally of it all gave Mac pause. Unsure of what to do or say, he stood, frozen.

"Kill a fucking Peacemaker, huh?" Rylin shouted, his voice cracking as he landed another punch. Moran's body started to sag to the pavement. Rylin pulled him up by his collar. "Oh no, you don't!"

Mac looked over his shoulder at the line of traffic, now completely stopped and sitting in the roadway. People stood outside their vehicles, their watching faces covered in horror and fear. Their expressions mirrored what Mac was feeling.

He stepped forward, putting a hand on Tobias's shoulder. "Rylin."

"Not now," Tobias said.

Mac persisted, squeezing his shoulder. "Peacemaker Rylin, that's enough."

Rylin hesitated mid-swing and looked back at Mac, his eyes filled with rage. "What did you say?"

"He's had enough."

"Enough?" Rylin let Moran's limp body fall to the ground. He leaned in close, speaking so only Mac could hear. "He's had enough when I say he's had enough, Rookie. Cop killers don't get to just walk into jail. I figured even you backwater Marshals would understand something like that. We protect our own out here, it's us versus them."

"This isn't protecting anyone."

Rylin held both of Mac's shoulders while he jabbed a finger into Mac's chest. "Listen up, Rook, and listen good. This is how it's done. Don't forget whose side you're on. You give these assholes an inch, they'll take you for a mile. You wanted to be a Peacemaker; this is what it's about. Murderers don't get any compassion from me, much less a murderer of a Peacemaker. There's a special place in hell for this asshole and those like him."

Moran moaned. "I didn't..."

Rylin turned and kicked him, hard, and the man gasped in pain. "Shut up!"

Sirens echoed in the distance. Mac looked up and was relieved to see a familiar flash of red and blue in the distance. He wondered who it would be. He'd had little contact with his old Marshal unit since he'd started training, one of the many requirements Rylin had imposed after he'd signed on with the Guild.

Please, don't let it be Tonks, he thought as the Marshal flyers dropped out of the sky.

Moran groaned again, rolling to his side, clutching his stomach, spitting blood onto the pavement. At that moment Mac felt something he'd never felt in his ten years as a cop, something he never *thought* he'd feel for a criminal. Sympathy. He tried to force it down, tried to ignore it, but it wouldn't go away. Instead, it grew, overwhelming him. His stomach turned.

Several Marshals ran up as Rylin finished putting Moran in cuffs. Tonks wasn't among them.

"Jessup Moran is in Peacemaker custody. We need to secure the area and get those people back. You two, escort the prisoner to our flyer." He turned to Mac as they escorted Moran away. "You have something you want to say?"

Though there were plenty of things he wanted to say, Mac simply shook his head. "No. No, I don't."

"Good. Get him loaded up and let's get the hell off this rock." Rylin turned and walked toward their flyer, ignoring the chaos around him.

Mac watched as the two Marshals led Moran to the flyer. The sympathy he'd felt only moments before was fading, replaced with something entirely different, determination. He'd spent the better half of his adult life on the road to becoming a Peacemaker, and now, here, when that goal was in sight, a stark realization came over him.

Macintosh Sacobi knew he would never be a Peacemaker.

* * * * *

Chapter Two

Mac wasn't a slow runner, but trying to keep up with an Amore at full sprint was damn near impossible, even for the fittest of Human runners. The Amore looked a lot like a Veetanho, but was leaner and *fast*. He caught brief glimpses of the furry alien as he bounded through the crowd. The more he thought about it, the more Mac was convinced his partner enjoyed startling the crap out of civilians. A woman screamed, throwing her hands into the air and backing away as Tonks abruptly changed direction, disappearing into an alley.

Mac reached the corner a second later, gasping for air. He heard another scream, but this time it was male. Halfway down the alley, Tonks was wrestling with their suspect. Both were scrambling for better position, but it was a losing battle, Mac knew. For his size, Tonks was a better-than-average scrapper and much stronger than he appeared.

Tonks snarled as the man grabbed for his long tail, trying to pull him off. Tonks lashed out, tearing the man's clothes to shreds with razor claws. The man pulled hard on his tail, causing the furry alien to squeal.

"I'll rip your damn face off for that!" Tonks yelled.

Mac skidded to a stop, leveling his pistol. "Enough, Sullivan. Don't make this harder than it has to be."

After another second of wrestling for a better position and neither finding one, they both stopped and stared up at the barrel of Mac's 10mm pistol.

"We done here?" Mac asked.

Sullivan relented. Keeping his gaze fixed on Mac, he rolled onto his stomach. Tonks cuffed him, stood, and stepped next to Mac, his head barely reaching the Human's chest.

"I almost had him."

Their prisoner flicked hair out of his face with a jerk of his head. "You didn't have anything you filthy little space-rat."

Tonks lunged forward to attack, but Mac caught him by the shoulder, pulling him back. "Whoa, hang on, Tonks. Now that wasn't very nice, Henry."

The man spit, pushing himself up to his knees. "Like I give a shit about what you or that rat thinks?"

"You might," Mac said. "He's the one that's going to be doing your booking paperwork, and sometimes it takes him hours to get the reports typed up."

Tonks held up his small, four-fingered hands, sneering. His razor-sharp teeth made Sullivan's eyes widen.

"Yeah," the Amore said. "That's what I thought."

Henry Sullivan, gambler, conman, and all around deplorable, didn't resist on their trek back to the street.

A Marshal prisoner transport kicked up a cloud of dust as it touched down beside their patrol cars. The transport officer had the back door open as the two Marshals and their prisoner approached.

Tonks gave Sullivan an extra kick as they ushered him into the transport.

"Hey," Sullivan cried, his voice echoing inside the metal enclosure. "You can't do that, I want your name and shield number."

"T-O-N-K-go screw yourself!" Tonks said, slamming the door shut with a clang.

The transport officer looked up from his slate. "Gees, Tonks, what'd he do to you, skin your sister?"

Tonks pointed a short, brown finger. "That's strike two, Binelli."

"What happens when I get to three?" Binelli asked, laughing.

"Bad things," Tonks told him in a low, ominous tone. "Very bad things."

The officer raised his hands above his head in mock surrender, eyes wide. "Oooooh."

Mac shook his head. "Make sure he gets straight to booking, Binelli. And have the escort team help you, he's squirrelly."

"Not a bad day's work, Mac. Glad to have you back. The streets of Nemis are in good hands."

"Not that they weren't while he was gone," Tonks said.

Mac grinned. "Good to be back."

"And don't forget," Tonks said as Binelli pulled himself into the driver's seat. "Fast and furry-ous my friend. Fast and furry-ous."

Binelli shook his head, and the two Marshals stepped back as the transport's engines spun up. Mac held up a hand, shielding his eyes as the transport lifted into the air, kicking up dust around them again. A second later it disappeared into the traffic above them.

"It *is* good to have you back, though," Tonks said.

"Nice to know I was missed."

"Eh, I wouldn't say that." Tonks reached down and pulled a small cylinder off the rear-end of Sullivan's car. "I knew you'd be back. It was just a matter of time. I won't say I told you so, but...I told you so."

Mac grunted. The Amore was right, not that he'd never admit it openly. "How'd you manage to get Command Staff to approve those things anyway?"

Tonks tossed the device in his hand. "What, this old thing? It's all in how you present it. They love it when you start throwing around phrases like 'reduced liability' and 'increased safety' and blah, blah, blah. Gave me a six-month test period, and had them installed on our units."

Mac held out his hand, and Tonks tossed it over. "And they'll track anywhere on the planet."

"Wouldn't be much good if they didn't."

A loud commotion across the street drew their attention.

"You're a real piece of shit, Boss!" a woman yelled.

"Whoa," Tonks said. "What's this?"

Two groups of mercenaries surrounded a man and woman who seemed to be in the middle of a really good argument. Mac cocked his head to the side, trying to hear.

"Oh, it's Boss now? What happened to Johnny?" The man leaned forward, speaking so only the woman could hear. The woman shook her head, pulling against a tall Besquith wearing a wolf's head helmet. To Mac's surprise, she actually managed to pull the massive alien off balance.

"You haven't changed, Boss," the woman said. "Always blaming everyone else for your problems. I told you going after Protness was a bad idea. Did you listen? You left us there to die!"

"You refused to exfiltrate when I gave the order!"

A transport flew past, its engines kicking up dust and drowning out all other sound. Mac cursed, looking away, protecting his face.

"...I divorced you the last time, Johnny Boss!" the woman said, pulling free of the Besquith. She turned and stormed away, her small group of mercenaries close in tow.

"And I thought my wife was crazy," Tonks said, pulling off his gun belt. "You working another double?"

"Yeah," Mac said, watching the other mercenary crew turn and make their way through the quarter.

"You really should take some time off, my friend. I know you feel guilty about leaving, but working all the time isn't going to do anything but burn you out."

Mac shrugged. "Don't have anything better to do I guess."

"Yeah, well, if I don't get home, Grinna will do more than just divorce me."

"You better get home then; I wouldn't want to find your body left in a field somewhere."

"Oh, trust me," Tonks said. "If my wife has anything to do with it, there won't be a body to find."

* * * * *

Chapter Three

Mac spent the next hour typing the Sullivan report, then returned to his patrol route above the city. His Marshal squad flew smoothly through the congested traffic skyways, soaking up information. Registration numbers, facial recognition programs, and active sound sensors provided Mac with an almost overwhelming amount of information, but aside from a few expired registrations, the night was relatively quiet.

Every so often his thoughts would drift back to the argument from the mercenary quarter, something nagged at him about it, but he couldn't pinpoint what it was. A search through the transit logs showed that Boss had arrived on a ship registered to the Ogre Fist Company, a small mercenary outfit. Mac's last option was a longshot, running it through the regional contract database. The less secure records weren't the most reliable, but they were better than nothing.

The OFC had bids on several low-priority contracts, nothing compared to what the Four Horseman groups would typically pull, but they appeared to make a livable wage at least. Most of their contracts were attached to back-water worlds where the Peacemakers and the larger mercenary groups didn't operate because the return on investment was next to nothing.

An alert flashed on his cockpit's display, a bar fight at the Twelve Gage Laser. Mac shook his head as he read. Two merc gangs fighting, several units en route. The bar was only a few kilometers outside his response area, and he knew from experience, mercs had a propensity to take things much further than they needed.

Mac adjusted his course, then turned back to his information on the Ogre Fist, scrolling to a list of registered members. He didn't recognize any of the names, but hadn't expected to. He clicked through to a list of past members. Halfway through the list his breath caught in his throat.

Jessup Moran.

Blood pounded in Mac's ears, remembering the pitiful look on the man's face as Rylin Tobias had dealt out his own, unique justice. Remembering his last day as a Peacemaker. He'd tried long and hard to forget, but every now and then the name would creep back into his thoughts, and he'd relive that horrible day.

Quickly he brought up Jessup's arrest record. His official file showed him being transferred to Super Max Prison Station 39 almost immediately after they'd arrested him. Just to settle his doubts, he queried the prison's records for Moran's status. The response was not what he was expecting.

"What the hell do you mean, 'classified'?"

The only information listed in the file was Moran's personal history sheet and his prison identification number; everything else had been redacted from the official record. There wasn't a listing for current housing block, and even his transfer records had been heavily edited.

Mac felt the hairs on the back of his neck stand up. His instincts told him Johnny Boss's arrival on Calista wasn't a chance thing, and then the radio squeaked to life. "All units, respond Code 3, large disturbance Twelve Gage Laser, all units respond. The gangs are tearing the place apart."

Mac punched his comms. "Dispatch, do we have any information on the gangs involved?"

"Looks like the Golden Feet Company and the Ogre Fists."

Mac slammed his hand on the flyer's controls, pushing its engines to maximum.

* * * * *

Chapter Four

"And no one has any idea why the fight started?" Mac asked.

He stood near the entrance to Twelve Gage Laser, looking over the wreckage strewn across the street.

Marshal Collins shook her head. "None. A few of the patrons thought it was some old rivalry, but they couldn't be specific on anything. Hell, no one has any idea who actually started the fight."

A medic team rolled a wounded man out of the bar to a waiting air ambulance, the bandage around his head stained red.

"How many injured?"

"Seven, but that's only those who couldn't leave on their own before we got here. There could be more."

"And none from the merc crews?"

"Bastards started a fire and just let it burn," Collins said. "I feel bad for the owner." She nodded to a short, balding man, working on putting his front door back in its frame.

"Any one talk to him yet?"

"Hystad did, for what it's worth."

Mac raised an eyebrow.

"He's not the hottest laser in the box. But his surveillance system is top notch."

"Good."

Mac introduced himself to the bartender, who eagerly led him inside, all too happy to share his video.

Mac stepped around a broken table, shaking his head. "They sure did a number in here, didn't they?"

"I don't know why it always has to be my bar they destroy," the bartender said, leading Mac into the back office. "Insurance company demanded I upgrade this thing the last time it happened."

"Impressive," Mac said.

Four large screens, mounted on one wall, displayed four different angles of the bar. A small control panel rested on a cluttered desk below the monitors. The bartender pulled a chair out and began working the controls. On the screens, the images started rewinding.

"Bastards just started going at it. Usually I have time to kick them all out before it gets too carried away, but this time...here, see."

On the screen, Johnny Boss stepped into the bar, accompanied by his gang. They paused just inside the door, as if they were looking for something, discussing something.

"Can we hear what they're saying?"

"Sorry, not wired for sound."

On the screen a tall, one-eyed albino, stepped up to Boss and said something. Almost immediately, Johnny's second in charge lashed out, punching him in the face. The fight was on. It sprawled across all four screens, growing as more and more people joined the melee.

Mac frowned, keeping his attention on Boss. The merc didn't seem to be paying attention to the fighting, instead, he pushed and shoved his way through the melee, making his way to the back of the bar. He disappeared into the back and vanished from the screens.

"Do you have shots of the back?"

The bartender shook his head. "No one's allowed back there."

Mac held back a curse as the fighting spilled out of the bar's front doors and into the street.

"But I do have a couple cameras in the back."

"Show me."

The bartender tapped a button and the view in the top two monitors changed to one of the bar's rear entrance and the alley. Two figures, Boss and his second, were chasing after a third. The second leaped and tackled the fleeing man, then rained down blow after blow to his victim's face. A moment later Boss caught up to them and jerked his second off the man. For a brief instant, the third man's face was visible, highlighted by the streetlights above.

"Freeze that," Mac said, his blood running cold. "It can't be."

Jessup Moran stared up at his attacker, his face frozen in terror.

"That's impossible."

* * * * *

Chapter Five

Rylin Tobias concentrated on the small bits of sediment floating in what remained of his tea, trying to clear his thoughts. There had to be a way to pawn off the recruit on someone else this time. Back-to-back recruit training hadn't been done before, as far as Tobias could remember. Not to mention the cluster-fuck that had happened with his last recruit.

There had to be a way to get out of this shithole. Tobias just needed to find the right leverage. One would've thought apprehending a known Peacemaker murderer would have been enough; Regional, however, thought differently.

He finished his tea, not taking his gaze from the view outside his window. To anyone else, the view might have been relaxing, even comforting, but Tobias hated this view. Nemis' cityscape was yet another reminder of his inability to break through into a regional directorship. The tall towers and busy skyways taunted him, laughed at him, much like the idiot no-loads above him did.

His leverage was out there somewhere, leverage that would give the guild's leadership no choice but to promote him. Leverage that would make his career. It made no difference where it came from; what mattered to Tobias was how effective the leverage was.

A chime sounded, and a female voice came through unseen speakers. "Peacemaker Tobias, you have a call from a Cindy Fowler."

Tobias gave the floating holographic image on the desk behind him a sidelong look, frowning. The name sounded vaguely familiar, but he had a hard time placing it. Then he remembered.

He sighed, maybe it would take his mind off Regional for a while. "Put her through."

The recorded image of Cindy Fowler disappeared, replaced by a live image.

"Ms. Fowler."

"Peacemaker Tobias, listen, I know it's been awhile, and I know you're probably still upset with me, but I have to tell you it wasn't my fault, and there were people after me, and I couldn't risk coming up for air. It wasn't my faul—"

"Ms. Fowler, please, let's just pretend for a minute that I'm not a complete idiot, and you're not a junked-out whore. I am extremely busy, I took your call as a one-time courtesy, which I'm already regretting, so why don't you get to the point."

Fowler stared back at Tobias for a moment, her face a mask of confusion. "I…uh…I…"

"Yes?"

The woman straightened. "Before the trial, you said that if I brought you good information, you would pay for it."

"Ms. Fowler, that was a long time ago. Besides, I seem to remember you not keeping up your end of the deal."

"Yeah, I told you, that wasn't my—"

"Wasn't your fault, I know."

Cindy sniffed. "Yeah, well, I'm sorry about that. But this, what I know, I think it might be worth a lot to you."

As unlikely as it was for this low-life to be well-informed about anything, Tobias decided to hear her out. "First, let's hear this so-called valuable information, then we'll decide how much it's worth."

Cindy's eyes shifted from side to side, as if she was looking for someone. "It's a fugitive."

"Runaways and absconders are of no interest to me. They're barely worth the cost of the transport fees."

"Even if they've escaped from a Super Max and are being hunted by their old mercenary crew?"

The Peacemaker straightened.

Cindy continued. "Rumor has it, this guy killed one of your buddies."

* * * * *

Chapter Six

"What the hell is an Ogre Fist?" Tonks asked, his tiny holographic image frowning. The projection cast an orange glow around the flyer's cockpit.

"Hell if I know," Mac said. "Doesn't matter; listen, we need to figure out where they went. If we lose them, Moran will disappear for good. We can't let that happen."

Tonks looked at something off camera. "Are you sure it was Moran, Mac? I mean, that's a big deal. Something would have been broadcast by now."

The thought hit Mac like a freight train. "The wife!"

"What are you talking about, man?"

Mac's fingers flew across his console. Why hadn't he thought of it before? "That couple arguing at the quarter, Johnny Boss and that woman. How much you want to bet she has connections here? There, Cindy Fowler, divorced from Boss two years ago." He scrolled through the information, pulse racing. He clapped once. "Told you, Fowler Agriculture."

Tonks's furry eyebrows raised expectantly. "You want to grow some plants?"

"A farming operation on the outskirts; the property is still registered to the family. It's far enough outside the city's network, they wouldn't have to worry about any prying eyes."

"I don't know, Mac. That's pretty thin."

"It's all we've got."

"But why in the hell would Moran come back here?"

"I don't know, Tonks." Mac punched in the heading for the farm.

"Do you want me to call it in?"

"No," Mac said. "No, we do that, and the Peacemakers'll be all over it."

"Well, at least let me come with you."

Mac shook his head. "No time. Let me figure out what's going on first. I'll get back with you."

"Mac, don't do anything stupid."

"You know me."

"I know, that's why I'm reminding you."

He reached the outskirts of the farm 15 minutes later. He flew in low, over what looked like a war zone. Fields all around the main homestead were burning. Craters marred the ground in hundreds of places, smoke still curling into the air from several. Small fires littered the property.

What the hell happened here, Mac wondered, setting the flyer down near the western edge of the farm proper. From the air, he'd only seen one flyer on the grounds, parked next to the large barn on the northeast side of the property.

Well, Mac thought as the flyer's canopy opened, *here goes nothing.*

He made his way across the property until he was in sight of the barn and flyer. Standing at the far corner of the farmhouse, Mac began to process the situation. A single guard, probably the pilot, stood with the aircraft. Another guard stood by the partially-open double doors leading into the barn, a sliver of light from inside cutting into the darkness.

It took 10 minutes to make his way around to the backside of the barn. The interior was lit by a line of photostrips hanging from the rafters. Moran sat, bound to a chair, facing away from Mac, toward the front of the barn. Even from behind it was clear the man had received a severe beating.

Two mercenaries stood off to one side, smoking and talking quietly. They gave Moran sidelong looks occasionally, but for the most part ignored the wounded man. One of the mercs, a woman, kept checking a personal slate. The other stamped out a finished smoke, only to immediately light up another.

What are you waiting for? Mac thought.

For a moment, Mac considered waiting for Tonks, but no. There was no telling how long the mercenaries would stay here. No telling how long before they decided to finish off Moran.

Mac centered himself on the small door, took a deep breath, trying to steady his nerves, then lunged forward, slamming his boot into the door. It smashed open, swinging aside in a cloud of dust and splinters. He rolled in, coming up on one knee several feet away from the door, and brought his pistol up.

"Calista Marshals, don't move!"

The woman's eyes snapped up from her slate, fixing on Mac.

The smoker turned his head slightly, finding Mac out of the corner of his eye. "The hell?"

"Don't move," Mac repeated. "You're under arrest."

It happened so fast Mac barely registered the movement.

The woman dropped her slate, letting it fall to the ground at the same time Smoker turned away from her. He cleared his jacket with one hand, drawing a large energy pulser from a holster under his arm in the other. The woman stepped backward, into the shadows of a stall, drawing her own weapon.

"No!" Mac shouted.

Everything slowed to a crawl. Mac squeezed the trigger.

Mac never heard the shot, never felt the recoil, but he did see the woman jerk back as a round took her in the shoulder, spinning her like a top. He got to his feet, already aiming for his next target. Smoker had spun completely around and was bringing his weapon up. The air cracked as the pulser fired.

Dodging behind a stall wall, Mac dropped to a knee as the heat from the energy bolts singed his hair. Smoker fired wildly as he moved down the length of the barn, away from Mac.

Mac stood and fired twice. His first shot missed, the bullet slamming into a post. His second shot hit Smoker's side, sending him crashing into a stable wall.

Metal creaked at the front of the barn. One of the mercs was pulling the door open, eyes wide in confusion and shock. The merc moved into the barn, obviously trying to comprehend the carnage he saw.

"What in the fuck?"

Mac brought his weapon up. "Calista Marshals, drop the gun!" Even as he said it, Mac knew it was pointless.

"Son of a bitch!" The merc shouted, bringing his pistol around.

Mac fired twice. Both rounds hit center-mass, sending the merc stumbling backwards. His shoulder collided with the still-opening barn door, and he spun backward into the darkness.

Mac kept his weapon trained on the door and moved toward the front of the barn. The pilot was still out there, if he hadn't just decided to bail and leave the rest of them behind. He took cover behind one of the stable walls and waited.

A second later the pilot appeared, rifle in hand, approaching out of the shadows. He moved cautiously and stopped just before stepping into the light.

"We can make a deal!" the pilot shouted.

"Sure thing," Mac said. "You drop your gun, and I won't kill you. Deal?"

A short barrage of rifle fire answered him. The shots tore through the front of the barn, several feet away from Mac. Even so, he flinched and backed away.

"This doesn't have to go down like this," Mac said. "We can all go home without unwanted holes. I'm here for Moran, not you."

"Can't have him! Besides, we already have the slate, he's worthless to you now."

Slate? Mac wondered. *What the hell is he talking about?* "I don't care about the slate, keep it. I just want Moran."

"Sorry, friend, only Boss can make that call. Now, I'm going to count to three, and then I'm going to come in blazing. If you value staying whole, you may want to vacate the premises and forget the name Jessup Moran. One."

Well, shit, that didn't work.

"Two."

There was only one other option.

"Thr—"

Mac stepped forward, aimed and fired.

The pilot's foot came an inch off the ground just as Mac's bullet slammed into the mercenary's forehead. His head snapped back, the impact sending him sprawling. He landed with a thud and didn't move.

Mac stepped up to the door, holstering his pistol. "Damn."

A loud crack echoed through the air, making Mac jump. His head snapped around just in time to see the woman stumbling back into a stable wall, clutching her chest. Then he saw Jessup standing where Smoker had fallen, the mercenary's pulser in his hand.

Mac put a hand on his pistol, but didn't draw. Moran didn't move. After several long moments, his hands fell to his sides, and his pulser dropped to the ground.

"I don't understand," Mac said.

"I don't kill cops, Marshal Sacobi."

* * * * *

Chapter Seven

"You better start talking," Mac said, turning sideways to face Moran in the flyer's cockpit.

The electrocuffs binding Moran's hands in front of him made it awkward to wipe the blood from his face, but he managed. "I feel like I've already been through this once today."

"Answer me."

"What are you going to do, shove bamboo under my fingernails? Beat me with a phone book?"

Mac considered the man for a second. "I could just turn you over to the Peacemakers."

Moran sniffed, but remained silent.

"Let's start with an easy one; how the hell did you get out of prison?"

"I know you're not going to believe me when I say this, but that wasn't my idea. Johnny and his crew broke me out. I didn't have anything to do with it."

"You're right, I don't believe you."

Moran shrugged. "Don't make it no less true. Trust me, considering the alternative, I'd much rather be stuck back in that cell."

"Some pretty good friends you have there to risk attacking a Super Max."

"Yeah, some friends, right?" Moran motioned to his swollen face with a thumb. "Trust me, it wasn't for an overabundance of loyalty, I can tell you that. Money is a great motivator."

"You're saying they broke you out of one of the most secure facilities in the galaxy for money? Must be one hell of a contract."

"You could say that."

"What is it? Why are you worth so much?"

"Ha. You got it all wrong, I'm not worth anything. But what I know, that's something completely different."

"So, this information you have, that's why they beat you half to death?"

"That's right, and if you hadn't shown up they probably would have finished the job when Johnny found out I lied to him."

"Lied to him about what?"

"The reason I'm in the whole shitty mess in the first place. The slate."

"Slate? Wait, you're not talking about the slate you took from that Peacemaker you killed?"

Moran groaned. "For the thousandth time, I didn't kill him. He was alive and well when I left him. I don't know how many times I can say it. I told you, I'm not a killer. Thief yes; killer no. I'd be willing to bet whoever *did* kill him was concerned about what was on that damn slate. Hell, if I'd known what was on it before I lifted it, I would never have touched it. I should've known it was a shit-job when the contract came through."

"What contract? What's so damned important about this slate?"

"Black-market job, masked client, and ridiculous amount of money. Should have known better. No one pays that much money for a 'Snatch and Grab.' I was in and out in under 15 minutes, and had it not been for Jenkin's death, I would've made it off-planet, no issues."

Mac frowned. "Who's Jenkins?"

"The Peacemaker I killed." Moran held up air-quotes.

Mac flushed slightly, embarrassed he hadn't recognized the name. He had known, but most of his energy and thoughts had been focused on Moran, the killer, not Jenkins the victim.

"But you didn't have the slate on you when we took you into custody."

"That's right, I didn't."

Mac paused, looking into the mercenary's eyes. "The slate's still here? On Calista? Boss broke you out of prison so he could force you to give him the slate?"

"Got it in one."

"But you said you lied to him?"

"Kind of a stupid thing to do I guess. But Davenport was going to kill me regardless of whether I told them where it was or not. I figured if I could point them in a direction where there was a chance they'd be taken out, it might give me a chance."

"So, where is it?"

Moran was silent for several seconds, almost as if he was trying to determine whether Mac was worthy or not. Finally, he said, "I'll take you to it."

* * * * *

Chapter Eight

"You know, it'd be a lot easier to do this if you took these off," Moran said, holding up his cuffed wrists.

"Yeah, not going to happen. You're lucky I'm not just taking you straight to Central Processing."

Mac climbed out of the flyer, then waited at the bottom as Moran struggled down the ladder.

"So, level with me," Moran said. "Why are you helping me?"

A voice from the shadows caused both men to jump. "I was wondering that exact same thing."

Mac spun, drawing his pistol and leveling it in the direction of the voice. He let out a sigh and lowered the gun as an angry-looking Amore stepped from the shadows.

"Jesus," Mac said. "Tonks, you scared the shit out of me."

The alien shrugged. "You pulled me away from a perfectly relaxing evening with a bottle of Black Label and the Misses. Seeing you almost shit your pants makes up for that a little."

"Great." Mac jammed the pistol back into its holster.

"Looks like you made a new friend," Tonks said, nodding to Moran.

"Well, I wouldn't say we're besties yet," Moran said, "but we're getting there."

Mac ignored him. "Did you bring the stuff I asked for?"

Tonks padded a pack slung over one arm. "Still not sure why you need them, but it's not the craziest thing you've ever asked for."

Mac gave his friend a knowing look. "We'll see." He turned to Moran. "Where are we heading?"

Moran nodded to the tall tenement building on one side of the service lot. "Sixth floor. Number 607."

"Let's get moving."

"Does it seem a little too quiet around here to you?" Moran asked as they walked.

"Peacemakers issued a planet-wide warning about your friends about an hour ago," Tonks said. "Nemis is on a city-wide curfew."

"Well, that's good for us, right?" Moran asked.

Mac held up a finger. "First, off, there is no *us*. Got that? We aren't in this together. There is no team. You are still a criminal and will be judged accordingly when this is over."

"Okay, okay!" Jessup said, holding his cuffed hands up in surrender. "Shit."

They continued in silence. They found the service entrance unlocked, and a few seconds later they were ascending the stairs to the sixth floor.

Unit 607 was situated in the middle of the floor, on the north side of a dimly-lit corridor. Several of the photostrips lining the ceiling flickered. Trash and dirt covered the floor, and graffiti covered the walls.

Mac tried the handle. Locked. He swiped his credentials across the panel, however, the door remained locked. "Huh, doesn't recognize my Marshal access."

"Let me try mine," Tonks said, stepping up to the panel. The light flashed red again, and the door didn't unlock. "Hmmmm."

"I've got a key," Moran said.

Both Marshals turned to him, sharing disbelieving expressions.

Moran dug one hand into a pocket. "It's right..." He lunged forward and slammed a boot into the door. The locking mechanism broke with a loud crack, and the door swung open.

"Very subtle," Tonks said. "Now the entire floor'll know we're here."

"No one pays attention to anything in these housing blocks," Moran said. "That's why I picked it. No one gets into anyone else's business."

"Come on," Mac said, stepping into the apartment.

The room was dark, lit only by the city lights outside the apartment's dirty windows. A small bed sat underneath the windows opposite the door. A small kitchenette was located to their right; a shower, toilet, and sink was on their left. The air was stale, and everything was covered by a thin layer of dust.

"You know, with a little paint, this place could be a little cozy space," Tonks said.

"We did an extensive check on you before we caught you," Mac said. "We never found any records of you ever renting or buying on the planet."

Moran gave Mac a sardonic smile. "Criminal."

Mac shook his head. "Okay, so where is this thing people are so willing to kill for?"

"Right," Moran said, moving across to the bed. "You want to give me a hand with this?"

Mac hesitated.

"Or you can take these off." Moran held up the cuffs again.

Mac lifted the mattress off the metal frame, and Moran reached underneath, stretching back toward the wall.

"Oh, come on," Tonks said. "You've got to be kidding."

Moran stood, holding up an unremarkable slate.

Tonks laughed. "You hid it under your mattress?"

"Worked, didn't it?"

Mac held out his hand. Moran hesitated.

"The stuff that's on this thing," Moran said. "There are people out there right now, high-ranking people, that wouldn't hesitate to kill anyone to get their hands on it. I'm not being overly dramatic, either. They've already killed at least one person that I know of, but I'm sure there are others. These are people you don't get away from."

"You're talking about Jenkins," Mac said, more a statement than a question.

Moran nodded. "I'm actually surprised I've lasted this long. I'm sure the only reason I'm alive is because of this." He waved the slate.

"Let's see it."

Moran handed the slate over, sighing as he let it go. Mac turned it on and waited as the device ran through its start-up sequence.

"Wow," Mac said, reading the data as it scrolled down the screen. "That's some pretty heavy-duty encryption. Almost looks like military grade."

"If it isn't, it's the next best thing," Moran said. "The guy I took it to before you said he'd only seen one slate like it, and that one was an Information Guild slate. Took him almost seven hours to crack it under containment. It's unlocked and safe now, but... don't say I didn't warn you."

"Oh, for shit's sake," Tonks said. He snatched the slate from Mac's fingers and scrolled through the data. He stopped after just a few seconds and looked up, eyes wide. "Holy shit. Mac this is incredible." He looked over at Moran. "There's enough dirt on this thing you could call in favors for life and still not run out of shit to hold over people."

"Now you see why people are dying for this thing."

Mac held out his hand, and, reluctantly, Tonks passed it over.

"What are you going to do with it?" Moran asked.

"There's only two options I see here. One, we destroy this thing and forget we ever saw it, or two, we turn it over—"

"No way," Moran interrupted. "No fucking way. You of all people know what happens when you try to do the right thing. You'll get a knife in the back as soon as you walk out of the guild hall. Or a flyer will run you over, or some freak electrical accident will fry your navigation system, and you'll crash into a building or something. They won't let this get out. Marshal or no, Peacemaker or no, these people don't care. They operate so far above the law, they don't even know what it is."

"He's got a point," Tonks said.

"So, we destroy it?" Mac asked, not liking that idea at all. "Let everyone implicated on this thing just go on getting away with everything?"

Moran pointed at the slate. "That right there, that's leverage."

"I'm not going to blackmail anyone, if that's what you're thinking."

"Well, then I truly don't know what to tell you. Because, that slate is priceless and deadly at the same time. Not only that, but I have no doubt there is tracking data in there somewhere, which will prove I was nowhere near Jenkins when he was killed. That alone is worth more than any other bullshit on that thing."

"We can shotgun it," Tonks suggested, climbing onto the bed. He pushed back the curtains and looked out over Nemis' skyline.

Mac could see the red, orange, and yellow glows refracted in the glass.

"We'd need a hell of a lot of bandwidth to push something this big."

Tonks turned away from the window. "Come on, man, I've got the tech section wrapped around my tail. We can load it remotely, compress it, then blast it out whenever we're ready."

"How long to upload?"

Tonks shrugged. "Ten to fifteen minutes."

He held the slate out to his partner. "Do it."

* * * * *

Chapter Nine

Tonks brought in his last bit of equipment, a large case almost as big as the alien himself, and opened it in the middle of the floor next to two others. The slate sat next to the first case, a thin black cable connecting the two.

"I could use some help here," Tonks said.

Mac nudged Moran toward the window. "Keep an eye out."

Mac moved to stand over the Amore, who slapped the center case with the palm of his paw, cursing the machine.

"Okay," Tonks said. "I've got a trace program up, our Marshal-net connection is running through this terminal here, and the third is a backup for the trace. Now, once we start we're not going to be able to shut it down. You sure you want to do this?"

"We don't have a choice," Mac said.

"All right." Tonks jabbed a furry finger down, and the program came to life. The slate's screen lit up, and the electronics hummed as they worked. Dialogue panels opened and closed, and lines of text flashed in seemingly random fractal line patterns, filling the screens. The terminal on the far right beeped, and a text box appeared, flashing red and white.

The Amore's ears perked up. "Shit!"

His fingers flew across the keyboard.

"What's up?"

"Someone's already tracing the line. Damn, that was fast."

Moran turned away from the window. "We need to get out of here."

Mac pointed at him. "Keep watching. How much time do you have before they lock on?"

"Hell…" Tonks said. "Maybe five, six minutes. Could be sooner; it's hard to say."

Mac clenched his fists. "Damn it."

"Oh, shit," Moran said, stepping back from the window.

Mac moved over to the window. "What is it?"

He pulled the curtain back and looked down at the street. Two flyers had just touched down, each disgorging a squad of armed men. Privately-contracted security forces—the Peacemakers used them sometimes to crack down on smaller operations throughout the fringe worlds.

"We've got company," Mac said.

"I still need a few minutes here. It's almost finished pre-loading."

"We don't have a few minutes, Tonks. We're out of time."

"Then we're screwed, Mac. How the hell did they find us so quick?"

"Has to be Tobias," Mac said.

"How the hell did he find us?"

Mac shook his head, frustrated. "I don't know. Maybe he was able to track us somehow. Maybe he got tipped off. I don't know, but it's the only explanation; if it was the Marshals, we'd have heard something."

"They're heading our direction," Moran said, pointing out the window.

Shit. Shit. Shit. Mac looked around the room, thinking. If Tobias was after them, he might not put forth the effort to arrest them. More likely, he'd simply kill them all to be rid of the irritation.

"How much time do you need?" Mac asked.

Tonks looked over his equipment. "Looks like the compression is finished, now it's just uploading the data to the proxy."

They couldn't stand and fight; they'd be overwhelmed in a matter of minutes. Tobias wouldn't be too far behind, if he wasn't here already, and then all bets were off. Security contractors were one thing, a fully-armed Peacemaker was another.

"We run," Mac said.

The two others looked at him, surprised.

He continued, "We run, and we lead them away from here. We only need to buy enough time for the package to upload to the proxy, then there won't be anything he can do to stop it. Push all that stuff under the bed and let's get out of here."

A minute later, they were running through the corridor toward the stairwell. Down was the only option. They reached Level 4 and stopped on the landing, listening. Boots pounded on the stairs below, gear rattled, and men spoke in short, clipped sentences.

Mac nodded at the exit. "Go."

Tonks was the first through the door, followed by Moran, and Mac brought up the rear. He heard one of the contractors shout something and cursed. They'd be on them in moments.

The building was shaped like a large "L." Just as they reached the building's elbow, the stairwell door they'd just come from slammed open. Mac caught a glimpse of three armed men filing through as he rounded the corner. Shouts to stop and surrender echoed after them, then gunshots, deafening in the confined space.

Plaster erupted from the wall behind Mac, sending dust and debris spraying.

"Go, go, go!" he shouted, pushing Moran forward.

They reached the far end of the corridor, where another door led to a secondary stairwell. Tonks launched himself through the air, slamming into the door, knocking it open. They flew down the stairs, barely even touching them. As they reached ground level, Mac heard the door slam open above them, followed by several more gunshots.

Bullets twanged off the metal railing and smacked into the floor. They raced from the stairwell into a long, dark corridor filled with trash and abandoned property.

"Quick," Mac said, grabbing a mattress. "Block the door."

Tonks cursed but moved to help. A few seconds later they'd created a barrier of junk that reached halfway up the door.

The trio fled down the corridor, then out through the exit into the service lot where both flyers sat.

"How much time?" Mac asked, making for his flyer, Moran and Tonks following.

"Four—"

The Amore's flyer, to their left, erupted into flames, the explosion ripping through one of its wings. The entire craft folded in on itself as wreckage sprayed into the air.

The explosion knocked Mac slightly off balance, slowing his progress to his own flyer. He cursed, raising a hand to shield his eyes from the brilliance of the flames.

"Son of a bitch!" Moran yelled, moving away from the flaming wreckage.

Tonks came to a stop, transfixed on the burning flyer. "Mother—"

A second explosion ripped open Mac's flyer. The drive compartment erupted in smoke and flames. Pieces of the flyer bounced off the brick wall behind them, and metal groaned as the chassis collapsed to the pavement.

Mac stuttered to stop, eyes darting back and forth between the two burning wrecks. The two fires cast eerie shadows around the darkened service lot.

"Well don't just stand there," Moran shouted, already heading past Tonks's flyer, down the alley. His stride was clumsy with his wrists still bound.

They'd almost reached the main access to the street, when a figure landed on the pavement in front of them. It stood; a human wrapped in Peacemaker assault armor. A loud, electronically enhanced voice boomed through the alley.

"STOP!"

"Son of a bitch!" Tonks yelled, bringing up his pistol. The Peacemaker shifted as Tonks fired, returning fire while dodging away from the Marshal's bullets. Sparks shot out from the Peacemaker's armor just as Tonks let out a blood-curdling scream.

Mac yelled as one of the Peacemaker's shots took Tonks in the chest, knocking him off his feet. He watched his friend roll several feet before coming to a stop, unmoving. He turned, bringing his pistol up, and saw the Peacemaker already had his weapon trained on him.

"I said stop," the electronic voice ordered.

Mac hesitated.

"Macintosh Sacobi, I knew you'd never cut it in the Guild; I should never have pulled you along like I did." The Peacemaker raised his helmet's face shield. Rylin Tobias grinned.

* * * * *

Chapter Ten

"I don't think law and order really is your thing," Tobias said, stepping forward. "Though, on a positive note, you'll probably have the record for shortest criminal career of all time."

Mac stared at the Peacemaker, feeling bile raise in the back of his throat. His arms shook with rage. "If you resemble anything close to law enforcement, I'm glad I don't measure up. You're not going to get away with this, Rylin. Not this time. I won't let you."

Tobias laughed. "Won't let me? I'm not sure how you have any control of tonight's events whatsoever."

Moran stepped up next to Mac.

"I will admit," Tobias said, his eyes turning to Moran. "I didn't see this little…partnership coming. Weren't satisfied with one cop dead, Moran? Needed to come back and pick up where you left off?"

Moran didn't answer.

"It actually makes my life a little easier, tell you the truth. An escaped cop killer kills two Marshals while they were trying to bring him in and is killed after firing on a Peacemaker. I don't think anyone will have any difficulty believing that."

"So, you're just going to kill us?"

"I guess there is one alternative. A way we can still both come out ahead on this deal."

"And that is?"

"Give me the slate. I know that's why your friend there came back. It's the only thing that makes sense. And the fact his friends went to such lengths to get their hands on it means it's very valuable indeed. Honestly, attacking a Super Max Prison with a low-level merc gang, to spring one man; that's a hell of a risk."

"I don't have it," Mac said.

"Oh, come on, do we really have to play this game? I know you have it. Come on, hand it over."

"No."

Tobias fired, the crack echoing around the alley. Moran doubled over, grabbing his stomach. The unexpected shot caught Mac off-guard. He stepped toward the injured man, keeping his pistol leveled at the Peacemaker.

"Damn it, Tobias!" Mac pulled Moran's arm over his shoulder, keeping the man on his feet.

Moran looked up, face etched in pain. "You're a real asshole."

"It doesn't have to be like this," Tobias said. "Just hand over the slate."

Moran groaned and slumped against Mac's grip. Mac's eyes bore into Tobias, every fiber of his being wishing to exact revenge on his old trainer. No, not vengeance, justice.

He lowered his pistol. "Okay, Tobias. You win." He reached into his jacket and produced the slate, holding it up. "Here it is."

"Good. Now slide it over."

Mac bent over and slid it over. The Peacemaker picked the device off the ground and examined it while keeping his weapon trained on the two men.

"I'll put in a good word for you, Mac," Tobias said. "Hell, I might even be able to get you a formal Guild funeral."

"No!"

The crack was deafening and Mac felt himself being flung back through the air. He just barely registered Moran shoving him out of the way, stepping in front of the Marshal. Moran's body jerked abruptly, taking the blast intended for Mac.

Mac screamed, rolling to the side as Moran dropped to his knees. Mac came up on one knee and fired. The bullet smacked into Tobias's weapon, knocking it from the Peacemaker's hand. Seeing his opportunity, Mac charged. Tobias turned and fled.

Gunfire echoed through the alley as Mac fired as he chased after Tobias. The Peacemaker rounded the corner at a full sprint. By the time Mac reached the corner, Tobias was dropping behind the controls of a Peacemaker flyer, and its cockpit windshield was closing.

Mac fired until he was empty, tiny bursts of sparks erupting across the flyer's fuselage. Mac cursed, turning and sprinting away as the flyer's cannons opened up. The street erupted in plumes of concrete and dust, the blasts cutting a path down the street into the mouth of the alley.

Mac launched himself into the alley as the cannon fire subsided, the last of the blasts hitting mere feet from where Mac rolled to a stop. The flyer's engines roared, then faded as it lifted into the night.

Mac lay still for several moments, trying to catch his breath. When he finally got back to his feet, his heart sank at the sight of his fallen companions.

Mac knelt next to Moran. Blood seeped from a wound in his chest.

"Why?" Mac asked, surprised at the anger and sadness he felt as the life faded from the man's eyes.

"I told you…I'm not a killer."

* * * * *

Chapter Eleven

Rylin Tobias locked the door to his office and tossed his harness over his chair.

The news cast on his wall screen displayed images of the carnage from the tenement building. Reporters were already linking the devastation to gang violence and mercenaries.

"Sources claim two Calista Marshals are among the casualties."

Tobias found himself whistling as he switched the slate on, barely able to contain his anticipation.

The main screen appeared, and he began working through the contents. He frowned, as he opened the first file, finding a list of intergalactic extradition attorneys.

"What the hell?"

The next file was more of the same. And the next.

"What the fuck is this?"

The female voice on the news broadcast was interrupted by a male. "I'm sorry, Diane, we have to interrupt you for a moment, we're just now receiving video that should shed some light on the developing situation there at the tenements. I should warn our viewers, what you're about to see is graphic and disturbing."

The image changed, the shot was behind two men, Tobias immediately recognized as Sacobi and Moran, and at the far end of the alley, he stood, weapon pointing at the two men.

There was sound, but it was difficult to pick up what was being said. Sacobi bent down, sliding the slate over. He watched himself pull the trigger, the flash turning the image into a grainy glare. He watched Moran shove the Marshal out of the way, taking the blast himself.

His stomach turned as he watched the brief chase, and then the street erupted in cannon fire. Blood pounded in his ears as Sacobi stood several moments later, then moved to Moran's side.

After a minute, the Marshal got to his feet and came back toward the camera.

"You okay?" Sacobi's voice asked.

Off camera, the Amore said, "I got shot in the leg, how the hell do you think I am?"

"Did you get it?"

"Yeah, I got it."

The image changed back to the reporter. "We have not been able to identify the Peacemaker as yet, and the Guild would not comment on the video. We are also receiving reports of a massive data dump across the Galnet, and our initial investigation seems to implicate a number of high level government officials engaging in a number of illegal activities, including smuggling, drug trafficking, and murder.

"For more on these developing stories, stay tuned to Calista News Network."

A pounding at his door jolted Tobias out of his daze. A muffled voice said, "Tobias, are you in there? Tobias, Regional Direction Kern is on the line. He's demanding to speak to you right now."

Tobias barely heard his secretary. He sat down in his chair, eyes fixed on the slate. His leverage.

His end.

* * * * *

Chapter Twelve

"**D**amn, Tonks," Mac said, stepping into the small sterile hospital room. "You look like shit."

The Amore coughed. "At least I have an excuse."

"Not a very good one."

Tonks snorted.

Mac stopped next to the bed. "How are you doing?"

"Since yesterday? I'm doing fine. Doc says I should be out beginning of next week. As long as you don't keep coming in here and interrupting my recovery. What's the word?"

Mac shrugged. "The fallout from the slate is pretty amazing. Three Information Guild execs were arrested last night, I hear there's going to be a handful of Merchant Guild operators dropping tomorrow."

"Hard to believe someone was able to get all that information compiled on a single slate like that. Whoever it was, they had to have some pretty phenomenal sources. Who'd have that kind of reach?"

"I don't care."

Tonks raised an eyebrow. "Really?"

"Conspiracies, back-room deals, corruption, it's never going to stop. I can only worry about what I can do something about. There's more than enough work here on Calista to keep me busy for a lifetime of cop work."

Tonks sniffed. "Yeah, you've got a point there."

"Which brings me to the point of my visit today."

"Oh?"

"I thought I'd tell you before you heard from anyone else, Sullivan got out today."

"Son of a bitch. What happened?"

"Apparently biting a suspect is frowned upon in certain circles."

"Bah," Tonks waved a hand through the air. "He had it coming."

"Yeah, I agree with you there. He'll mess up again, and we'll catch him again. That's how this game works."

"I guess."

"Anyway, hurry up and stopping milking this scratch, we have work to do."

# # # # #

Luck Of The Draw
by J.R. Handley
& Corey D. Truax

Luck of the Draw Cantina, Planet Saxet

The Luck of the Draw Cantina was a smoky hole filled with cheering bodies. Amidst the ruckus, Ivan Petrov sat with his boots lazily resting on the table in front of him. He clutched a six-sided die in one hand and a mostly empty tankard of the gambling den's cheapest swill in the other. He felt at home.

The walls and ceilings around Ivan appeared to be little more than metal sheets tacked onto a wooden frame. The entire ramshackle of a building looked like it could collapse at any second, but he didn't come for the decor. What mattered to him was the money the place had invested in gaining unfettered access to live video feeds.

The bar erupted into shouts and other odd noises as some of the patrons jumped to their feet, baptizing the sludge-covered floorboards with whatever bizarre drinks they had clutched in their hands. He had opened his mouth to join in the cacophony; however, the cantina barkeep walked past and pushed his boots off the table. Ivan simply held his tankard out for a refill in response.

179

The Cochkala, which looked like an over-sized badger, made high-pitched chittering sounds while it filled Ivan's oversized drinking vessel. A beep came from his slate, indicating his Universal Account Access Card (UACC)—pronounced *yack* by humans—had been charged for the drink. He was descending more into debt by the minute.

Ivan took three gulps of the coldish brew and felt the room spin a bit. The tipsy feeling, paired with the thrill of a high-stakes bet, made him forget about what a shit life he had. Much like the two gladiators he watched on the screen, he had been through an arena of sorts...only he had lost everything in the contest.

"Come on Gilly, kick his ass!" he shouted as he watched the melee unfold. The underdog, a metal-fisted human, knocked the champion onto his backside.

He rolled his brother's die across the tabletop. The metal cube with hand-carved dots landed on a six. This was a good sign, and Ivan jumped to his feet.

Every eye in the room had turned to the fight, as if mesmerized by the chance the champion might be unseated. It appeared the conclusion was at hand. The two contestants, battered and bruised, had regained their footing and continued pummeling each other.

Ivan needed the underdog to win. He didn't technically have the credits he had wagered on the bout. The pale-skinned bounty hunter was so engrossed in the thrill of the fight he missed the angry bookie approaching him.

"Time to pay up!" said Crovax as he pushed Ivan from behind.

He felt his chest and face hit the table. The force of the wooden face-plant caused his brother's die to jump on the tabletop, roll, and land on one. His free hand was able to scoop up the precious me-

mento just in time for two henchmen to drag him out of the building and into the alley behind.

The two meatheads Crovax employed as security chucked Ivan onto the ground the moment they cleared the swinging back door. A kick to the ribs flipped him onto his back. He struggled to breathe, but the dust made it hard. Ivan could see the two hired hands were both carrying illegal, merc-grade weapons. One of them had already unholstered a pistol and aimed it at Ivan's chest.

"You all don't want to kill an employee of the Peacemaker Guild, right?" Ivan asked as he raised both of his hands defensively in front of his face.

Crovax hissed between his pointy teeth and crossed his fur-covered arms in front of his chest. It was hard for Ivan to focus on the creature towering above him while the pinpricks of light danced in his vision. The pistol trained on his chest was distracting, too.

"Bounty hunters are *not* Peacemakers," said Crovax. "You are the toys they employ to do work for them. Now, where are my credits? I want what I'm owed, or else…"

The pause was followed by the weasel squatting next to him. The slave collar the bookie wore became more visible as the Zuparti's beady, blood-red eyes narrowed at Ivan. The alien's appearance wasn't nearly as frightening as the six-inch stiletto he produced and placed on Ivan's cheek.

"I promise, I'm good for it," said Ivan. He didn't dare move as the knife would sink into his flesh, possibly even gouging an eye. He felt his pistol being pulled from his holster by one of the goons.

"I want my credits." The universal translator Ivan wore struggled to keep up with the angry weasel. "I want them now, or I slice you up and sell you for parts."

"I've got them. I think I just won big on the Gilly fight. It'll pay you back, with interest!"

Squinting, Crovax used his free hand to pull out his slate. He glanced at the screen and laughed.

"You idiot, when you want to hedge your bets and put credits on both sides, you have to account for the odds. Plus, my master *owns* the other house you put credits down at. One last time, where are my credits?"

"There's a couple contracts waiting for me at the be-hop," he said, referring to the Bounty Hunter Orbital Platform. "I can earn the credits I owe, and interest, if you just let me do my job."

It was a lie, and the look on the weasel's face told Ivan it hadn't worked.

"You are *barely* a bounty hunter." The weasel pushed his blade into Ivan's cheek, breaking the skin. "If anything, you are a glorified prisoner guard for the real hunters. The point—" Crovax stopped to lick the blood from the blade, "—is there isn't a job an unranked, useless, hunter like you could take to break even."

Crovax paused in thought, stood, then nodded to his two flunkies. The knuckle dragger who had a gun trained on Ivan holstered it.

"You made the right choice, Crovax," said Ivan, pushing out a breath of relief.

"Having you beaten to death? I agree; it was the right choice."

Ivan went for the pistol holstered on his leg, but only found air. His other hand, the one still grasping his brother's die, defensively covered his face as the two henchmen kicked the shit out of him. Rolling onto his knees and attempting to crawl, he shouted for help.

Four hands grabbed his back, and for a moment he was airborne. His body came to a crashing halt against the back wall of the cantina.

The flimsy metal surface didn't hurt, but the beam it was nailed to did. The force of the blow caused his slate to fly out from beneath the duster he wore. The poor device was already dated and barely functioning, just like Ivan. To his surprise, the speakers still managed to sputter out a message.

"Ivan Petrov, badge number eight-seven-zero-five, congratulations on your advancement to apprentice," the smooth, female robotic voice droned. "You have been selected for a Tier-4 contract. Meet with the bounty hunter that selected you at the Bounty Hunter Orbital Platform, immediately."

The message continued to repeat as Crovax lifted his hand, stopping the beating. Ivan showed his appreciation by puking the contents of his stomach onto the dust and sand-covered ground.

"Nice try," said Crovax. "You record that yourself?"

Groaning, Ivan used a sleeve to wipe away some of the vomit clinging to his unkempt beard. He didn't have a clue what the hell the message was about, or why he'd been inexplicably advanced to apprentice. He'd been an un-tiered bounty hunter for a long time, by choice.

"That's an official be-hop communique; just look at the transmission codes. If you kill me, the Tier-4 bounty hunter that selected me for this mission is going to come sniffing around. Let me do my job, and you will get your credits, with interest."

Crovax's long whiskers twitched. The weasel whispered something to one of his goons. Before Ivan could react, a small, needle-tipped dagger pierced his shoulder. He yelped in pain as the blade was withdrawn, then he was lifted to his feet. Soft fur tickled his cheek as the little beast whispered into his ear.

"You owe me and my boss, so I'll let you go collect this bounty. I'm adding another twenty percent interest to your balance. You try to disappear, we'll find you."

The moment Crovax stopped speaking, the hands supporting Ivan were gone, and he fell to his knees. His pistol landed in front of him, now covered in grit, and he looked up to watch the trio head back into the bar. After the door closed, he slumped back to his butt.

Why the fuck have I been selected for a Tier-4 bounty? he wondered as he inspected the tiny, bleeding hole in his shoulder. He knew there was only one way to figure out what the hell was going on and dig himself out of this hole; he'd have to pretend to be a real bounty hunter for a change.

Bounty Hunter Orbital Platform, near Planet Saxet

The be-hop was coming into view as Ivan slumped in the passenger compartment of the taxi shuttle. He had gone home to clean up, but water was pay-to-use on Saxet. He had managed to change clothes, oil his weapon, and wipe himself off with some liquor-dampened rags. Everything that mattered to him was stuffed into a duffel he slung over his shoulder.

He had decided against shaving the unruly beard and shoulder-length black hair. The jet-black swell of hair served as a mask. Fully shaved and groomed, he looked exactly like his dead twin, Viktor. He didn't want to see the ghost of his best friend in the mirror; that would defeat the purpose of his self-imposed isolation on Saxet.

The shuttle lurched and reminded Ivan of his earlier beat down. He tried to silence the pain by focusing on the be-hop. He'd only been there once when he received his badge.

The extent of his dealings as a bounty hunter were largely digital. Jobs came to him through his slate. Sure, he dumped prisoners at the docks of the be-hop, but only legitimate hunters went inside the structure. They would use the resources within to plan missions and securely catalogue evidence for the Peacemakers. To Ivan, those things sounded a lot like work and responsibility, two things the past had proven he should avoid.

Ivan picked dirt out from under his fingernails while he looked out the window. The orbital platform had the basic shape of a sideways cylinder, surrounded by a series of rotating rings. There were docking ports and struts for the thrusters that kept the platform solidly in the LaGrange Point. He knew other species referred to these locations by different names, but they could go to hell. Ivan was a human with roots back to Mother Earth, even if he'd been languishing on Saxet for the past several years.

The shuttle vibrated as it docked with the platform. Ivan scanned his yack to pay for the ride and was a little surprised to see the payment go through. He tried to tell himself he didn't smell that badly while he waited for the last airlock to cycle. When it opened, he was stopped by an imposing Tier-2 hunter who was standing sentry. Everything about the mid-tier hunter was spotless, including the large rifle resting in his hands.

Tithing service, rather than credits, allowed hunters to keep even more of their earnings. These plum rent-a-cop assignments were never trusted to the un-tiered. On-duty guards wore slick, reflective face shields.

"Stop. All non-hunters are required to be escorted beyond this point," the guard said through the robotic voice of his helmet.

Somewhat embarrassed he'd forgotten to display his badge, Ivan reached into his coat and began fumbling around. "Name's Ivan Petrov, I'm an apprentice. I was selected for a—"

Ivan was interrupted by the guard's muzzle poking his chest.

"Remove your hand and slowly open that ridiculous cape-looking jacket so I can see what you are reaching for," the guard commanded.

"It's not a cape. It's a duster," Ivan retorted. Frowning at his forgetfulness, he located his badge and held it out.

"This portion of the be-hop is restricted to Tier-4 hunters, *apprentice*. Now, run along."

Before Ivan could say anything to make his reception worse, a large Zuul stalked up to them on all fours. Standing on its hind legs, he saw its badge had four stars above the Peacemaker crest. This indicated that the shaggy canine was a Tier-4 hunter. Ivan had seen a few Zuuls before and knew they were formidable trackers and hunters, using their dog-like senses to sniff out their prey.

"This…hunter, is reporting to me," the Zuul said in a clearly female voice, "let him through."

The guard responded by stepping back for Ivan to pass. Not wanting to linger, he followed the Zuul through the airlocks. The walkway opened into a larger space full of tables and Tri-V displays. Hunters crowded around tables with maps and blueprints projected in front of them. The walk quickened and up they went, at least three curving decks. Out of breath, Ivan was happy when he was pointed to a table.

"Sit," the Zuul ordered.

Ivan took a moment to look at his guide. She had a long, angular snout and a face full of whiskers. One ear perked up as she looked back at him. Her big brown eyes were startling, and almost made him want to reach out and pet her behind the ears. Knowing that would be ill-advised, Ivan refocused.

"What the hell is this all about?" he said. "Who am I supposed to be meeting here? You?"

Instead of answering, she looked at Ivan's badge and stalked away. Pulling the die from his pocket, he compulsively tumbled it in his hand as he glanced around. The walls were lined with glowing screens that scrolled a list of open contracts. Ivan could feel a lot of eyes lingering on him. When he returned the gazes, he saw a collection of intimidating-looking aliens in advanced combat armor, scarred and pitted from use.

Unlike mine, he thought to himself. *What am I getting into?*

After asking the silent question, Ivan rolled the die. Looking down, it had landed on a three. It was a non-committal response from Viktor.

"Really, brother? You don't have any advice for me?" Ivan whispered.

Padding on all fours, the Tier-4 Zuul returned and sat on the table edge in front of him. She looked curiously at the die on the table.

"It seems you really are Ivan Petrov, just with significantly more fur than your old picture reflects. My name is Boudicca, and I'm the reason you're here. The Peacemakers have given me the authority to offer you a once-in-a-lifetime opportunity to crawl out the miserable pit you've dug. You'll be able to clear your debts and wipe some of the grime off your reputation. Are you interested?"

"Interested in *what*," Ivan asked. "What could you need from me?"

"We need someone to fit a certain role. You're the only hunter dumb enough to get into bed with a Bizon Syndicate bookie. At first I thought you were working an inside angle; it appears this is not the case."

"I'm in debt to a weasel over at Luck of the Draw. When did the Bizons come into play?" Ivan asked in disbelief.

Boudicca burst into laughter. "How can you be a hunter and not know the cantina is a front?"

"Having a suspicion and giving a shit are two different things. Regardless, I'm un-tiered so that's all above my paygrade," Ivan tossed the die into his pocket. "I just do this hunter thing to clear the bills."

"Guess what, *apprentice*, it's time to pop your smelly ass out of the stands and back into the game. This is a one-time offer. If you don't take it, the guild will probably arrest you to leverage the access they need."

"Well, I mean, how many credits are we talking about?" Ivan replied.

"If you plan on accepting, follow me to my ship. If not, wait here and security will gather you up shortly."

Boudicca stood and walked away. Ivan, forced to commit, jumped up to follow.

RNS Mabinogion, near Planet Saxet

Thu shuttle ride to Boudicca's ship was silent. The furry, plus-sized pup didn't seem to be a conversationalist. Ivan passed the time looking at the ship they were destined for. The vessel was a slate-gray color, like bare metal, with fading neon-green accents. Oddly, some of the paint seemed to form a racing stripe down the length of the ship.

What a dumb color scheme for a ship, he thought.

As he stared, focusing more closely on the gracefully conical shape of the craft, he realized it was an Old Republic destroyer. He vaguely remembered seeing images of them while he and his brother were still kids back on Earth.

"It's the RNS *Mabinogion*, one of the Olwen Class destroyers," Boudicca said to his unspoken question. "We call her 'The Mab' for short. She's a relic, but she still has a few tricks up her sleeve."

"I know the feeling," said Ivan.

"Unlike you, she doesn't run on stale booze and wisecracks," she replied. "We're headed there to get you out of those rags and into something practical. We've a small side mission to complete; otherwise, the guild can't *officially* make you an apprentice bounty hunter."

"But my badge changed. There's a little *A* under my name, now. Doesn't that mean I'm already an apprentice?"

"Right now, your tier jump is interim. You must complete a supervised apprentice-level contract before it's official. If you aren't a confirmed apprentice, the Peacemaker Guild specifications of the Tier-4 contract can't be fulfilled, and then nobody gets paid."

"Okay, so what's this side mission?" Ivan asked

"Just an escort mission. We pick up some prisoners here, take them there—even you can't foul it up."

Ivan wanted to ask for more information, but any further questions were cut short as Boudicca announced they were about to begin final docking procedures. Not wanting to lose his lunch in front of her, he closed his eyes and waited for the all clear. Surprisingly, instead of coupling to the side of the vessel, as was the norm, the shuttle glided gently into a hangar bay.

Ivan imagined the large hangar bay doors making loud clanking noises as they slid shut. With the shuttle on the deck, and the pressure re-establishing itself, Boudicca powered down.

"Move your feet," Boudicca said as she activated the magnetic boots she had donned.

Ivan mimicked her actions and followed behind.

"We'll go to the quarters I've assigned you and then straight to medical."

"Medical? I'm fit as a fiddle," he protested, still unsure where his father had got that expression.

"Nevertheless, the contract requires we verify all parties are of sound mind and body. When the contract says you do it, you do it." She stopped in her tracks and looked Ivan straight in the eyes before continuing. "As long as you're not too drunk, you should be okay. If you fail, we wipe the results, flush your system, and do it again. You *will* pass this physical."

Not another word was said until they reached the end of a winding series of passageways. The entire trip was strange, as he expected to run into a crew of some sort. The mag-boots he had slipped into on the shuttle were already wearing his legs out. Boudicca stopped abruptly, and Ivan ran into her back. Growling, she turned and stared him down until he backed up, offering his hands to show his good will.

"These are your quarters, drop your garbage inside."

He rushed inside the space. There was a bed, a locker, a sink, and a toilet. He placed his duffel bag in a locker and couldn't help but notice what looked like an enclosed shower cabinet in the corner. Awestruck, he stepped toward it.

"Yes, it works. And yes, you will be rinsing your hindquarters when we're done in medical. The air scrubbers have to work hard enough without your stench taxing them more. You might shear your face as well. Let's move."

Ivan wanted to jump for joy. Instead, he followed his new boss. The little room she had just given him was infinitely better than the seedy hole he called home on Saxet. And a shower, too. It'd been a lot of years since he experienced something like that.

They walked through another series of passageways, this time encountering a crew member. Not able to identify the species, Ivan made space for it to pass and continued after Boudicca. She stopped at a hatch and motioned for him to enter. Following behind him, she addressed what appeared to be an autonomous medical device.

"Medical Unit 12 Alpha, perform standard apprentice physical diagnostic. Patient name, Ivan Petrov. Scan his badge into the system."

The machine, which looked like a trashcan with arms, responded with a series of beeps. Boudicca waved her paw toward a gurney, and he drifted down and strapped himself to it. His heart thumped faster as the gurney vibrated, then pulled him into a tunnel where he was scanned.

"You idiot," she growled as his gurney pushed back out of the scanning tube, "your bookie put a tracker in you. How'd you not know he slipped one into your arm?"

Rubbing the puncture wound on his shoulder, he shrugged.

"I noticed the delivery tool. Just didn't know there was a tracker. Trust me, if I could have stopped them, I would have. It was three on one. Plus, I may have been a little drunk."

"You are shaping up to be the worst apprentice I've ever had. Regardless, I can make your mistake work for us, later. Meet me in the armory in one hour so we can get you some gear. First, go take a shower and clean up. Once we've got you looking halfway respectable, we'll pick up the prisoners and their guard contingent and get this qualifying contract out of the way."

* * *

Ivan sat in the Mab's armory, performing daily maintenance on his gear as they headed back to Saxet. The weeks he'd spent playing nursemaid to the jailers weren't sexy or fun, but he'd earned twice what he owed Crovax on this one jaunt. Not that he planned on paying the runt.

He'd also scored some new gear and was officially advanced to apprentice, which he was sure would impress the ladies at the cantina.

Before he started cleaning his pistol, he habitually removed his brother's die from his inside pocket and released it into the air. The die was made of magnetic metal, and after it spun weightless for a few moments, Ivan knocked it toward the table. It clicked loudly as it stuck to the surface.

"I know I cleaned it yesterday," he muttered quietly as he disassembled the pistol and placed it on the mag-lock portion of the table.

"I feel like I'm pretending to be a merc again. That didn't work out for us so well last time, did it, Viktor?"

"Why is it you speak to a speckled cube when no one is looking?"

Ivan jumped at Boudicca's sudden intrusion, then he scooped the die from the tabletop and re-pocketed it.

"Talking to inanimate objects is unnerving," she continued. "Despite this concern, your performance on the last mission was outstanding."

Ivan chuckled. "Most of my un-tiered bounties have been prisoner transports, so I'm not out of practice. This one was just a little longer than my normal contracts."

Boudicca approached the area where he was tethered and pulled a pistol component from the mag-lock to inspect it. She smiled, revealing her white canines, and placed it back.

"Your record indicates you were a formidable warrior when you were hairless of face. Why did you leave mercenary work?"

Turning to address the dog-faced whelp, Ivan was startled. He didn't see judgment in her expression; instead, there was curiosity, or perhaps even concern, which put him at ease.

"You probably know this already, but for humans to be selected for mercenary work, we must take a test called the Voluntary Off-World assessments, or VOWs. My twin brother Viktor, he did better on the VOWs than anyone for our cycle. I barely passed. He could've gone anywhere he wanted, but he compromised so we could stay together."

Ivan swallowed as he pulled the die from his pocket and held it in his hand.

"Slowly, I got better. No matter how good I was, everything was a competition between me and Viktor."

He let go of the die and let it float in the air. This was a conversation he never got to have with anyone that mattered. Boudicca reached for the silver-colored cube, paused, and looked at him. He nodded that it was okay and pretended to clean the worn surface of his pistol's magazine well while she looked at the die.

"The die was both of ours. When there wasn't a spot for both of us on a mission, we would roll it to determine who got to go. The day he was...lost, he won the roll."

Boudicca placed the die on the table with care.

"My father was already lonely and depressed when we left. We were all he had. When he found out about Viktor, it was too much. He killed himself. I lost everyone I loved in a span of weeks. I never went back to Earth, and I got out of the merc business. If it wasn't for me, Viktor would have gone to a top-notch company. Hell, he'd probably be running it by now."

He reached out and took the die and put it back into his pocket. Boudicca ran a finger along the scar on her face and turned toward the hatch.

"I know what it is to lose your pack," she said. "We can only honor them with our future actions."

Before he could respond, she was gone. Regardless, he felt like a great weight had been lifted from his shoulders. Things were starting to look up.

Luck of the Draw Cantina, Planet Saxet

The sandstorms made it a rough shuttle ride to the surface of Saxet, but Ivan was happy to suffer through it. The credits he had accumulated from the transport job were burning a hole in his yack, and he needed to unload some of them. After being stuck on the Mab so long, he also needed to blow off some steam.

Combat tactics and weapons drills, weapons drills and combat tactics; this had been his life for the last two weeks. Ivan understood the need to train, but weeks spent sparring with an overzealous pup weren't going to change things that much. Despite the pace Boudicca kept, the clean room, shower, credits, and gear she provided made up for it.

He smiled as the shuttle touched down.

"Do you need to go to your home for anything before we begin?" she asked as they disembarked. "Once we initiate contact with your bookie it may be a while before we can return."

"Nah, I've got everything I need in my pockets."

Ivan didn't mention the fact he was currently homeless. In the time that had passed since they left, he hadn't paid rent. He'd received a notice of eviction when the credits from the transport job cleared his yack.

"Now, remember, you aren't here to play. Just make a show of gambling and lure your bookie out. I understand you have credits to spend; just don't get carried away."

Ivan laughed as he straightened his new gear and increased his pace toward the Luck of the Draw. He had kept his badass duster, despite being told not to, but everything underneath it was practically new. Most importantly, he could walk through the front door of the cantina with his chest out, instead of skulking in the shadows.

Saxet was a sandy, dust-covered planet, and the Luck of the Draw was situated on the edge of the slums. Ivan knew three alternate routes into the building, but was happy to use the front door for a change.

When they finally reached the gates to the courtyard, they met a four-armed hulk of a guard. Unlike before, Ivan proudly allowed his yack to be scanned. The surplus of credits confirmed his entry.

"Thanks, Tiny," he said as he brushed past the brute.

Boudicca walked in first, and Ivan waited a few minutes to follow. Once inside, he could see she was leaning against the rearmost wall, just a few feet from the door to the back alley. The bar was buzzing with activity, and everyone was on their feet cheering some big event. Ivan found the closest table to his boss, took a seat, then put his feet up on the table. Genuinely interested in the commotion, he pulled out his slate to see what was available to bet on.

"Do you never learn?" Crovax asked from behind him.

The large weasel's head, neck, and shoulders all slipped around Ivan. The furry bastard was staring him right in the face. Ivan had heard Zupartis could fit their entire bodies through a hole if they managed to get their heads through. He just hoped the weasel wouldn't be able to fit his head through the bars in the Mab's brig.

"Crovax, how've you been?"

Staring at him with no expression, the bookie stabbed at Ivan's chest with his furry little fingers. "Cut the chatter and pay up."

Ivan nodded and punched some commands into his slate. In a moment, his debts were paid. Seeing the notification scroll across the screen of his own tablet, Crovax motioned for his guards to disperse.

"Well done, so let's talk about your next line of credit," the weasel said in a purring, coaxing manner, rubbing his paws together and blinking his eyes. The sudden change in demeanor was alarming.

The bookie wouldn't have been so happy if he knew the truth: the credits Ivan had just sent weren't real. In an hour or so, thanks to a computer code Boudicca provided, the payment would bounce like a bad line of credit.

"Crovax, my friend," said Ivan as he patted the top of the weasel's head, "I don't need your fucking help anymore."

Ivan pulled his feet off the table, which was the signal for Boudicca to send tranquilizer darts into the bookie's back. The timing was perfect, because whatever was happening on the Tri-Vs had everyone on their feet and was creating a needed distraction.

"Nighty night, asshole," Ivan whispered as Crovax's wide, red eyes drooped and then closed. He didn't feel as slick when the animal's deadweight landed on his chest and almost caused his chair to flip backwards.

Lurching to his feet and lifting the knocked-out bookie, he braced as Boudicca approached and grabbed the weasel. She was much larger than Crovax and easily hoisted him. She squatted as she carried him out the back entrance to the alley. Ivan followed behind, wondering where the goon who normally manned the back door had gone.

"Hold him for a moment," said Boudicca. She tossed the weasel onto his shoulder, and he felt his knees almost give out. "Get moving; I'll take care of this door."

Ivan shuffled down the alley, careful not to trip over the body of the missing guard. The four-armed humanoid had three metallic darts sticking out of the side of his neck and was bleeding from the nose and mouth. Grit was already caking the crimson fluid, devouring it. Ivan pulled goggles down over his eyes with a free arm as the sandstorm picked up. A loud hissing noise pulled his attention backward.

Boudicca was spraying yellowish foam onto the door. The puffy spackle adhered to the cracks of the door and began expanding. In a few moments, the entire exit was covered. When she finished with the door, she caught up with Ivan and snatched the bookie away from him.

The run to their shuttle was exhausting. How Boudicca could keep such a pace while carrying the bookie was beyond his understanding. They were home free once they cleared the city proper and entered the docks, although it took them another few minutes to reach the shuttle. There, they restrained the unconscious Zuparti and prepared for takeoff.

"That was smooth," Boudicca said as she started the pre-flight checks.

The rest of the departure was filled with stony silence. Ivan's chest heaved as he tried to slow his breathing. Once his heart stopped pounding, his mind started to wander.

"I can never go back," he said. "We just kidnapped Crovax and took out a guard."

"We're bounty hunters, and this scumbag bookie of yours has a detainment warrant for failure to declare taxable commerce," said Boudicca. "You knew this would be the outcome."

"I did," Ivan replied. "I just hadn't considered what the next step would be, or what I would do once we turn him over and collect our pay for the Tier-4 contract."

Boudicca's laughter almost ruined her smooth takeoff.

"Turn him over? Did you honestly think your Zuparti bookie was the Tier-4 target? We were given provisional authority to detain him so we could interrogate him. I believe he's the first step toward a high-priority target, and I convinced the Peacemaker Guild to have an arrest warrant on standby if this is true."

"Who is the main target?" asked Ivan. "Why wasn't I told of any of this?"

Boudicca laughed, again.

"Your old bookie will tell us about the main target. As for sharing, I wasn't sure if I could trust you with this information. Regardless, now you know. Continue to improve and you'll see your access increase."

Ivan stared out the window. He felt too old to be playing these games. Worse, now he didn't have a home. Would he have to go back to Earth? Looking at the Mab approaching on the shuttle sensors, he began scheming how to make his temporary dwelling on board more permanent.

RNS *Mabinogion*, near Planet Saxet

Crovax floated, still unconscious, in the Mab's brig until Boudicca initiated a series of high-pitched sounds. The noise was ear splitting and shook the metal cage in which the drugged Zuparti drifted. With a screeching noise, the bookie's red eyes shot open, and his entire body began to flail in panic.

"Relax, you're in a zero-g environment. You're not falling to your doom...for now," said Boudicca. "You have been detained by order of the Peacemaker Guild regarding illegal, unreported, and untaxed gambling income. Do you have anything to say for yourself?"

Crovax's long, slim body twisted in the air to view the source of the accusation. His whiskers twitched as he looked at his canine captor. But when the bookie saw Ivan, he growled and bared his teeth. Boudicca ignored the outburst and continued speaking. Her face and body language betrayed little emotion.

"The provisions granted to me by the Peacemakers allow me to utilize any interrogation method I see fit, if it does not result in the detainee's death or permanent disfigurement. This is fortunate for me, not so much for you."

She flipped a switch on the cage surrounding the bookie, which activated high-powered, adjustable electromagnets. Crovax shouted as the metal cuffs that had been attached to his wrists and ankles suddenly began to pull taut, as if they were bound by invisible chains. Instead of drifting, his body hovered rigidly in a spread-eagle.

"This is the lowest setting. Let's see how long it takes before my medical robot has to repair your connective tissues."

The unfolding spectacle was made all the sweeter when Ivan thought back to the beating Crovax and his goons had given him. The weasel let out a squeal as Boudicca increased the magnetic pull on his limbs.

"Ask! Please! Just ask!" the bookie yelped. "You haven't asked me anything!"

Boudicca glanced back at Ivan and gave him a shrug. "Sometimes silence is the best interrogation tool. Well, that and some high-powered magnets."

She turned her attention back to their captive. Ivan hadn't seen this side of her before, and decided he would avoid getting on her shit-list.

"I know who you work for and," —while she spoke, she slowly increased the power— "your only way out of this is to lead me to him. Otherwise, you'll spend the rest of your life in servitude. *After*, I dislocate all of your joints—"

"Lucky! They call him Lucky," Crovax shouted, cutting her off midsentence. "He leads the Tarva branch of the Bizons. I'll take you to him, but you've got to let me go. Tarvas are insane; they'll kill me for sure."

She reduced the power, and the bookie sagged in mid-air as some tension was relieved. Crovax took advantage of the lull and continued.

"Lucky is establishing a hunting enterprise called *the Game*. He's managing the formation and supervising the hunts."

Boudicca stared at the sniveling Zuparti with a blank expression then made her demands.

"Tell me everything: when, where, and how many credits it will take to convince your master to allow us to participate."

RNS Mabinogion, near Planet Sierra 2282

The trip to Sierra 2282, a recently discovered planet, was uneventful. This was the location Crovax claimed Lucky was using to set up an off-the-books enterprise that organized the hunting of sentient beings. While the Mab navigated on auto-pilot, Ivan and Boudicca spent their time digging up all the information they could find on Lucky, the Tarva species, and the Bizon Syndicate.

Ivan enjoyed their frequent trips down to the brig to pick Crovax's mind. His ex-bookie was now more willing to share, so he'd been receiving better treatment. Boudicca recorded these softer interrogation sessions to provide to the Peacemakers. She explained to him how she tweaked her contracts to allow for higher payments, simply by providing extra intelligence information to the guild. Ivan couldn't argue with extra credits.

He felt an odd closeness to Boudicca. It was almost like they were becoming friends. This sort of connection was something he hadn't allowed himself to feel since Viktor died. The more time he spent strategizing about the mission, the less time he spent talking to his ghosts.

Just do it, Ivan. The worst she can do is say no, he told himself while he shaved. He'd been working up the courage to ask Boudicca to allow him to stay on as her apprentice. He didn't have a home anymore, and going back to Earth wasn't something he was ready for.

The focus on grooming, he hoped, would make him appear more professional. His long black hair was now shorter and slicked back, and his wild beard was trimmed into a goatee. The hair being kempt made the veins of gray running through it more apparent.

Ivan jumped as the speaker in his room squelched.

"We are approaching the planet. Get up here," said Boudicca.

Ivan glanced into the mirror one more time, trying to shake the feeling Viktor was staring back, then he turned toward the hatch and used a handheld magnetic tether to navigate down the passageways to the bridge. The small device used compressed air to launch a tethered magnet at moderate speed. Then the user was pulled along toward the lock-point. The process was simple: fire, attach, glide, detach, and repeat as necessary.

Once Ivan reached the bridge, he activated his mag-boots and walked the final few steps. He hated how much work the metal-soled boots were, but he also knew flying headfirst into the compartment wasn't advisable. Ivan was surprised to see a large number of crewmembers working on the bridge as he strutted in.

"What's going on, boss?"

Boudicca looked up from the sensor readings she was studying.

"The planet is currently locked in an ownership stalemate between three massive corporations. While there are some surveyors on the planet mapping out potential building locations, there shouldn't be *anyone* in this location."

Boudicca pointed to an area of thick vegetation with a cleared area in the middle in the shape of a square. A number of tiny dots indicated a cluster of lifeforms. Ivan leaned in toward the sensor screens to examine closer.

"Do you think the Bizons are paying to play there, or do you think they are squatting?" he asked.

"That is the correct question," she replied, giving him a nod of acknowledgement. "The implications of the Syndicate paying a corporation to run untaxed enterprises on a locked planet would certainly be news to the Peacemakers and the Merchants Guild."

Boudicca opened a comms line to the brig and asked for Crovax be escorted to the bridge while Ivan studied the readings from the planet. There appeared to be some small craft flying around the surface near a makeshift camp or fortification.

Once the bookie made it to the bridge, he was reminded of the deal they had struck. If Crovax's actions led to the capture of the high-priority target, he could walk away from the whole situation untouched. Better yet, with his master gone, he'd be free. Gripping the communicator in both of his paws like it was a piece of food, Crovax chittered into it.

"All nearby pilots, I'm bringing in a customer to Lucky. My authentication code and slave ID are attached to this data packet. We will transfer to the planet via shuttle."

Crovax sounded supremely confident when he spoke, but his entire body trembled as he handed the comms device back to Boudicca.

"Affirmative. Follow the landing beacons and wait to disembark until your escort arrives," said the disembodied voice over the bridge speakers.

With the landing data from the security craft, the three boarded the Mab's short-range shuttle and headed out the hangar bay. Just prior to entering the planet's atmosphere, a single craft joined them as an escort.

"Stick to the plan, you two," said Boudicca. "We'll be on the ground soon. If this is going to work, we need to sell it."

Lucky's Encampment, Planet Sierra 2282

The cleared area Lucky used for his encampment was centered in a marshy area. The closer Boudicca piloted them in, the more details Ivan could see below.

"They've built some primitive fortifications," he stated. "Looks like a bunch of sharpened tree trunks stabbed into the ground to create a wall, and there is a guard tower in each of the four corners. They've placed some automated guns in the towers."

"Noted," Boudicca replied. "It changes nothing. Automation usually indicates a lack of manpower. We proceed as planned."

The shuttle shook as Boudicca brought it down. Ivan reached into his pocket and pulled his brother's die out. He held it for a moment, turning it over in his fingers. Instead of rolling it, he stuck it gently to the wall next to where he was sitting. He made sure the six dots were facing him. Tapping the top of the metal cube with a fingertip, he took in a big breath and narrowed his eyes.

Boudicca and Ivan took turns checking the advanced body armor they both wore while they waited for their escort. Crovax had been given concealable lightweight armor. It had to be mutilated and stitched together to fit around his tubular weasel frame.

Banging on the shuttle's exit cut their nervous preparations short. Boudicca repeated the mantra one last time.

"Stick to the plan."

When she finished speaking, she walked to the hatch and opened the door. Stepping out with a hand on her pistol grip, she leaned back in through the opening and shouted.

"Mr. Petrov, it's secure!"

Ivan liked this part of the plan. Being treated like a high-roller was a dream come true. That didn't do much to ease the nervous sickness he felt in his stomach.

Don't fuck this up, Ivan. Stick to the plan, he reminded himself.

With those positive affirmations out of the way, Ivan stuck out his chest and strode down the ramp, stopping just shy of the waiting guards. Crovax followed on his heels.

"Crovax, my man, this is the shithole you promised would bring me fortune?" said Ivan. "Seriously? It looks like it's only going to bring me a case of trench-foot. Now, where's this boss of yours?"

The brown-furred weasel sighed, then glided past him to address the guards.

"We're here to see Lucky. I've got a big fish looking to swim."

After grabbing the weasel by the face and pushing him away, the head guard, a four-armed Lumar, scanned the three for weapons. Ivan and Boudicca were both armed, but it seemed the guards just wanted to know who had what. They appeared confident in their ability to squash any problems.

"Let's go," the burly, seven-foot tall Lumar said.

Two of the security team moved to the rear, and the giant guard led the way. The landing zone was roughly a mile from the camp. Despite the weightlessness he had endured on the trip, Ivan didn't lose his breath during the walk. He figured the gravity on the planet had more to do with it than his physical conditioning he had been dedicating time to.

Arriving at the wooden palisade, their party was passed off to a new set of guards. Walking through the 20-foot tall gateway into the makeshift fortress, Ivan couldn't help but chuckle. Aside from one gigantic tent, some storage containers, and a smattering of fancy smaller tents, there wasn't much inside the walls. He also found it amusing that the wood everywhere was fake. It looked to be some sort of synthetic material.

The guards stopped at the entrance to the sprawling tent and motioned for the three to go inside. Ivan approached slowly, then ran his hand over the speckled wooden posts the tent was fastened to.

"It's a polymer that inhibits digital surveillance and protects against small caliber chem rounds. Should deflect weaker lasers, but a plasma pulse would light this thing up," Boudicca said.

Ivan nodded his head to acknowledge her as they moved inside. The giant tent seemed to be broken up into many smaller spaces. It had a high canopy above and a table that was at least 20 feet long running the length of it. On top of the table were the remains of a feast.

"That's why my security team scans newcomers for anything that could emit a plasma pulse," a deep voice said. "Can't have trigger-happy idiots burning my tent down."

"It's Lucky," Crovax whimpered as the ground thundered.

Crovax moved behind Boudicca as the eight-foot-tall Tarva ducked under a flap in the far corner. The quasi-minotaur barely cleared the opening with his two bull-like horns. Lucky blew air out of his bovine snout as he stomped to the head of the table, flanked by a couple of toothy Besquith security guards.

Ivan and Boudicca had studied the Tarva, but the colossal mountain of fur and muscle was far more imposing standing above you. Half of Lucky's right horn was missing, he had bones braided into his beard, and he was wearing some sort of leather gladiatorial girdle.

"Lucky, this is Ivan," said Crovax. Ivan glanced over to see the bookie's beady eyes were looking at the ground. "He is one of my regular patrons who normally can't pick a winner in a one-man race—"

Lucky's fist hit the table in a sudden motion. The action cut the weasel off and caused all the dishes and plates to jump. Ivan jumped, too…but only a little.

"When I want the words of a slave, I'll demand them! Speak again, and I'll break your neck and make a blanket out of you. Now, Ivan, is it? Who are you, and why are you here?"

From their research, Ivan knew he couldn't show this creature fear. Tarva were bullies who took pleasure in torturing the weak. There was also their berserker rage, which he didn't even want to think about.

He jumped onto the table and approached the beast. Leaning down, he scooped up what appeared to be an animal leg of some kind and took a bite as he walked closer. When he was within striking distance of Lucky, he took a bite, then bowed deeply in a ridiculous flourish. This was *not* part of Boudicca's plan.

"Ivan Petrov: ex-merc, failed bounty hunter, and suddenly a wealthy gambler. I struck it big with the Spice Cartel and wanted to keep my luck rolling. Betting with anyone named *Lucky* just made sense. But the fighting pits just don't get my juices flowing anymore. The stakes are too low. I want more blood, more excitement, and more risk. Was your furry little slave correct? Are you the one to see for this?"

He wasn't sure if his voice was trembling, or if his heart was just racing too fast. Regardless, Ivan did his best to not choke on the foul-tasting meat while he waited for a response. He noticed Lucky didn't appear to be armed, but his one good horn was encased in metal.

"And the Zuul?" Lucky enquired menacingly, having to slightly look upward at Ivan.

"My puppy? Come on, a man can't be too careful. Hell, you have a couple wolves of your own," he replied, motioning toward the

Besquiths. "This business venture could go south, so I made assurances for my own safety."

Lucky gestured toward the beast on his right. The bipedal wolf pulled a slate from its pocket and handed it to him. The tablet looked tiny in the Tarva's oversized hands. After a few moments, the bull's mouth twisted into a smile.

"It seems like you're a very wealthy little human. But do you have the fire in your belly to bet on the ultimate fight? *The Game* is an apex hunt, with species from all over the galaxy being brought here to serve as prey. You can bet, or play the role of a hunter. Hunting costs extra."

Ivan pretended to be bored with the concept and held his hand out lazily.

"I'm in. Hand me your slate, and I'll read the stats myself. I'll start off betting, but will probably get bored and join the hunt. I suppose you have some Tri-Vs somewhere for me to watch this unfold?"

After studying the information provided, Ivan was going to bet on one of the Zuul runners, but a scan of the hunters showed too many who looked promising, so he bet on the underrated Flatar. The odds of the foot-tall chipmunk winning the day were slim, but he knew looks could be deceiving. After putting his yack on the reader, Ivan placed his bet and held onto the slate.

"You mind if I keep this?" Ivan asked. "My slate broke on the way here. You can put it on my tab."

He jumped down from the table and pretended to be preoccupied with the slate. Inside, he was just hoping he hadn't gone overboard. He could feel Boudicca staring through the side of his head in disbelief.

Lucky waved off his guards and told the group to follow him deeper into the tent. They passed through some private viewing rooms into a larger area that was complete with a bar and multiple Tri-Vs. The room was empty except for a few patrons, the bartender, and a handful of guards loitering around. Ivan figured the elite gamblers likely had private viewing tents.

With no one to compete with for the bartender's attention, Ivan went to the bar and ordered a large tankard of booze while Crovax and Boudicca secured a table. Wooden tables, made of the fake wood, added to the rustic look the tent seemed to be going for. None of the credits being accessed from his yack were legit, so he didn't mind splurging.

"So now what?" Ivan said as he approached his companions and sat down.

"Did you *really* call me a puppy?" Boudicca put her hands on her head and sighed. Leaning in and lowering her voice to a whisper, she continued. "I'm not sure what the play is. It's beyond the scope of what we can hope to accomplish. We're not going to be able to use a few darts and carry him out of here without getting killed. Plus, even if we bag him and manage to get him to my shuttle, it doesn't have guns. We'll get blasted out of the sky before we break atmosphere."

Ivan didn't have a clue what to do either. Instead, he worked on finishing his drink while he brainstormed. Reaching into his duster's inside pocket for his brother's die, he remembered he had left it behind. Knowing ghosts wouldn't help him, he pushed the slate he had procured from Lucky over to Crovax.

"Can you do anything with this? Perhaps create a distraction or something? You said you had some access. This is your chance to get rid of that slave collar."

The weasel grabbed the slate and began tapping away on it. Ivan turned his attention up to the Tri-V displays. It wasn't like watching the fighting pits, where two beings chose to battle each other to the death. This was murder, plain and simple.

Ivan and Boudicca both jumped out of their chairs as automatic gunfire erupted from somewhere just outside of the tent. Crovax didn't flinch at all; his hands continued working.

"I just accessed those automated turrets outside! They are firing at anything that moves. Is that a good enough distraction?"

"Lower your voice! Wait…what?" Boudicca growled. "With *that* slate?!"

Before she could get an answer, Lucky ripped a hole through the tent with his horns as he ran into the room. He snorted, stomped a meaty leg to the ground, and charged at their table like a deranged bull. Everything was knocked out of his way or trampled underfoot as he sprinted toward them. This included two patrons who screamed as he backhanded them out of his way.

Ivan threw himself sideways, just missing a fast-moving horn. A guttural screaming noise filled the area. Crovax had been impaled. The weasel's body twisted and writhed as he attempted to lift his body off the gore-covered spike running through his back and sprouting out of his chest. The struggle didn't last long. Lucky grabbed the limp body off his horn and threw it at Boudicca with both arms, knocking her flat.

Ivan un-holstered his CL-32 pistol and pointed it at Lucky's back, which was now covered in blood.

"Don't kill him!" Boudicca shouted as she rolled away from one massive Tarva foot. Her pistol flew from her paw as Lucky kicked her in the side. She yelped as the tree-sized leg sent her rolling a good 10 feet.

Ivan felt calm, oddly so. It was a feeling of déjà vu mixed with nausea. His finger squeezed the trigger twice, and Lucky roared as his immense weight was suddenly supported by obliterated knees. While the beast tumbled to the floor, projectiles and lasers began to cut through the air around Ivan. Returning fire, he ran toward where his mentor was lying.

Moving past the thrashing Tarva, he flipped a table on its side to serve as a barricade and started shaking Boudicca with his non-firing hand. Small-arms fire pounded the table, and he wondered how long it would hold. A groan indicated she was alive.

"We're fucked!" Ivan shouted down toward her. He peeked over the synthetic table and put down two guards that were approaching. He fired clean shots, hitting just above the sternum in the un-armored throat area.

"Maybe," she responded rolling onto a knee and yelping in pain. Her ribs were likely shattered, or worse. "There's good news, though."

"Yeah, what?"

"You aren't the worst apprentice I've ever had."

Ivan laughed for a moment, then a fur-covered hand the size of his chest grabbed the table and pushed it out of the way. Lucky had dragged his crippled body across the floor by his arms. Snot hit Ivan's freshly trimmed face as the crazed bull snorted at him from the ground.

Ripping his duster free from his back, Ivan threw it over Lucky's head. He tossed his pistol to Boudicca and moved on all fours past

Lucky, trying to keep low. While he skittered forward like an animal, he heard her firing.

Grabbing the pistol she had dropped, he flipped the fire-select lever above the dual-magazine release button, which switched the pistol from laser to tranquilizer darts. Unsure how many to use, he fired all ten of them into the bull's meaty ribs.

The moment the last dart impacted flesh, Lucky went limp. Ivan crawled forward, awkwardly dragging a table behind him. Once he was close enough, he gripped Lucky's gore-covered horn in one hand and pressed the muzzle of his pistol into the bull's head with the other.

Holding the Tarva head in front of his chest, he kicked the table out of the way. If the remaining security team wanted him, they'd have to shoot through their boss.

He smiled as the two remaining Besquith guards and the one Lumar stopped firing and ran to flank him. Boudicca didn't let them move far, pinging them with laser fire before they could take a handful of steps. With no threats remaining, and the automatic turrets outside going silent, Ivan dropped Lucky's head to the canvas deck with a thud.

"Get him shackled," Boudicca said, while she struggled to stand.

Ivan had to use three pairs of electromagnetic cuffs to successfully bind the giant Tarva's arms behind his back.

"How are we going to carry this big—"

His question was cut short as an object punched a hole through the tent's canopy and landed in a blast of rocket fire. In the center of the newly formed crater was a stark black CASPer with bright golden markings and the seal of a blue tree on the chest. Ivan knew a little bit about CASPers, but this seven-and-a-half foot mech suit looked regal as fuck.

"I am Peacemaker Enforcer Erlor Tram," the CASPer's speakers blared. "Surrender your weapons or face immediate verdict!"

Ivan tossed his pistol to the deck. Boudicca sighed, handed it back to him, then limped toward the CASPer with her badge out in front of her, motioning for Ivan to do the same.

The CASPer took three earth-shaking steps toward them and scanned their badges. When finished, Enforcer Tram looked around the space, taking obvious note of Lucky.

"Fine work, Bounty Hunter Boudicca," Enforcer Tram stated via loudspeakers. "You and your apprentice have stumbled into a larger investigation into the Syndicate. After I dismantle this operation and secure those who have been kidnapped, I will meet you on your vessel to discuss the evidence you have collected and question your quarry."

Enforcer Tram marched away in his machine of death and destruction. Ivan righted a chair and let Boudicca sit down. Crovax was dead, Lucky was tranquillized, and the contract would be fulfilled. There was only one thing left for him to do.

"Boudicca, you mind if I stay on with you for a while?"

"Ivan, you've earned a place on my ship, but not as my apprentice. I'll recommend you for advancement to Tier-1. What do you say? Partners?"

"Deal."

# # # # #

Contract Fulfilled
by Tim C. Taylor

Chapter 1

“That’s the last of our drones,” replied the MinSha from the acceleration cocoon secured near the combat information center’s, or CIC’s, dorsal bulkhead. “Five missiles got through. Seventy-eight seconds to impact.”

Branco sensed a question hanging in the air, an unspoken hesitation. The whole setup of this starship made no sense, though; maybe he was picking up on another epic-level incongruence. For a start, instead of using Tri-V holos or implant virtual spaces, the deck officers were wearing virtual reality glasses straight out of a museum.

“Helm, estimate time to transition.” The captain’s words were beginning to sound strained, which was disappointing. Branco had her down as the type of captain who never showed anxiety, no matter what.

“Ninety-one seconds, ma’am.”

Ah, that was the unspoken issue: they were all going to die.

“Captain,” said the weasel-like Zuparti who seemed to be the XO, “you nearly got away. You did well. Gloriana would rather you release the tail than lose the *Midnight Blue*.”

215

"True," replied the captain, "but she would be pissed nonetheless, and angering our silent partner is not on my list of priorities. We are in disagreement, Venix. Should we ask our prisoner for his unbiased judgement? Mr. Branco, are you hearing this? The tail my XO speaks of is the outer shell of the ship, which we can jettison as a last resort. If we allow the missiles to catch our tail, perhaps we can break free of their pursuit long enough to make it through the stargate. What do you say?"

Branco tried to twist around to see Captain Sue Blue's face, but the *Midnight Blue's* acceleration pinned him in position as if the mass of the entire ship were resting on his ribcage. "I say…" he started, but the acceleration was squeezing his voice too hard. That wasn't all it was squeezing. His poor, suffering testicles were demanding a frank discussion when this was all over about what he was subjecting them to. How did those spacers manage this? Branco tried raising his pitch and managed to gasp out a reply. "I say you make up your fucking mind, and you do it fast."

What were these idiots thinking of, with just a handful of seconds before the missiles blew them to hell…? Or would they? Was this all just an elaborate piece of theater for his benefit? That would explain the weirdness he was sensing.

"Make up your mind, he tells me," purred the captain. "Very well."

Branco had the uncomfortable sense he was a saucer of cream that Captain Blue was licking up with sensual delight. She was toying with him.

"Oh!" she said suddenly. "Mr. Branco, I perceive from your facial expression you suspect me of subterfuge. You should compare notes with my XO, Commander Venix, who has been placed here to be professionally suspicious of everything I do, and yet none of these second guesses will mean a damn in approximately 28 seconds because we shall all be dead."

"Use the tail!" urged Venix.

Manic laughter came from the captain's acceleration cocoon, although it quickly descended into a wet cough. The captain cleared her throat of some constriction and announced her orders. "Helm, spin 180 degrees. All batteries, five missiles are trying to ram themselves up our tail pipe. Ready fire pattern delta."

Captain Blue sighed, a tremor of pleasure mixed with hurt.

"Impact in eight seconds," said the MinSha. Was it Branco's imagination or was the alien's chitinous flesh deepening from blue to purple?

"Please use the tail," begged the Zuparti.

"Recommendation noted and denied," said the captain.

Branco screamed, though not from fear.

Oh, he was terrified all right, and despite his cocoon's buffering, the acceleration was like a squad of Besquith practicing yoga on his chest—with malicious intent. His body's capacity to express his fear had been crushed out of him.

The scream sounded in his head because someone—presumably the captain—had hacked his implants and thrown him inside the ship's sensor view.

Outwardly, the ship's data systems appeared as obsolete as clay tablets and tickertape, but it clearly had hidden capabilities, because Branco's perception had been forcibly ripped from his body and sent out into space. He was the ship. He was the *Midnight Blue*.

When he'd first come aboard the ancient vessel, he'd thought it was the strangest ship he'd ever seen. Although practically empty, she was big enough to carry an enhanced battalion of mercs, and the strangest thing of all was its hull—a polished sphere with a blindingly high albedo.

Now that he was the ship, her configuration didn't seem strange at all. The central compartments, including the CIC, were conventionally oriented, so that under acceleration the force trying to pull him down through the deck was directed to the stern. Decks of the outer compartments, though, pointed outward through the spherical hull. And now that the outer hull had rotated 180° about the ship's core, he realized some of those outer compartments would be better described as gun turrets.

The captain spoke a single word: "Fire!"

Space lit up with flames and weapon exhaust gases. Starlight reflected off a steady hail of enhanced-metal defensive munitions, quickly whipped away into a long tail at *Midnight Blue's* ferocious speed—and the slightly faster the pursuing missiles. Hooked into the ship sensors, Branco felt ammo feeds pulsing through his body like blood as well as the ship's joy as one, two, three, four missiles exploded...

And the dismay at the fifth that made it through the point defense.

The missile crashed against the hull.

And bounced off.

"EMP scrambled its fuse," he heard an alien voice say back in the CIC. The system identified the speaker as the tactical officer, Lieutenant Flkk'Sss, which was a MinSha name if ever he'd heard one.

They'd survived. He was going to live.

Then he remembered where he was.

Branco rotated his cone of vision all the way around the hull until it faced the direction of travel. There it was. The Taphao-47 stargate.

The sight was beautiful. A rip in reality caught inside a gleaming metal frame, which shimmered in every wavelength as exotic particles ionized along its outer edge.

And they were about to go through.

He shut his eyes.

But that made no difference. He wasn't seeing any of this through his eyes.

I'm gonna see transition in full fidelity. No one has ever done that.

He screamed once more and was wrenched back into his body.

For several seconds, he couldn't work out who he was, let alone where or why. Then it all came flooding back.

He was Saisho Branco, safely inside hyperspace and locked into an acceleration cocoon by the mercs who'd kidnapped him. He might be trapped, but his lurching gut told him they'd ceased accelerating, and they were now floating in zero-g.

Branco vomited into the air.

"Well done, Captain," he gasped when the retching eased. "Can someone release me? I gotta wipe my face."

Ow! The Zuparti XO gave him a well-aimed kick to his face. "Shut up, filthy human creature," it snarled, but its tube-shaped body had already shot past him to attend more pressing matters.

Branco twisted round and lifted his head through the top of the cocoon still clamped around him. He couldn't see clearly, but Venix had halted by the captain. "Medics!" shouted the XO. "To the CIC, STAT."

"Is someone hurt?" Branco asked, feeling foolish the moment he uttered the words.

"Yes," answered the Zuparti. The XO mumbled a mix of curses and commands under his breath that resulted in Branco's cocoon retracting. It helped him out with a little parting gift of momentum that pushed him into the globules of puke, and the air-scrubber micro-drones swarming over to clean up his mess.

Branco had 100 pounds of mass on the XO, but the little weasel didn't break sweat as he grabbed the human by the cuffs that bound his wrists and twisted him around so he was facing Captain Blue.

A cloud of scrubber drones hovered over the captain, sucking up the writhing bulbs of thick red fluid streaming out from her open cocoon.

Jesus, there was so much blood!

Captain Sue Blue was a striking-looking woman. He had known the instant he'd walked in on her negotiating a merc contract with the Oriflamme, and seen the blue topknot crowning her otherwise completely hairless head. That had been three days ago. Now her most striking feature was the left side of her torso, where the mangled ruins of her light body armor merged with her charred and torn flesh. And through that wound, her still-beating heart pumped a geyser of blood like the sulfur volcanoes of Cap-Soufre that threw their plumes hundreds of miles into space.

Crap.

He thought the captain had only been lightly wounded during his kidnapping. Being wrong about that could prove a problem, because it was he, Saisho Branco, senior weapons designer at Cap-Soufre Base, who had shot her.

Branco looked at the CIC crew. He tried holding up his hands in supplication, but forgot they were cuffed. "Hey, I'm sorry about Captain Blue, but you can't blame me for resisting my own kidnapping."

Venix drew up close and pushed his be-whiskered snout into Branco's face. "You're wasting your breath, wondering what we think. It's Major Sun Sue you should be shitting yourself about."

Branco followed the Zuparti's gaze. The CIC main hatch had opened, and a medical team were coming through, pushing trauma kits and a stretcher sled before them.

Following them was a human woman sailing through the air with the effortless grace of a superlative athlete. If not for the lush eyebrows that framed her dark eyes, this could be Captain Blue. But she was dressed in black shipboard fatigues with a major's insignia on her collar.

"Where is he?" shouted the woman. "Where's the fucker who shot my sister?"

Branco allowed the fear to bloom across his face, and to be fair, it wasn't difficult as the woman rounded on him with fury blazing in her eyes.

But inwardly, he clung to a thread of hope his implants had given him after he'd re-queried with this new data: Captain Sue Blue had a sister.

His implants finally found a match within the forbidden records he kept in his head, wrapped in the ultimate encryption known to humanity. The two women were sisters, all right. But that was about the only truth going in these parts.

Neither Captain Sue Blue nor Major Sun Sue were who they claimed to be.

And neither was he.

Chapter 2

"**S**he dies, you die," said Sun, sneering at the brig's only prisoner.

Blue had purred like a cat in heat when she had first described this Saisho Branco—or whatever his name really was. Blue had allowed this man to apparently chance across her as she ran through a fake merc garrison contract with the boss of this sickly yellow moon, a human with the unlikely title of Oriflamme. But Blue didn't just sound like she was in heat when she mixed with dangerous men—which was why they'd been forced to flee their original merc contract in the first place.

Honestly, sometimes Sun thought it was better Momma thought they were dead than realize what the nanites had turned her favorite daughter into.

She sighed hard. Branco didn't look much of a catch right now. In fact, he looked like spoiled meat. The brig was subject to low gravity from the centrifugal effect of the spinning hull, but this was only pseudo-gravity. Given the prisoner's pallor, Branco's gut had not been fooled.

"I'm sorry about your sister," he said.

"Sorry? You fucking shot her!"

"I won't apologize about that," he said, seeming to grow a little backbone in his stance as he did so. "I was being kidnapped. Of course I fired in self-defense."

"Fair point," Sun admitted. "If you'd missed, we would be laughing about it right now. My sister would be seducing you, and we'd be trying to pretend we didn't know that at the end of our journey, we would hand you over to our client for the brief remnant of your life. But you didn't miss, did you? I won't apologize for killing you if my twin sister dies."

"I thought mercs cared only about profit," said Branco. "Kill me, and your client won't pay out."

"Mercs know loyalty too. So do sisters."

Branco rose unsteadily to his feet, and paced slowly in the low gravity to the edge of his cell. "Look, Major, my superiors have resources, very deep pockets. You know I must be valuable because you've taken a contract on me already. Whatever your client has offered you, my superiors will more than match it."

Sun shook her head. This guy was a disappointment after all. "Not going to work, Branco. It's one thing for you to die under interrogation. That's an unfortunate accident that will void the contract. But for us to swap clients midway through a deal...Have you any idea of what the Merc Guild would do to us?"

Sun shuddered at the thought, and then watched intrigued as Branco bit his lip for a moment before seeming to arrive at a decision.

"You're human," he said, as if it were an accusation.

Sun frowned. "Well spotted."

"Your merc company—the Midnight Sun Free Company—it's not registered with the Earth branch of the Merc Guild."

"True."

"How come humans lead an alien-registered merc company?"

"Now that is a very interesting story. But as you've seen fit to remind me, mercenaries feel the profit motive, and it is not profitable for me to tell that tale right now."

"Your twin explained about the nanites," he said. "Back on Cap-Soufre." He had the decency to blush a little, but she couldn't see where this was leading.

She shrugged. "Some kids get themselves a pornographic morphogenic tattoo and regret it the rest of their life. My sister wanted more. She went for an illegal nanite package that amplified all the pleasure centers in the brain, and it worked beyond her expectations. Except the off switch failed. I'm still searching for one that works. Until I find one, Blue remains a pleasure addict."

Sun narrowed her eyes and waited for the bastard to smirk, daring him to think the idea of a pleasure addiction was amusing. "So you know our dirty little secret," she said when he didn't. "So what?"

"So I had the opportunity to take a DNA sample of your sister, back on the moon. I needed several, because she's running some serious DNA obfuscation, and I bet you are too. But it's not impenetrable. I know who you really are, Sun-Yin Solara, and your twin sister, Sun-Yin Midnight. Officially, you're dead. Your legitimate merc company even paid out your death benefits to your mother."

"You're a stupid man. You've just talked yourself into a death sentence. How the hell did you know about us anyway? And how come you had our DNA on file? That's seriously classified."

He grimaced as if admitting to an embarrassing misdeed. "Because you've worn a CASPer at some point. Usage telemetry is constantly assembled into data packets and quietly streamed back to Earth. It's in the small print. To improve the suits, we need to know how they perform in the field, and for that we have to know about the people inside too."

Shock pummeled Sun's guts. She blinked. She already knew Branco was worth money, but she had no idea how big a deal she was getting into. She knew, and he knew she knew, but she whispered it anyway. "You mean you work for—"

"Yes. Binnig."

"Jesus Christ, Mister. When you said your superiors had money...No one on Earth has more money than the corporation who builds the CASPers." She smiled triumphantly, because they had bested the little prick. It took a couple of seconds before Branco realized something was badly wrong—he had miscalculated.

Sun laughed. "I know you're watching," she announced into the air. "Make yourself presentable, Blue, and come join us."

The prisoner protested and pleaded, but Sun was bored of him now and ignored the man. He didn't shut up until the hatch opened, and her twin sister bounded through in the low-gee.

"But...?"

Blue winked at Branco. "Oh, I'm fine, sweetie. I was just messing with you. We wanted to put a little pressure onto our corporate spy."

Sis beamed with pleasure. Sun recognized the warning signs: her twin was enjoying this just a little too much. She gave her sister a quick kick to the ankle and brought her back to her senses.

"Helm, change course," Blue ordered. "We've finished with Mr. Branco sooner than we expected. As soon as we transition back to normal space, organize a turnaround back to Taphoe-47 in the next slot available."

"No!" Branco was really frantic now. "You can't. I need to return to Earth. If you don't, the Oriflamme will find me and kill me. Earth needs to know what he's up to."

"We're the Midnight Sun Free Company," said Blue. "We always fulfill our contract."

"But the Oriflamme is stealing secrets and equipment from Binnig, and a dozen other organizations. His fingers run deep into the corporation, and I know he's working on behalf of someone else. This could be a prelude to an attack on Earth. Humanity can't afford for Binnig to be compromised, for the CASPers to be hacked. Your former brothers and sisters in the merc companies need you. Don't you even care?"

The twins exchanged glances. Branco had a point.

"Of course we care," said Blue, "but our first loyalty is to whoever pays our contract. And our client would be especially displeased if we did as you said."

"Who is it? Maybe Binnig can negotiate with them. Who paid the acquisition contract?"

"Acquisition?" teased Blue, raising what had once been an eyebrow. "Our client is your boss, the Oriflamme. He knew you were a very naughty spy, but he didn't know who you were working for. That was our job, to pretend to kidnap you and shake you up to reveal clues to your true purpose."

"We were contracted to provide a lead on your employer," said Sun. "But you went and told us everything. Binnig." She gave a low whistle. "That's a fat bonus for us."

The man looked from one sister to the other, but didn't find what he sought there. "Have you no honor?"

"I've already explained," said Blue in a voice edged with sharpened steel. "We are the Midnight Sun Free Company, and we always get the job done. And you, Mr. Binnig-Spy, mean contract fulfilled."

Chapter 3

Blue didn't bother speaking, she simply stuck her hands on her naked hips and cocked an eyebrow at the pair of CASPers standing guard over the Oriflamme's fancy chambers.

At least, she raised the ridge of flesh over her eye where a brow had grown until the day every hair follicle ejected from her body. At first, she had hated the side effect of her DNA obfuscation. Now she reveled in her distinctiveness—and the effect it had on people.

The CASPers guarding the Oriflamme regarded her impassively. She couldn't see inside their helmets, but she wanted to believe the show she was putting on was making the troopers inside sweat inside their haptic suits. She bit her lip and tried hard not to groan, because she was getting a serious thrill from all that deadly hardware standing before her. For all she knew, the CASPers might be women, but the suits they wore were oh-so-masculine.

"As you can see," she told them, "the Oriflamme's rather enthusiastic security insects thought any clothing was threatening. You know how Jeha can be."

She padded about in bare feet, cushioned by the thick carpet and the moon's low gravity. "As you can also see," she said, "I'm not armed with any clothing, dangerous or otherwise. Now, your master, the Oriflamme, invited me to share a little nightcap in his private chambers. He can share a drink if that's what he wants, but I intend to fuck his brains out before we transition away tomorrow. Maybe a little playtime is on his mind too. So are you going to let me in or explain to your boss why he has to drink alone?"

"The Oriflamme says come through now," said one of the CASPers through his external speakers.

Blue ran a hand over the machine's metal chest. Interesting. It was like a Mark 8 suit, but the neck armor was thinner and the faint hum of its capacitors was pitched higher.

The exotic configuration made the occupant seem even more dangerous. Excitingly so.

"Step away from the suit, ma'am."

"Shame we're leaving tomorrow," said Blue. "I would have liked to know you better, trooper."

"The galaxy is frequently a disappointment, ma'am. Now, go on through, the Oriflamme is waiting."

Blue shrugged, pushed through a wooden door wrapped in metal bands, and entered the Oriflamme's inner sanctum.

He was waiting for her inside, elbow resting on the mantelpiece over a roaring hearth.

Oh, please. Really?

Cap-Soufre was an airless moon, but the Oriflamme inhabited a make-believe world that was far grander. From the crystal glass tumbler in his hand, filled with a gleaming dark liquid, to the fake logs and a fake hearth, and the silk kimono coating his broad chest like an invitation to stroke him, the Oriflamme's tastes were a throwback to the 20th century on Earth.

He gestured to a matching tumbler waiting for her on the glass table.

"You don't need to ply me with drink, Oriflamme."

"I want to see the effect."

She drank the fluid. It was whiskey, rich and smoky, that sent sweet fire coursing through her veins. She trembled with giddy anticipation. "So do I."

He laughed, a very deep but also a quintessentially human and masculine sound. He beckoned her to sit on the deep leather sofa beside the table.

"Why are you really here?" he asked, as he watched her take her seat while taking a sip of his drink.

"We've had the after-contract party. Thank you, it was delicious. You've paid us in full for shaking up your spy, and paid us again for revealing the Binnig connection." She gave a languid shrug. "I guess I never did know when to finish a good party."

He smiled indulgently, and she had to look away because she was choking up with the prospect of toying with this dangerous man.

"You are former mercenary trooper Sun-Yin Midnight," he said looking down at her in judgment from his post at the mantelpiece.

Blue felt a sudden chill. Two people had seen through her disguise in the past few days. She would have to hide better if she got out of here alive.

The Oriflamme enjoyed her disquiet. "You underwent viral rewriting of your DNA to change your appearance and identity, and you couldn't resist adding in a reworking of your hair pigmentation to render it midnight blue to reflect your name. Leaving this giveaway clue was bad enough, but made worse because the viral rewriting had a side effect. You lost all your hair other than your topknot. That, at least, is what my researchers tell me, but I think they're wrong about your hair loss. My dear, it is not a loss at all but an exquisitely exotic veneer. Truly, you are a delight to someone such as myself, who considers himself a connoisseur of beauty."

She sniffed with disdain, the way she imagined a haughty twentieth-century aristo might. "I research my clients too. You are the de facto governor of Cap-Soufre. To the galaxy outside, you are conducting research on synthesizing F11 from the core of Phobetor, the gas giant we orbit. How convenient it would be if one could source F11 without the tedious necessity of waiting for dying stars to blast away the atmospheres of their gas giants first." She looked up. The colored bands of Phobetor cast a beautiful and eerie light through the upper view bubble.

"If your research succeeds, Mr. Oriflamme, you'll be rich beyond imagination, but my ship has some impressive sensors, and she says there's far more to this base than you pretend. You have a fusion power plant, for instance…that was the first clue."

The Oriflamme sat down beside her. "Everyone has a fusion plant," he said, with a quick laugh, but his eyes were teasing.

"Yes, but yours is sufficient only for your visible needs. You also extensively energy-mine the moon's volcanism. Why? To power the hidden parts of your operation, of course."

He nodded, impressed. "Bravo, Mademoiselle. You are beautiful, resourceful, intelligent…" He leaned forward, close enough for her to inhale the strong perfume on his face. "Most of all, you are suspicious. I like that in a woman."

He sat back, and she saw the triumph in his eyes. He had meant what he said. He admired her, which to him made it all the more exciting that he was also outwitting her. And that confirmed what had until then been only a strong suspicion: the Oriflamme did not intend her to leave this moon alive.

She blew out her cheeks in relief, blowing too her game of pretending to be a cultured sophisticate. While most of the company had been enjoying the lavish party earlier that night, she'd ordered two squads to freeze their fur off, getting into position on the plateau that curved around the northern end of the base. Now that she was sure the Oriflamme was going to betray them, Blue felt better about her mercs sweating in their suits as they hauled enough heavy weapons to blast away the base's anti-ship batteries.

There was a standard twelve-hour handover clause in the contract, which would expire in half an hour. After that, neither party owed an obligation to the other. Things would get interesting real quick.

She moaned with pleasure, her steady breath racing into gasps. She couldn't help herself. It was the Oriflamme—he was so very, very delightfully wicked. But Blue wasn't going to let him blow her ship out of orbit. And if there was one thing sexier than a very bad man, it was a bad man she was in the process of outsmarting.

She licked her lips at the prospect, but then shook her head furiously to clear it. Too soon! She had to wrench herself back into control of events. It was the drink—it was firing her up too soon.

"I know your other secret," he said. "Your teenage nanite experiment went wrong. Your pleasure centers are permanently wired to the max. You're a thrill addict. That's the only reason why I agreed to meet you here."

"You should try using nanites yourself."

"I do well enough without them," he replied and then scowled. "Where is your sister? I expected the pleasure of you both."

"She had to run an errand first."

"But she will be here?" He frowned, disappointed.

"Oh, trust me. She will be here. She's not a helpless thrill junkie like me, but she can't stop herself from keeping an eye out for her sister."

He held her gaze, unsmiling.

Fear started to sober Blue. Was he suspicious enough to kill her now? She began looking around for a weapon, but the Oriflamme's expression softened. "Some music," he asked, "while we wait?"

The roaring log fire disappeared—or rather the illusion of it did—to be replaced by a Tri-V virtual music library.

She walked over to the controls, making sure the Oriflamme had a good view of her rear profile.

"I've heard bad things about you," she said as she rifled through his collection.

"I expect they are all true."

"You know what afflicts me," she said quickly and hotly. "I'm easily excited but I can never get enough. Tell me all the bad things you've done."

"No."

"At least tell me how you arrived at your name."

He looked away, briefly ashamed. "It is an embarrassing legacy of my youth, rather as your teenaged years, Captain, left you with the legacy of your nanites. For me to assume that name was a crass masculine boast, a reference to the royal standard of my native France. In the medieval period, when the King of France ordered the Oriflamme to be raised on the field of battle, it was a signal no prisoners would be taken. The sight was said to drive enemies fleeing in terror from the battlefield. Captain Blue, do you feel afraid?"

She turned her face and closed her eyes, letting out a gasp of pleasure. "I won't wait for my sister. She'll be here soon enough."

He laughed. "You are most passionate, Mademoiselle."

"Oh, you have no idea. Come, Oriflamme, let me steal you before my sister arrives…"

Chapter 4

"Human not permitted here," growled the Lumar. The four-armed mound of muscle blocked Sun's route along the passageway, its four fellows taking up aggressive positions behind.

Lumar weren't too bright in her experience, but they excelled at looming. There was no way she could push past or through them. Instead, Sun raised her hands slowly. "Easy, big bears. I'm a guest. Your boss authorized me and my sister."

"Not in this zone," the alien replied, scratching idly at the back of its neck.

"I've been a mercenary for nearly 20 years," said Sun. "It's too late for you now, but it's my professional observation that unauthorized intruders should be shot first and debated with later."

The Lumar growled, its lips rolling right up to reveal the full length of its teeth. "I am not debating. I am telling you to leave." It drew its laser pistol. "Now!"

"Oh. Fair point. My mistake. And in the interest of full transparency, I will admit I'm not so much debating as distracting you. Here's a little question for y'all—paws up anyone who felt a little prick in the back of their necks a few moments ago?" The Lumar commander's eyes bulged in horror.

"Oh," said Sun sweetly. "I'm sorry. I forgot. You can't lift anything. Your limbs are already paralyzed. Drone! Set safe mode, then return."

As the micro drone made its way back to the pouch on her shoulder, she clicked her tongue in frustration at these annoying Lumar. Even paralyzed, the alien guards still blocked her way.

"Sorry, boys," she said, and gave the leader a hard shove to its chest, sending the whole group crashing to the floor like bowling pins.

After rifling the still-living Lumar, she came away with a key tab. A few seconds later, and she was at Branco's cell. He looked up at her in surprise, which only grew when she opened the door and extended the ladder down to the pit in which he was trapped.

"Why?" he asked.

"Your little speech about loyalty worked better than you realized. The Midnight Sun Free Company has fulfilled our contract with the Oriflamme, and the contractual handover period will expire in just a few minutes, after which we will be open to negotiate fresh contracts. Is it possible Binnig Corporation might be in need of a mercenary company to retrieve you, and would pay extra for information on the Oriflamme's activities?"

"Yes! Yes!" shouted Branco in triumph as he climbed the ladder.

"Did you have a company in mind?" asked Sun innocently.

Branco paused for breath at the lip of his pit. His face was bloodied, and his wince of pain suggested bruised ribs, but he looked game for an escape bid. In fact, there was a coldness to him, a tension in those muscles that made her think the Oriflamme had miscalculated by not killing this man when he had the chance. She approved of revenge.

"On behalf of Binnig Corporation," he said, "I wish to contract you to get me home to Earth. Safely. Alive."

Sun shrugged. "Regrettably any such contract must be sanctioned by an authorized Merc Guild representative. As none are available at this present time, I must decline your request." She accessed the timer in her implants. "However, in these exceptional circumstances, in about 20 seconds I shall be available to negotiate an agreement, which we can formalize as a contract later under proper guild rules."

"Fine, let's do that. Now cease yapping, and let's get out of here."

They jogged down the passageway, Branco trying to ignore the pain in his ribs but not entirely managing it. As they stepped over the cooling alien corpses, Sun nodded with approval as Branco bent over to loot a laser pistol. He clearly wasn't intending to be a passenger or a victim.

"I've an errand to run first," she told him.

Branco looked up from the Lumar and blinked at her. "A fucking what?"

"I'm going to collect the Oriflamme. We're bringing him with us."

"No. No, we're not. This is important. No heroics. No madness. Not a game. We just go home."

"Well, that's the problem, Saisho Branco. If we don't kidnap the Oriflamme first, none of us will leave Cap-Soufre alive."

Chapter 5

"Until the viral rewriting went wrong, we looked identical, my sister and I." Blue cocked an eye ridge. "Now that we don't, do you prefer me or my sister?"

The Oriflamme pushed himself up on the bed and regarded the naked form of Captain Sue Blue, the woman he thought he was toying with. His scrutiny was bracingly honest.

"I'd have to see you together first," he said, practically licking his lips in anticipation.

Yeah, like sis would ever play that sort of game, thought Blue. But she hid her thoughts and wriggled under the attention. "But you do like me...despite my condition?"

"Mademoiselle, you are an exquisite jewel, as I have already re-marked."

"Prove it," she said with a teasing wriggle.

He laughed and moved down to kiss her belly.

"I think it's about time to let my hair down," she announced, wriggling and squirming as she lifted her hands up and fiddled with her topknot. "Funny thing," she said as she loosened the thick strands of midnight blue coiled atop her head. "The idea that the hair would fall out all over my body, except for the very top of my head. Don't you think that's strange?"

"It is a...wonder." There was horror in that last word, as the Ori-flamme suddenly guessed something was wrong.

He looked up just in time to see Blue's heel smack into his nose. He roared in pain and anger.

"I thought you liked it rough, Oriflamme. No prisoners, remem-ber?" Before he could struggle up to a position from which to attack, she whipped the blue strands across his back, driving a scream from his body.

"Oh, the hair is real," she explained. "It's my sister's, dyed blue." She cracked the whip across his back, sending a surge of electricity through his organs.

"And the ELH7 electro-whip inside...do you think that's real, my exquisite jewel of a man? Let's see, shall we?" As he lay gasping, sprawled on the bed, she wrapped the whip around his neck and delivered electric pain, jerking a hand back and screaming herself when a power backwash jolted into her.

"Tricky things, aren't they? But I bet you hurt a whole lot worse than me."

"Stop, please, I beg you!"

"No," she replied and sent him pain that left him spasming on his own bed.

"And that's another funny thing," she said. "Your security didn't strip me naked. I just wanted your guards to convince themselves I was unarmed. And no one thought to question why I had no clothes." She made him scream again. "Oh, dear, Oriflamme. Do try to remember. You don't take any prisoners in here. I bet your CAS-Pers out there are incapacitated with laughter at your noisy frolics with the exotic-looking merc woman. Now, you've been a very bad man. Stealing equipment and secrets from those nice people at Binnig. Tell me everything…"

Chapter 6

"What can you see?" whispered Branco.

Sun's eyes bore through him like a full-spectrum security scan, and yet it wasn't her perceptiveness that impressed him most. Major Sun Sue was beautiful, and her eyes, blazing like black sapphires, were impossible to ignore. But as much as he wanted to appreciate her eyes, her lithe physique, and her cheekbones that were sharp enough to cut steel, those qualities were cold data points, as uninvigorating as height or blood pressure. He bit his lip hard. The joys of life had been driven from his body for a good reason.

"Here," said Sun, adjusting the front of her armor to draw virtual glasses out of an inner pouch.

Branco donned the glasses, telling himself to ignore the warmth Sun had supplied them with from her body.

The spy drone was only 20 paces away, bouncing a tight microwave comm beam off the polished stone bulkheads to the hidden recess behind a stairwell where they hid. Reception was perfect, and the two CASPers standing guard outside the Oriflamme's chamber showed no sign they were aware of their surveillance—a failing he'd have to report back to the Binnig labs...if he ever got back.

The thought made him shudder. Those CASPer suits weren't just eight-foot high monsters of super-dense steel and advanced composites, which held operators who would kill him without compunction, they were prototypes stolen from the heart of Binnig's most secure facilities. How the hell did the Oriflamme get hold of them? And why? Maybe the mad sisters were right to go for broke and kidnap the Oriflamme too. Whatever was really going on here was bigger than any of their lives.

Pushing those thoughts away, Branco let his training wash over him and concentrated on the scene.

From a marbled observation deck that offered spectacular views of Phobetor's colorful atmosphere, a pair of ornate stairwells swept down to a carpeted hallway where the two CASPers stood guard with perfect fields of fire. Behind them was a wooden door covered with ornate metal bands. Oriflamme's personal rooms lay beyond.

Taking off the glasses, Branco raised the gun he'd looted from the Lumar—wincing from his abused ribs—and then glanced meaningfully at Sun's still-holstered CL32 Peacemaker.

Sun smiled innocently as she replaced the glasses, and then grabbed something from a hip pouch.

"You've got to be kidding," Branco whispered, staring wide-eyed at the pair of EMP grenades she was holding out. "Have you even fought CASPers before? The suits are hardened against that kind of attack…although, in this case, you might knock out the jump-jets."

"Relax, Spy Boy. We're just the distraction here. My sister shares my brains even if she lacks the looks. She'll have this Oriflamme jerk under wraps by now, and she's armed with something that will take even a CASPer offline long enough for us to get away with the prize."

"Armed with what? Witty banter?"

"A customized DiHong Industries ELH7 superconducting electro-whip, with enough Jaha energy clusters to set smoke coming from those mercs' teeth."

"I don't know. Those are Mark 8-bis suits. Binnig was working on hardening the EMP shielding, though I don't know how far they got."

"Mark 8 who?"

"Mark 8-bis. That's why this is so serious. It's an abandoned prototype model. Abandoned but supposedly secret and secure."

"I do understand, you know? CASPers give Earth just enough muscle to stop the rest of the galaxy from walking over us at will. If Binnig's been compromised, maybe our suits have too. Our mecha might be as much use as wearing rubber gimp suits. So stop yapping, and let's pick up the bad guy already."

"Shouldn't we wait for the rest of the company?"

"No, because…talk of the devil…" Her eyes glazed as her attention shifted to something unseen and unheard.

An alarm rang out throughout the base.

Shit!

"Venix tells me he's done the hard work and is sending us a spare squad," reported Sun, untroubled by the wailing noise and flashing lights. "He's left nothing standing to shoot at our ship. All we've got to do is pick up this Oriflamme and get the hell out of Cap-Soufre." She tossed her grenade over the stairwell in a graceful arc aimed at two CASPers who, thanks to the alarm, were already alerted to the prospect of a fight.

"You coming?" she asked, raising an eyebrow in challenge. Without waiting for a reply, she sauntered out from behind cover over to the CASPer guards.

Branco watched her, speechless. Was Sun Sue a brilliant tactician or the most stupid person he'd ever encountered? He opened his mouth to deploy his secret weapon, to save her from her own audacity. Then he thought better. Audacity was who Sun was, and he wanted to see her shine in her own way. He lobbed his own grenade and scrambled to catch up. Brilliant or stupid? Didn't matter which she was, he decided. Sun was magnificent in either case.

The scene he emerged into was truly bizarre. Against the unlikely backdrop of a low-gee mansion thinly disguised as a research base, a barely-armed Major Sun Sue confronted two Mark 8-bis CASPers. She held her Peacemaker out vaguely, not wanting to look too threatening.

"Surrender immediately," commanded the amplified voice from one of the CASPers. The arms of both suits shook in uncontrolled spasms, which meant the EMP grenades were interfering with the signals from the haptic suits the mercs inside were wearing. It was the only explanation for why Sun hadn't been shredded by the lasers mounted in the mecha arms. But even as he formed his assessment, the spasms eased as the troopers regained control.

Then the metal-banded door burst open, and Blue ran out, wearing nothing but a shirt several sizes too big for her. It was one item of clothing up on the Oriflamme, though, who sprawled naked at her feet. Blue rushed one of the CASPers, lashing out with the customized ELH7. In the instant before the electro-whip hit, sparks leapt from the weapon to the mecha suit. Then it snapped against its target, full force. Branco's teeth hummed so hard he felt sure they would shatter, but to the trooper inside the suit it would feel like sticking your head inside a neutron star. He doubted the trooper would be hurt badly, but the haptic connections to his suit must be fried to a crisp.

The other CASPer fired up the jumpjuice and flew high out of the whip's reach. The suit twisted around in mid-air to get a good shot at Blue, and Branco decided it was time for him to intervene.

He opened his mouth and...said nothing. There was no need. The CASPer's jets spluttered and cut out.

Cap-Soufre's gravity was weak, but the CASPer fell hard.

"We removed the motor shielding to work on uprated jumpjets," said Branco defensively. "Then we abandoned the prototype before replacing the shielding. It's the only reason your grenades blew its jets."

"Understood," said Blue. "Binnig screws you on the small print, but still builds reliable shit. But with this being a half-finished prototype and all, I get to do this..." She lashed the downed CASPer, sending more than enough power through it to be sure it wasn't getting up any time soon.

Sun stepped around the fallen CASPers and gave their employer a kick. "We need your data. Are you going to surrender it nicely, or do we need to give you some more motivation first?"

"No need," said Blue. "I've already learned he trusts no one and nothing, so he stores everything in his implants. We take him with us and hack his mind at our leisure back on the *Midnight Blue*."

"Not going to happen, my pretty merc girls." Oriflamme rose unsteadily to his feet. "My CASPers can kill you hard, here and now, or you can surrender for a little interrogation first. You'll die either way, but I swear upon my honor in front of my employees that if you surrender, I shall let your ship and its crew go free."

Sun and Branco moved out across the hallway and scanned the area in alarm. What CASPers? What employees?

Blue remained where she was, and coiled the electro-whip around Oriflamme's neck. "If you try," she told him, "I fry your brain."

The Oriflamme laughed. "There's nothing you could possibly threaten me with that my employer would not do to me a hundred times worse, if I let you capture me."

A sudden thumping noise made Branco look up to the marbled viewing area above them. The bulkheads were hung with framed paintings of gas giant cores scoured clean by long-ago stellar explosions, and now colonized by mining operations.

One of the pictures revealed itself to be a fake projection when it began flickering. CASPers came flooding through, lighting up their jets and circling above their heads, weaponized arms pointing down at Sun, Blue, and Branco.

One CASPer remained standing, leaning casually over the railing above the Oriflamme's room.

"Squad's suited up and on its way to wipe out the intruders," said the commander, in a voice that sounded as if she breakfasted on whiskey, razor blades, and the body parts of anyone who displeased her. Branco recognized the voice as belonging to the merc leader,

Lieutenant Taj. "Figured you might need support too, sir. Permission for main group to use heavy weapons?"

"Denied. For now. I would rather not damage this facility because your people are scared of this third-rate rabble. More to the point, Taj, my employer would not approve. Use heavy weapons only if your CASPers are threatened with defeat."

"Never gonna happen, sir."

"I should think not. With those suits you should be able to rip them apart. Blood is much easier to clean up than the damage to property from explosive decompression. Besides, recycled flesh makes such a good fertilizer for the atrium plants."

"With pleasure," growled Taj. "Sandford, Goran, Chedjou! Secure the prisoners."

Three CASPers descended from the air to pick off the intruders.

Before the CASPers could reach them, Sun turned to Branco with an urgency in those dark eyes he'd never seen before. "Help me," she said. "Guess we took one chance too many and...I don't want to be captured alive. Shoot my sister for me. I can't bring myself to do it."

"No."

The CASPers were almost upon them. "Please. I swear I'll shoot you after. Their torturers will not be gentle."

Branco shook his head in disbelief. "I can't believe you based your plan on a single electro-whip!"

Defiance returned to Sun's face. "A human girl's gotta take a few chances to get ahead in this galaxy. Now, do it! Fire!"

"I can't shoot her."

"Don't move!" shouted one of the CASPers. The monsters of war were upon them. One of them grabbed Sun's Peacemaker.

She glared at Branco with a look of contempt that could slice through hull armor. "Bet you wouldn't have a problem if I asked you to shoot Venix. Blue finally worked her seductive magic on you, didn't she? Thought you were different. Thought you were a man worth getting to know."

Branco felt a smooth gust of air as a two-foot super-dense alloy combat blade snapped out from the nearest CASPer's arm, ending less than an inch from his throat.

"Hold that thought," he told Sun, ignoring the CASPer. "If anyone's making my heart beat a little faster, it's not your sister. It can't be. Binnig made me immune to her allure. Blue had her pleasure centers permanently stimulated, but Binnig switched mine off. It's their way to avoid distractions while I'm under contract. The only way I get my body returned to me is to return to Binnig with my contract fulfilled."

"Impressive employee motivation," said the CASPer. "Now hand over the fucking gun!"

"No," Sun screamed. "Shoot Blue!"

Even if he wanted to fire on the mercenary captain, the CASPers were deliberately blocking his line of fire. He safed his weapon and handed it to the CASPer.

Branco looked at Sun's face and saw the disappointment written there. He much preferred the astonishment that replaced it when he gave her a cheeky wink.

"Listen to me," Branco shouted at the CASPers "You all know by now where I'm from. I have a message for you from Binnig, from the development lab that your suits came from."

With his hands held up in surrender, he nonetheless dodged around the nearest CASPer so he could look the Oriflamme in the eye and see the look of assured victory there.

"Mit luftpudefartøj…" Branco began, enjoying it as the certainty deserted his enemy's face. "Er fyldt med ål."

"Kill them!" roared the Oriflamme. "Kill them now!"

His CASPers did not respond.

"What's wrong with you? Shoot them, or I'll have you begging for death."

With a hiss of pressure releasing, the clamshell fronts of the suits opened up to reveal the unarmed and very confused troopers within, wearing haptic suits wired to suddenly useless hulks of metal and advanced carbon materials.

Branco's capacity for joy had been shut down, but he felt a distant memory of satisfaction to see so much confusion wrought by a single phrase of nonsense, apparently a little Danish joke. "Don't you know it's standard lab procedure to fit a kill switch to prototype weapons systems?"

"I do now," said Sun as she grabbed her CL32 Peacemaker back off her escort. "Impressive. Will the phrase work on the other suits?"

"Already done," Branco replied. "Any suit of this model within comm range has just shut itself down."

"Very impressive," said Blue, dodging the rain of mecha falling from the air, and dragging a semi-conscious Oriflamme across the smooth floor. "Now, about those suits. I think they would look good stored securely in *Midnight Blue's* hold. Can you think of anyone who would want to buy experimental 8-bis prototypes?"

"Binnig will pay 100,000 GCU per suit," Branco replied. He'd already worked out his offer.

"Agreed," said Blue, "subject to formal ratification."

"You'll need to clean them out first," said Venix, arriving at the head of two squads or mercenaries, who began ripping the confused CASPer pilots first out of their mecha and then out of their haptic suits. Two of them advanced with extreme menace on Branco, until Sun shook her head.

"Wait," said the Zuparti, shoving his whiskers in Branco's face. "Do we like this human male now?"

"We do," said Blue, passing the Oriflamme over to company mercs. "In his revised capacity as agent representing a new employer, I expect great profits from him."

Venix's whiskers twitched with suspicion, but the XO was a Zuparti: mistrust came more naturally to them than breathing. "You humans," he said, running a long, narrow tongue over his nose. "You're devious, unpredictable, and can sniff a profit out of a vacuum."

"Thank you," said Blue.

"Although you are kinda disgusting about sex. Breed like bacteria, you lot. Why you can't keep it in your pants until a mating period, like a respectable species, is beyond me. Still…I had my doubts when Gloriana put you two humans in charge. But after the stunt you've pulled off on this job, I have to admit she knew what she was doing. You two are tolerably competent."

"Will you stop with the chitter-chatter?" shouted Branco. "We're still in a hostile environment, and we're not away yet."

"Are you sure we have to take him with us?" Venix asked, sniffing Branco. "He makes me feel suspicious…"

Chapter 7

"When this is all over," said Branco, "I'd like to stick with you. Figured we've developed a relationship worth exploring."

Blue's face turned icy cold, and she looked incredulously across at her sister, although Branco still didn't understand why Blue had asked her sister to join them in the captain's space cabin, a private office just off the CIC.

They were two jumps clear of Cap-Soufre and the Taphao-47 system, just one away from a trading world where they could ratify their agreements. So far there had been no obvious signs of pursuit. If this wasn't a good time to make his request then there surely wouldn't be a better one.

"Am I understanding this correctly?" asked Blue. "You asked to speak with me in private because you imagine we have a relationship worth exploring?"

"Let me rephrase," said Branco. "When I conclude my contract with Binnig, I'll be looking for my next berth. It's time for me to move on, and I'd like to join your company."

Sun made a brief choking noise, and that was when Branco realized the nanites that had supposedly wiped his capacity to experience joy must have been faulty, because when Sun's lips tightened first into an 'O', and then widened into a smile, the sight whipped a thrill through his heart.

The two sisters exchanged a lengthy glance.

"I have no use for you," said Blue. "You're not entirely without skills, but you're not what I need, and the Midnight Sun Free Company does not carry passengers, hangers on, or hired eye candy. Not for anyone's benefit. Now, if you'll excuse me, we have multiple active contracts with Binnig, and it's my responsibility to see they are completed. Some of us work for a living."

She pushed off and floated through the hatch, which opened automatically and then sealed behind her.

Sun grabbed a bulkhead hold to follow her sister, but hesitated before pushing off. "Blue runs the ship," she explained, "but I run the merc squads. I might have a vacancy in Shock Squad. Might. You'd have to do your internship, and you'll have a limited window of opportunity to impress your squad leader and convince me to offer you a contract."

"How long do I have?"

Sun looked back at Branco, tilting her head in mock disappointment.

Branco rolled his eyes. "I got it." He grinned. "Until contract fulfilled."

# # # # #

Emancipation
by Mark Wandrey

They moved in a single column, heads hanging almost to the ground. The slightly-rounded dome of their mostly-flattened shells reflected the bright bluish sunlight, protecting vital internal organs. They resembled box tortoises with rather long legs, and a lower shell that had a protrusion, allowing them to settle to the ground and use their front limbs as hands. Now they only used them to walk.

Spaced along the column every dozen meters, the guards watched the creatures' slow progress with the same bored indifference all prison guards developed. These guards were only slightly more interested because, unlike common prisoners, the ones they oversaw represented an impressive bottom line.

"Not many more of these left," a guard named Oso said to his KzSha leader, Koto. They wore a form of combat environmental suit, carefully formed to their thick insect bodies. Their wings projected through ingenious locks at the back of the suit, and, at the point of their abdomen, another lock allowed their stinger to be used in close combat, something they dearly loved. The other KzSha buzzed his wings twice, their version of the ubiquitous shrug all intelligent races seemed to develop.

"Who is to care?" He reached out with one of his fighting limbs and took a swipe at the nearest Aku. It didn't try to dodge, and the KzSha overseer's razor-sharp blade rebounded with a splash of sparks. The shell showed a deep score, and the Aku shuffled a little faster. "They're tough, at least in parts." The other nodded and turned his head slightly so compound eyes could focus on the pile of viscera and cracked shell lying nearby in the foliage. A few bones were scattered haphazardly.

"Expensive meal," Oso said. "We get as much as a million each for these things."

"It disobeyed," the Koto said, and then clicked his mouthparts savoring the taste. Too bad they were so useful as slaves; they could tolerate inconceivable amounts of radiation for a mammal and had the ability to breathe under water. But they were ever so delicious. His combat armor's computer beeped to tell him he'd passed the halfway mark for allowable radiation absorption for that day.

"We need to get them aboard," Oso said, no doubt responding to his own radiation warning. "I guess it's just as well we've almost exhausted this planet. This entropy-cursed radiation never ceases, even at night. Maybe we'll take the last for breeding stock." Koto nodded in appreciation. That was a good idea. If they had enough of the Aku, then the surplus could be utilized as prey and food! If they went extinct, it was no concern of his.

Koto passed along the instruction to his platoon to try to speed up the slothful beasts. He didn't want any of his platoon to take too much radiation. If they had to use nanites to counter the damage, it would eat into their profit margin. He watched up and down the line as his troopers began to jab, poke, and prod them onwards. They may have sped up a little bit. Maybe. One of the Aku nearby stopped, and Koto buzzed his wings at it angrily.

"Move along you!" he snapped, but the mammal ignored his master, its armored head craning to look up with naturally shielded eyes at the sky. "What are you doing!" he snapped, getting angry. He didn't want another million-credit meal, but if this insolent beast didn't listen to him it might still happen. He snatched his laser rifle from the magnetic retention point on his armor and moved closer, getting ready to butt-stroke the being when his antenna picked up a sharp and reverberating BOOM echoing in the planetary morning.

Koto looked up, his antenna swinging back and forth to test the air for more sounds. He was about to discount it as an atmospheric effect when two things happened—the alarm sounded over the platoon's radio, and a rattling string of additional booms sounded from the sky.

"Incoming ballistic radar signatures," the nearest ship's sensor technician called over the radio.

"How many?" Koto demanded. A series of optical enhancements dropped down over his multifaceted eyes. They revealed a sky full of burning streaks.

"Looks like 40," the technician replied.

"We are going to engage them with lasers before they get below engagement height," the ship's captain, Eshto, reported. "Order your men to abandon the village!" On the ship, half a kilometer down the ravine, Koto saw two of the mobile laser turrets come alive and begin pivoting. He used an antenna to tap the controls on the combat armor and change frequencies while looking up, eager to watch the attackers explode. His suit said the lowest was still over 30 kilometers up. Perfect. The ship's batteries fired a single pulse of coherent light, and lightning struck.

A white beam lanced from orbit, white-hot like a welding torch, and connected with the ship. The entire rear section of the ship exploded, sending armor and debris careening in all directions. KzSha troopers scrambled for cover. The Aku performed an incredibly fast sweeping motion with their feet, digging into the ground a half meter, and dropped into the resulting hole. Only the angled tops of their shells were still visible as partially melted starship parts tore through the ranks.

Koto saw two of his squad drop off the status board, cut down by scything debris. Another was yellow, wounded but still operational. A wounded KzSha was more formidable than the healthy troopers of many other merc races.

"They fired from orbit!" Oso said, rising up from where he'd taken refuge behind a dug-in Aku. The creature's head popped up a few centimeters, big eyes examining the situation before going back into the dirt.

"Peacemakers," Koto said. The other ship, five kilometers away on the other side of the ravine, opened fire with its lasers. It didn't fire at the plummeting streaks, though, it fired into space. "No, you fools," Koto said, but he was on the wrong frequency, so he addressed his men. "Orbital assault underway, rally at the village!"

More lasers lanced up to the sky, and a missile streaked away, accelerating at incredible speed. Fire didn't rain down on that ship like it had on the other one. He changed frequencies. "Ship Two, do you have any of the mammals aboard?"

"Yes, we have almost 100," came the immediate reply. Another missile raced away; this one was shot down in just a few seconds. So the ship in space hadn't been disabled—they were holding their fire because of the slaves!

"Change of orders, make for the other ship," he said, "bring as many of the slave creatures as you can."

"But commander," Oso complained, "they are too slow!"

"Carry them if you must! The Peacemakers won't kill beings who they believe are innocent bystanders."

"Weaklings," Oso laughed, snatching up a shocked Aku.

"Indeed," Koto agreed, ripping one from its hiding place as well, and the two KzSha used their powerful rear legs to explode into the sky, wings coming alive in a parabolic arc towards their objective. A dozen more troopers followed close behind. The other ship spared some laser fire for the plummeting streaks. The 40 falling stars instantly bloomed into hundreds of tumbling, flashing, burning meteoric fires. Koto ground his mouthparts together. He knew what that meant. "Humans."

* * *

"Incoming laser fire," the computer spoke.

"Buddha, deploy shields!" Jim Cartwright, commander of Cartwright's Cavaliers, ordered over the squadnet.

"You got it, Jim!" his top sergeant said. Jim tensed his muscles against the suit's harness and used his pinlink to trigger his own orbital drop shell. There was a tiny explosion, followed by a roar of racing wind from his descent as it ripped away the eight petals of his drop shield.

"Successful deployment," his suit's computer told him and autonomously applied some braking and lateral thrust from his jumpjets. Now free of the protective shield, the Combat Assault System, Personal, or CASPer, could paint his environment in better detail. The bulbous canopy in front of him, where the chest of the roughly Human shaped suit sat, became a Tri-V holographic projection of wherever he looked. The computer also fed him live visual feeds to his pinplants, allowing 360-degree vision. You couldn't sneak up on an alert pinplanted CASPer driver.

The suit fired its jets randomly again, making it look like one of the deployed shield parts, and Jim's back thumped painfully against the pads. He wasn't a small guy, tipping the scales at just over 310lbs, but he was down a good 40lbs from the first time he'd strapped into a CASPer. He wasn't used to getting bumped around like this, though. The problem was, he still had a lot to lose if he wanted to wedge his fat ass into a MK 8 CASPer, like most of his squad were using. For now, he stayed in the bigger, roomier MK 7, just like Buddha.

"How you doing, little Jimmy?" Buddha asked. The computer flashed the Tri-V image of the other MK 7 with his top sergeant in it. Buddha might look like a fat guy, but he was really 250lbs of badass muscle, with about 30lbs of baby fat around his waist. At least that's what he said his mother told him.

"AOK," Jim said. He'd have given Buddha a thumbs up with the suit, except the arms were still locked at his side. Air speed indicated they were falling at more than 500 miles per hour and descending below 15 miles. The only remaining part of his shield was a cone-shaped segment his feet were embedded in, helping his aerodynamics, and the flight pack on his back. "How you doing down there?" Jim said towards his thigh.

"Splunk good, <Skee!>" the Fae replied. Jim couldn't see her, but he knew the furry little alien would be nestled in the relatively spacious area behind his right thigh. He also suspected by the smell of pepperoni swirling through the air system that she'd helped herself to a snack before they'd dropped from *Bucephalus*.

"Sergeant Ortega reports Second Squad is all accounted for," Buddha said. Jim nodded and changed to the command channel.

"All good, Hargrave?"

"One slight damage, kid," the gravelly voice of his second in command, who had A Company, 2nd Platoon, for this drop. B Company was still on the cruiser, with 1st platoon in its drop tubes and 2nd platoon in Phoenix dropships. Just in case. "How are your troops?"

"We're all good," Jim replied and consulted his drop computer through his pinplants, "three minutes to touchdown. No change to target plan."

"Be safe, commander."

"And you as well," Jim said, and he switched back to the squad-net and consulted his altimeter. "Ten seconds," he told the men in his direct command. "Hang on, Splunk."

"Kick ass, <Proo!>" she asked.

"Yep," he said, triggering his play list. "Radioactive" by a long-dead band called Imagine Dragons began to blare in the suit. "Kick ass time." The nose shield blew away, and he was in complete control.

Unlike the mothballed and salvaged CASPer he'd used in the previous months since taking command, the MK 7 he piloted now was both brand new and customized. Made for orbital drops, it had lighter armor and a powerful flight pack, although its weapons were less impressive. The suit excelled at quick deployments and lightning strikes, just like this mission called for.

"Okay," he said over the squadnet, "let's do this by the numbers. Watch for collateral damage, pick your targets, and everybody goes home."

"All up!" Buddha called.

"Lead the charge!" all nine of his squad replied as one. Jim smiled in pride. Many of the men were new to the Cavaliers, but all were proud to be with one of the Four Horsemen.

He checked his radar and saw he was under a mile above ground. There were a pair of APCs visible, just beginning to move, dozens of huge insect shapes, and a long line of little round shapes. He thought about them and his face turned from a smile to a snarl.

"Buddha, heavy weapons, take out those APCs."

"On it," his Top said. A second later two rockets shot out from the CASPers, and the APCs were no more. He nodded as a second later he oriented and fired the suit's jumpjets long and hard, feeling almost 4 gravities crush against him. The proximity alarm pinged in his mind through the pinplants, he bent his knees, and the suit grounded with a boom.

"Cartwright's Actual, I'm down," he transmitted on the command channel and cut the music. "*Bucephalus*, status update."

"Commander," the voice of Captain Kim Su, the commanding officer of the *Bucephalus*, replied from orbit, "we have retreated to a somewhat higher orbit to present less of a target. There was no damage from the attack. The first ship was eliminated on the Peacemaker's instructions; we cannot engage the second ship as it holds hostages."

"Understood," Jim said as he released the now expended orbital drop thrusters and pulled the CASPer-sized laser rifle from its retainer on the suit's thigh. "Have 2nd Platoon, B Company prepare to deploy. Tell Major Alvarado we might have a remote listening post, based on the accurate orbital fire."

"Understood," the captain said, only a hint of her native Mandarin accent evident. "Stay safe, commander. Your mechanic sends her regards."

Jim felt his cheeks getting hot. The company's chief CASPer mechanical engineer, Adayn Christopher, was quite a bit more than his friend.

"Call 'em out, Buddha!" Jim barked after verifying there were no immediate threats.

"All down and operational," the big Samoan said.

"Very good." He consulted his battlespace, a Tri-V generated view of the area around his troopers and himself. Fed from live datalinks with all the CASPers within range, it gave an amalgamated view from 20 different suits scattered over a square mile. It was a very detailed map. His CASPer was a bit lighter because of the extra sensors and computing power needed to run the battalion, although he only had one company to wrangle now. "I mark 10 bogies in our immediate area," he said, and flashed them in red to the entire platoon. Two glowing points showed APC wreckage. "Scouts out, move east," he ordered. The radiation was so bad, there really was no discernable magnetic north. Courses were based on preset gyro readings from their suits. "And watch your rad counts."

The platoon formed a skirmish line and moved east as he'd directed. Two MK 8-equipped troopers ranged out front, one from each squad, moving much faster and with better point sensors. Private Stodden from First Squad and Private Howell from Second Squad, the two scouts, worked well together. A little too well, truth be told. Jim had separated them only a month ago, because they caused too much trouble off-duty. While too green as mercs to earn a handle, Jim thought of them as Rick and Morty.

"Skirmish only, Stodden and Howell," Jim ordered. "Do I make myself clear?"

"Yes sir," Stodden said.

"You can trust us," Howell added, but there was a hint of mischief in his voice. Jim sighed.

He watched on his sensors as the two smaller MK 8 CASPers ran/bounded forward in the planet's relatively light gravity. They moved with surprising grace, never jumping more than twice their height, and never in exactly the same direction twice. It was as close to random as you could get.

The planet's strange, radiation resistant vegetation didn't grow more than 10 feet tall, an aberration for most low G worlds where you might find 200-foot-tall trees or other megaflora. The radiation seemed to favor short, wide-leafed plants that reminded Jim of a cross between a palm tree and a broad leaf maple. Using visual, he could see the two CASPers bound over them intermittently as they raced away. It was both a way to get good forward views, and to draw fire. Scout and skirmish. It didn't take long.

A laser pulsed across the sky, then another. Jim's computer logged the beams of coherent light, invisible to the naked eye but perfectly visible to his suit's sensors.

"Contact!" Private Stodden said. "Medium laser rifles."

"Can you ident the race?" Jim asked.

"Looks like wasps," Private Hartman said.

"We could tell that much from the air," Hartman's squad leader, Sgt. Ester "Buckshot" Martin said. "Give the commander a positive ID."

"Should I walk up and get a better look?" Stodden asked, the sound of his suit's jumpjets audible over the radio.

"Stow that shit," his sergeant barked. More and more lasers crisscrossed the sky, evidence the two skirmishers were stirring up the slavers.

"Knock it off," Buddha said, his deep Samoan voice booming out. "We need to know if they're SleSha or KzSha. SleSha don't have wings. Can you see wings?"

They were at the edge of Jim's effective battlespace, and there was a lot of clutter, but two of the bogies suddenly jumped into the sky and flew at Hartman.

"KzSha," Jim said. He cursed. The SleSha were a handful because they had a hivemind; the queens could control the warriors with a sort of telepathy, and the warriors fought to the last breath and were tough. The KzSha, though, were *really* hard to kill, as they were individually sentient and 10 times as tough. More massive than a Human, they wore top-notch, unenhanced combat armor, could fly in low gravity (like here), and had two bladed middle arms tough enough to cut steel or punch through carbon-ceramic armor.

The Peacemaker who'd contracted them to bring down these slavers had been tracing them for a decade, but he'd never gotten close enough to verify what race they were or to track them to their base. He'd thought they were likely SleSha, who were already a disgraced merc race known for piracy. The KzSha were active in the guild, though, both powerful fighters and shrewd at playing the political game. That they'd picked the planet Soo-Aku spoke of the latter. The Aku, native to the planet, weren't members of the Union, which afforded them little protection. However, enslaving an entire race was one of those basic protections even the naïve enjoyed.

"Break off," Jim ordered, "bring them to us." The pair bounded a couple more times, fired a few magnetic accelerator cannon, or MAC, rounds, then retreated. "First Squad on me. Buddha, Second Squad around to the north and envelope."

"You got it, boss," Buddha said, and the other eight members of his squad, minus its skirmisher, quickly cut away, moving low and fast.

"They're coming hot," Hartman called out. "Looks like we kicked over a hornet's nest."

"So original," Stodden said. A missile shot up over the low vegetation and instantly angled towards Hartman, who was in the air. Stodden took it out with a flurry of laser shots from the counterfire system on his suit.

"Much appreciated," Hartman said as he grounded and covered his partner. Their skirmish/scout model MK 8s only had a shoulder-mounted MAC and defensive laser counterfire systems for weapons, as well as a dozen CASPer-sized grenades called K bombs. Hartman pitched a K bomb in the general direction of their pursuers before heading off again, this time staying on the ground and using the foliage as cover.

Jim saw the detonation and ground his teeth, hoping it wouldn't deter the enemy pursuit. From what he'd heard about the KzSha, though, he didn't think it would. As he started to move, he felt Splunk stir against his thigh. She'd probably been asleep.

"Wake up buddy," he said down his suit's interior, "trouble's coming."

"Fight now, <Cheek!>" she asked.

"Yep," he said and removed the safeties on his heavy weapon. "First Squad, here they come," he broadcast on the squadnet.

"Second Squad is coming around," Buddha told him.

As his top sergeant, Buddha had only coordinated the troop movements while staying alongside Jim; he suspected Hargrave had something to do with that. Less than a minute later, Stodden and Hartman bounded past Jim's line, and he prepared to fire.

His suit sensors showed radar reports of the onrushing KzSha, yet he waited for more direct targeting. The reputation of hard to kill was a formidable motivation. He felt Splunk move upwards a bit, into a better position if he needed her technical expertise. A second later the first group of four KzSha burst through the underbrush.

Jim blanched at the sight of them. He'd faced down waves of huge spiders known as Tortantulas and had even taken on a massive fusion-powered tank single-handedly once, but the sight of the four-foot-tall, armored wasps was sobering. When the aliens saw the line of CASPers, they didn't hesitate for even a second. They leaped into the air like grasshoppers, wings a blur, and fired at the Humans as they came.

"Engage!" Jim barked, and all 10 of First Squad's troopers opened up with a combination of laser, chain gun, and MAC rounds.

Two of the KzSha were blown apart in sprays of greenish blood, the result of multiple weapons impacts. Another took at least two hits, one of which severed a pair of legs and a wing, sending the insect crashing to the ground. Enemy fire fell among the Cavaliers but was deflected or absorbed by the formidable Human armor. The final enemy was also hit, but the single laser that found it splashed off its armor without effect.

The trooper just to Jim's right, Private Rick Partlow, swung his CASPer-sized laser rifle from right to left like a huge baseball bat. The MK 7's mechanical muscles drove the weapon with armor-cracking force into the hurtling KzSha, which had just angled its abdomen forward, intending to impale Partlow with its huge gleaming stinger. The laser rifle was designed for CASPer melee use, the KzSha wasn't. Partlow cracked its armor and broke its leg, but it rebounded away toward Jim, still ready to fight.

Jim just had time to deploy his left arm shield and partly turn before several hundred pounds of armored wasp slammed into his suit. A razor-sharp forearm aimed at his cockpit glanced off the shield as they crashed together. The inertia took him off his feet, and the two went down in a tangle of arms, legs, and weapons.

"Damn it, Partlow!" Buddha yelled. "Check your down range!"

"I...got...this..." Jim grunted as he gave a well-timed thrust with his legs, rolling over on top of the wildly-flailing alien. One of the alien's arms flashed and sparks flew off Jim's armor. "Oh, you want to play it that way?" he yelled, using his pinplants to release the right arm's three-foot-long, molecularly-hardened, chromium steel blade. It flicked out and locked into place, and Jim pistoned it down with all his machine-enhanced strength, pinning the KzSha trooper to the ground with a sickening *Crrruch!* of shattered armor and a splash of green blood.

He gave his jumpjets a bump and bunny-hopped backward, jerking the blade free, just as the alien's stinger shot up. It only scraped against his boot as he cleared the threat. Corporal Ramsey fired three thudding MAC rounds into the alien, blowing it to pieces.

"I'm sorry, Commander!" Private Partlow said, sounding chagrined.

"No damage done, Private," Jim said, "just listen to Top and watch your follow through."

"Yes sir!"

"Those were the skirmishers," Buddha warned, "here comes the main force." Jim checked his battlespace and saw at least two dozen more KzSha troopers racing at them, flying just a few feet off the ground.

"Volley fire!" Jim barked. All ten CASPers fired in a line, each along a corridor directly towards the enemy. There wasn't as much overlap this time and almost all the weapons hit, with varying degrees of effectiveness. Jim noted that all the laser shots were nearly ineffective, except against the difficult to target wings.

"Switch to ballistics only!" he ordered. "Any trooper without ballistic weapons, hold for hand-to-hand." Weapons were magnetically secured and blades snapped into place. It was Corporal Nick Sharps, while stowing his weapon, who spotted the new threat.

"Heavy weapons!" he called an instant before a medium MAC round exploded through his cockpit, pulverizing his entire upper torso. Jim didn't see him take the hit, but the First Squad corporal's icon went red all the same.

"Damn it," he said. Jim was one of only two troopers with both energy and ballistic weapons. He pivoted the MAC down over his shoulder, setting the crosshairs on one of the two huge wasps with its own MAC, and blew it to hell. The round punched through its head and out its rear in a spectacular fountain of gore. Buddha hit the second one, but just as it fired.

The round caught Jim's CASPer in the upper left, spinning him around from the inertia of the hit. He threw himself forward, feeling a dizzying lag in the suit's response, but managed to take a knee.

"Cartwright actual," he called, "I'm hit, but not hurt." He shut the mic down and spoke. "Splunk, I've got motive damage."

"Splunk fix <Skaa!>" the Fae said, and he felt her scrambling up the more cramped back area to open an inside access point. He smelled ozone and a tinge of smoke. "Small fire <Pree!>"

"Well how do you think I feel about it?" he asked, a little peeved. Outside his troopers were blazing away at the advancing KzSha troopers. They'd dropped five of the aliens, including the two Buddha and he had killed. The rest grounded and raced at them in an erratic zigzag pattern.

"K bombs," Buddha yelled a half second before Jim could give the same order. Unfortunately, his arm gave a stuttering jolt when he reached toward his own bombs, and he only managed to dig a handful of dirt from the ground next to him.

"Oh, Adayn is going to be pissed," he moaned. She spent more time repairing his suits than any other trooper in the outfit. And this one had been brand new. Still, he was better off than poor Sharps. His command and control computer seemed fine, so he watched as the men fought. Another suit went from green to yellow. It didn't flash, so the trooper wasn't seriously injured, at least. A line of explosions threw great gouts of dirt into the air and brought the KzSha to a stop, just as Second Squad got into position.

"All set," Second Squad Sergeant Jesus "Lamb" Ortega called out.

"Open fire," Jim ordered, then on the open squadnet. "Clean them up!"

First Squad fired from straight ahead, and Second Squad from 90 degrees off, putting the remaining KzSha in a lethal crossfire. Able to shoot from an oblique angle, the lasers of Second Squad were more effective. Only one alien trooper closed to melee range, and a pair of Cavaliers cleaved it down.

"Clear!" rang out up and down the line, and Jim heaved a sigh of relief. Private Paula "Vorpal" Handley, the platoon medic from Second Squad, bounded over and checked on Corporal Sharps, confirming he was KIA. The other trooper had sustained a hit to his power supply. Repairable, but not quickly. There was a snap, a chirping curse, and his suit function lights all turned green.

"All fixed, <Skee!>"

"Thanks, Splunk," he said and stood carefully. There was almost no after effects from the damage. He noted a secondary radio was now offline, and suspected his little companion had turned it into spare parts. "2nd Platoon, report!" he called.

"We got them cut off from the transport," Hargrave said over the radio. Jim could hear the whine and thump of weapons fire. "They're dug in pretty deep and have a bunch of the Aku as hostages. What do you want us to do?"

Jim checked the man down with a damaged suit. In normal conditions, he'd have had Splunk go fix the suit. Soo-Aku though was far too bright for her sensitive biology, and the radiation was horrendous. After confirming the trooper's life support was still working, he called the *Bucephalus* and ordered Phoenix Dropship #2, which held only an evac and support team, down on their position.

"Pick up one disabled trooper and one KIA," he told the drop ship pilot, "then hold on station for possible close air support and reinforcements."

"Acknowledged," the pilot said. "Dropping in one minute." Jim changed to the squadnet and addressed the disabled trooper.

"You going to be okay, Private Biggs?"

"Yes sir, I'm sorry to leave you down another."

"Don't be; it happens. Keep your survival gear in hand; it can save your life. Trust me, I know." Most of the Cavaliers had heard the story of Jim's month in the wilderness of Kash-kah, having been all but given up for dead, only to come walking out under his own power with Splunk as his new friend.

"I fix, <Skaa!>" Splunk complained.

"Not this time," Jim said, "it's too radioactive outside. Besides, we have another date."

* * *

The ship's heavy lasers fired so close to Koto that the blazing UV temporarily blinded him. It was playing hell with their communications as well. However, as best as he could tell, they'd yet to hit anything except foliage.

As he'd thought when he saw the contrails from plummeting troopers, it was the damned Humans. As mercs went, they were physically weak, easy to kill if caught unaware, and particularly tasty. The problem was they liked powered armor. They liked it a lot. So much so they'd developed their own. Very few races bothered with powered armor; it was too expensive.

It had been laughable at first, little better than modified industrial exoskeletons. Now a century later, they were turning out quality suits. A Human did a short, jet-assisted jump and shot the trooper next to Koto dead with a shoulder-mounted MAC round. The projectile almost perfectly split his soldier's head in two and completely missed the Aku he'd been carrying. The Human fell out of view before anyone could aim at it. This latest iteration of the entropy-cursed armor was *really* good. Someone should complain to the guild; it was an unfair advantage.

Koto looked behind him. It was another 100 meters to the ship, which had its landing ramp down and was openly inviting their escape. He'd lost a ship and some soldiers, but they could be replaced. Oso's idea of breeding the Aku was a good one. Koto would feast on one of the creatures and toast to Oso's memory. The idea would serve as his memorial. Koto hadn't seen Oso since a Human laser cut his wings off and forced them to leave him behind.

Fifty yards, they were almost there. The ship's lasers ceased firing as Koto and his surviving team approached. He turned from laying down covering fire and prepared to make the final dash to the ship. Once inside, they could negotiate a withdrawal. He'd heard many of the Humans were gullible and would parley if innocents were in the cross fire. When he turned to fly into the ship, he saw a Human standing on the ramp, a huge MAC weapon pointed at him. Entropy. Koto pulled the weakly struggling Aku higher so it was between the Human and most of his vital organs.

"You will lower your weapons or we will kill these creatures." He made sure his antenna were aimed at the armored suit. He knew they would have a translator that could pick up his speech, even though the Humans used sound waves to communicate while his species used light pulses. As he'd thought, a moment later the Human suit was flashing back at him in a language he could understand.

"You're done here," it said. "We have your ship, and your base on the moon was destroyed an hour ago." Koto ground his mouthparts together, his mind working desperately to find a way out.

"Passage off this entropy-cursed world in exchange for these creatures, then." He was past considering how to profit; now he was just trying to survive. The Human didn't reply and, for a moment, Koto thought it was going to work. Then an Oogar walked past the armored suit and to the bottom of the boarding ramp. It was the height of the armored Human, despite not wearing powered armor, although it did wear an environmental suit. Koto could see its purple muzzle and tiny black eyes through the faceplate. He started to aim a weapon at the huge ursine when he saw the blue tree logo of the Peacemakers Guild emblazoned on its chest. Koto felt his blood begin to settle in his thorax.

"You have been accused of slavery with the intent to commit genocide by servitude against the Aku, a non-union race of the planet Soo-Aku," the Oogar Peacemaker's suit flashed to him from a translator. "I judge this charge correct, and my pronouncement is death." All the other KzSha sat down on their abdomens. A few lowered their weapons and/or released their hostages, while others clung to them in desperation. "Any who surrender and aid in our investigation will gain consideration for that act. Decide."

Koto's compound eyes could see his troopers were no longer prepared to fight. He started to raise his laser, and it all happened in an instant.

The Oogar Enforcer moved far faster than a being his size should have been capable of, raising and firing a ballistic hand weapon the size of a small artillery piece. The entire left side of Koto's helmet was blown to pieces, along with the head inside it. He slumped to the side, dropping his laser and the Aku he'd been holding. At the same instant, 30 Cartwright's Cavaliers fired, killing every remaining KzSha.

"Check the hostages!" Jim called out while loping in from the perimeter, and the medics from both platoons fell out to round up the dazed Aku. A minute later, he got the news. Nineteen of the twenty-two hostages were unhurt and two were injured; one was dead. The 100 already in the slavers' ship were being released. The Peacemaker walked among the dead KzSha, checking for any survivors. He shook his head from side to side.

"I asked for survivors," he growled at Jim who'd joined him.

"We discussed this, and you agreed the hostages were more important." The Peacemaker turned his purple head to regard the armored war machine standing next to him. After a moment, he nodded his assent.

"You are correct, Commander Cartwright. The Science Guild estimates no more than four hundred Aku left on the planet. It may already be below viable population, even with these. If they'd joined the Union, they might have bought some protection with the wealth this world offers."

"They just wanted to be left alone," Jim said.

"Now they will have the peace of the grave," the Peacemaker snorted.

"Commander," Buddha said, bounding into the clearing.

"Report, Top," Jim said.

"Partlow and Stodden were sweeping the perimeter, and they found something for you." Jim was about to ask what it was when the two scouts in their MK 8 suits bounded into view. They were supporting a KzSha between them. When they landed, it was apparent the alien was much the worse for wear, but obviously alive. They'd hosed it down with secure-foam, an instant-hardening goop used on many multi-limbed aliens in lieu of the Human's own ubiquitous handcuffs. They tossed the alien trooper at the Peacemaker's feet, where it landed with a crash and rolled over. Its wings were gone, and several limbs.

"Present for you, Peacemaker," Partlow said, and gave the Oogar a thumbs up. The gesture was lost on the alien as he examined his prize.

"Well done," he said, turning to Jim. "Per the contract, you will get the 10% bonus." In his suit, Jim grinned. Then he had a thought.

"Hargrave?" The CASPer which had been standing on the loading ramp turned to him.

"Boss?"

"What's the condition of that ship?"

"Smells like wasps."

"Yeah, no shit. I mean will it fly?"

"Oh, sure. It's worth a couple million; I already logged it as fortunes of war." Jim thought for a second, looking down at the KzSha, and gave it a little kick. "Hey, what's your name?" he asked.

"I am called Oso," it flashed. "Why haven't you killed me?"

"Because we're not savages," Jim said. The bug regarded him with its huge multifaceted eyes. "Do you want to go on living?"

"Of course," it said.

"Good," Jim said. He grabbed it by a leg and started dragging it toward the ship. The alien's antenna flashed bright and the translator rendered it as screams of pain. Good.

"That is my prisoner," the Peacemaker said.

"We haven't formally handed it over yet," Jim said. "There was a 200% special bonus contingency on that contract, was there not?"

"Of course, but considering the situation, I see little chance of your collecting it." Jim shrugged.

"As my father used to say, there's always a chance." He dragged the KzSha up the ramp, careful to not pull its leg off. "Let's see how helpful Oso can be."

* * *

Several hours later Jim stood by his CASPer, stretching and drinking a cool sports drink. He hurt in all the wrong places, but he was also smiling the smile he got when things went right. Corporal Sharps had been the only casualty in the operation. Two others were injured—one from radiation and the other from a through-and-through laser wound to his thigh. It severed the femoral but luckily cauterized the wound. He was already on *Bucephalus* and in nanosurgery. The prognosis to save the leg was good. He hated losing anyone, however the KzSha were tough cookies, and the Cavaliers had wiped the floor with them.

Inside the cargo hold of the Phoenix drop ship were a dozen of the native Aku, looking around curiously at the machinery and sniffing the air that no doubt smelled strange to them. Soo-Aku's atmosphere wasn't poisonous to Humans; the radiation it carried was. Jim's sports drink had a minor dose of scrubber nanites that would find any radioactive particles in his body, isolate them, and flush them out.

He took another drink and turned to the leader of the Aku, who called himself Chiss, and handed him a translator on a cord. The being looked at it and then took it in both hands.

"I am sad for your losses, and that we couldn't save your fellow at the end." Chiss looked surprised as the translator spoke in his own language. Before he'd spoken to them in a halting version of Buma, the only other language their race knew. "Please accept a present of these translators," Jim continued, and one of his techs placed a box with two dozen of the devices next to the alien. "They may help you in the future."

"I am confused," Chiss said, pausing to marvel at the translator now speaking in English. "Why do you do this for us?"

"We are paid by the Peacemakers. Your people's plight is wrong."

"We understand you get paid, but it is not much." Jim nodded slowly. Splunk was sitting on his CASPer's shoulder, eating the meat from a sandwich. Jim suspected one of his people was wondering where their lunch had gone. "We tried to ask for help, but anyone who would come wanted to take much. Entire island, or all of a mineral. We hold our world sacred and do not believe in this. Still, you come, you fight, and you die here for us. Why, when no others will?"

"Because we're Humans, and we don't like seeing people killed for no reason," Jim explained. "There are so few of you left."

"Yes," Chiss agreed, "the scientists from your Union say maybe not enough. We may perish."

"Not if I can help it," Jim said, and left Chiss to examine the gift.

"Pretty words," the Peacemaker grumbled, coming down from the cockpit where he'd been using the radio to talk to his ship in orbit. "You Humans like killing as much as the rest."

"There might be some truth to that," Jim admitted.

"Some truth?" the Peacemaker asked, then laughed. Out of his suit now, the Oogar towered over Jim. The alien was eight feet of muscle, fur, and claws, with a mouth full of bright white, sharp teeth. He came right up to Jim, who stood his ground, despite how imposing the alien was. "We study all the races of the Union, especially the merc races; it's part of our job. With so few merc races, we study them in great detail. After all, they tend to cause the most trouble. Your race has one of the top ten bloodiest histories of all the races in the galaxy. At least those still alive.

"Merc race are naturals at fighting and killing, but you Humans made it an art form! Such glorious slaughter you've done to each other, sometimes wiping out entire ethnic groups. You are no better than the Besquith or the Tortantula."

"The difference between us and them," Jim said, poking the bear in the chest, "is we fucking learn from our mistakes. When's the last time the Tortantula or the Besquith took one of your piss-paying contracts, Peacemaker?" He was a little surprised at himself for poking the huge purple bear. Wasn't there an old adage about that? The Peacemaker regarded him with its tiny black eyes.

"Don't act all superior Human, just because you did a good deed."

"We do a lot of good deeds," Jim said. "I know for a fact Humans take more Peacemaker contracts than nearly all the rest of the merc races combined."

"And why is that?" the Peacemaker asked, not denying what Jim said. The Cartwright's commander pointed at the small turtle-like Aku.

"Because we care about those who can't help themselves," he said. "Humans always root for the underdog." The Peacemaker cocked his head, no doubt listening to the translation from his pin-plants.

"What does a short Zuul have to do with this?" he asked, and Jim laughed. The Zuul were a canine race, and the translator had no doubt caught the dog part and went the wrong way. He explained the meaning. "Ah, I see. You root for the likely loser?"

"Not really," Jim said. "Maybe it's too complicated for me to easily explain."

"Maybe you Humans are just crazy." Jim shrugged. Before he could think of a retort, the ship's air lock opened, and a figure in an environmental suit ran up and jumped on him. For once Jim was glad he was fat; otherwise, he'd probably have been tackled like a rag doll. Adayn ripped her helmet off and kissed him, long and hard.

"Hi honey," he said eventually.

"I will leave you with your mate," the Peacemaker said, the translation holding an obvious edge of distaste.

"Hello Funwork, <Cooo!>" Splunk said between bites, using his nickname for Adayn.

"How's my little Watchmaker?" she asked with her nickname for Splunk. The Fae cooed her appreciation that everything was as it should be. That was when Adayn saw the access panel open and twisted metal. Her face darkened.

"It's just minor damage," Jim said, putting her down.

"It was brand new!" she said, walking around to see the impact. "Oh, Jim, you are so hard on my toys!"

"Your toys?" he spluttered. "Who pays for all this?"

She gave him a lopsided grin. "Okay, point." Adayn came back around the CASPer. "So, we going home?"

"That's the plan," he said. Adayn smiled and gave him a kiss. "We could all use a few weeks on Earth."

Smiling, she went over to discuss fixing Jim's CASPer with Splunk. Jim finished his drink and looked at Chiss for a moment. Two other Aku were discussing the gifts he'd given them. They might well be the last of their race. Jim found the imminent extinction of the Aku intolerable.

"Peacemaker?" Jim called. The Oogar came back over, after first making sure Adayn wasn't there to perform any more mating rituals.

"Yes, Commander?"

"How many of the Aku do you believe might be being held right now?"

"We estimate several thousand, at least, based on the slavery market we've monitored." Jim nodded then went over to Chiss.

"I want to suggest a plan," he said to the leader of the survivors. "It presents some risk to you, but may also be of great benefit." He outlined his idea, with both the Aku and the Peacemaker listening.

"You are willing to risk this?" the Peacemaker asked, looking from Jim to the Aku. "Both of you?" Chiss spoke with his fellows for a moment, then addressed the Peacemaker.

"If the Cavalier thinks it is possible, we believe it is worth the risk."

"Then you are just as crazy as this Human," the Peacemaker said, "but I will go along with it."

"Okay!" Jim said, slapping his hands together and smiling. He glanced up at his girlfriend who he'd just told was going home, and his grin faded. Only one hitch, he thought, then used his radio. "Hargrave?"

"Yeah boss."

"Detail a squad to collect as many intact or partly intact KzSha combat armor suits as you can."

"Sure," the older man said, "but why?" Jim told him. Hargrave just laughed.

* * *

"But why do you need to go yourself?" Adayn asked, tickling the not-quite mustache Jim had been cultivating. It had doggedly refused to grow in seriously, and he'd secretly looked up some nanite treatments. It was hard to concentrate with her lithe body curled next to him in the hammock, even after what they'd spent the last hour doing.

"Merc law," he explained yet again. "If it's not a commander or XO, there can be some denial of claim."

"Then send Hargrave," she suggested. Jim sighed. The hammock jostled as *Bucephalus* maneuvered slightly, holding its position at the stargate.

"I won't send someone else to do something that's my responsibility, just because there's risk." The cabin was almost dark, and he could still see her frown from the dim glow of the room's status controls next to the door. He liked the ship; it was more modern and comfortable than *Traveler* had been. Captain Kim Su was also an excellent ship's master, having been found in a recommendation left by Winslow prior to his death. It didn't hurt that she'd been trained by none other than the Winged Hussars at their secret space naval academy.

He still missed the old British gentleman who'd been the *Traveler's* captain; he had been one of the first men Jim had lost under his command. "He won't be the last," Hargrave's voice echoed in his mind.

"The commander can't take every risk himself."

"True," he agreed, and he felt her tense, "but I'm taking this one." She took a breath to offer another argument, and he quickly cut her off. "This is how it's going to be, so drop it."

"Is that an order, sir?" she asked coldly.

"If you force me to make it an order, then yes." She didn't say anything. "I have a feeling I need to follow through with this myself. No, I don't know why." She gave a deep sigh and relaxed against him. "Can we just enjoy the next week before I have to go?"

"Sure," she said. He knew she wasn't happy, and there was nothing he could do about it. Ever since he'd taken over the company after his mother had nearly destroyed it, he'd needed to make tough calls, sometimes without enough information. He'd had a marvelous series of success, though the jury was out on whether it was a chain of brilliant successes or incredible luck. He dearly hoped his instinct was still working well.

He napped for a bit, and time slipped by. He was awoken by the ship's computer announcing they were about to make transition to hyperspace. He'd done it so often in the last two years it wasn't even interesting anymore. An instant of uncreation, and they were in hyperspace.

"Prepare for spin," Captain Kim Su said over the intercom, and a second later the hammock swung to one side, and he felt the spin creating pseudo gravity. After a few minutes, it settled at ¼ of a G. Adayn half woke, repositioning in the gravity, and drifted back to sleep. He knew she was tired after two days of custom robotic builds. If it hadn't been for Splunk's unbelievable ability to improvise with machines, and Adayn's knowhow, they would never have been able to manage his crazy plan.

Jim didn't want to wake his girlfriend up, so he stayed where he was and used his pinplants to do company paperwork. There was always plenty to keep him occupied. He noted the loss of a CASPer and damage to six in the last mission, including his own. Then he authorized the payment of death benefits to the dependents of Corporal Nick Sharps. He accessed the dead man's file. Wife and two kids. He remembered when Sharps signed on, so incredibly proud to be one of the Four Horsemen. Now he was dead. He knew not to dwell on such things, so he composed a quick letter to the man's widow and sent it to the outbound transmit queue, to be delivered to the next stargate they passed. The Information Guild would see it got back to earth. By the time Mrs. Sharps knew her husband was dead, months may have gone by. Jim hoped the credits would lessen the blow, but he knew that was unlikely.

It was almost 2:00 a.m., ship time, when he finished the necessary work and started thinking about sleep. Only a couple messages remained unread, both received from the stargate just before they'd made transition. One was a note from his cadre commander back in Houston. Charlie Company training was coming along well, as was project Spartan. He smiled at that and turned to the last email. As he read, his smile turned to a frown.

"Damn it," he muttered, Adayn shifting and snoring slightly. He reread the email before saving it with a flag. There was nothing he could do about it right now anyway, not thousands of light years from Earth and going in the wrong direction. He'd have to make some arrangements after they returned to normal space in a week. His mother had died three weeks previously.

* * *

The small ship dropped through the planet's outer atmosphere, its hull glowing white hot as it burned off velocity to slow. Computers linked up and exchanged codes. The ship's identity was verified, and a controller came on the radio.

"Gatherer G-12, you are overdue. Where is G-09?"

"Lost," the ship's pilot replied. "We were attacked by Human mercenaries." The channel was silent for a moment.

"Where is commander Koto?"

"He was on G-09," the pilot said. "This is Oso, in command. I managed to escape with 40 slaves."

"How many of your troopers survived?"

"Myself, and one other."

"Entropy!" the other said. "Still, the slaves will offset some of the costs. Did you make the Humans pay?"

"Dearly," the pilot said.

"Then you did your duty. Follow the approach beacon to the landing field by Slave Processing Camp Two. Welcome home."

The ground crew watched the ship approach, immediately noting it was damaged. Two of the cargo pods were holed to space, and one of the lifter engines was missing. The pilot brought it down roughly, more of a controlled crash than a landing. Emergency robots stood by, just in case. They stood down when nothing exploded or caught fire, and the boarding ramp fell.

Slave Camp Two's administrator, Jolo, buzzed out of the flier he'd arrived in and landed at the base of the ramp. The pilot, one of only two survivors of the expedition he'd been told, came down the ramp.

"Where are your wings?" Jolo said in surprise. "And why are you still wearing armor?"

"I was badly injured by the Human mercs," Oso explained, "it was only luck I escaped with this ship. The Humans were overconfident, so I stole the ship and got away with the slaves. The armor is still trying to heal my injuries." At the only intact cargo pod, a dozen KzSha were opening it up and using shock probes to move the slow Aku off the ship. "Be easy on those slaves!" Oso barked. Jolo looked at him, waving his antenna in incredulity. "They're the last profit we'll see from these creatures," Oso said quickly, and Jolo snapped his mouthparts in agreement.

The other surviving trooper came down behind Oso. Jolo didn't notice the trooper also wore combat armor. The Aku were meekly lined up, and a robot used a laser to etch an identification number on each of their shells. Oso watched it all, obviously intent on making sure his share of the profit was secure. When they were finished, he fell in with the processors.

"You should see the physician," Jolo said. "They will help facilitate your wing budding."

"Once these slaves are processed and logged into my record," he insisted.

"Your diligence is admirable, but your trooper can do this."

"I must insist," Oso said. Finally, Jolo relented, and the procession moved toward the camp.

The planet was cool, and the light from its yellow star mellow compared to Soo-Aku. The Aku all moved extra slowly, having trouble seeing in the, to them, dim light. In the camp, bright lighting was set up to aid in training the new slaves in their future duties as equipment handlers in high-radiation jobs. The trooper, which had arrived with Oso, flew alongside the formation, but kept turning this way and that, apparently curious about the surroundings. Jolo noticed this behavior.

"What is wrong with him?" he asked, pointing with a limb.

"He has been a little out of sorts since the tasty batch of the color seven," Oso said, and Jolo looked at the trooper in confusion.

"What?"

"The sun is crunchy, and provides a wonderful smell in the yellow blood." Jolo stopped and looked at Oso, trying to make sense of the wounded trooper. Meanwhile, the other armored trooper had flown to the camp's perimeter fence and hovered there, seemingly observing the hundreds of Aku who were being trained to move machinery. Jolo turned to look closer at Oso, and saw one of the trooper's antennae disappear and then reappear inside his helmet.

"What in entropy is going on?"

There was a banging sound inside the armor, almost like something was pounding on it. A second later the trooper's head seemed to disappear and was replaced with another. This head was not a KzSha at all, but a Human!

"Fuck," Jim said as the Tri-V projector failed completely. He activated the remote on his pinplants. "Go, go, go!" he ordered. From the hold of the ship, dozens of KzSha combat armored suits flew up and out, spreading in all directions. Only their wings weren't buzzing as they flew, each was powered by four tiny lift fans, and their heads were replaced with Tri-V cameras.

"What is going on?" Jolo demanded. Jim had no idea what the alien was saying, the translator built into the suit had failed along with the mimic software he'd cobbled together. His personal translator was inside the armor, not in view of the supervisor. He abandoned all pretenses and ran right into the stunned camp administrator, bowling Jolo over with a crash. "Stop him!" Jolo flashed at the slave handlers, who had stopped herding the new slaves and were watching the rampaging armored trooper in amazement.

Meanwhile the other trooper had deployed tiny lasers and disabled the camp perimeter defenses nearest to it and had flown over the fence and out of view.

"It is a break out attempt!" Jolo called on the radio, "Summon a platoon from the barracks!"

The camps had never had any trouble with the slow, docile Aku, so the summons took some time to accomplish. Jim managed to crash through the camp fence near where the trooper had wrecked the defenses, and he charged into the midst of the Aku being trained. Their trainers, non-combat KzSha, backed away in confusion at the combat armor, even more rattled by the alien head inside.

Jim managed to get the suit to stop in the middle of a huge group of Aku, whereupon the cobbled together automation committed suicide and blew out entirely. The armor thudded to the ground, all the limbs spasming randomly. Coughing from the smoke, Jim hit the eject control and the front of the suit popped off. He slowly and ponderously extracted his bulk, grumbling and cursing the whole time. When he stood up, there were a dozen KzSha troopers pointing lasers at him.

"Hi!" he said and lifted the other item that took up most of the space in the armor with him. It was the warhead from one of the Type 4 ship-to-ship missiles on *Bucephalus*. Essentially, it was a 200 kiloton micro-nuke. All the alien troopers froze. "Translator?" he asked and very slowly reached inside his Cavaliers uniform to lift it out so it could flash visible signals.

"Who are you?" he immediately heard from the pendant.

"Jim Cartwright, commander of Cartwright's Cavaliers." The commander of the KzSha troopers landed and examined Jim.

"Well, commander, your attempt to free these creatures was ill-conceived. Your drones are being rounded up—they did no damage—and the other trooper you brought will soon be captured, as well. It pointed at the warhead. "You humans aren't known for your willingness to die for no effect. Using that weapon will not free our slaves."

"It wasn't an attempt to free them," Jim said, making sure his thumb didn't come off the bomb's trigger, "and my friend should be back any second." Time passed, and the alien commander watched him. "Any second now…" Jim said, starting to sweat. His thumb threatened to cramp. Just as he was starting to get worried, the other suit of KzSha combat armor flew up. A dozen real KzSha troopers tracked it with weapons, watching its every move. The suit landed lightly, and its torso popped open. This one didn't hold another Human; Splunk hopped out and looked around.

"Stupid bugs, <Skaa!>" she said.

"Easy, Splunk," Jim suggested. His friend adjusted her goggles and hopped over to land on Jim's shoulder. She looked at the warhead, then the alien commander, and smiled. The alien trooper commander watched it all carefully.

"If you weren't trying to free them, what were you doing? I'd like to know before we kill you."

"You are no more suicidal than I am," Jim admitted, "but you want to hold off on that for a minute."

"And why is that?"

Jim triggered his pinplant link to the transmitter on his belt. "Peacemaker, have you been recording the remote data?"

"I have, Commander Cartwright." Jim knew the KzSha back at the starport would be looking on in amazement as the Peacemaker came walking out of Jim's ship. One of the cargo holds only appeared destroyed; it was instead carefully shielded to avoid anyone detecting the person inside. "I must thank you," the Oogar said. "I've been here three times before and never saw a single slave. They could detect my transition into the system and hid these camps. Riding in with you gave me the perfect cover. I'm transmitting to their government now." Jim waited for a tense minute, knowing there was still no guarantee. They could just kill him anyway. It was a huge gamble with the nuke; it could provide a near perfect cover for the mess. Murdering a merc commander wasn't much when compared with a charge of genocidal slavery. Kaboom, and no witnesses.

At last the troopers began lowering their weapons. The unit commander was the final one to do so, and Jim could tell he really didn't want to. The gambit had paid off. In the Merc Guild rule book, there wasn't anything against slavery; however, what they'd been doing to the Aku was against one of the few Union laws—genocide—and that law had real teeth. Jim had the feeling the guild wouldn't forgive and forget, this time.

"Get off our planet," the KzSha commander said.

"Gladly," Jim said and he walked with Splunk back toward the ship. "And we're taking that ship; it's already registered with the guild as a war prize." Chiss was waiting by the ship, wearing one of the translators Jim had given the alien.

"We will not forget this act of kindness," he said to Jim.

"Glad to help," Jim said, patting the alien on the shell. The laser-etched numbers made him grind his teeth. "The Peacemaker will begin processing the evidence and arrange transport for you and your people to go back home. If you ever need us, just call."

He walked back aboard the ship and into the cockpit, almost falling into the seat. He was shaking so hard he almost forgot about the bomb he'd been holding. Luckily, Splunk hadn't. She took it from him, reactivating the safety, and stowed it away. Adayn hadn't known it was a real warhead. Jim had no choice in that, if they'd scanned it and found it to be a fake, they would simply have shot him.

"I don't believe that worked," he said.

"Jim crazy, <Cooo!>" Splunk said.

"You can say that again." It took him a few minutes to stop shaking enough to program the ship for takeoff, and he watched the screen all the way to orbit, not certain he wouldn't get blown to atoms. He made it up safely and set the ship to head for the stargate. The Peacemaker had sent him a message confirming the extra pay for finding the slavers' base and providing definitive proof of slaver activity. The KzSha were in deep shit, and the Cavaliers were to blame. He shrugged, what's another pissed off alien race? They could take a number.

He was halfway to the stargate when he realized Splunk was playing with one of the slates they'd brought with them to control the alien ship's non-standard controls. She had a datachip interfaced and was reviewing images.

"What do you have there?" he asked. She detached the slate and handed it to him with one of the images frozen and enhanced. He'd been wondering why she'd taken so long to return. The original plan was for a quick sweep over the other nearby camp to photograph as many slaves as possible and return. She'd taken a detour through a series of huge warehouses. There were dozens of buildings, all full of trade goods. No doubt things the slavers had gotten in exchange for the Aku. Suddenly, he stopped and backed up.

There, on the slate's high definition screen, was the unmistakable shape of a Raknar—one of the giant mecha warbots the long-dead Dusman had used to defeat the Kahraman and their Canavar terror creatures. Jim had gotten a couple of them running with Splunk's help, and just one had defeated a thousand Tortantula warriors and three of the not-quite extinct Canavars, which had been used in a plot by the Besquith to try to corner the F11 market. It had been a bold plot, and it would have made the Besquith powerful beyond belief.

"Oh!" he said, examining the almost ape-like visage of the 20,000-year-old war machine.

Splunk reached a finger over and delicately tapped the frame advance and another Raknar appeared, and another, and another. They all looked like they were in excellent condition. Some seemed almost new.

"Raknar, Jim," Splunk said, a huge toothy grin on her face. "Many Raknar, <Skee!>" His smile was just as big as hers. Now they just had to figure out how to get the Raknar from the KzSha, who were certainly not going to be in the mood to trade. For now, though, he needed to go home. The KzSha planet fell away behind them.

# # # # #

Forbidden Science
by Terry Mixon

"Antimatter."

The whispered word hung in the cafeteria air as if supported by antigravity, an admittedly unobtainable scientific fantasy.

Jeff Peters frowned and leaned a little closer to Saren, his friend and fellow engineering student. The large millipede's—at least that was the closest analog Jeff could think of for the Jeha—voice was soft at the best of times. Right now, it was almost inaudible.

His translation pendant made his friend's whisper seem furtive. That was damned impressive. None of the other models he'd owned had come close to that level of discernment.

One of his instructors was breaking ground on the cutting edge of the translation field, and Jeff was helping test a next-gen version of the tech. Well, something past the next generation, probably.

It wasn't always this sensitive, but the professor had taken steps to ensure it was as accurate as her research could make it. At least so far as the races her test subjects were most likely to encounter here at the university.

That wasn't to say he hadn't run into a few glitches. Mostly revolving around cursing, of all things. Some of the translations were hilariously wrong. He'd made note of each occurrence and would return that with the pendant at the end of the semester.

"I'm sorry," Jeff said after a long moment. "Could you speak up? I thought you said antimatter?"

"Shhhh!" the Jeha said anxiously. "Keep your voice down."

"As far as I know, antimatter isn't a big secret," he said dryly. "Humans made some before the Union found us."

It was amazing how impressive his friend's version of a flat stare was, since he didn't have eyes.

"So have we, Monkey Boy, but only numbered in atoms and at great cost. Professor Xaltar is rumored to have discovered a theory that might lead to the creation of significant quantities of the stuff relatively cheaply. They say that's why the Council is debating expelling him from the Science Guild."

Jeff leaned back in his chair, took a sip of his juice, and considered that. The food in the university cafeteria was universally terrible, but the juices were terrific.

It had taken him a while to get past his astonishment that a cafeteria at a major Science Guild university produced food for its students that prisons on Earth would have rejected on humanitarian grounds, but he was beginning to suspect foul play. Seriously, there wasn't a single species that found any of the dishes here to their taste. Not a single one.

That was statistically unlikely and fueled his growing suspicion that the food servers were Guild researchers performing some obscure research project on their fellow students. If so, he didn't want to encourage that kind of thing by giving them data.

They might tag him for special study, and he could only imagine how that would manifest itself. He shuddered and pushed the thought away.

"So, wouldn't that be a good thing?" he finally asked. "The power generating capabilities would be impressive."

"As would the destructiveness of the weapons. It is Forbidden Science."

Jeff could actually hear the capitalization of the words.

That was a term one didn't expect to hear at a Science Guild university. In fact, Jeff had never heard anything like it in the six years he'd been studying here.

"Is there such a thing as Forbidden Science? I thought the Science Guild explored all lines of research. It said so in the welcome packet when I arrived for classes."

"This is no joking matter," the Jeha said sternly. "Some types of research are too dangerous to explore. The destructive power of antimatter would be unimaginable. Visualize how many lives an antimatter bomb could extinguish. Would your people use such a weapon?"

Probably, but Jeff shook his head in negation anyway.

His race's status as one of the few species that produced mercenaries was a sore point between him and his friend. Jeff wasn't going to admit that he knew humans would use weapons like that if they could. Saren wouldn't believe humans had the restraint.

Even though Jeff knew humanity would impose firm rules on the use of such a weapon, there were others in the universe who would exterminate billions without the slightest qualm. So, Saren's point was still valid.

Jeff considered his friend for a long moment before he continued. "I thought the practical limitations of producing the stuff were so stringent that it cost an amazing amount of resources and took a huge amount of equipment to create. How could Professor Xaltar have found a way around that?"

The Jeha rippled, his race's version of a shrug. "I don't know. The only fact I can confirm at all is he was here looking for another lab assistant this morning. He spoke to Dean Wandrey. Well, perhaps 'spoke' is too mild a word. Let us say that words were exchanged at a volume sufficient to allow people throughout the building to gather the basic points of their disagreement."

That mental image made Jeff chuckle. In fact, he suspected his friend was understating it a little.

Dean Wandrey might be human, but that didn't mean Jeff was exempt from being eviscerated by the man's sharp tongue. The head of the engineering department had a well-earned reputation that occasionally fell somewhat short of reality.

Rumor said the man had once flipped a desk during a heated discussion with a colleague. Ironically, about antimatter, if he remembered correctly. Jeff wondered if that associate had been Professor Xaltar.

All Jeff knew for certain was that he had no desire to get on Dean Wandrey's bad side. Even the man's good side was almost comically irascible. For God's sake, he had a mat in front of his office door that said *Get off my lawn* and an official closed-door policy.

Thankfully, he had a very capable assistant that shielded him from having to interact with any of the student body. Assistant Dean Yusstic, a Zuul, got along with most people. Jeff had interacted with him on several occasions and had no complaints.

He was about to ask his friend for more details when he saw Assistant Dean Yusstic enter the cafeteria and start scanning the crowd. The canine-like being could operate in either biped or quadruped mode. For the moment, the dean was standing on his hind legs for a better view.

Yusstic's scanning stopped when he looked at their table. He dropped to all fours and started in their direction.

"Dean Yusstic is here," Jeff said quietly. "That can't be a coincidence. How many people did you tell this story to?"

"Just you. He can't be here to chastise me for gossiping. What did you do this time?"

The Zuul stopped at their table and showed his teeth in his version of a smile. One that, while not as intimidating as a Besquith, was still unsettling to most humans.

"Good afternoon, gentle beings. Saren, might I speak with Jeff in private?"

Saren wasted no time bowing his head and leaving Jeff to his fate. The rat.

Jeff spent the next few seconds reviewing his recent conduct. Nothing popped out as worthy of a visit by the leadership of the engineering department. Well, maybe he shouldn't have built that robot for the gladiatorial games last month, but most of the parts had survived the experience and made it back to the lab.

"Is something wrong, Dean Yusstic?" he asked once they were alone.

The Zuul turned his attention to Jeff. "In a manner of speaking. Nothing you've done, I assure you, but it does impact you.

"As you are no doubt aware, all graduate students are required to perform work under a professor as part of their doctoral studies. In most cases, the professor will approach a promising student they already have an existing relationship with. However, that is not always the case.

"In a few circumstances, the professor requests the department assign someone to support them. When that happens, we use random selection to identify potential candidates and the first one that meets the professor's requirements is sent to assist them in their research for the mandated period of one year."

The dean seemed to sigh. "It is my unfortunate duty to inform you that this has occurred, and you have been selected. I realize this likely comes at an inopportune moment and is likely a shock, but your sabbatical begins today."

This turn of events did shock Jeff. He'd had no idea they could just grab someone at random and send them off to work for someone they'd potentially never met.

He'd already entered discussions with one of his favorite instructors about joining her team at the end of the semester. Speaking of that, he was in the middle of preparing to take his exams. He couldn't just leave before he did that.

"Dean Yusstic, I'm getting ready to take my examinations."

The Zuul nodded. "That is being taken into consideration. I've already spoken with your instructors—who are universally complimentary of your performance, by the way. They will not require any further testing to grant you top tier scores on your finals, based on your current progress. Well done."

Jeff wasn't certain he'd have earned top marks in all his classes, but he knew he'd have passed every class. It sounded as if they were sweetening the deal so he couldn't complain. He wracked his brain for any other potential objections and came up blank.

Lacking any option, he nodded at the dean. "I see."

"I very seriously doubt that, but you understand the basics of the situation. Why don't you finish your juice and accompany me to my office? I can fill you in on the specifics of your assignment and the ramifications for your remaining study."

Jeff pushed the juice away. He wasn't thirsty. "I'm ready now."

The two of them made their way to the dean's office, and Jeff took the seat in front of the Zuul's desk. The chair was constructed for humans, so the dean had expected to return with him.

It was sinking in that Jeff really didn't have a choice in this matter. He wondered what would happen if he refused.

Like many offices in academia, the dean's was small and packed with books, even though they could all have fit on a single slate. It also had shelves with memorabilia—the dean seemed to be a collector of sports-related knick-knacks—and the bare walls held numerous images of the dean with other people.

It seemed as if many of the people with him were from outside the halls of learning. Some seemed to be politicians, others business leaders, and some were mercenaries.

Although the Zuul were a mercenary race, they weren't devoted to being mercenaries like humanity. They did plenty of other work. Jeff thought of them as dabblers, even if that wasn't precisely so.

Dean Yusstic settled into a seat that was more of a padded bench designed to support his torso. It raised the Zuul up so he could see over the desk.

"I'd imagine you have many questions. Ask them, and I shall do my best to give you complete and coherent answers."

Why not start with the big one?

"Am I really obligated to do this? What happens if I decline the offer?"

"That would set off an unfortunate series of events cumulating with your expulsion from this august institution. You signed papers agreeing to this eventuality when you arrived. I would deeply regret losing such a promising scholar, so I urge you to turn away from that path."

Jeff didn't remember signing any such document, but he probably had. There had been so many, and it had been six years. Counting the year he'd agreed to work with a professor's research, he was only two years away from defending his own doctorate. He couldn't throw that away.

He sighed. "Well, that being the case, I suppose I'd best hear what kind of work I'll be doing. What can you tell me about the research I'll be assisting with?"

The dean looked uncomfortable. "I'm afraid I don't have very much information. The specifics are not available. All I can tell you with any certainty is the project revolves around the potential generation of antimatter. The lead researcher is Professor Xaltar, by the way. Have you ever met him?"

Jeff shook his head. "No, sir. I never had any classes under him, and I can't recall anyone ever pointing him out to me. In fact, I know very little about him other than he specializes in particle physics. How does my engineering background play into generating antimatter? Which, by the way, I thought we already knew how to generate."

"My apologies for being imprecise." The dean showed his teeth again. "We do know how to generate antimatter an atom or two at a time and at incredibly great cost. Professor Xaltar is exploring the potential of *commercial* generation.

"He mentioned creating a gram of the stuff to Dean Wandrey before their...ahem, disagreement became too...ah, boisterous. And before you insist that is preposterous, I will tell you up front that I agree with your assessment."

Jeff frowned. "Then why is he wasting his time, and by extension, mine?"

Dean Yusstic drummed his claws on the desk. "That is a complicated matter. One beyond the scope of your involvement. The Council is considering his work, and the potential impact it might have. Allow me to assure you their deliberations will not affect you, since we are obligated to provide him with an assistant, and you have no choice in the matter.

"I believe it likely the Council will terminate Professor Xaltar's research in the near future. Should that happen, you will have met your requirement to serve as a research assistant. Potentially, you could shave a year off your remaining time with us and accelerate your graduation."

He leaned forward and fixed Jeff with an unblinking stare. "In fact, if you are willing to assist me in a related matter, I could make absolutely certain you are offered a position here when you do. As I said, your work has been exemplary."

At that point, the Zuul smiled again.

This only caused Jeff's unease to increase. The dean's proposition sounded very much like the apocryphal "offer he couldn't refuse." The implied complement in this binary solution was that Dean Yusstic could make things very hard for Jeff if he didn't help.

Oh, nothing in the dean's words hinted at that outcome, but discerning the unstated was an important skill for someone working in academia. Those in the learning fields tended to be subtle, and there was always some kind of unspoken tension in the air.

Students who hadn't made it to the graduate level often missed the slow currents that flowed around them, but anyone who intended to be a teacher or researcher had to see the world as it really was. That was actually part of their education, even if it never made it onto any official syllabus.

It wasn't as if he had any choice in the matter. He might as well reap any benefit he could from a bad situation.

"I'd be happy to help you in any way I can, Dean Yusstic," he said with as clear an expression as he could manage. He didn't know how good the other being was at reading other species, and he wasn't going to take any chances.

The dean sat up straighter. "Excellent. It's always a pleasure dealing with the brightest minds the Union has to offer. I promise my requirements will not be onerous. I simply wish you to keep me informed as to Professor Xaltar's progress. Particularly if he has any notable successes. Or safety violations, of course."

Jeff barely stopped his eyes from narrowing. The dean said this as if what the dean asked was nothing out of the ordinary. It was unprecedented and violated every rule about working on a research project. Trust under those circumstances had to be paramount.

Furthermore, the part about the dean worrying about the safety of the project rang just a bit false. In a human, Jeff would've been certain he'd heard things correctly, including the insincerity of the last bit. In an alien, there was room for misunderstanding, but Jeff was still inclined to trust the translation.

Once again, the sensitivity of his translation pendant amazed him. The versions available to the public—even the priciest models—might not have picked up on something so subtle.

They probably wouldn't have, he admitted. Once again, he was lucky to have the very best or he might have walked into something without looking at the situation closely enough.

The dean lowered his seat and stood on two legs. "I shouldn't keep you any longer. You'll need the rest of the day to purchase sufficient supplies to last for some time and pack."

Jeff stood and frowned. "He isn't doing his research here? I suppose that makes sense. Any significant amount of antimatter would be ludicrously dangerous."

"Indeed. Professor Xaltar is using an obsolete research station the Guild had slated for reclamation. Thankfully for us both, it's located in this system so the travel time won't be onerous.

"Nor will it be difficult to make reports." He pulled out a communications unit and slid it across the desk to Jeff. "This will interface with the systems on the station and allow you to send messages without troubling anyone for access. There are repeater units that will forward your messages to the main net. It will be public, so be discreet."

Jeff took the unit, looked at it for a moment while trying to hide his nervousness, then slid it into his jacket.

The dean gestured toward the door. "The intrasystem craft will pick you up first thing in the morning. Don't be late." He smiled one last time. "And as you humans say, don't forget to write."

* * *

Jeff arrived at the university landing pad at the scheduled time. Barely. He'd been up late packing everything he owned into bags. That included everything he could think of he might need for a year.

The manic shopping spree to fill that list had drained his funds, so he'd damned well better be able to get by with this stuff for a year.

A boxy intrasystem hauler of some kind sat waiting for him as he dragged the cart holding all his galactic possessions onto the pad. A five-foot-tall humanoid with brownish skin stood waiting for him.

Her eyes sat on either side of a central mouth and she had four arms, marking her as a Pendal. He'd never met one before, but he knew of them. Members of their race made for some of the finest pilots in the Union.

She wore sturdy-looking trousers and a heavy leather jacket. It probably wasn't authentic leather, as it was much less expensive to manufacture synthetic hide than raise living beings. It had to be beastly hot, though.

The woman stepped forward and extended one of her lower hands, the ones used for finer manipulation. "Jeff Peters?"

He nodded and found the right balance of firmness in shaking her hand. "That's me. Let me get this inside, and we can lift. Sorry if I'm late."

"You're right on time," she assured him. "I'm Sash. I'll help with the smaller pieces."

She used her upper arms to grab a few precarious bags from the top of the pile and headed up the ramp.

He followed slowly, maneuvering the cart to minimize the chances of an avalanche and only lost one bag. That was a victory, no matter how one calculated it.

Speaking of calculating, he'd spent some of his precious time last night calculating how dangerous a single gram of antimatter would be.

The answer was terrifying. 1.8×10^{14} Joules of energy might potentially be released. That was the equivalent to forty-three thousand tons of old-style TNT. Roughly the same amount of energy as the nuclear weapons dropped on Hiroshima and Nagasaki on Earth in what they called World War Two.

Saren's comments about the use of antimatter had come back to haunt Jeff's dreams. If one gram of antimatter could do that, how much would be needed to wreck an entire planet? Surely no more than a few kilograms, if spread out appropriately.

Mercenaries were forbidden to fire weapons at a planet from above ten miles in height. That prevented things like orbital bombardment. Supposedly. Jeff knew some races would be willing to risk the repercussions in spite of the draconian penalties, if the price were right.

"Put all your bags into these bins," Sash told him. "Use the straps to secure them so they don't come loose if we need to maneuver. I'll leave the hatch to the control area open so you can join me when you're done."

Jeff froze. "You want me to sit up there while you fly?"

She raised an eyebrow. "The Professor accepted you as part of his team. I'm assuming that means you don't intend to hijack me. You're not a pirate, are you, Jeff Peters?"

Her matter of fact tone made him smile. "No. Just an engineer. We aren't that dangerous, I suppose."

"That depends on the engineer. I've met some very dangerous engineers in my time. A few even meant to be. See you in a few minutes."

She actually winked at him as she headed toward the front of the hauler. He'd never seen any alien with that level of familiarity with human interaction before. She did it so casually, yet it had to mean she knew far more about human society than most of his instructors.

Or, was it possible the Pendal winked, too? He promised himself he'd do the research as soon as he had the free time.

Jeff secured his bags and made his way up to the control area. It was a cramped compartment with several bulky seats in front of control consoles. Sash sat in the one on the right, working on her console.

"You can have the left one," she said as she glanced over her shoulder at him. "I've disabled the controls so there is no danger of you touching anything critical."

He'd flown in small craft before—mostly atmospheric—but had never had the opportunity to observe the control area in flight. He sat down in the heavy couch and it adjusted slowly to his frame.

"Pull the webbing over you before we lift. If there's an inflight emergency, you won't have time to put it on."

He found the webbing and pulled it across his body, quickly locating the points to secure it.

She nodded approvingly. "Very good. I usually have to do that. You're clever. The Professor will be pleased."

"What can you tell me about the Professor?" he asked. "I've only heard general rumors."

Her smile widened. "Allow me to say the rumors don't do him justice. Anything you heard needs to be taken to the next level. The

Professor is an exuberant scientist and much larger than life. In fact, you might say that he is the quintessential scientist of the old school."

That was a big word for a pilot. He wondered how good her vocabulary was in her native tongue.

Then he felt ashamed for looking down on someone just because they weren't an engineer or scientist. Wasn't that just like some of the people he hated the most?

"An old school scientist, eh?" He smiled at Sash. "I can hardly imagine what that means."

"You'll find out soon enough," she replied with a twinkle in her eye. The translation pendant rendered her smug tone so clearly he almost grinned.

And then he almost slapped himself on the forehead. He'd forgotten to return the damned thing. His professor was going to be pissed. Oh well, it was a little late to worry about now. He'd call her once he'd settled in and make arrangements to get it back to her.

Sash pulled a headset designed to go over one ear from a hook near her head, slipped it on, and murmured into it, presumably to get permission to lift off. Once she finished, she manipulated the controls, and the hauler lifted smoothly into the air.

Jeff watched the university stretch out below them with more than a hint of wistfulness. He was going to miss this place. He would miss his friends even more.

The trip to orbit didn't take long, and he enjoyed the view far more than he would've expected. The bright sky slowly faded to black, and the stars emerged. It was just like something out of an old movie.

The world below looked so fragile. The thin coating of atmosphere was all that protected the billions living on its surface.

He couldn't stop himself from imagining the world rent by massive explosions that shot giant mushroom clouds into the sky. It took an effort of will to push that image away.

Despite all the talk, he knew the likelihood of anyone discovering a method to generate and hold significant quantities of antimatter was extremely unlikely. Plenty of theories sounded good until you tried to put them into practice. The history of engineering was filled with failures. Good ideas that never worked.

The Council would never allow anything so dangerous to get out. They'd stop Professor Xaltar if it came to something like that. At least Jeff hoped they would. He'd do his part and call in with regular updates for Dean Yusstic if things looked bad.

"You're very quiet," Sash said as they pulled out of orbit. "Most people can't stop chattering once they see space like this."

He smiled at her. "Don't mistake my silence for lack of awe. It's beautiful. I just have a lot of things on my mind. Things I really can't control."

She nodded knowingly. "Like becoming Professor Xaltar's research assistant? The last one felt much the same way. The Professor has been gone from the university long enough that most students have never met him. Their assignment to assist him always comes as a great shock."

"Did the last one work out?"

"Well enough, though she was a social creature. The isolation disturbed her more than she admitted. She was glad to get back to the university. Still, I believe she enjoyed her time with us in her own way and learned a great deal."

Jeff turned in his seat and eyed her. "If you don't mind my asking, what is your part in all this? Does the Professor often need pilots?"

"More than you might think," she said agreeably. "He conducts experiments at some distance from the station for safety reasons. I also assist him in more prosaic tasks. He's not as young as he thinks and simply moving bulky equipment around can prove challenging.

"Still, the Professor can be a rather…peculiar man. He has his own eccentricities that make having someone more levelheaded nearby a good thing, even if I can't help him in his research directly. He also pays very well for me to humor his sense of the dramatic."

Jeff had no idea what she was talking about, but he imagined he'd find out soon enough. "How far out to the station?"

"It's parked at what you humans call the L2 Lagrange point, just on the other side of the moon. Well, parked is something of a misnomer. It's actually in a halo orbit. This point is one of the unstable ones."

He cocked his head. "A halo orbit?"

She nodded. "The gravity there balances out, but staying in place is akin to balancing on the tip of a stylus. In practice, it's easier to simply orbit the station around the Lagrange point. Like a little halo for one of your Human angels, I believe, if you're looking for the source of the word."

Jeff had never been particularly religious, but he immediately caught the meaning. "Got it. Why put a station there? The moon is directly between it and the planet. Why not use one of the other points?"

"You'd have to ask the Professor to be sure, but I'll wager it has to do with the lack of neighbors. After all, who would put something worthwhile in such an isolated location? That keeps his research secure and provides a buffer for any...accidents."

He raised an eyebrow. "What kind of accidents?"

"I'll let the Professor brief you on that."

Her voice was level and uninflected. Jeff wondered if she knew what kind of research the Professor was conducting out here. Still, she was right. He needed to hear everything from the man himself.

The trip around the moon was unexpectedly beautiful. Sash took them far closer to the surface than he'd imagined beforehand. The sight of all the craters and sharp hills were stark and imposing.

All too soon, they pulled away from the surface and skimmed into the darkness of space. Oh, he could see well enough. The sun was at a favorable angle, so they weren't in the pitch blackness of deep space, but there wasn't any orbital traffic for the light to reveal.

Then he saw a small dot growing brighter in the distance. "Is that it?"

"It is," she said. "It's not much to look at without a frame of reference, but it'll make quite the impression once we get closer."

He had no idea what that meant, so he watched the station grow larger in silence. Once it was close enough for him to start seeing details, Jeff knew exactly what she meant.

The place was a floating wreck.

Well, that wasn't very precise. It was a run down, decaying structure that looked to be mostly abandoned. Partially stripped, too. Large sections of hull plating were missing. It was a floating skeleton.

Most space stations were well lit and had numerous position lights to avoid accidents. This one was brightly lit by the star, but no floodlights provided backup illumination. It would vanish into the shadows once the moon took it around the curve of the planet hidden behind the moon.

It also had no functioning position lights other than the ones at a single docking hatch. The impression of abandonment grew stronger the closer the hauler came. Frankly, he couldn't imagine how the damned thing kept an atmosphere inside even the intact portions of the hull.

The open pits beyond the missing hull plates were spookily similar to what he'd imagine the eye sockets in a skull looked like. All that was missing in transforming the station into a space-based haunted house were spider webs. He idly wondered if the place were haunted.

The station was rotating, of course. Without centrifugal force, there would be no interior gravity. That implied a certain amount of structural integrity.

"Did they condemn it?" he asked hesitantly.

"By they, I assume you mean the planetary authorities. No, but the station isn't certified for habitation, and it's slated for reclamation at some point in the next few years."

She smiled a little. "That doesn't mean it's completely unsafe. The Professor's laboratory and the habitation section are airtight and safe, if not always comfortable. I made sure of that."

"And the planetary authorities were fine with that?"

"The Science Guild wrangled a waiver for research purposes. They made me sign a different kind of waiver, too. Didn't you?"

"Probably," he said sourly. "I really need to read documents a little more closely in the future and ask questions before I sign them."

Her smile widened. "A wise precaution here in the Union. Now, if you'll excuse me, I need to focus on docking. The Professor hates it when I bang into the hull."

Jeff hoped she was joking.

The pilot deftly brought the hauler around to the operational docking hatch and tapped her controls to open it up. The massive slab of metal slid ponderously aside, revealing a gapping maw of darkness.

He almost asked if it was safe going into the dark like this before he remembered she'd asked for some peace and quiet to work in. The last thing he wanted to do was distract her at a critical moment.

The overhead lights came on as the hauler slid into the station. "On" being something of an overstatement as the bay was about as well-lit as the exterior of the station. Only a few lights near the far bulkhead flickered to life, but it was seemingly enough for Sash to guide her craft in.

He couldn't be sure, but he thought there were other vessels squatting in the darkness. There was no way to be certain they were even functional. On this station, he nursed his doubts.

Sash turned the hauler so they could see the exterior hatch, now appearing to sit in the floor due to the gravity caused by the station's rotation.

"I want to make sure it closes this time," she confided. "It's a pain in my donkey when it gets hung up, and I have to suit up to crank it shut manually."

Jeff felt the corners of his mouth quirk up. The translation pendant had struck again. He was sure she'd made a reference to her anatomy rather than a beast of burden. Not for the first time, he wondered if the professor who designed the prototype had intentionally skewed the results for curse words.

The massive hatch slid closed without issue. Jeff watched as Sash manipulated the controls and the sharp shadows outside began to soften. She'd started the pressurization process.

Once her console beeped, she stripped off her headset, hung it up, and undid her safety webbing. "We're good. Let's get you settled into your cabin. Once that's done, I'll take you to meet the Professor."

He discovered the pressurization process hadn't done a thing for the ambient temperature. As soon as the hauler's hatch opened, his breath puffed into large clouds of vapor, and he felt the small hairs inside his nose crinkle. It had to be below the freezing point of water in there.

By the time they'd piled his belongings onto the cart and headed into the bay, he was shivering. Sash's leather jacket suddenly made a lot more sense.

That situation improved only marginally once they entered the station proper. He was suddenly glad he'd packed some sweaters. He'd need them. He made a mental note to add thicker socks to his shopping list for his next trip planet-side.

The corridors in the habitation module were dark and dingy. Housecleaning and lighting seemed to be low on the priority list. Thankfully, their journey to his new accommodations was short.

To his surprise, his room turned out to be a set of rooms. An actual suite, and one in good order. The place was clean and well-lit. The furniture seemed to be made up of odds and ends, but everything was in decent shape.

There were even some pictures on the walls. Mostly scenes from planet-side. Not the world they orbited, he suspected, but many different places. That made him wonder how far and wide hotel art from Earth had made its way in the galaxy, passing from hand to hand, system to system.

"Jensta kept it in good repair while she was here," Sash said. "That's your job now. I take care of the air systems and general maintenance, but cleaning this place is all on you. I expect you to be diligent. If I stop by and it smells like cigarettes, I'll have your hide."

Jeff narrowed his eyes speculatively. She probably hadn't said "cigarettes."

He settled on "butt" as the most likely source word that his translator had mangled. He'd long ago learned that asking for clarification was usually a waste of time. An occasionally hilarious waste of time, but still less productive than he needed to be right now.

"Will do," he assured her. "I'll just park the cart here, and you can introduce me to the Professor, if you have time. After I get a sweater."

That made her laugh. "About all I have out here is time. I'll be waiting outside for you."

It only took a few minutes to find a sweater and slip it over his shirt. It helped immensely with the chill. He slipped the communicator into his pocket, too. That wasn't the kind of thing he wanted anyone to ask awkward questions about.

Sash didn't have a key for him, but he imagined larceny wasn't much of a concern on an abandoned space station with just two potential suspects. That presupposed he had anything worth stealing. Which he didn't. Name any serious student without a wealthy family that did.

Rather than lead him around the ring—which was probably a good thing considering its condition—she led him toward the central core through one of the spokes. The gravity dropped quickly as they made their way inward until it was gone.

What he found in the central core left him speechless. In fact, it shocked him so badly he let go of the handhold and drifted away from it before he could stop himself.

She deftly snagged him by the belt and hauled him back. "His lab has that effect on everyone. I keep meaning to record people's reactions, but I'm always too busy laughing. Inside, you understand."

Under normal circumstances, he'd have had some kind of witty reply, but the scene in front of him left no room for clear thought. And "scene" was exactly the right word, too. It looked like something out of an old movie. A *really* old movie.

In fact, he was sure the Tesla coils on the right side of what was obviously a mad scientist's lab were exact replicas of ones he'd seen before. The massive arcs of power shot in every direction with crackles of barely-restrained energy. Energy that ultimately did nothing except provide a dramatic show.

Other props from various ancient monster movies hung from the walls, and a massive glowing ball hung from the ceiling. There was no gravity, so that had to be for show. And what a show it was.

Jeff hauled himself around and stared at what appeared to be a wooden platform against the nearest wall. One with indecipherable equipment and modern controls arrayed around it. One supporting the most striking figure he'd ever seen in his life. This must be the being he was here to meet.

Professor Xaltar was a tall, bipedal humanoid almost seven feet tall. His appearance would be considered nondescript except for the wild spray of white hair shooting in every direction from his head, and the thick, bright green gloves he wore over the sleeves of his lab coat.

Not a modern lab coat, either, Jeff saw. A white double-breasted coat with two rows of prominent buttons down the front. He also wore what looked like welding goggles. They had to be for show, because Jeff was sure he saw a pair of eyestalks sticking from the hair.

That had to be a wig. It just had to be.

"Professor," Sash shouted. "We have company!"

Jeff suddenly realized the pilot had no choice other than shouting. How could he have missed the organ music playing like some kind of ancient dirge at an almost deafening volume? It had fit into the setting so seamlessly that his conscious mind had passed right over it.

Of course there was organ music. What else could there be?

The man turned and stared down at them as if shocked he had company. A wave of his hand over the nearest console killed the music. The sudden silence was like a hammer blow to the ears.

"Great Scott!" Professor Xaltar said as he walked down from the platform. The thick, black, knee-length boots had to be magnetic. "I had no idea so much time had passed! Welcome to my laboratory, Mister Peters. I'd meant to come meet you in the landing bay. My deepest apologies. I tend to get lost in my research."

He pronounced the word as "la-bore-a-tory," with his accent just so. In actual English, no less.

The alien—one whose race he was unfamiliar with—held out a hand. So, of course Jeff released his handhold when he took it. Like an idiot.

The Professor proceeded to shake Jeff's hand vigorously, which had a profoundly disorienting effect as it pumped Jeff up and down in time with the movements.

"Professor, you should let him hold onto something," Sash said dryly.

"What? Oh! Quite right. My continued apologies, Mister Peters." How did he manage to sound *just* like Christopher Lloyd? He even looked like the long-dead actor.

Jeff managed to get a grip back on the handhold. "It's alright, Professor. Ah, allow me to say that I love what you've done to the lab."

The man's smile turned into a grin and his eyestalks waved from side to side. "I have a weakness for Terran monster movies. The old ones, obviously. And the Back to the Future movies. Oh, how I wish time travel were truly possible."

"So I see," Jeff said faintly. It was amazing how human-like the Professor's head was, with the exception of the missing eyes and added eye stalks. The hair was indeed a wig, he now saw. One obviously crafted to look just like the actor in the movies.

"Imagine how difficult it is for me to fit into his fantasy," Sash said in a sotto voice. "Do you have any idea how hard it is to do an Igor impression in zero-G?"

"Preposterous," Professor Xaltar declared firmly. "Magnetic boots take all the challenge out of it." He half turned to face Jeff. "Believe me, she's worth the premium she charges just for the way she walks like a humpback and says, 'Yes, Master.'"

Jeff wondered if they'd managed to drug him somehow. This was surreal.

"In any case, welcome aboard!" the Professor said. "I assume my capable pilot and all around handywoman has seen you settled into your quarters, so we should take a tour of the lab. I have so much to show you. Sash, why don't you make some of your fabulous lusras stew?"

"Yes, Master." Sash made a credible show of a hunchbacked limp as she hauled herself back down the spoke toward the station's ring.

"What an incredible woman," the Professor murmured. "If only I were a few centuries younger. And of the correct species, of course."

He clapped his hands together as he turned back toward Jeff. "The first thing we need to do is get you outfitted with magnetic boots. We can't have you floating into one of the Tesla coils."

That was something Jeff could get behind.

Professor Xaltar opened a locker beside the spoke and extracted a set of boots. "These have some adjustment capability and look to be about the right size for you. I'll hold you steady while you strap them in place."

The boots did indeed fit fairly well. They'd never look stylish, but they'd hold him down.

Once he'd activated them and was firmly attached to the deck, the Professor released him and gestured toward the platform. "The central controls for all my equipment are up there. Do you know what we'll be working on?"

Jeff had some difficulty getting the boots to release their hold without yanking them up. He'd have to practice. Still, he managed to follow the Professor.

"Someone told me you might be working on commercial applications for antimatter generation."

Professor Xaltar stopped abruptly and frowned. "Someone in a position of authority at the university or part of the student body?"

"Both, actually. Apparently, your discussion with Dean Wandrey was a bit…energetic."

He grunted and resumed walking toward the platform. "That man vexes me. Cantankerous old fuddy duddy. It's hard to believe the wide-eyed young man I shepherded through his course of study has become so set in his ways in only 40 years.

"I expect to hear he's had an aneurysm at some point. Probably just after I tell him I've cracked the secret of generating significant quantities of antimatter. The word makes the vein on his temple throb. It's very distracting. He should get his blood pressure checked.

"You should have seen him as a young man. He'd have tried anything just to learn something new. Now all he does is rave about how much this project costs. As if he has to pay it out of his own paycheck, I might add. Sad really."

Jeff didn't know how to respond to that, so he changed the subject and trudged along after the man. "If I might say, your English is excellent."

The Professor beamed over his shoulder as he started climbing the steps. "Thank you! I've worked hard at it, particularly the accent. I'm grateful Oristian physiology is sufficiently close to Human to allow it. I'd wager my antics wouldn't be nearly so entertaining through a translation pendant."

Jeff wasn't so certain that was true. The Professor was one of a kind.

"Well, to answer your earlier question, one of my friends said a number of people overheard you and Dean Wandrey arguing, and the word antimatter was bandied about with sufficient volume to be clear.

"I didn't get any real details until I spoke with Assistant Dean Yusstic. He's the one that briefed me on the project. Not in much detail, though. On the plus side, I don't believe any of them think you have much chance of success. Sorry."

The Professor stepped up beside the consoles and grinned. "Then won't they be surprised when they hear I've cracked the secret? I've already created more antimatter than every species in the Union combined."

He gestured toward the glowing ball that hung from the ceiling. "Behold! My finest creation!"

Jeff stared at it uncertainly. "Is this part of the act, Professor? You can't really make antimatter, can you?"

The Oristian put his hands on his hips and bestowed a disapproving stare on his new research assistant. "This isn't an act, Mister Peters. This is science! If one can create antimatter in miniscule amounts, then one can do so in larger quantities. There is no such thing as being a little pregnant. Well, unless you're a Deryran, but that's hardly relevant to this discussion.

"To address your skepticism, I have indeed created more antimatter than anyone imagined possible. That sphere is a magnetic containment chamber containing approximately one gram of the most destructive material known."

Jeff stared at the ball in shock. Part of his mind marveled that the Professor was discussing the exact amount of antimatter Jeff had calculated the energy release for. The rest of his intellect screamed that he was standing beside what amounted to a nuclear weapon.

"Is it safe? Not that it would matter to us what the scope of any explosion would be, but we're talking about 1.8×10^{14} Joules of energy."

The Professor turned to face him abruptly and smiled widely. "You did that calculation in your head? Most impressive, Mister Peters. Most impressive"

"Actually, I just happened to use that amount in a calculation I ran last night," he admitted with a little embarrassment. "Coincidence, I'm afraid."

The Professor nodded, still smiling. "Nevertheless, I think you'll fit right in. You're correct to be concerned about the danger, but I assure you that I've designed ample safety precautions for our situation. Also, do you see that hatch over there in the bulkhead?

"It leads to an emergency ejection system. If there are any serious problems, we can duck inside, and it will shoot us away from the station at the very highest rate of speed modern technology can manage."

Jeff didn't think that would be of much help if the containment fluctuated. A cold chill ran down his spine as he considered the implications.

"Professor, aren't you concerned about the potential misuses of your research?" he asked somewhat doubtfully. "This could make a terrible weapon."

The man smiled a bit sadly. "Pure research shouldn't be avoided because of what others might do. Let's have some of Sash's wonderful stew, and I'll explain my reasoning to you."

As the two of them made their way to the spoke, shed their magnetic boots, and climbed down into the gravity of the ring, Jeff considered his options. He really didn't have a choice. He had to notify Dean Yusstic.

He felt bad about throwing the Professor under the bus, but the potential damage was literally beyond imagining.

Professor Xaltar brought them to a small compartment off what had once been a full-sized commercial kitchen. Something smelled wonderful.

Sash waved from behind the counter. "I just got it heated up."

"Then I'd best clean up. Do you have a handy washroom?"

Once the Professor pointed it out to him, Jeff went inside and sat on the commode. He then pulled the communications unit out and accessed it. He'd need to connect with the station's network in order to access the larger transmitters.

His conscience warred with his integrity. Did he have the right to be the informer that ruined a man's work like this? Or did he have an obligation to speak up?

Maybe he should listen some more before he made any decisions he couldn't take back.

Still, it wouldn't hurt to connect the communications unit to the station's network. He brought up the menu and saw it had already connected. How was that possible?

It took a few moments rooting through the menus to discover the unit had been set to autoconnect. He'd been linked into the station since he'd boarded it. That wouldn't have worked if there was a network password, but the Professor must not have bothered.

That's when he saw the connection wasn't the only thing set to auto. The voice memo feature was on. It was set to record all conversations and save them to internal memory.

No. Not just to internal memory. It was sending them out once the recordings accumulated to more than fifteen minutes. The contact didn't have a name, but Jeff knew who it had to be.

Cold washed over him, as if someone had just doused him in ice water. Dean Yusstic was spying on him. Spying on the Professor.

Oh crap.

A quick check revealed the conversation they'd just had was already uploaded. Jeff cursed and disabled the function. As an added precaution, he removed the unit's power cell.

He sat for a minute as rage built inside him, making him tremble. How dare the man? Jeff had rights, and he'd already agreed to tell the dean everything important.

Dean Yusstic obviously didn't trust Jeff to be completely forthcoming. That scared him. What was the man up to?

Whatever it was, it couldn't be good. Yusstic wouldn't have had to go to all this trouble if he was just compiling information for the Council. There was something more sinister at work.

He had to warn the Professor.

Jeff actually did wash his hands. Some habits were difficult to break, after all.

Professor Xaltar and Sash were seated at one of the tables. They had bowls of thick stew, large hunks of bread, and what looked like tea set out. Including a place at the table for him, something he no longer thought he deserved.

The Professor gestured for him to join them. "Sit and eat. You'll love the lusras stew. It tastes even better than it smells."

Jeff sat, but made no move to touch his food. "I'm afraid I've made a terrible mistake."

The scientist waved his hand dismissively. "Don't rush to judgement, my boy. This will never become a weapon. Not with the current level of technology in the Union, in any case. The containment issues are too pervasive for that.

"Any gravity—including exceptionally low acceleration—will cause the antimatter to leak across the magnetic boundary. Even a single atom is more than enough to disrupt the containment vessel with catastrophic disruption of the protective field.

"That's why I have the containment vessel at the center of this station where it can experience no gravity or acceleration whatsoever. Even so, I have to encase it inside an intensely powerful magnetic field to assure our safety.

"No one can use antimatter in any meaningful manner, including as a weapon. All I've managed to do is create the material and hold it. Nothing more. Perhaps the only task it is capable of fulfilling at this point is becoming the most epic self-destruct device imaginable."

"I brought a communicator that Dean Yusstic gave me," Jeff said woodenly. "He told me to call him if you had any success. He claimed it was to notify the Council. I didn't want to, but I didn't feel as if I had a choice.

"I just found out it was recording this entire time and has already sent the conversations we've had to him. He knows you've succeeded. I took out the power supply, but it's too late now."

It all came out in a rush. Jeff heard the shame in his voice. He deserved every possible rebuke. He'd help betray this man.

They both stared at him a long moment. Then Sash stood abruptly and made her way to a wall panel. She brought up a screen, stared at it for a moment, and whirled to face them.

"Oatmeal muffins! There's a hauler almost on top of us! They're jamming all the channels!"

The Professor stood. "We need to get back to my lab. We must warn them away from attempting to move the containment vessel."

"They're bypassing the ring entirely and heading directly for the hub," Sash said. "We only have a few minutes."

"Then we have no time to spare. Come with me, Mister Peters."

Jeff blinked. "But I betrayed you."

The Oristian scientist shook his head. "We only have time for the short version of this conversation, so listen up. I've already informed the Council of my success. I sent a hardcopy message on the same excursion when Sash picked you up.

"In fact, they probably have my summary in their hands already. That's old-fashioned, but when you live as long as my people, you find tradition very important.

"I realize this is somewhat unfair to you, as the Council will undoubtedly shut my project down as soon as their flunkies realize the potential repercussions. I assure you I have other ventures you'll find quite engrossing as reparation.

"In any case, I hold none of this against you, my boy. The fact you informed me carries a lot of weight, in fact. I respect the courage that took. Now stop stuttering apologies and help us stop these idiots from causing the worst disaster ever seen in this system."

Jeff rose to his feet and followed the two of them out. They hurried to the spoke and up toward the hub. They'd just arrived when a loud clang reverberated through the lab.

Sash dove toward the dock, which was on the opposite side of the hub from the spoke. It opened just before she reached the controls, and three men with weapons in their hands came through.

Their leader gestured for Sash to back up. "That's right, get back there with the others, lady poodle."

With no choice, Sash pushed away, floating toward the area where the Professor and Jeff had ended up near the emergency pod. She expertly brought herself to a stop as a fourth figure came through the lock: Assistant Dean Yusstic.

The Zuul shot them a toothy grin. "Well, it seems the study group has gathered. I'll admit I never expected to take possession of this gem so soon, Mister Peters. I actually never expected the mad scientist to succeed.

"Well done, by the way. Too bad no one will associate you with the discovery."

"If it's to become a weapon, I can live without the recognition," the Professor said with cold dignity. "I'd never have expected this of you, Yusstic."

The dean turned to his men. "And never say 'lady poodle' again or I'll rip your throat out. My people find it extremely offensive."

Part of Jeff's mind prompted that he should try to figure out what the real phrase had been, but this really wasn't the time.

Once the minion nodded, the dean continued. "Go get the portable power connections. We have to move the containment vessel, and we'll need to provide the energy it needs during the transfer."

"You have no idea what you're doing," the Professor continued. "The containment vessel is far too unstable to move. You've come all this way for nothing, I'm afraid. What did you hope to gain anyway? The Guild will expel you, so it can't simply be stealing my research."

The dean laughed long and hard. "Oh, that is entirely too rich. All you can see are scholarly papers and knowledge for its own sake.

"No, I have aspirations of a more prosaic nature. I'm going to sell the technology and antimatter to some people who can put it to very lucrative use. And don't think for a moment that you can fool me into believing the ridiculous claim that I can't leave with my prize, either. Now, where are your research notes?"

"He keeps the data chips in the room behind us," Jeff said before the Professor could respond. "I want my share. You used me, but I can give you the research in exchange for a share. He has the drives encrypted, but he gave me the codes."

Yusstic considered Jeff for a long moment and then smiled. "I believe we can arrange something, Mister Peters. Get the chips and don't try anything heroic, or you'll disappear right along with these two."

With a deep breath, Jeff opened the hatch and looked inside. It was laid out similarly to the hauler, but had four couches that were significantly heavier than the ones in the first vehicle. Well, the Professor had said that this thing used the fastest technology available.

He was about to turn and grab the Professor when Sash hurled them both through the hatch. One of the goons shouted and opened fire. Something bounced off the hatch as it slid smoothly closed.

"Into the couches," Sash shouted as she raced to the front of the craft.

Moments later, they were all in place, with Jeff and the Professor in the second row. Jeff was still looking for the restraints when the hand of God tried to crush him.

The screen at the front of the ship came to life and showed the station receding at an incredible rate. In moments, it became a dot.

"I do hope...they don't...attempt to disconnect the power...from the containment vessel. Even that has...significant risks. It won't remain…stable while they…switch to an…alternate means of—"

The receding dot suddenly blossomed into hellish life. It expanded in a sphere of actinic light that raced after the life pod as if to devour it.

"Great Scott," the Professor murmured.

For one long moment, Jeff knew this was the end, but the light rapidly dimmed as they raced clear of its destructive radius. In moments, it guttered out and was gone.

"Reduce the…acceleration," the Professor said.

Seconds later, the weight lifted. Jeff stared at the black screen. The station was gone as if it had never been. And so were all his worldly possessions, he belatedly realized.

"Well, that was a significantly poorer outcome than I'd hoped for," the Professor said tiredly.

"I'm sorry you lost everything, Professor," Jeff said, resting his hand on the scientist's shoulder. "Perhaps it's best the research on antimatter is lost."

Xaltar shook his head reprovingly. "What kind of researcher do you take me for, Mister Peters? I never go anywhere without backing up the data to my slate, which is safely in my pocket.

"Though you are correct that my lab is gone, along with all the equipment for generating the antimatter in the first place. Still, we can rebuild, and the time will not be wasted.

"In all the hubbub, I had an idea for something that could be used to make the transport and storage of antimatter possible. It will require some groundbreaking work from both of us, but I am feeling confident we can crack this as yet unsolved mystery."

Jeff felt his jaw drop. Surely the Professor didn't intend to keep working on this mad scheme.

"What solution is that, Professor?" he heard himself ask weakly.

Xaltar grinned, leaned toward Jeff, and whispered.

"Antigravity."

# # # # #

Change of Command
by Thomas A. Mays

Major Nick "Papa Smurf" Smithfield's first act upon assuming command of the Terrible Texans' Bravo Company was to get himself decapitated by a three-foot length of obsidian shrapnel.

His second act was to collapse off the ruin's platform, and his third was presumably to die on the alien grass analog, but Staff Sergeant Sheila Murphy was no longer watching what happened to him. Instead, she dove for cover just like the rest of "B" Company. *Gods damn it*, she thought, *the friggin' Zuul would pick NOW to complicate the contract.*

Normally, Sheila and all 211 of her Bravo brethren would either be kitted up in armored CASPers or else safely ensconced within the walls of the garrison, but today was *special*. Today, Bravo Company got to wear their fanciest, neatly pressed utilities and stand in ranks beneath the mysterious obsidian bowl of the impossibly ancient alien amphitheater—well outside the facility's defensive perimeter—listening to speeches as Major Graves was relieved by Major Smithfield after two years of commanding Bravo Company on contract after successful contract.

Sheila understood it. The dog-and-pony show of a formal Change of Command was important to some folks, but dammit, you had to balance ceremony with tactical realities—even if the sheer absence of any hostilities during their whole tenure here might lead one to complacency. Those hostilities had arrived at last, however.

Moments after Smithfield had returned Graves' salute and taken over as CO, a mortar explosion shattered the overhanging black volcanic glass bowl of the amphitheater ruins and rained shrapnel down on the unarmored company. Along with Smithfield, two other nearby mercs had also been bisected, and there were dozens of less serious debris wounds and injuries due to the explosive overpressure. Of Major Graves or the Exec, there was no sign.

Sheila herself felt dizzy and disoriented by the blast above them, but she remained functional. She made it to the tables full of hors d'oeuvres and drinks, knocked one over to conceal herself, and dragged another over her head for protection, as if the table might be any more durable than the stone overhang had been. Another merc—a young private right out of his VOWs who had just joined the company and transited out with Smithfield—dove behind the dubious cover of the tables beside her. "Staff Sergeant! The Commander! He's dead!" he cried.

She shrugged. "Uh, probably."

The private's eyes widened. "So, who's in charge? What do we do next?"

"Well, answering in reverse order, we A) try not to get killed our own selves, and B) if it doesn't matter at the moment, refer back to A." Sheila peeked over the toppled table. Chaos reigned as mercs either scrambled for cover like she had or ran back toward the garrison for their armor. No one knew when the Zuul dogs of war might lob their next mortar, or come yapping and barking from over the hill, magnetic accelerator cannons, or MACs, blasting away like some nightmare vision of Fido gone wrong.

The ancient amphitheater pre-dated the establishment of the GenSha commercial farm or their garrison contract, and—Sheila had to admit—was quite attractive if you ignored the smoking hole smashed through the black-glass bowl. It had been a nice locale for the Change of Command ceremony, rampant with natural floral excess and a fetching mixture of green, blue, and purple alien grasses. The special soil here had been the reason the GenSha had set up their grow-op and hired the Terrible Texans to provide security for the last year, a year that had proven about as exciting as watching the extraterrestrial grass grow.

Well, it certainly seemed "exciting" now. She watched in horror as the guys who had run for their armor hit the halfway point between her concealed position and the outer line of Bravo Company's defenses. A second mortar round whistled down and burst thirty feet above the ground. It went off close enough for her to feel the heat and the trailing edge of the blast, but not close enough for the overpressure to liquefy her organs, pulverize her bones, or pepper her with shrapnel—not like the dozen mercs beneath it.

Sheila wasn't sure what was so special about the soil here, but it had now been watered by the blood of her comrades. That made it sacred. She was going to make those pups pay if it was the last thing she did.

Had she been by herself, she might have gone for it, tried an alternate route back to the compound, CASPered up, and played "Bad Dog" with their canine Zuul attackers, but she couldn't abandon the utterly green private. Instead, she gestured east. "Hey! Here's what we're gonna do. Threat sector's that-a-way, where the Zuul are guarding a rival grow-op. We don't know why they picked now to burn us, but there's nobody else on the continent with the balls to try. Don't give 'em a shot! Move, concealment to concealment, favoring cover to the east. Follow me. Gotta find the Exec, get organized, get air cover, and then get us some back. Got it?"

"Yes, Staff Sergeant!" Clear direction seemed to ground the panicked merc, even if that direction was essentially to find someone else to ask for help.

Sheila and the private moved fast and low, crouching, sliding, and scooting from uncertain concealment to dubious cover, especially since she could not be *certain* the dogs were indeed approaching from the east. Without sensors to inform them otherwise, the mortars could have been fired from any direction. Others saw her moving, and since no one else wanted to attempt another open run back to the garrison, they followed suit until she led a ragged phalanx, hunting for leadership.

They found the old CO, Major Graves, and the Exec, Captain Foster, behind the western side of the amphitheater's stage, using its concrete analog and the floral overgrowth to protect them from any threats to the east. Major Smithfield's headless corpse stained the multicolored grass a uniform crimson. The three officers had been armed only with decorative swords for the ceremony, but one of them had at least squirreled away a pistol, which the wild-eyed Foster aimed at Sheila as she came around the corner.

She held up one hand while keeping another gripping the stage, ready to pull herself back fast if the Exec proved to be *too* rattled. He checked his aim, however, and went back to scanning the area, covering Major Graves as that man wielded their strongest weapon: an encrypted comm back to the garrison.

Technically, Captain Foster was CO now. Smithfield had assumed command, properly relieving Graves, if only for about 30 seconds. With his demise, the Exec became the boss...but looking at the pair of them now, there was no question who was in charge. Sheila didn't know if there had been any discussion between the men about the situation, or any formal reversion to the old order, but Graves was back in command, barking orders into the comm and getting the armed reserve at the garrison into the fray.

Better late than never.

At last, Sheila heard the drone of armored flyers and felt the rhythmic thump-thump of CASPers running their way. Missiles dropped from rails and streaked over the horizon at the yet-unseen pups. Lasers snapped and the MACs chattered, hopefully targeting the attacking Zuul mortar section and tearing it all to hell.

Sheila shook her head and risked standing. "What a friggin' waste of a cake contract."

In a few moments, CASPers ringed the amphitheater and flyers orbited as close air support, preventing any further sucker punches. Bravo Company's medical section streamed in, checking on the wounded and pronouncing over the dead. There were far too many of both.

Major Graves, again in charge, finally stood. He looked proudly at the new defensive perimeter, and with sadness at the demolished ruins and all of his unfortunate casualties. With a sigh, he dropped the comm to his side and gestured Foster and Sheila over.

Before he could pass his orders, though, a final snap sounded. A laser bolt from the west streaked in and flashed a narrow cylinder of the Major's chest into pure plasma, which then exploded outward in a fountain of gore. He fell like a marionette with its strings cut.

And command devolved to the Exec once more.

* * *

"**O**kay, what the sam-fuck is goin' on 'round here?" demanded First Sergeant Brenda Reeves.

The portly GenSha running the agricultural team the Texans were guarding scrunched its massive head down into its even more massive body. The tiger-striped bipedal bison-oid might have appeared imposing due to its sheer size, but trying to go turtle in order to escape the wrath of a senior merc NCO tended to undercut the alien's innate intimidation factor. It clearly wanted to escape its own agricultural directorate office, but 1SGT Reeves offered it no way out.

Sheila would have thought it amusing had she not just washed off her old CO's blood.

Realizing it had no way out of the room, the GenSha director shuddered in some alien gesture and finally talked. "Terrible Texans contracted to protect GenSha grow-op here in probable 'car' valley."

Across from Sheila on the other side of the director's office, Captain Foster suddenly looked nervous, but he nodded. "Yes, Glashthul, and we've performed as contracted. But it's remained quiet for the whole last year. What's changed now?"

The GenSha director nodded in a purposefully human manner. "Zuul guard Jeha grow-op in next valley over. Also potential 'car' valley, but rockier. Less absorbent clay in soil strata." The director spread its hoof-hands as if that was explanation enough.

"So the hell what?" Reeves yelled. "They guard one farm, we guard another. Why the hell would those mangy curs pull a sneak attack now after a year o' complete silence!?"

Glashthul pointed east, toward the other operation. "Miscalculation. Target crop unable to extract desired resources from soil. Failure. Wasted effort. Expenditure unmet. Paid 'car' prices, lack 'car' payoff. Here, crop yields bounty. Success. Essence of 'car' industry ready for extraction, interstellar trans-shipment. Jeha-Zuul partnership seek profitable harvest through alternative means. Assault. Theft."

The First Sergeant backed off from the GenSha director, nodding. "I get it now. The hungry, hungry caterpillars watched their grow-op go all Oklahoma Dustbowl on 'em, so they sic their guard dogs on us to take ours. Nice. The Jeha must have offered the Zuul a *reeeaaal* hefty bonus to change the terms of their contract."

Sheila still felt confused, however. "What's all this 'car' stuff though? I don't think you're talking about automobiles."

Captain Foster stood hastily. "That's hardly of paramount importance at the moment, Staff Sergeant Murphy. I appreciate your help rallying after the attack, and I'm sorry for what you personally experienced there at the last, but we really do need to get ready for the Zuul, should they attack again. Please return to Second Platoon and see to your preps."

"But—"

"That is all, Staff Sergeant. Reeves, you as well, please."

Brenda Reeves narrowed her eyes, but she complied. The 1SGT ushered Sheila out ahead of her and closed the door on the Captain and Glashthul. Outside the modular office, the sun shone brightly overhead, and the grow-op stretched out in front of them.

Instead of the multicolored alien grasses and rampant flowers at the wrecked pavilion, things looked far more industrial here. Tanks, pumps, and irrigation lines served acres upon acres of the GenSha's target crop, laid out in neat rows. Three concentric perimeters of fence-line, modular walls, and active barriers protected the alien bounty, backed up by four platoons of Terrible Texan mercs and their associated support units.

Sheila had no idea what their bison-ish employers were growing, but it sure wasn't wheat. Known only as C117, the plants were not unlike giant eggplants, if eggplants pulsed with their own glowing internal radiance. All she knew was that the GenSha workers shuddered in fear every time one of the Texans joked about frying up a mess of C117 for chow.

Reeves marched past her, headed for the main gate. Sheila rushed to catch up. "Bren! Why do I feel like I just got the big brush-off?"

Reeves grinned. "Probably because you just got brushed off bigtime."

"What the hell is going on here? Really?"

Reeves relented and stood still. She put her hands upon her muscular hips and flexed her well-defined arms unconsciously. "Not shittin' ya, Sheila, but I have no goddamn clue. This job's always been hinky, though. No one pays a merc outfit as much as our contract calls for unless the payoff is worth it, and the threat is real. We've been in la-la-land since day one, but the fuckin' beast that's always slumbered in the shadows has well and truly woken the hell up. And truth be told, this is the last goddamn outfit I'd wanna be part of when the shit went down. Unfortunate for us, huh?"

That took Sheila aback. "What makes you say that? You and I served with Graves for the last two years. The Major was a straight shooter."

"Yeah, he was, but we also never really got into the shit with him. We've provided rear echelon support to a bunch of assault companies, some low-intensity peace-making, and garrison jobs like this. Compared to other outfits, the Terrible Texans are a low-margin, high-volume, budget enterprise. The ad copy may try to sell us as the "Fifth Horseman," but that's just cynical corporate branding, right down to the bucking bronco they put on our logo. One of the Four Horsemen we ain't. Every one of our companies look prepared, but you best not scratch the surface, Bravo Company included."

Sheila's face grew hot. Reeves practically sounded treasonous. "Fuck you, Brenda. I'd pit my Second Platoon against any friggin' outfit you care to name. We're ready to fight!"

Reeves smiled. "I like the fire in your belly, Sheila, and I'd bet on you and yours in any stand-up fight. But that doesn't change the fact most of our officers are just lawyers or corporate drones in uniform with hardly a bit of tactical experience between 'em. Graves was the exception. Foster and Smithfield? They may have had the appropriate VOWs scores and all the same management courses, but they were *not* cut from the same cloth as him. Who the hell else would think a pomp-and-circumstance Change of Command ceremony *unarmed and outside the defensive perimeter* was a good idea, no history of hostilities or not?

"Then there's the intel failure. We should have known the pups and the 'pillars were planning something. And—your personal pride notwithstanding—we are ill-prepared for a hard-scrabble, dug-in defense of this farm. We don't understand our enemy or his tactics well enough, we lack info on his current deployment or his tactical options, and—yes, while we are ready to fight hard and soldier on—we don't have the legs to fight as long as we might need. There's no defense in depth here, and the merc corp doesn't have the ready resources to augment us or send in a ship should our garrison come under sustained attack. What we see is all we get.

"I'm sorry, Sheila, but Bravo Company was gambling on this farm staying low-intensity, just enough to repel local raiders, thieves, or pirates. Deterrence through presence ops. Put on a good show. Against another similarly-sized garrison of alien mercs as tenacious and resourceful as the Zuul? We're kinda fucked."

Sheila deflated, her shoulders slumping. "Crap. Really?"

Reeves shrugged. "Don't worry about it overmuch. Foster ain't stupid. He won't push for a last-gal-standing defense. He'll realize we're outmatched soon enough, and he'll either cut a deal with the GenSha and Jeha to pass along some of the GenSha's mystery crop so everybody profits, or he'll cry to corporate and advise default, withdrawing us from this contract. The Texans might get a black eye which could affect what we're offered in the future, but the company will survive. A pencil-pusher like him will never take the bold option."

Sheila frowned. The Terrible Texans were the third merc outfit she had worked for since completing her Voluntary Off-World assessments. Not the best and not the boldest, but they had a great bottom-line and the lowest loss rate of any outfit she had seen, even if their per-op profit margin was a bit low. She thought that meant they knew what they were doing, not that they were well-practiced at avoiding doing it.

The 1SGT put an arm around her and walked them both toward the gate. "Trust me! This time tomorrow, we'll either be compromising with the Zuul or packin' up to get out of their way. It'll suck for our own bottom-line, but better alive, toasting our good fortune, and able to quit this chicken-shit outfit than dead and on a wall of Honored Dead."

* * *

Captain Foster neither cut a deal the next day, nor ordered a withdrawal. Instead, he himself joined the ranks of the Terrible Texans' Honored Dead.

And so did First Sergeant Brenda Reeves.

Disconcerted by what Reeves had laid out for her, Sheila returned to the comforting chaos of Second Platoon. The squads were just about to go on rotation outside the outer perimeter. They were all on edge, but they covered their uneasiness well with good-natured trash talk, some wholly inappropriate gallows humor, and exaggerated posturing. To the uninitiated, their forced joviality might have looked uncaring or insane. After all, Second had lost three mercs in the mortar attack. Banter, boasting, and grab-ass were the last things someone might expect, but the vast majority coped as such.

Not all were as sanguine, though. First Lieutenant Jamal Smith, Second's platoon leader, was not taking it well. He barked orders and grew visibly angry if the mercs cutting up did not immediately jump to comply. A sheen of sweat was visible on his forehead, even in the cool temps.

Sheila shoved her own concerns, questions, and doubts to the rear. "All right, you dumb-as-fuck jokers, square your shit away and hop to when the L-T says, or you're gonna have to mod your CAS-Per's to make room for my boot up your ass! You feel me, Second?! Move it!!!"

Once they were engaged, Sheila hung back and pulled Smith aside. "L-T, you good? Need to re-center yourself maybe? Before you climb in your CASPer and short it out from all the sweat pouring off you?"

Looks of confusion, anger, and then embarrassment flashed over his face before he was able to wipe his brow and put on an expression of faux-stoicism. "I beg your pardon, Staff Sergeant?"

Sheila shook her head. "Never mind, sir." She almost let him go, but then grasped his arm again. "L-T, when we deployed, the TOE had enough sealed gear listed to sustain us for up to 30 days of full combat ops before we required augment or re-supply. More than enough to defend this farm from a whole brigade until reinforcements could be flown in. A big investment in resources which you signed for as the inventory control officer. You stand by that signature still, sir?"

His mouth opened and closed without saying anything. After a moment, he stood straighter and looked her squarely in the eye. "Sarge, we have exactly the resources we expected to need and were meant to have. Now, I think we should get on with relieving First Platoon on the perimeter."

Shit, she thought.

The night passed tensely, but without any further attacks. Sensors picked up some small, moving heat signatures on the horizon, but recon drones and a few patrols beyond their lines did not reveal any Zuul. Either the mutts were good at hiding or they were indeed biding their time.

Six hours later, with the sun not yet risen, Third Platoon trotted out and relieved them. The reveille watch sucked, beaten only in terms of circadian rhythm ruination by the six hours of the mid-watch Second had just stood. And Sheila had the sinking feeling the Zuul had slept a full night, secure in the knowledge that—rather than counterattack—the human mercs would opt instead to redouble their defensive line. She sighed, parked her CASPer in its mainte-nance alcove to charge, made sure the rest of the platoon was stowed and settled, then shuffled off to breakfast while the sun began to rise.

The farm went from different shapes of black, to indistinct grays, to finally the riotous colors of this world, muted in intensity only by the cool light of dawn. As the light rose, Sheila could see others had been at labor while she had been on watch. Hundreds of transport crates had been loaded full of the glowing eggplant-ish C117 plants. GenSha workers toiled to fill even more, leaving only the few imma-ture plants in the soil. She understood that harvest was not intended for another two months. What did this mean?

Catching 1SGT Reeve's eye, Sheila trotted over. "Been busy?"

Reeves nodded. "Plan C. The GenSha figure they've already har-vested more than they anticipated, so they contacted the Jeha and offered a compromise. No more attacks, we depart early, and the Jeha are welcome to shift their failed farm to here. Win-win. We complete our contract, the customer makes its profit, and the enemy gets a second chance."

Sheila frowned. "Yeah, the only ones that get screwed are the poor bastards that got blown up before the deal was done."

"No deal would bring them back, Sheila."

"Nope," she acknowledged. "But they go unavenged all the same."

Reeves averted her gaze. "Think what you want, Murphy. I'm less interested in revenge than I am in survival and contract completion. If it sits that badly with you, go free-agent when we get back to Karma. Join a more daring outfit than the Terrible Texans. Hell, I might opt out, too—with the first round of drinks on me—but that's all for after the contract. For now, I gotta help Foster with closing this negotiation." She stalked off, away from the growing stacks of transport containers and toward the flyer field.

Sheila shook her head and continued on toward the mess. If this was the way it was, so be it. She wanted to live, to have a chance to go back to Earth, to family and friends, and to enjoy some of the credits she had saved up. And, yes, now that she had seen how the sausage was made in an outfit like the Texans, she was anxious to move on. Doing something half-assed did not suit her. It was not how she had been raised, where being a Texan was a source of pride, not a disingenuous form of advertising.

Still, she was surprised they were getting off this easy. Based on everything she had ever heard about the Zuul, they were a greedy, resourceful species, more akin to hyenas than the bipedal mastiffs they looked like. She was surprised they would allow the GenSha to take the harvest they had already gathered when a second yield from this valley was just another gamble.

Just before she entered the mess, she heard a whine of servo motors from overhead and looked up. A quad-mounted air defense MAC atop a middle perimeter post swung down from its ceaseless scan of the sky and locked in its maintenance position. Around the farm, all the other air defense stations did the same.

With alarm, Sheila sought out and grabbed a corporal from the operations cadre. "What's with the air defense!?"

He looked at her like she was an idiot. "It's for the Zuul. They're flying in to parley and inspect the facility before the Jeha agree to this turnover deal. They refused unless we showed good faith by masking our weapons."

Panicked, Sheila looked to the flyer field. Captain Foster, Glashthul, 1SGT Reeves, First Platoon's lieutenant, and a small contingent of senior personnel all stood next to an empty landing pad. Foster keyed a handheld comm and spoke, presumably to give the Zuul the go-ahead for a safe landing. Sheila ran a few steps toward them, then stopped, stumbling, unsure. Surely, they wouldn't—

The white hot lance of a hyper-velocity penetrator struck the ground in the center of the assembled personnel. Ten megajoules of kinetic energy instantly converted itself to heat, sound, and pressure, blossoming outward at many times the speed of sound.

The equivalent of two kilograms of TNT, it was a targeted meteorite of death. The explosion ripped apart Bravo Company's leadership and wrecked the nearest flyers, but left the containers of C117 untouched.

Alarms sounded, and the air defenses came back up, searching for radar and lidar tracks. Two quad-pack MACs picked up the trail of whatever had fired off the HVP and fired back. Streams of magnetically accelerated coil gun rounds scythed through the morning sky until an explosion answered, just above the distant horizon.

Sheila picked herself up from where the detonation had knocked her on her ass. She looked to the smoking crater where Foster, Reeves, and the others had been. Questions filled her mind. What do we do? Who's in charge? How soon can we get off this rock? Can we take them in a stand up fight? And what the hell are we really doing here?

The only answer she received was rushing, aimless chaos.

"We are so screwed," she said to herself.

* * *

"It's really quite fascinating from a strategic, xeno-anthropological standpoint."

"You're talking out your ass, Meyers. And shouldn't that just be xenopological?"

"That's not a word, Poretti. But vernacular aside, that's what we're seeing here: 'Alpha-oriented predation.'"

The surviving officers of Bravo Company, one first lieutenant and two second lieutenants, stood in the ops center, arguing back and forth. 2LT Dina Poretti was strident and assured, if lacking in experience, while 2LT Ben Meyers was bookish and haughty…and also lacking in experience. Of the three, 1LT Jamal Smith had the most authority and experience, but seemed least able to exercise it. His dusky skin had traded its sheen of sweat for the gray pallor of abject terror.

And Sheila didn't feel any bit too confident looking at him from her spot by the door with the other platoon NCOs.

Smith spoke softly. "Alpha-oriented predation. You mean the Zuul are gunning for whoever's in command?"

Meyers nodded. "More or less. We usually only tend to notice examples of convergent evolution in animals, like dolphins and fish exhibiting the same form even though their backgrounds are completely different…but there's no reason we cannot apply those same principles to alien species. The Zuul are a dog-like, mercenary, interstellar race, but they are not dogs. Dogs are more closely related to humans than they would be to the Zuul—but it is not outside the realms of reason to surmise that, given their outward appearance, they may still have evolved to fill roles and develop behaviors not unlike those of earthly dogs."

Poretti chuckled in derision. "But instead of 'fetch' or 'roll-over,' the dog-like behavior the Zuul just happen to mimic is boss-murder?"

"Well, I would never reduce the issue so simplistically, but yes. Canids are often pack animals. When two packs meet, their individual members may clash, but it's just as likely only the alpha of each pack will vie for dominance, or a single member of a pack will challenge the alpha for dominance. Evolutionarily, that's far more efficient than both packs fighting down to the last member for supremacy. Strategically, going after leadership rather than the rank and file makes perfect sense—"

"Perfect sense if your damn leaders keep exposing themselves," Poretti interrupted.

Meyers kept going like she had not even spoken. "—and it's been a time-honored tradition among resistance movements and guerilla factions opposing superior forces. We rarely use it as our primary stratagem, though, as we tend to focus upon objective-based maneuver, accomplishing a specific mission rather than just 'gunning for the boss.'"

"Oh shit, oh shit, oh shit," Smith chanted, pacing. "I'm senior. I'm in charge. I'm next on their list. This isn't what I signed on for. Oh shit, oh shit, oh shit…"

Third Platoon's NCO, SSGT Cuchinello, grunted from his spot on the wall next to Sheila. "I'll tell you one thing, I don't think I'm willing to trust any of those twits to lead me into battle," he said in a low voice.

From her other side, SGT Evanston chuckled. "Yeah. I'm thinking a good, old-fashioned fragging might be in order…"

This is getting out of control, Sheila thought. She felt she had to rescue LT Smith from himself. Pushing off the wall, she approached the trio and stopped the pacing Smith with a gentle hand. "Sir, you are senior. That puts you in charge, but it doesn't mean you have some sort of death sentence. Your best bet—and that of every other merc around you—is to figure out a way to counter the Zuul directly, to act instead of react."

He looked at her with a small glimmer of comprehension, but it was soon enough supplanted by the same gibbering fear. "No, no, no, I can't…go out there. I can't expose myself."

"Sir, you have to," Sheila pleaded.

Poretti walked up and pulled her hand off Smith's shoulder. "No, screw that. He steps down. I'm in command now. Bravo Company is to form up under me and we are going on the goddamn offensive. The mutts want to take me out, they can try it as I ram my armored fist up their asses!"

Meyers raised a hand. "Technically, Dina, I believe I'm senior to you. If Jamal abdicates, I'm in charge—"

"Fuck you, Meyers! You couldn't lead an elementary school fire drill, much less Bravo." 2LT Poretti turned to the NCOs glaring at them. "Who's with me!? Who wants to give those mangy mongrels some payback!? Who wants to show them you don't friggin' trifle with the Terrible Texans!!?"

She pumped her fist and yelled, and—sure enough—the NCOs began to match her fervor and bloody-minded enthusiasm. Even LT

Meyers recovered from the upset and managed to pump his fist too. LT Smith just sat down and stared forward blankly. Sheila felt pity for him, but a certain level of contempt as well. Poretti might be a hot-head, but better to err on the side of violence than to just sit here, waiting for the next raid.

Fifteen minutes later, the whole garrison was afire with activity. Sheila briefed the mercs of Second Platoon by herself—LT Smith was nowhere to be seen—and they set to, switching the loadouts on their CASPers from light patrol to heavy assault. While they worked, Sheila used a universal key (a crowbar) on the door to the sealed combat resupply containers. It took some doing. The containers were sufficiently armored to survive an unaided drop from orbit into a hostile fire zone. But Sheila was determined.

What she found inside was depressing, but not that surprising, given what 1SGT Reeves had told her. Each container was supposed to be a squad-in-a-box, with enough ammo, rations, repair parts, and sundry to re-equip a whole CASPer squad for three days of sustained combat. For 30 days sustainment for four combat platoons and support staff, that meant 100 containers of stuff. On the plus side, there were indeed 100 containers. Within the containers, however, the mix of stuff was a bit...off.

Inside each box she pried open, she found a few cartons of ammo, some random, non-matching repair parts, and more rations than a squad could eat through in a year of gluttony. While they might not starve on this planet, they'd be hard-pressed to defend themselves from the Zuul in a protracted fight—unless the pups reacted worse to "Stew, Vegetarian Beef (Simulated), w/Goat Cheezee Puffs" than the mercs did.

Sheila informed Poretti, who shrugged. "Guess we better kick their asses in round one, then. No need to hold anything back," the lieutenant said.

"Yes, ma'am. And I know it's not in my lane, but with the demise of the company HQ staff who'd normally do this…"

"Out with it, Staff Sergeant."

"Have we communicated with Karma and the home office yet? That sort of thing sometimes gets frowned on by company officers worried about the optics of it."

LT Poretti frowned, but nodded. "It does, and I'm sorry for that reality. But I wanna survive. I want all of us to survive, even if it means telling the whole galaxy we couldn't handle things on our own. Yes, Sarge, I already sent the balloon up. We sent a priority skip drone back to Karma, requesting relief and assault support. But they reasonably won't reach us for at least two weeks at the earliest. More likely 3-4 weeks, which is why we had those combat stores…"

"Yes, ma'am," Sheila responded, resigned.

Poretti looked around. "This is a farm, ain't it? Hit up the GenSha. At this point, I'd even take an improvised ANFO bomb if it can add to that first assault."

Sheila did just that, and received the GenSha equivalent of a shrug in response.

Burblann—Glashthul's replacement after that worthy individual had been blown up with the rest of the leadership—answered her. "No. No ammonium nitrate or any other type of fertilizer. Object of farm to remove specialized 'car' compounds from valley soil, not sow nitrates. C117 not organic plant. C117 is archeological/industrial resource extraction device, nanotech-enabled pseudo-organics. No fertilizer required. All necessary process energy come from 'car' soil."

Sheila screwed up her face. She was tired of everyone keeping her and her people in the dark. She encroached upon Burblann. "What is all this 'car' stuff!? Cars? Like *vroom,* cars that you can drive around?"

"No, no!" the GenSha answered, hastily. "Very sorry. Homonym. 'Car' is K-A-H-R in your spelling. As in Kahraman, ancient despots from 1,000 years ago, creators of the Canavar destructors. Analysis indicates this valley owned by Kahraman before the Fall and Galactic Union. Theory suggests certain locations involved in creation, processing, or rendering of Canavar monsters. This valley may have been…ecological dump of requisite chemical compounds, concentrated and stabilized by intervening centuries. No longer immediately deadly."

No longer *immediately* deadly. *Great,* Sheila thought. For the last year they had been living on the alien equivalent of a New Jersey Superfund site, left behind by galactic Nazis from many millennia past. "So, what sort of chemicals are you bringing up? Anything we can use?"

Burblann did the shrug-thing again. "Doubtful. Will get you list."

* * *

"What do you see out there, Meyers?" LT Poretti asked. The new leadership of Bravo Company nestled at the base of a hill, just a half-mile from the Jeha-Zuul farm. The moons were down, and the darkness was so deep that a merc could not even make out the blacked-out CASPer next to him.

LT Meyers nonetheless smiled, and it gave off the faintest glow through his open suit hatch. They were not risking radio comms this close. "What do I see? There is no Dana…"

"Only Zuul," several people answered back.

"Har-dee-har-har, fucker," Poretti hissed. "Now how about some intel instead of old movie references?"

His smile dropped, and he referenced the IR drone footage transmitted via laser point-to-point comms to his pinplants. "Standard pup patrol platoon on duty. No plus-ups, no extra active sensors. Nothing to indicate they're expecting an attack. It's just after the midpoint of their nightly rotation, so likely the nadir of their awareness and focus. Attacking later during the shift change might leave them more confused…"

"But they'd have twice as many guns on station. We do this now. All or nothin'." Poretti turned to the NCOs, Sheila included, who had all become her de facto platoon leadership. "You've got your assignments. Radio silence. We hit in five mikes. Move it."

Sheila rolled away and fled to her platoon's position on the right flank as quickly as possible, while still keeping as low and as quiet as a half-ton CASPer could. Overhead, the recon flyer was stealthed and at high altitude. The strike flyers were still below the horizon and not radiating any of their emitters. On the ground, the CASPers and tanks were also maintaining a total blackout, with all active search, targeting, and comms silent. In addition, the blacked-out shells of the CASPers were also masking their IR signatures, venting their waste heat over strap-on dry ice heat sinks. Those thermal suppressors would not last long and had a real tendency to back waste heat up into the cockpit, but while they were configured, the whole CASPer would radiate heat exactly at the background air temp—a good feature when going up against dogs who could see into the infrared.

The plan was bold, violent, and textbook to perfection. Sneak in as close as possible, start with air strikes all around, but concentrating on the Zuul main access—a rookie move, hitting where the enemy was strongest, but that was what you got when you knocked out the pack alpha. Back up the naïve power play with an oversized frontal assault using the remains of First and Fourth Platoons against the strongest section of the Zuul defensive works. Once the Zuul committed to reinforcing their front, the Texans would spring the envelopment on both flanks. It could only be done if the Texans committed all their troops and operated without a reserve; it wasn't something a force prepared for a long defensive siege would attempt. But they knew something the Zuul did not: their own home office had screwed them, making a protracted siege untenable.

It was bold and reckless, but sound. The NCOs had signed off and *not* fragged the enthusiastic, young second lieutenant. So now Sheila waited, crouched with the rest of Second, poised to strike.

Five minutes passed, and the strike flyers boosted to a nine-mile altitude and let loose with all their ordnance. Missiles with shaped-charge warheads, focused EMPs, and HVP carriers streaked to their targets in coordinated-time-on-top waves, followed by stream-raids of follow-up hits. Zuul compound MACs, particle weapons, and lasers snapped into action, taking a ruinous tithe on the human weapons, but they could not kill all of the incoming rounds, not once their targeting queues became overwhelmed.

Every defense has a saturation point.

Explosions blossomed around the Jeha farm compound, and several fixed-place defenses fell silent. An opening in the center could be seen! Poretti, Myers, Cuchinello, and Evanston stood and charged, along with the combined, armored might of two Terrible Texan platoons.

Zuul mortars and direct-fire poured into their ranks, but these were not the sucker punches the unarmored humans had endured before. Most of the CASPers just shrugged off the light arms and shrapnel and kept firing, kept charging forward.

The Zuul in the compound shifted, moving to reinforce their front, such that not even two platoons of assault-ready humans could penetrate it. It was what Sheila and the flank platoons had waited for. What did it matter that fewer Zuul than expected had rushed out to reinforce the defensive front? Were there fewer dogs within, or did they think what they had were sufficient numbers?

Sheila stood and yelled, "*Attack!*" into her comm.

And that's when the heavy weapons that had been missing from the farm's defense opened up *from behind them.* Unarmored Zuul rose from the mud or threw off multicolored grass roofs from their foxholes in the approaches the Texans had already passed through. *How the hell long have those mutts been waiting there in the dirt?* Sheila wondered, dismayed. They had seen *nothing* moving ever since the first mortar attack. Were the Zuul that sneaky, or that patient and prescient?

MACs and heavy chemical lasers snapped and laid waste to First and Fourth. Screams and cries of anguish and confusion filled the comms channels where there had only been silence. In Sheila's blue-force-tracker, the icon for LT Poretti winked out. Then Cuchinello, Evanston, and Meyers. And down the line, as if the pups had a sequential list of their hierarchy and followed it to a fault.

Others were hit and died, of course, but it seemed as if the dogs only aimed at someone—anyone—who had their shit together and tried to rally the remains of the broken assault. The alien fire worked its way out to either side and into the flanks where Third Platoon had waited.

And into her own Second Platoon.

The plan gone to hell, Sheila yelled, "Retreat! Fall back by fire team to the south! Concentrate covering fire on the forces to our rear—we are abandoning the objective!"

Second held their shit together, she noted proudly, and fell back away from both the Jeha farm and the mud-pups, though they would eventually have to curve around and head back for home. Fire teams and squads covered one another and poured bullets, rockets, and energy weapons into the now-exposed dogs. Going primitive might well have allowed the Zuul to sneak about and lie low better than the humans had anticipated, but it also meant they had virtually no armor to shrug off returning fire. The mutts were massacred...but the damage was already done.

Eventually, the Zuuls' leader-oriented focus turned its attention to Sheila herself. A heavy laser sliced through her CASPer's left leg and left arm. She tried to compensate, picking up a hopping gait, but then a glancing HVP spun her about and planted her in the mud.

Sheila blew the cockpit hatch and jumped out, landing in a clump of flowering grasses. She regained her footing just in time to stare down the distant maw of a magnetic accelerator cannon pointed straight at her.

The enemy MAC fired, but the round failed to obliterate her. Instead, a lone CASPer dropped down on its jets right in front of her and took the coil gun round center of mass, directly through the cockpit. Sheila stumbled back and fell, and the mech collapsed, sprawling, where she had been. Through the shattered armor of the cockpit, she saw the lifeless face of a young merc whose name she had never bothered to learn.

It was the fresh, young private who had hid out with her under the canapes during the battle at the Change of Command.

* * *

Back at the relative safety of the GenSha farm, Sheila took stock of what remained.

It wasn't a lot.

Of the 212 mercs in the original complement of Bravo Company, 116 remained, scattered among four shattered combat platoons, the flyer sections, medical cadre, and catering/support. The headquarters element was all but gone, and if she wanted to reform functional platoons, she would have to cut down from four to two, with a couple of orphan squads left over.

But that was just numbers. The losses were much deeper than that. For her own part, Sheila could not un-see the faces of her compatriots, now forever lost. Each of the Texans' Honored Dead— mercs she had served beside for years in some cases, along with a smattering of friends and frenemies, former lovers and major assholes alike—all of them looked back at Sheila in her mind's eye. They glared at her, demanding vengeance for their restless souls— and she was now the only one who could give it to them.

In regards to leadership, and with LT Smith in a state of shocked catatonia, Staff Sergeant Sheila Murphy was the senior Terrible Texan on this nameless hunk of paradise. And she had no idea what to do now.

An alien *harrumph* sounded just behind Sheila. She turned around and cast a weary gaze at Burblann, waiting excitedly just beyond the crowd of her surviving mercs. Sheila nodded and the bisonoid alien rushed up.

"How did the battle fare, Staff Sergeant? Has Lieutenant Poretti returned as well?"

Sheila exaggeratedly looked around her, and then checked the bottom of her bloody boot. "Nope, no Lieutenant Poretti here!" she said, as sarcastically and as viciously as she could, hoping that some of it might make it through the GenSha's translation algorithms. "Whups! Looks like we must have left her behind, along with the 56 other poor sods who died covering our retreat. The battle? It didn't fare well, Burblann, not well at all."

She grabbed the alien by its elbow and led it away from her remaining men and women. Out of earshot, she turned to the GenSha. "We did a lot of damage to the Zuul and to the Jeha farm's perimeter, but they pretty much ate our lunch. Bravo Company is less than half effective now, and I have no idea of how that compares to what the Zuul left in reserve. If I had to give you a firm answer though, it's this: The Texans can no longer protect your farm. About all we can do now is provide cover for a retreat of personnel only to the planetary debarkation point."

"No transport crates?" the alien asked, carefully.

Sheila shook her head. "I'm not even sure we can get away with that. We pull out now, leave everything behind, the Jeha and the Zuul have no reason to waste ammo on us. Try to retreat with everything in tow, they'll attack us as the sole means to protect their investment."

Burblann appeared very distressed. "Failure to protect shipment amounts to breach of contract! GenSha will not pay! Will lodge complaint with mercenary guild and leave scathing review on Gal-Net!"

Sheila roared and leapt into the GenSha's face, knocking the top-heavy bisonoid down. "Do you think I give a shit about that? About this contract, about this farm, or about the goddamn Texans? I'd give anything to win, just once, but all I can offer you is a chance to survive. Do you not get that?"

Behind them, all the mercs silently stared at her. She was in command of Bravo Company for now, but that might not last long if the survivors thought her erratic and decided to frag her.

Being in charge was a terminal condition on this rock.

Sheila reached down to grasp Burblann's hoof-hand and hauled the massive alien to its feet. Looking down, she saw it had a sheet of paper crumpled there.

Burblann saw her looking and held the paper out. "What you asked for. List of C117 harvested chemicals."

She took the sheet and read it over. It was a mix of complicated organic chemistry formulas, common names for compounds, and lists of rare elements and isotopes. Sheila recognized a number of aromatic hydrocarbons, some truly nasty heavy metal poisons, certain DNA analogs, and a number of things she had no idea what they were. The soil here, supposedly used in the processing of the ancient, terrifying Canavar, yielded a treasure trove of important chemicals, but there was nothing that could help them.

It had been a pipe dream anyways, she supposed. After all, they had never received any warning about the pseudo-plant pods, nothing to tell them how nasty they were on the inside, or any alerts from their chemical sniffers.

Sheila looked back at the sheet, giving it another once-over. There was one compound that raised the hackles on the back of her neck, but she couldn't think of why. She pointed it out to Burblann. "This one here, this PABF. What is that? It sounds familiar."

Burblann told her.

* * *

"**A**re you in command of this garrison, human?"

Sheila looked out the open hatch of her unarmed, borrowed CASPer at the battle-armored mutt standing before her. Behind the alpha, three heavy platoons of equally impressive canid Zuul mercs were lined up, all with weapons pointed at her, alone and very, very much afraid, standing before the GenSha farm's main gate.

In answer, Sheila shook her head. "Not really. It looks to me like you're in command of everything."

"So, you surrender?"

"We withdraw, as discussed. The GenSha farm team and my mercs walk out safely, with no arms larger than a sidearm. We leave behind the C117 harvest, all equipment, all live plants, etc. and declare you the rightful owners of the site, registered with the Merchants' Guild on the GalNet, but set to automatically revert to the GenSha if we don't make it back to Karma safely. You win, we live, everybody's happy."

"All but the dead."

"Yeah. All but the dead." She stared at the doglike alien, but it was hard to register how sincere the growling beast might be. Hell, she didn't even know whether it was a bitch or a cur.

Well, we'll see in a minute who's the bigger bitch here, Sheila thought.

The Zuul alpha chuffed a bark and gestured her aside. She stepped over and motioned for her people to start. Slowly, a line of lightly-armed CASPers, uniformed humans, and dejected GenSha exited the compound, all under the guns of the victorious Zuul. As they trundled out, the mutts marched in, along with a contingent of millipede-like Jeha agricultural engineers.

A security squad of Zuul guarded them as they walked past the ruined amphitheater, out of the valley, over the hills, and to their designated landing site. Looking back toward their valley, Sheila could well imagine the mood of the Zuul and Jeha in her old garrison/farm: cautious but ecstatic, their contract saved through the precise exercise of violence. They'd be looking over their haul, the abandoned weapons and supplies, and the transport crate upon transport crate full of near-priceless C117 pods. They'd be careful, as Sheila would have in their place, watchful for any booby traps or subterfuge, scanning continuously for the telltale chemical gas molecules of high explosives.

But they would find nothing like that.

Sheila also knew they would find piles upon piles of discarded military meals and mismatched CASPer spare parts. And they might notice that many of the transport crates were not full. Most, in fact, were empty, except for a few placed in strategic locales around the garrison, half full of C117 pods, C117 pods that had taken the highest percentage of PABF.

Peraza Buckminster Fullerene.

The explosion that knocked both the humans and their Zuul minders down was powerful enough to strip the tops of each and every intervening hill to bare granite, and shook the ground like the footfalls of the Canavar that had long ago been born here. A mushroom cloud worthy of a full-scale orbital bombardment or an old-school nuke roiled up into the heavens, carrying along with it the souls of every single Zuul and Jeha that had entered their camp or had stood guard well outside the compound.

The Texans, desperate and forewarned of the apocalyptic blast, fell upon their Zuul guards and overwhelmed them, lack of weapons or not. When the dogs were down, Sheila looked upon her and her people's works with grim satisfaction. "Okay, Bravo, we ain't done yet! Let's get back, kit up, and take this fight to them!"

* * *

"Peraza Buckminster Fullerene? I'm sorry, Staff Sergeant, you'll have to elaborate. I know what fullerenes are, but I'm unfamiliar with that one."

Sheila, dressed in her Terrible Texans' dress uniform, but conspicuously missing the bucking bronco patch of her old company, nodded and answered the question from the senior Mercenary Guild auditor in Bartertown on Karma. "PABF, otherwise known as N_{60}, is a metastable allotrope of nitrogen. When I grew up in Midland-Odessa, Texas, chemistry was sort of everybody's pastime, a holdover from the oil-field days. We learned all about the math and the chemistry of explosives. Most chemical explosives are nitrogenated organic hydrocarbons, with the carbon, oxygen, and hydrogen compounds forming a stable base for the energetic nitrogen bonds.

That's also what your chemical sniffers pick up to register the presence of explosives—aromatic hydrocarbon residue. But it's the constrained nitrogen bonds that give explosives most of their boom factor. Increase the number of nitrogens, you increase the boom, but you also increase the instability. The biggest, most unstable booms come from pure nitrogen allotropes, like octaazacubane or N_8.

"Now take the single largest self-contained stable carbon molecule: C_{60}, or buckyballs, and replace every carbon with a nitrogen azide. A 'per-azide buckyball'…Peraza Buckminster Fullerene, the largest allotrope of nitrogen that could theoretically exist, with a yield just short of a tactical nuclear device."

"And the GenSha are farming this out of the ground there?" the Guild auditor asked.

"Yes, sir, them and the Jeha. That and a whole bunch of useful chemicals that they theorize were by-products of ancient Canavar creation. PABF should be unstable as hell, but something about the centuries it spent soaked into the soil stabilized it enough for the C117 to extract it safely. And since allotropes don't set off explosive sniffers, we never realized the GenSha were farming explosives. For that matter, neither did the Zuul. We loaded our weapons and most of the C117 pods into the shock-proof cases our misallocated supplies came in, then set up the transport pods with PABF-heavy C117s and an electrically initiated thermite grenade on a timer. After the farm blew up, we retrieved our surviving gear and took down the skeleton crew left behind at the Jeha/Zuul compound. The GenSha farm's a total loss, but they were able to recover enough C117 to still turn a profit."

"Thus the Terrible Texans successfully completed another contract."

Sheila grimaced. "No, sir, my people and I successfully completed the Texans' contract, in spite of *everything* they did wrong to set us up. My first act after getting back and picking up my pay and bonus was to resign from the whole outfit. My second act was to tell you all here at the guild."

The auditor, a scarred, old, rat-like Veetanho, stood from her seat and approached Sheila. "Staff Sergeant Murphy, thank you. What the Zuul did to you is part of the game, and it appears you ended with the upper hand in the end. But what your own merc company did to you and yours is unconscionable. We will be taking action to censure them."

Sheila nodded and could feel the ghosts of all those she had lost calm just a bit, not to mention the restlessness of her own spirit. "Thank you, ma'am."

"And for you? Using your newfound cache as a successful freelancer to get on with one of the Four Horsemen? With your sudden record of success in command, you could pretty much name your own price."

Sheila sighed and smiled back. The flamboyant figure of First Sergeant Brenda Reeves came to mind. "I don't think so. Not yet anyway. I've had my fill of command. For the foreseeable future, the only thing I plan to be in charge of is a bar stool and a glass.

"There are some dear, departed friends I have to toast."

# # # # #

A Family Tradition
by Ian J. Malone

Kicking out over an open hill, Taylor threw his CASPer into high gear and vaulted the summit, soaring some 30 feet through the air.

"Woo!" he shouted, the full North Florida moon at his back. Water plumed in a mushroom of mud and lily pads when Taylor struck the marsh, then just like that, he was off and running again.

Taylor loved it in the swamp, almost as much as he loved piloting a 10-foot-tall, battle-armored war suit like the CASPer. Ever since he'd come out camping for the first time as a kid with his late father, he'd felt drawn to it, as if he were connected to it somehow. There was a peace out here, a tranquility, that couldn't be found in the everyday hustle and bustle of city life. Then again, Taylor thought, in a metropolis the size of Jacksonville, North Florida, with its population of 1.8 million, that was sort of a given.

Skidding to a halt alongside a riverbank, Taylor popped his CASPer's canopy and removed his helmet, instantly feeling the night humidity on his skin. All around him, frogs croaked, birds cooed, and crickets chirped. Meanwhile, a mild splash rippled the otherwise glassy surface some 20 yards out from his feet. He keyed his spotlight to dim and glanced that way; two red eyes looked back.

Gator. Taylor threw the beast a nod—one predator to another—then returned to the serenity of his surroundings. Only, they weren't there anymore. Instead, Taylor was standing in the mess hall of a starship—an *Akaga*-class cruiser, if he guessed right. The place was filled with uniformed personnel—mercenaries mostly, judging by their battle-dress fatigues and standard-issue hardware. They were all laughing and joking over cocktails, as if there weren't a care in the world to consider.

But that wasn't the case. Not on this ship, and most certainly not on this day.

Taylor's eyes bulged in revelation. *Oh please, God, no.* He whirled. "Terry!"

No one acknowledged him.

"Terry!" he screamed again, panic growing. How had they not heard him?

Taylor darted his eyes around the room, searching frantically for the one face in the crowd he longed so very much to see.

A familiar laugh chortled from the back corner, and Taylor snapped his gaze that way. His older brother, Terry, was sharing a beer with one of the others from his company. He was just as Taylor remembered—rugged-lean looks with a tight, blond brush cut and a swagger that'd never failed to brighten a room. He looked happy, too. Or at least, that's how Taylor had always imagined him in this moment.

Time slowed to a crawl as Taylor bounded forward. He thrust out a hand, lips formed into the one word he'd have given all to scream when it mattered. "*Run!*"

A massive thunderbolt rocked the scene as a white light slashed at Taylor's eyes, blinding him. He threw up his arm to cover, but as always it was no use. Nerve endings ignited as flesh seared from the bone—and all the while, his brother just stood there, laughing.

"Terry!"

Taylor bolted upright in bed. *What the...*It took a second to find his bearings, but eventually they came. He sucked in a breath, heart pounding in his throat, as the last vestiges of his nightmare retreated to his subconscious. *Terry...*

Someone knocked at his bedroom door.

"Yeah?" Taylor gulped.

His older sister, Rita, peaked inside, her long auburn hair draped in a bedhead of curls over her gray Georgia Bulldogs t-shirt. "You okay?"

Taylor rubbed his eyes as heat became frostbite. He grabbed a sheet, sweat-soaked as it was, and wrapped it around him for warmth. "Yeah, I...I think so."

"You sure?" Rita kept her voice low to avoid waking the others. "I ain't heard you holler like that in a long time—real long."

"I'm fine." Taylor tightened his grasp on the covers. "Just bad dreams. Ain't nothin' to worry over. Go back to bed."

Rita chewed her lip. "You were there again, weren't you?"

Taylor shivered, and that was all the confirmation his sister needed.

"Try to get some sleep," Rita said, pulling the door to. "Tomorrow's gonna be a long day, for all of us."

* * *

Waking the next morning, Taylor rose from his hand-me-down bunk and headed for the Jack and Jill bathroom he shared with his two sisters. He hated—*hated*—sharing bathrooms. However, the aging craftsman bungalow in which they now lived only had two, and his mother needed the second for its wheelchair access. That'd been one of the reasons they'd picked the place. That, and it'd been all the bank would finance them for after the bankruptcy hearing.

At least we're back in the old neighborhood, Taylor thought. Then again, if the bars on their windows were any indication, the old neighborhood wasn't what it used to be.

Knocking on the bathroom door and getting no answer—a small victory in itself—Taylor slipped inside and shuffled across the scarred linoleum floor to splash some water on his face at the sink. It felt warm and life-giving, like it always did just after dawn.

Taylor inspected himself in the mirror. His hair, long and blond, hung in matted clumps past his tattooed shoulders. He also looked paler this morning than usual, a fact unaided by his two-day beard and the Goodyear-like bags under his eyes.

"So, what'll it be, hoss?" Taylor asked his reflection. Today was the day, and a decision had to be made. He weighed his options, along with the out he'd gotten last night from his general manager.

After a hard minute of introspection, the mirror man rendered the answer. *Nope, ain't doin' it.*

That was good enough for Taylor. Laying out a fresh change of clothes—his usual wardrobe of faded jeans, t-shirt, and his dad's old arrowhead necklace—he flipped on the shower to start his day.

"Mornin', sleepy head." Rita was already seated at the kitchen table, coffee in hand, when Taylor entered. "You get any more sleep last night?"

He shrugged in route to the cabinet for a mug of his own. "I got enough."

"Gotta work on that," Rita said.

Taylor threw her a cursory smirk as he fixed himself a coffee. Then, turning, he raised an eyebrow at the sight of her nurse's scrubs. "I thought you were off today."

"I'm just goin' in for the mornin' shift," Rita said. "Dr. Newlin agreed to let me off at lunch so I could bus it back here to pick up mom for the ceremony. We'll meet you downtown."

Taylor frowned, drawing a perplexed look from his sister.

"You are plannin' on bein' there, right?" she asked, sea-blue eyes narrowing.

And here we go. Taylor exhaled.

"Taylor?" Rita pressed.

"Ziggy called last night," Taylor said. "Apparently, Harvick's Hurricanes just fulfilled a sizable garrison contract, and they're due back later today. Sizable contracts typically mean sizable celebrations, and sizable celebrations typically mean sizable tips. We need all of those we can get these days."

A touch of red flashed in Rita's cheeks. "There'll be other chances to get tips. Tell Ziggy to find somebody else."

"Can't do it," Taylor said. "Deal's done made. I gotta be at The Hell House by 11:00 to prep for open."

"But the whole family's gonna be there," Rita protested. "You can't just bail on us like this, Taylor. It's the five-year anniversary!"

Taylor raised a shoulder. "Sorry, sis. I'm just doin' what I thought was best for everyone involved."

Rita huffed in disbelief. "He'd want you to be there. You know that, right? He'd kick your ass for hangin' us out to dry this way."

"Yeah well, he ain't exactly here wearin' the boots, now is he?"

Rita's gaze plummeted, and Taylor hated himself immediately. He rubbed his temples. "I'm sorry, Rita. I didn't mean to—"

"It's all right." She stayed him with a palm. "Today's a tough day for all of us. I get that. If you feel you've gotta go, then go. I'll cover for ya with the others."

Now Taylor really felt like crap. His focus drifted to the hallway in search of a new topic. "Where's Jolene? She not up yet?"

Rita returned to her coffee. "She was out late again last night. I expect she'll be up in an hour or so."

"Just long enough to pop some more stims and head back out, right?" Taylor rolled his eyes. "Typical Jo. Heaven forbid she'd ever help around here."

"Jolene's dealin' with her issues like the rest of us," Rita said. "Her ways are just a little different than ours."

"Yeah, but our ways don't take us to rehab," Taylor shot back.

"So says the boy with his head over a commode three nights ago while I held back his hair," Rita said.

Taylor had no answer for that.

"Jolene's family, plain and simple. For all her faults, she's still one of ours, and ain't nothin' gonna change that." One of Rita's auburn curls fell across her face as she peered into her mug. "Family sticks together, Taylor. Has to. It's the only way we survive days like to-day."

A soft groan carried from the master suite down the hall.

"Mom's up," Taylor said.

"Been up all night." Rita sighed as she rose from her chair.

"Want me to handle it?" Taylor asked.

"Nah, I'm already up," Rita said. "You go ahead and take off before you get the third degree for skippin' the service. I've got this."

"Hey Rita?" Taylor asked.

"Yeah?" She held at the corner.

Taylor pursed his lips. "You deserve a break on occasion, too, you know."

Rita swallowed, staring off into nowhere. She looked so much older now. Between the growing wrinkles on her forehead and the deepening lines on her face, it was easy to forget that she was only 27.

"That's...a real nice thought, baby brother." Rita forced a smile and pointed to the stove. "There's biscuits in the oven. Take one for the road so you don't go to work hungry."

* * *

Closing the door behind him, Taylor threw the lock to their stucco house in the old Riverside neighborhood and descended the weed-covered driveway to the sidewalk across the street. From there, it was over three blocks to the corner of Saint Johns and Cherry, where he'd pick up the JTA redline bound for Jacksonville Startown. Thankfully, the wait wasn't long, only about five minutes. Once the bus arrived, Taylor boarded the armored tube on dual rollerballs, paid the robotic driver via UACC, or Yack as most called it, then assumed his usual spot near the back. If he'd had his own transportation, the startown commute would only have been about 10 minutes door-to-door. Via public transit, however, the trip was more like 90 minutes.

Man, what I wouldn't do to have my flyer back. Taylor missed having a personal vehicle almost as much as he missed having his own bathroom. He'd had a sweet one, too. With her candy-apple paint scheme, black racing stripes, and modified capacitor system for max thrust, she'd been the envy of most of his friends. He'd even taken her Daytona for a handful of amateur racing events, although that'd been before the bank had taken it all away.

Damn money-suckin' vultures. Taylor fished his biscuit from his knapsack and thought of something else.

Several stops and a station transfer later, the Jacksonville skyline crested the horizon in Taylor's window. He'd always found it an amazing sight, in part for its sprawling expansiveness, though mostly for how much it'd changed, even in his lifetime.

Taylor had been lucky. He'd grown up at a time when Jax had ranked among the top cities in America, but it hadn't always been that way. Toward the end of the 21st century, after decades of political feuding with the so-called "Panhandle Rednecks" up north, the citizens of South Florida had petitioned the federal government for the right to independent statehood. The request was granted, and in the year 2085 the American flag saw the addition of a fifty-second star to its pattern.

Naturally, most of Florida's powerhouse tourism drivers— Disney, Universal Studios, the cruise industry, and so forth—had supported the move, as had many others who fled south to join them in the new South Florida capital of Orlando. This left North Florida—and therefore cities like Jax—with nothing on which to hang their hats for commerce. Soon, empty shopping parks, rotting factories, and decimated property values were commonplace from the Volusia County line to the Alabama border. By the year 2096, the state's lawmakers faced a grim choice: "we either change, or we die."

In a stunning break from tradition, the North Florida Congress passed sweeping legislation that slashed its entire tax code and replaced it with a 1% consumption tax on retail goods and services. In effect, this took the state from being among the nation's highest taxers to one of the cheapest places in the country to do business. Almost overnight, companies from across the country flocked to cities like Pensacola, Destin, Tallahassee, and Gainesville to seize the new incentives. Every industry was represented—from textiles to tech—though none more so than the mercenary field, which, by then, had become the backbone of the global economy. Fast-forward to the present, and, while the South Florida economy languished under bloated deficits and an overabundance of entitlement programs, North Florida's economy was alive and vibrant, and flush with billions in hard-earned mercenary cash.

And guns. Lots and lots of guns.

Feeling the bus halt alongside the A1A strip, Taylor spotted his stop through the window, Cocktail Junction, and rose to get off. Once outside, he shouldered his knapsack and lobbed his biscuit wrapper into the trash as a *Douglas*-class frigate flew by overhead.

Cocktail Junction was the northernmost stop at the Jacksonville Startown. Partially named for its array of bars and restaurants, and partially in homage to The World's Greatest Cocktail Party (the annual rivalry game between the Universities of Florida and Georgia), the Junction occupied most of the old Neptune Beach area. The rest of the region—the towns of Mayport, Jax Beach, Atlantic Beach, and much of Ponte Vedra—were all now private property, owned by merc companies. Throw in Jax Starport, the largest east of Houston, and Jacksonville Startown was never short on action.

Strolling down the strip, sea breeze rustling his ponytail, Taylor soon arrived at the Junction bar where he spent most of his time. The sign out front read simply, The Hell House, in bold red font. Legend had it the faded red splotch beside it in the logo had once been a caricature of the devil, but no one had been able to corroborate that for years.

Fishing the keys from his pocket, Taylor offered a quick wave to the bar's custodian and house Dobro player, Mr. Lowe, in route to the door. Once inside, he flipped the light switch then waited as, one by one, the florescent bulbs over the main hall hummed to life.

By all rights, The Hell House was a total dive, although most agreed this was part of its charm. After all, not every pub on the coast needed a cabana with a thatch roof, umbrella drinks, and a beach deck. Sometimes people just wanted a bar—a dingy, dumpy, crap-hole bar—and it was in that capacity The Hell House had proudly served for more than 32 years.

Taylor rounded the horseshoe bar, with its array of scratches and scars, and headed for the 1950s-era jukebox in the corner. Granted, it was by no means an original—more like a novelty knockoff built in Grand Rapids, Michigan. However, it still carried the look and design of the old machines, which was cool, plus a full library of music thanks to its direct uplink to Earth's Aethernet.

Taylor keyed in his manager's code then toggled to his personal playlist. *Yep, that oughta do.* A few seconds later, *Statesboro Blues* from the Allman Brothers Band was blaring through the speakers.

"Aw, damnit," a voice grumbled behind him. The accent was a thick Bostonian.

Taylor turned to find Rex, The Hell House's resident metal-head, frowning behind him wearing frayed jeans, Doc Martins, and a tour t-shirt for the slasher band, Napalm.

"I knew I shoulda come in early," Rex muttered. "Now I've gotta sit here and be subjected to another one of your hick-shtick twang-athons until we open. Because, you know, that's awesome."

Taylor folded his arms. "Rules of the bar, hoss. He who opens picks the prep tunes. He who follows shuts his pie-hole and listens."

Rex scowled beneath the brim of his Boston Red Sox hat, but he wasn't surprised. This was, after all, the same debate they always had when paired on shifts together.

"I can call in Karl," Taylor said. "He could sub in for you."

"Oh, hell no," Rex said. "With the Hurricanes coming back into port today, there's no way I'd miss this shift—twang-athons or not. You catch the word on that contract?"

Taylor shrugged. "I heard it's impressive."

"Impressive my ass." Rex scoffed. "Historic is more like it. Rumor has it the elSha made a hard pitch to land one of the Horsemen for this gig but it was too small potatoes. That left all the mid-card firms jockeying for the deal, and somehow old man Harvick managed to nab it. Can you believe that shit?"

Taylor could, actually. "What was the payout?"

"Somewhere north of 30 million credits," Rex said. "That's all I got."

Taylor whistled. Thirty million credits were an impressive sum for any merc outfit, but especially one the size of Harvick's Hurricanes. At the current exchange rate, that would net them somewhere around 210 million dollars.

Good for you, Pete. Taylor's family had known the Hurricanes' owner since his move up from Miami 15 years ago to build his own company. If anyone deserved a payday, it was Harvick.

Taylor glanced at the clock. They had an hour until opening. "We gotta get to work."

"Yes sir, Captain Hillbilly, sir." Rex threw him a mock salute in route to the Tri-V down the bar. He switched it on, causing its three-dimensional image to flutter above the device's base. The picture was muted, of course; however, the closing crew the previous night must've been watching the playoff game, because the channel had been left on the local network affiliate. The picture showed a crowd of hundreds outside of Jacksonville City Hall, many of them holding signs with phrases like "Eagles Fly Free" or "Eagles Never Die." Others wore t-shirts and ball caps featuring a logo that any kid from Duval County—especially one from Riverside—would've known on sight.

Taylor dropped his eyes.

"Huh." Rex pulled at his goatee. "I forgot that was happening today." Then, as if a light had gone off in his head, the metal-head turned a perplexed look to his co-worker. "Wait a second. Why are you here and not downtown with everyone else?"

Taylor kept his eyes off the screen. He'd already read the caption—*Hometown Heroes honored five years after tragedy*—and that'd been enough. "I, um…had stuff to do."

"Stuff." Rex blinked. "The mayor is giving your family the keys to the city today. Maybe I'm a little off base, but it seems to me you should carve a little time out of your schedule for that sorta thing."

"Drop it, Rex." Taylor locked eyes this time. "I've got my reasons, and ain't none of 'em concern you. Understand?"

Rex put up his hands. "Fine, man. Whatever floats your taco. I'll get started on the keg duty if you'll scope our glassware."

Taylor shot him a final glare then snatched up a towel and went to work.

* * *

As expected, the afternoon came and went with quite the uptick in sales as several members of Harvick's Hurricanes dropped in with the desire to party. A few of them had been regulars once, and it did Taylor good to see them. He liked hanging out with mercs. He always had, a fact which surprised no one given his family's history with their trade.

By the time 1830 rolled around, orders had slowed to a crawl as most customers had either cleared out to find food or someone to pilot them home. All that remained were a handful of regulars and a couple early birds hoping to claim stools at the bar before the night crowd swarmed the place. Either way, Taylor saw it as an opening to leave early so he could catch the pharmacy on his way home. Rita had left him a message earlier. Apparently their mom had had a pretty rough time at the memorial ceremony and was almost out of meds. No one wanted that, especially not today.

"Hey Rex?" Taylor turned to his co-worker. "If you don't mind, I'm gonna—"

The front door swung open, and another customer appeared. He was tall, about six feet, with a slender frame, freckled features, and peppermint-colored hair that touched his shoulders.

Every eye in The Hell House turned to study the newcomer, not for his physique but rather his attire. Unlike the rest of the crowd who sported jeans, fatigues, and casual tees, this man wore a tailor-made suit of navy-blue silk that doubtless cost more than most non-mercs saw in a month.

Attorney, maybe? Taylor despised lawyers.

"G'day, gents," the stranger said in a cheerful Australian tone. He got a few grumbles back but that was about it. Undaunted, the man glided over the concrete floor and pulled up a stool in front of Taylor. "I'll have a whiskey, please. Neat."

"This is a bar." Taylor smirked. "We've got a few of those. Would you care to be a little more specific? Jack? Jim? Johnny Walker? Crown?"

The stranger waved off the suggestions. "No, none of that. I think I'm in the mood for something a bit more…indigenous."

Taylor wasn't sure he'd ever heard that word used in the context of booze before. Maybe it was an Aussie thing. "Caballero Distilleries is based out of Saint Augustine. They've got a blonde that's pretty popular."

"Excellent." The stranger beamed. "I'll have that then."

Turning for the plywood liquor shelf at his back, Taylor plucked out a square bottle with a Spanish matador on the label and placed it on the bar. From there, he grabbed a tumbler from the dry-rack and tipped the bottle over its lip for a three-count. He then cut the pour with wrist-turn and slid the glass of golden liquid to his customer. "That'll be six dollars."

The redhead frowned. "Sadly, I don't carry cash. You do take credits, though, yeah?"

"This is a startown, ain't it?" Taylor replied.

The stranger reached into his coat and came back with a Yack, placing it onto the counter with an audible *click*.

"Be right back," Taylor said.

The man sat on his stool, staring.

Not that kind of bar, chief. Taylor scooped up the card and swiped it through his slate to process the transaction. Once it was done, he handed it back to the redhead. "Will there be anything else?"

The stranger seemed to consider the question. "Yes, actually. There is."

Taylor waited.

"I'm here on something of a recruiting trip," the man said. "I represent a gentleman from Atlanta with an eye toward the mercenary trade. Specifically, he wishes to invest in a firm."

Taylor shrugged. "He's come to the right place. There's plenty around here to choose from, plus a ton more in Houston if he really wants into the bigtime."

The stranger shook his head. "As a native of the South, my employer prefers to keep his interests based in the region—hence his fascination with Jacksonville." He paused, catching himself. "Ah, where are my manners. Please, allow me to introduce myself. My name is Remington. Raymond Remington."

Taylor accepted the man's handshake. "Good to meetcha. So your boss wants to stay local, huh?"

Remington nodded.

"Well, he's in luck," Taylor said. "Word around port is there's an outfit in town from San Diego that's lookin' to move south but they need backers to help finance the relo. They left a card with one of the other bartenders if you're interested."

Remington sipped his whiskey. "That's an interesting proposition for someone, but not us."

Taylor leaned on the counter next to the beer taps. "Fair enough. What did you have in mind?"

Slowly, the stranger reached into his back pocket and came back with something. It was one of the ball caps from the news footage he'd seen earlier.

Taylor froze, eyes fixed to the logo on the garment's crown. It showcased a screaming eagle astride crisscrossed muskets with a bright, green palmetto leaf for a background. The sides of the design were laced in Spanish moss while the top featured a black banner with the company's name in stylized gold font. It even had their slogan: Semper Proficias.

Always move forward.

"What can you tell me about Swamp Eagle Security?" Remington asked.

Taylor swallowed. "I can tell you they're closed for business. Have been for some time now."

Remington's smile faltered. "That's too bloody bad. As I understand it, the Eagles were quite the celebrities around these parts. Five young men from Robert E. Lee High School banded together after graduation to form a small-time mercenary outfit, only to rise through the ranks of Terra's merc scene to become a solid mid-level player. That's an impressive feat for anyone, much less a pack of roughnecks from the hard side of town." He cocked his head. "But you'd know all about that wouldn't you, Taylor?"

Taylor's eyes narrowed. "Listen, mister. I ain't sure what you're up to but my brother's company died with him five years ago. There's nothin' else to say about it. Now if you'll excuse me, I've got—"

"And what a tragedy that was." Remington's expression turned rueful. "Your brother's passing, I mean. Remind me again how that happened. Engine failure, wasn't it?"

Taylor nodded but didn't elaborate.

"Such a pity." Remington clicked his tongue. "And to think, if only the engineering crew had done its job, the whole thing might've been averted."

Taylor rocketed out a finger, unable to hold his tongue this time. "That's a bunch of propaganda bullshit. Steve Collins was a great engineer. Hell, some even called him a savant. He and Terry went all the way back to Lee together, and I'm here to tell ya, nobody ran a tighter ship in an engineering room. Nobody."

Remington raised his palms. "My apologies. I didn't mean to offend. It's just that negligence was cited in the official report as the attributing cause of the accident."

"Please." Taylor snorted. "Steve didn't understand the meaning of the word negligence. You'd know that if you were from around here."

The redhead grinned, sensing a challenge. "Very well then, mate. Here's your chance to educate me. I'll tell you what I know. You tell me where I'm wrong. Sound like a deal?"

An occasional angler himself, Taylor knew when he was being baited. He chose to roll with it to see where the man was going. "All right, fine. Let's hear what you've got."

"According to the Science Guild's report, something went awry with one of the *Eagle's* engines on their way back from Karma Station. Once that happened, the hyperspace generator failed, thereby casting the ship and her crew into oblivion before they could reemerge." Remington glanced up. "How am I doing so far?"

Taylor raised a shoulder. "Pretty good, if you trust the Science Guild."

"And you don't?" Remington asked.

"I don't trust anyone who keeps that many secrets," Taylor said. "Here's what I do know. The ship the Eagles were travelin' on was a shiny new *Akaga*-class cruiser, purchased straight off the line two months prior to that contract. I know this because Terry gushed about her for weeks after buyin' her."

"Why's that?" Remington asked.

"She was the first cruiser the Eagles had ever owned," Taylor said. "Prior to that, they'd been forced to lease transportation from other companies come deployment time. Anyway, Terry was proud as hell of that ship, and so was Steve. The man literally lived in her engine room that first month, learnin' every nook and cranny of her operations. By the time they broke orbit, there wasn't an inch of that cruiser Steve didn't know, save for one exception."

Remington reclined on his stool. "The hyperspace generator."

"Bingo." Taylor snapped his fingers. "Those units were new and had come straight from the Science Guild with just enough information for our engineers to know how to work them but not much else. Hyperspace travel is one of the few things mankind still don't fully understand, and those greedy alien bastards have gone to great lengths to keep it that way. They want us in the dark, otherwise they'd have released the specs to those drives years ago."

The corners of Remington's mouth trailed downward. "Are you suggesting that the Galactic Union's Science Guild—one of the most powerful entities in the Milky Way—sabotaged your brother's ship?"

Taylor shook his head. "Nah, nothin' that nefarious. I think the more likely answer is the Guild sold my brother a bum generator, and rather than fess up about it when the unit failed in transit, they opted to pin their screw-up on the poor dead engineer who ain't around to say different. It's classic CYA, man. The whole situation reeks of it." Taylor pointed for the door. "Now if we're done with story time here, I've got stuff to do. There's the exit when you're ready."

Remington bit his lip. "Might I be so bold as to make an assertion?"

"You're on your own time now, bossman." Taylor shouldered his knapsack to go. "Make all the assertions you want."

"The legacy of Swamp Eagle Security extends far beyond their wealth, achievements, or the tragedy of their end. It's a legacy of commitment and dedication, of pulling one's self up by the bootstraps to build a better life." Remington tapped a finger on the bar top. "That's a legacy worth preserving, Taylor, though not in memoriam. In perseverance."

Taylor made a face. "What are you gettin' at?"

"The man I represent wishes to resurrect your brother's company for a return to the field, a mission he hopes to achieve with you at the helm."

Taylor dropped his bag. "You can't be serious."

"I assure you I am." Remington laced his fingers. "My employer can't bring back your brother, Taylor, but he can continue his work. Help us do that, and in doing so, help yourself and your family."

A string of past events and corresponding life choices played like a highlight reel through Taylor's mind. "I'm sorry, but that can't happen."

"Why not?" Remington asked.

"For starters, you'd need permission from Terry's surviving partners to bring back the Eagle's name, and that won't come easy. After the accident they swore they'd never field another contract as Swamp Eagle Security again. That's a vow they won't soon break, for you or anyone else."

Remington didn't miss a beat. "They're already onboard."

"What?" Taylor blinked.

"I met with them this morning before the ceremony. I told them of our plans moving forward, and how we mean to honor the Eagle's legacy as a cornerstone of those plans. They've agreed to participate on one condition." Remington aimed his glass at Taylor. "That you, and only you, lead them into the company's next era."

Taylor slouched back against the counter and rubbed his temples. He couldn't believe this. Gary, Leon, and Ed were like uncles to him, and why he could believe they'd make such a demand. At the same time, Taylor had never been a businessman—a wannabe merc and stargazer in his youth, maybe, but not a leader. He exhaled, searching for a reason to pass that sounded less cowardly. "Swamp Eagle Security sold off most of its assets when it was dissolved. The rest are in the North Florida History Museum in Tallahassee. That means we'd be startin' from scratch, so unless your employer's name is Dave Ramsey IV, you can expect to run out of capital by the end of week one."

Remington flashed a wry smile. "That won't be a problem."

"Really." Taylor chuckled. "And how is ole Dave these days?"

"My employer's name isn't Dave," Remington said. "It's Daryl. Daryl Dominic."

Taylor could've used a crane to haul his jaw off the floor. *Holy shit.*

Daryl Dominic was the owner of MCA Creative, the multi-billion-dollar tech firm based in Atlanta, Georgia. The "A" in the name stood for Apple, as in one of the myriad companies MC had absorbed during the late-21st century in route to dominating the American tech landscape.

On a related note, if Taylor had any lingering doubts about the legitimacy of Remington's offer, they'd just vanished like a fart in a nor'easter.

"Well?" Remington knit his arms. "What do you say?"

Taylor's head swam with questions. However one in particular rose above them all. "Why me?"

Remington glanced from side to side. "As I said, your brother's partners—"

"I know why they want me," Taylor said. "At least, I think I do. But why would Mr. Dominic? I'm sure he's got a laundry list of candidates who'd be way more qualified to run this company than me. I mean, look at me." He gestured to his surroundings. "I tend bar, for cryin' out loud. What do I know about bein' a merc?"

Remington's expression turned lopsided. "You mean aside from the fact that you were practically raised by them?"

"You know what I mean," Taylor said.

Remington bellowed a sigh. "You sell yourself short, Taylor. I've seen your VOWs scores. Six years ago, the Duval Public School System graduated forty-eight thousand seniors. Of those, thirty-two thousand took the VOWs to become mercenaries." He leaned in. "You ranked twenty-fifth among them, eleventh among those pursuing an MOS as a CASPer pilot. Even your brother didn't test that high."

Taylor threw up his hands. "So I'm decent in a simulator. Big deal! That still don't qualify me to run an outfit!"

Remington wasn't convinced. "Make all the excuses you like, mate, but you and I both know you were born to do this. It's in your blood. As for your lack of business acumen, there's no worries there, either. We'll surround you with the best and brightest to help you make sound decisions until you're comfortable making them on your own. Frankly, that's just good leadership."

Taylor stroked his whiskers and wished like crazy this had come eight years ago. Like most kids of his generation, he'd dreamed of piloting a CASPer from the time he'd been big enough to clutch one of their toy figurines. He'd loved those machines, and studied everything about them through grade school: their operations, ordnance, and performance records. He'd even done a project on the history of their various models while in junior high. But then had come Terry's accident, and with it their mother's decree that none of her other children would ever follow him into the mercenary trade. The angry 16-year-old Taylor had hated her for that, for depriving him of his dream. Deep down, though, he'd understood why she'd felt that way. That's why nowadays he served drinks to mercs instead of fighting alongside them.

"I'm sorry, Mr. Remington." Taylor held his eyes on the floor. "I appreciate the kind words. Really, I do. And in another life, I'd have taken your offer 10 minutes ago. Unfortunately, this ain't that life, and I must respectfully decline."

Remington drummed his fingers on the edge of the bar. "You mentioned my employer's reputation for luring talent earlier. Well, if you know him, then you also know his reputation for something else: philanthropy. Swamp Eagle Security left a mark on this city—on the

American South, for that matter—that will never be forgotten. At a time when outsiders came from as far out as Great Britain to seize on Floridian promise, here were five men who rose from these very swamps to conquer the world and build lives for themselves that few can even imagine. Yet no matter the heights they soared to nor the money they made, the Eagles never lost sight of those roots. Anyone who doubts that need only look to their leader for assurance."

Taylor smiled at the memory.

"Terry was the quintessential Southern Man," Remington said. "Fiery, charismatic, sometimes even brash, but driven as hell and loyal as a hound to anyone he called friend. These were the traits that defined him and his company, be that in the hell fires of an alien battlefield or a pep rally in his high school gymnasium. Terry's only flaw, as far as I can see, was his inability to care for his own interests with the same fervor he cared for those of others."

On that, Remington had a point. For all his savvy as an entrepreneur, Terry had made one critical error: he'd neglected to leave a proper will in the event of his passing. Taylor had cursed his brother for that, especially when they'd lost the house. *Still, how many single guys with no kids worry about wills at age twenty-nine?*

"You asked why Mr. Dominic wants you for this position," Remington said. "Well, if I had to guess I'd say it's because he knows what I learned when I started digging into you. There are others who could lead Swamp Eagle Security. But in the end, you're the only one who should."

Taylor held there, speechless.

"All right then." The redhead glanced at his watch. "I really must be going."

384 | KENNEDY & WANDREY

"Whoa, what?" Taylor piped up. "You sure I can't get you another drink? It's on the house."

Remington shook his head and fished out a business card, laying it on the bar. "I'm staying at the Duke's Club near Sawgrass until the morning. That's when my flight leaves for New Orleans. You should know that while your brother's company is Mr. Dominic's first choice for this venture, there are others, as well as a timetable we must adhere to. I'd therefore urge you to make your decision quickly." He tapped the card for emphasis. "Fate has dealt you an opportunity to change your future forever, mate. I suppose the only question now is, do you have the intestinal fortitude to take it?" And with that, the stranger strolled from the room with the same careless ease he'd entered with.

Taylor stood motionless for a long moment, head spinning like a top with all that'd been said. There was so much to consider, from his brother's legacy to the promise he'd made his mother in the wake of Terry's accident. There was also her health to factor in, plus the mountain of medical debt that was already threatening to overwhelm their finances.

Finally, Taylor's thoughts turned to the resident superhero of his life. *Rita.* She deserved so very much more than she had. And yet no matter how bad things had gotten, she'd never once complained. Not one time. She just sucked it up and soldiered on, because that's what heroes do. Still, even heroes have their limits, and at the rate Rita was going—three jobs plus her role as their mother's primary caregiver—Taylor knew it was only a matter of time before she burned out.

Something had to change.

"Yo, hillbilly!" a voice called.

Taylor turned to see Rex standing in the doorframe to The Hell House's corner office.

"You got a call," the metal-head said.

Now what? Heaving a sigh, Taylor headed for the space and waited for his co-worker to take his leave. Once Rex had gone, he closed the door for privacy and placed a thumb to the aging comm's *respond* key.

"Van Zant here."

# # # # #

Go For Bait
by Troy Carrol Bucher

"This is Cochkala shit, Chief," the young, female noncom's voice rang in Mackey's earpiece. "Guarding an underground maglev station on some backwater, crap-smelling farm planet."

The transport door opened, and Mackey squinted against the harsh sunlight of a 48-degree Celsius day on Geomide II. It was less than an hour until full dark, and the air still felt like the inside of an exhaust port. At least it would be dark soon, and they would get a little respite from the heat.

Mackey jumped down from the back of the transport into 10 centimeters of powdery soil the consistency of volcanic ash. Behind him, three squads piled out, sending up clouds of dust that would wreak havoc on the platoon's equipment. The dust had an acrid, metallic smell similar to copper. It tasted worse. Mackey unlatched his vapor mask and spit, but it did little to remove the gritty film already coating his teeth and tongue.

"Why do we get all the shit jobs?" the female noncom asked.

Mackey could correct Thavy for her attitude, but decided against it. She was young for a squad leader and hot tempered. If he reprimanded her, she'd only bottle it up until she exploded on her soldiers later. Might as well let her vent what the rest of the platoon was thinking. Soldiers have always been the same. They don't care if you have the ability to change things, only that you acknowledge their complaints. Besides, she was the only one pinned in the platoon, and it was never a good idea to piss off the communications specialist, especially when she was the one pinlinked to your recon drones.

Mara, the Third Squad leader, was the last soldier to exit the transport. "Would you look at this place?"

For endless kilometers in every direction, the fields around them were littered with scattered and broken pod shells left behind by harvester machines. The broken shells were thicker than Mackey's thigh, and more than a few were the size of the transport. In the distance, four-hundred-ton harvesters inched their way across the horizon, sucking up soil and shattering the massive pods to get at the crystalized murculite inside. Behind each, ejected soil and shell fragments swirled with the power of an F5 tornado. The only manmade structures visible in any direction, besides the entrance to the transfer station where they'd landed, were the scattered dumpchutes the harvesters used to drop their cargo onto underground conveyors.

"LT says this mission is important to our contract, so we do it." He pointed up. "What's the PRD show?"

Thavy flicked down the SyncSlate embedded in the front of her combat armor. The screen lit up with an aerial view from the platoon reconnaissance drone two kilometers overhead. She cycled through sensors—thermal, infrared, movement tracking, k- and x-band, ultraviolet, hydrometric—without touching a button. The display was all for him. Thavy had no need of the slate. She processed the images raw through her pinplants.

"All clear, Chief."

"And the AMWARN?"

On screen, he could see her run a diagnostic on the system. It lit up green. The AMWARN would give them five or six seconds' warning prior to incoming artillery or missiles. The insurgents didn't have any missiles as far as Mackey knew, but he wasn't taking any chances.

Satisfied with their systems, Mackey moved to the maintenance entrance for the transfer station. The door was only half a meter tall. The indigenous population were short, furred, and sported long flat front teeth—sort of like walking rodents without the ears or tails. Shaking hands with one of their long-clawed employers had been like shaking hands with a large, exotic pet. Mackey shook his head. This place must have had one hell of a strange ecosystem for them to wind up on top of the food chain. But as long as they paid, who was he to judge? Legionaries Inc. certainly didn't care.

He wiped dust from a keypad next to the door and punched in a code. It beeped at him, but the door didn't move. He frowned and punched it again. Nothing happened. "Friggin locals. Useless," he mumbled. He wrapped his knuckles on the door. The muted thud told him they weren't going to force it open. That changed things. LT wanted a squad belowground guarding the transfer station.

Mackey backed up and looked toward the top of the structure. About 30 meters wide and 10 tall, the fibercrete walls of the facility rose up like a round culvert stood on its end. The top was capped, and the small door was the only blemish on the smooth surface. Stenciled above the door was the number 17. He flipped his com switch so the whole platoon could hear him speak. "All the drop-chutes you see lead to a transfer station below us where the murculite gets dumped into maglev cars. From here, it runs to a refinement center on the coast. Intel says the rebels plan on hitting it tonight. If they destroy the transfer station, they shut down the whole region."

"If it's so important, why isn't the LT here?" Mara asked.

"Shut it, Mara." While Mackey believed in the age-old soldier mantra of reward in public, chastise in private, Mara was more experienced and knew better than to mouth off on the platoon net. He was also good enough to get his own platoon if he'd just learn to shut up and color when told. "LT's at a briefing with the boss and the rest of the company officers. He'll be here with fourth squad when it's over."

Mara said something into his mic, but it wasn't on the platoon frequency. Several of his squad members laughed.

Mackey would have a little talk with Mara later. Right now, it was time for business. There was something about this place that had him on edge, although he couldn't have said what it was exactly. Glitches, like the door code not working, always came in threes, and when little things went wrong, big things tended to follow. "Change of plans. Thavy, your squad has the transport and the main gun. Taber, you have zero to one-eighty. Mara, you have the other side. Fifty meters out and dig in. Crew-served weapons set at cardinal directions. I want the second PRD up and circling 20 kays out." He thumbed toward the fibercrete structure. "And put a sniper team on top of that thing. We'll worry about getting inside when the LT shows up."

There were a few grumbles at the command to "dig in," but they would do it. They were professionals. While most company hires called themselves mercs, the Legionaries considered themselves soldiers—a class above the rest. For the most part, they were right.

Mackey pulled off his helmet and ran a hand over his close-cropped, gray hair. His hand came away gritty and wet with sweat. Beside him, Thavy threw a pack down and dug around for something. She had a jagged scar running from her temple, across her left eye, and over the bridge of her nose. The eye had been replaced with an implant, and she'd gone with one that made no attempt to hide the loss. It looked like someone shoved a crude, chrome-ringed camera lens into the socket. This close to her, he could hear it whir and click as it zoomed in and out.

Behind Thavy, her squad prepped the transport for combat support, opening ports on each side and mounting weapons. The transport didn't have the armor to make it a true armored personnel carrier, it was really more of a souped-up flyer, but it sported plates thick enough to stop the local projectile weapons. It also had a 20mm magnetic accelerator cannon that would level any platform the insurgents could muster against them. At least that's what the Trade Guild intel said in the contract.

So why did he feel like a cat in a room full of rocking chairs? After the three-jump trip to Geomide in cramped quarters, maybe it was simply the wide-open space that gave him the heebie-jeebies. Still, he would've felt more relaxed with a few CASPers to augment the platoon. Unfortunately, the company didn't have the resources to waste CASPers on guard duty.

Thavy found what she was looking for and pulled out a water pouch. "Hydrate or die, Chief," she said and winked with her good eye, making light of the company motto *Pugna eul Morietur*—Latin for *Fight or Die*. She pulled out a second water pouch for him.

It bothered the others when she winked like that—it made her look inhuman—but not Mackey. All he cared about was that she was good at her job, and she was tops.

He wiped the sweat from his hand onto his combat armor, leaving a grimy streak, and took the pouch from Thavy. She was all smiles and dimples under a face full of freckles. If it weren't for the scar and the eye, she'd be the sweetest, most innocent-looking killer you'd ever meet.

He held the water pouch up in a mock toast. "Hydrate or die, it is."

* * *

The blare of the AMWARN startled Mackey. He leapt up from where he dozed against the fibercrete—exactly the opposite of hitting the dirt like a good soldier should when under artillery or missile attack—and flipped his goggles to night vision. A blinking icon told him the direction of the single incoming projectile.

"I'm on it, Chief," Thavy called out over the com.

A missile streaked up from the transport, quickly followed by a second. The counter-missile missiles were small, but the flare still turned Mackey's vision white.

"Intercept in three...two...damn. Countermeasures. Changing the second CMM to k-band. Locked...and...impact." There was an explosion a thousand meters or so out. "Take that, polla-fucker!"

"What'd they send at us?" He had no idea what a polla was, but he didn't ask.

"Hell if I know, Chief. Some kind of advanced missile. Thought you said these rebels only had projectile weapons."

The return of the AMWARN cut off his response.

"Two more inbound. Launching CMMs."

Again his vision flared white as, one after another, four more CMMs streaked off toward the incoming missiles.

"K-band is jammed. Let's try...got you."

There was a detonation in the distance, closer than the last one.

"Better hide your asses. The second one's going to be close," Thavy said over the net.

Mackey knelt low to the ground. Around him soldiers disappeared into fighting positions like frightened groundhogs scurrying back into their dens. Two more CMMs streaked away from the transport.

There was an eerie moment of quite before an explosion blossomed no more than a hundred meters away.

"Hope they don't have too many more of those babies. You'd think—"

"Cut the chatter." The transport had a basic load of twenty CMMs, normally enough to protect it from a few missiles while the pilot hunted and killed whoever launched them. That meant only twelve left. "Do you have a fix on the shooter?"

"Negative, Chief. Missiles came out of thin air at Mach 2. I don't read anything other than the harvesters moving out there. Either they've got a soft launch system and they're hiding, or they're using a platform with ghosting equipment more sophisticated than our sensors."

Mackey flipped down his own SyncSlate and pulled off his goggles. "Give me the harvesters and the missile tracks. Play it through from the first missile." A few seconds later, Mackey frowned.

"Looks like they're using the harvesters to mask the launch."

That wasn't quite right. "Maybe...look up instead of at the ground. Zoom to max width." Aside from more harvesters, the slate remained blank. He looked at the time. It was near mid-night on a planet with a twenty-seven-point-four hour rotation.

"That's out to a hundred kays, Chief. According to both the PRD and the transport's LIDAR, there's nothing flying out there."

"Have you sent up a situation report?"

"Yeah, I sent a sitrep about point-three seconds after the attack." He could hear irritation in her voice. She was impatient with those who weren't pinned. "No response from Lieutenant Shale or Ops."

Of course the comms would be out—glitch number two. "What's the LT's ETA?"

"Her pilot pinged me when they launched. ETA of zero-one-thirty, so ninety-four minutes out."

Mackey did the math in his head. "We'll be able to pick her up with sensors in sixty minutes."

"Sixty-four-point three, to be exact."

Two clocks appeared on Mackey's slate—one for the LT's time to sensor range and one for time to arrival.

"Keep pinging the LT and Ops. Let me know when either one responds."

"Yes, Chief."

Mackey switched over to the platoon net.

"Listen up. LT and fourth squad are about ninety minutes out. Kill the rest plan. Everyone stays on full alert 'til she arrives. Intel said these rebels used only civilian flyers and projectile weapons. Looks like intel was wrong. Nothing new there. I would love to use the transport to go H&K whoever launched those missiles, but I'm not moving our only protection away from this facility. I've a feeling we're going to need it again before the LT gets here. Thavy, send the second PRD out around those harvesters. Put a 20mm round through anything that moves."

Each of the three squad leaders acknowledged his orders. Damn, he hated being on the defense. It gave all the advantages to whoever was out there in the dark.

* * *

Sixty-six minutes and two missile attacks later, neither the LT nor Ops had responded. Nothing showed on the sensors.

"LT could be out there, Chief. There's a lot of interference from the dust."

She was grasping at straws. He had a hunch things were about to go south.

Mackey flipped down his slate. "Pull up the first missile tracks again and overlay the next two attacks."

Mara walked up next to him. "What are you looking for, Chief?"

"I don't know. Seven missiles, with no trace of who or what launched them. Doesn't make sense." Mackey scratched his chin. "Color code the three attacks and show where the harvesters were located during each."

"What about the dropchutes? Could they be using those to hide?" Mara asked.

"Not inside." Thavy said. "I'm tapped into the local maintenance net. None of the dropchutes have been tampered with."

"Give me a 200-meter ring around where each of the missiles showed up." Glowing rings formed an arc to the northwest. Two of the rings included dropchutes, but the other five did not. Four came from behind harvesters, but three were not within five kays of one. The only similarity was altitude—each of the missiles was picked up at just over 40 meters above the ground—but that still didn't tell him if they were ground- or air-launched. A good soft-launch system would float a missile out over 100 meters before the main engine ignited in order to prevent counter-fire from coming back down the shooter's throat.

"They all came from the northwest," Mara said. "We could fly the transport out that way and try to find them before they launch again. With only four CMMs remaining, we're going to run out of indirect protection here anyway, and I wouldn't want to fly out there with zero counter-missiles. Might as well paint a big bull's eye on the transport and broadcast 'shoot me I'm defenseless' in the clear if you do that."

"Thavy, what will one of those incoming missiles do to the maintenance facility?" Mackey asked.

"I've looked at the schematics. Not much. Blow a big hole in the fibercrete, but they could topple the whole structure, and it wouldn't interfere with the maglev station. The generators and cars are too far down."

Mackey was reluctant to send out the transport. Aside from the four CMMs remaining, the 20mm main gun was their only real defense if the rebels had any more surprises. On the other hand, if he could kill whoever was launching the missiles, it might get inside the enemy's decision cycle and halt any plans to attack the station.

"Fuck it." He snapped the SyncSlate closed. The LT wasn't here to make the call. "Thavy, go find and kill those bastards would you?" It was better to go on the offense than sit and wait for more missiles to rain down on their heads.

"Fight or die, Chief!" The transport's semi-enclosed rotary blades spun up, filling the air with dust.

"And Thavy..."

"Yes, Chief?"

"Don't lose the transport. It's a long walk back to the capitol."

"Yes, Chief."

"What about me?" Mara asked.

"You and I, along with the rest of the platoon, are going to dig our fighting positions a little bit deeper."

* * *

A missile screamed over Mackey's head and exploded in the dirt 20 meters behind him. The ground heaved, and the concussion knocked him against the wall of his fighting position. Dirt splashed over him like an ocean wave, and dust blanketed him in a heavy fog. Even with his earpieces filtering out most of the sound, his ears still rang.

The ground shook with another explosion further away and again when a third hit somewhere between the first and second. The AM-WARN alert tone ceased.

Mackey coughed and waved his arms, trying to clear the air. "Casualties?" He asked on the command net.

"None in Third."

"One in Second," Taber said. "Direct hit on Damon's position. Doesn't look like there's much left—just a crater."

Mackey tried to picture Damon in his head. He was one of the new guys. The one with a mustache and narrow eyes. This was his first contract out of the mercenary service track, or MST, if Mackey had it right. It shamed him that he wasn't certain. It was his job to know everyone in the platoon like he knew his own mother. He pushed the feeling away. There would be plenty of time to beat himself up about it later.

"Well, at least they're using rockets and not missiles," Mara said, stating the obvious. "Crater analysis says 150 millimeter."

Mara was correct. Missiles locked on a target. Rockets were precision guided to a location, and one-fifties made a big hole when they got there.

"They're shooting blind. Picking spots at random around the station in the hopes of reducing our numbers." Mackey changed his comms to a direct feed to Thavy. "It would be real nice if you found whoever is shooting at us."

"I'm trying, Chief. I'm already at the launch point for the last salvo and there's not a damned thing here. Just dirt piles and pod fragments."

"Well something's out there."

"Chief, I'm using every sensor I've got. They're all empty."

"Then quit relying on the sensors and use that one good eye of yours to look." Mackey switched to the platoon frequency. Before he could speak, the blare of the AMWARN kicked in again. He dropped down low. The HUD in his goggles told him three more rockets were inbound.

"Man, I'm going to seriously fuck up some rodents for this!"

"Ya. Fuck those little, buck-toothed gopher-looking bastards."

There was laughter on the net. Mackey needed to shut that down. It was never good to use slurs for your employer's race, even when their rebellious cousins were trying to kill you. Once an offensive nickname stuck with soldiers, stopping it would be like putting milk back into a cow, and that wouldn't be fun for either side involved. Let them run with the name, and it would only be a matter of time before someone used the term at the wrong moment. It didn't help that the soldier was right. The locals did kind of look like gophers.

The first rocket hit. The concussion felt like a hammer slamming into every part of Mackey's body. One moment, he was looking up at the stars, and the next, all was black. A giant was standing on top of his chest. He couldn't move his arms or legs. Angry bees filled his ears, and he couldn't breathe. He twisted and turned, fighting against whatever held him.

Slowly the bees became words. "Chief!" Mara yelled over the net. "Chief!"

Mackey forced himself to calm down. "I'm...alive," he croaked through a mouthful of dirt.

"We're coming for you."

He heard scratching above him for a long agonizing minute before rough hands dragged him out of the ground and pulled him to his feet. He doubled over coughing. Someone shoved a water pouch at him, and he used it to rinse his mouth and flush out his goggles.

A blackened crater was carved out of the ground next to them. Flames danced at the bottom of the depression. Little remained to mark his fighting position. Mara and another soldier stood to either side of him, holding him up by his body armor.

"Thought those fucking gophers took you out, Chief." Mara said.

Mackey shook his helmet out. "If you'd dug any slower, they might have, and don't call them..." Mackey froze. Furred bodies. Long, flat teeth. Clawed hands. "...gophers. Well, fuck me."

"What is it?" Mara asked.

Mackey ignored him. "Thavy, you there?"

"Roger, Chief. Moving to the launch point of the last salvo. About five kays from it."

"Thavy, what do you have that'll let us see movement underground."

"Underground, Chief?"

"Yes. Underground."

"I suppose I could reconfigure the x-band. There isn't a lot of power on the PRDs, so it will only reach a couple meters in depth, and there'll be a lot of holes. It won't see through all those pod shells."

"Do it, and send the results to my screen." Mackey pulled down his SyncSlate. There was a crack down the right side, but it still lit up. Mara and the other soldier who'd helped dig him out huddled around it.

Onscreen Mackey could see icons for his personnel and the transport, along with range rings around the PRDs. One of the two recon drones was straight above the platoon and the other shadowed the transport.

"Here goes, Chief. It's not going to give you much more than a kay or two radius."

At first nothing happened. Then, as the computer onboard the PRD began tagging movement, icon after icon populated on the screen. The area to the south of their location became a solid mass, with the leading edge no more than fifty meters away from their positions. To the north, near the transport, sporadic icons popped onto the screen.

"Holy shit!" Mara said.

Mackey looked up from the slate. Through his night vision goggles, the fields to the south were empty. He had no idea how close the little bastards would come before they attacked, but he was sure there wasn't much time. Any minute now, they'd be overwhelmed by a thousand rebels popping up out of the dirt, or even worse, they'd dig right into the fighting positions. Mackey had their defense set all wrong. "Everyone out of their holes, now!" he yelled over the platoon net.

"What do we do, Chief?" Mara asked.

Mackey took a long look around them. Setting up an ambush for child-sized gophers wasn't exactly something they taught during MST. He looked at the pod shells and the maintenance facility. There were very few options. He flipped back to the command net.

"Taber, split your squad east and west of the building. Get people up onto the biggest pod shells they can find. Crew served on the flanks. I want them ready to lay grazing fire across our front along a final protective line. They'd better be prepared to protect our rear as well."

"Moving, Chief."

"Mara, get your squad on the roof."

Mara nodded and began shouting orders.

Mackey glanced at the time on his display. It read zero-one-twenty-six. "Thavy, start killing those launchers. If I were a betting man, I'd say there was going to be one final artillery prep before they attack. You've got about four minutes to kill as many as you can before it happens."

In the distance, he heard the boom of a 20mm projectile going supersonic.

"Was only waiting for the order, Chief. Just smoked the first one. Twenty-three more to go."

That girl will make one hell of a chief someday...if she didn't get hired as a platoon leader first. Mackey smiled as another thought came to him. "Taber," he called over the net.

"Yes, Chief."

"How many trip wires do you have?"

* * *

Thavy didn't get all the launchers. Whether they were too far apart or some had remained still and gone undetected, it didn't matter. The moment Mackey's display hit zero-one-thirty, the AMWARN went off for what he hoped would be the final time. Eight red icons lit up the display in his goggles.

Mackey, lying flat on top of the maintenance facility with the rest of Third Squad, looked north. The display helped him locate the inbound rockets. The glowing pinpoints grew larger, coming straight for them. He was guessing the rebels wouldn't target the entrance to the maglev station, but his instincts still yelled at him to run like hell.

He forced himself to turn away. "Forget the rockets, watch the south," he told the platoon, as much to stop himself from worrying as focus the soldiers.

The incoming rockets pounded the ground north of the platoon's new formation in a staccato of deafening explosions that shook the building and rattled Mackey's teeth. He imagined what twenty or thirty of them would have done if they were still in their fighting positions. No doubt it would have been a sad-faced day for the visiting team.

The quiet stillness of the night returned, as if the darkness attempted to hide all trace of the destruction that had already occurred...or the carnage about to happen. To the south, there wasn't a hint of movement, but Mackey knew the enemy was there, clawing their way through the soil.

As he and the rest of the platoon waited, a dozen scenarios ran through his mind. What if they dug straight into the facility? He should have blown the door open and sent a squad down into the station. That was dumb. There was no way they could dig through the fibercrete, and the platoon was already shorthanded. What if the enemy came out behind them? "Stop it, Mackey," he told himself. This was the best course of action for the limited time available.

Still, it was hard to push the apprehension away. He always doubted himself in the silent moments before combat. There were some who loved to fight—who lived for the rush and the power. The wait turned people like that into coiled springs ready to unleash destruction. Not Mackey. He kept his emotions out of it. People who lived for a fight had a way of finding them a little too often for his taste, and at some point, the odds of survival always fell to zero. No. Mackey loved easy contracts, and he loved soldiers, and he loved being alive to spend his pay. It was those three things that made him a good chief. While he would always accomplish the mission, he would never waste a soldier's life, or his own for that matter, and he never took the missions personally.

An explosion at the southernmost fighting position batted the self-reflection from his thoughts. The positions to the left and right of the first flashed a moment later. "Surprise," Mackey whispered. He'd had Taber string tripwires attached to grenades inside those three. It wouldn't take out many, but it was certainly worth the effort...and it felt damned good. It was the little things that kept a person motivated.

Mackey flipped down the SyncSlate for a final glance. There were icons inside the original perimeter, closing fast on the building beneath them. He switched to the platoon net one last time. "Get ready people. Watch your sectors and conserve ammo. Remember, they don't have to kill us to win. Don't let any get inside the maglev station."

About 20 meters from the building, the icons halted. Mackey snatched one of the two grenades he carried from a side pouch and pulled the pin. "It's about that time ladies and gentlemen. Fight or die, people. Fight or die."

"Fight or die, Chief!" echoed across the net.

In front of the platoon, sinkholes formed. Each reminded Mackey of sand emptying from the top of an hourglass, counting down the seconds. They were short timers, because in less than a minute, the area was littered with gaping holes. Men and women around Mackey hunched over their rifles, eyes pressed to thermal sights. Mackey cocked his arm back, ready to throw.

There was no audible signal. One moment a dirty, furred and goggled face appeared in one of the holes. The next, more than a hundred rebels leapt out of the ground yelling and spraying automatic fire.

"Big mistake." Mackey threw the grenade he held and drew his pistol as Second and Third Squads opened up, mowing down the lead rebels. Even with the deafening sound of both sides firing, Mackey heard projectiles smack the fibercrete beneath him and whiz overhead.

Explosions dotted the enemy's front ranks as his and a dozen other grenades detonated—he hadn't been the only one ready to throw when the rebels appeared. To his left, a man screamed as a projectile found a seam in his combat armor. Mackey ignored the soldier and calmly blew a hole through the forehead of a rebel with a two-millimeter, depleted uranium round traveling at a hair over 1,500 meters per second. He looked for another target.

A rebel leapt forward. In his clawed hand he held a heavy satchel. Mackey put two rounds through his chest plate before the rebel pitched forward and dropped it. The depleted uranium rounds the Legionaries used were expensive as hell, but they were very effective against all but the best combat armor.

A second rebel picked up the satchel and advanced.

The unmistakable hammering of a crew-served weapon came from Mackey's left. Eight-millimeter rounds at grazing-fire height raked along the enemy's front. Against humans, it would have cut the legs out from under them. Against the short-statured natives, it tore heads from shoulders. The rebel with the satchel lost half his face. He stood confused for a moment before toppling over—sometimes it took the body a moment to realize it was dead.

The platoon continued to pour depleted uranium rounds into the onslaught, and the bodies stacked up. The second wave used the first for cover, but it did them little good. Rounds punched through the dead to reach the living. Still they kept coming.

Mackey continued to fire into the mass. Another rebel reached the satchel and hurled it as he died. It cartwheeled through the air and disappeared beneath Mackey's sight. An explosion rocked the building, and Mackey found himself sliding forward and down as the front of the maintenance facility collapsed. He hurled himself forward and rolled when he hit the ground. Hulking sections of fibercrete tumbled around him.

The destruction wasn't limited to the building. The front ranks of the rebels were scattered by the blast. A weaponless rebel with his fur on fire materialized in front of Mackey. The creature screeched and slapped at the flames before disappearing into the billowing smoke and dust. For a brief moment the pungent smell of burning hair and flesh overpowered the metallic smell of the soil in Mackey's nose.

"Don't let them in the building!" he shouted into the net. Around him, deadly projectiles ricocheted from the fibercrete. Several bounced off his combat armor, and one tore painfully through the joint of his wrist. He needed to get to cover before the enemy reorganized. Mackey scrabbled back, climbing the rubble. He reached out for a broken chunk of fibercrete to pull himself up and realized he was holding the protruding leg of a soldier buried in the wreckage.

Suddenly Mara was next to him, skating down the debris and firing his rifle on automatic to cover Mackey's retreat. Together they worked their way to the top of the rubble and dove down the back side into the remains of the maintenance facility. Tool bins and lockers lay toppled and burning. A broken winch swung loosely above a wide, square hole with a ladder leading down to the maglev station. Fully a third of the structure had collapsed, leaving a 20-meter gap on the south side of the circular building.

The remains of Third Squad were positioned behind the rubble in the breach. Mackey climbed next to one of the soldiers, but he'd lost his pistol in the fall. Somebody shoved a rifle at him. Mara took up a position on the left side, using the wall for cover. To his right, two soldiers struggled to get a crew-served up and firing.

"SITREPs," Mackey yelled.

Thavy was first on the net. "I'm a few minutes out, Chief. The last of the rocket launchers are bugging out to the north."

"This is Gooden. Taber is down. Second squad's at sixty percent. Both heavy-weapons are operational, but they're already amber on ammo. The enemy is still pouring out of those holes."

"Third is at fifty," Mara said. "I lost three men and one crew-served in the blast. Two others are wounded, and I've got two on the roof. I can't see shit through the dust."

"Roger all," Mackey said. "We hold until Thavy arrives with First Squad. Thavy, drop your squad to the east in order to flank them and then close those holes with the 20mm."

"Get ready to have guests, Chief," Gooden said. "The heavies need to reload."

First one and then the other of Second Squad's crew-served weapons cut out. Mackey pushed himself up onto his elbows. His wrist and hand were numb, but his fingers still worked—sort of. Awkwardly, he checked the magazine, and sighted down the rifle. The thermal sight was broken, but at close range he wouldn't need it. He fumbled the sight free and tossed it aside, leaving streaks of blood wherever his injured hand went.

Out of the dust, the enemy came at them with feral determination. Mackey pulled the trigger again and again, firing two-round bursts that cut through armor and bodies. There was no shortage of targets. Bullets pummeled his position as the rebels gained ground in front of him. Mara's remaining crew-served weapon thundered next to him, the sound deafening in the semi-enclosed space. It was simple math. The enemy was fighting bullets with bodies, and it would continue until one side or the other ran out.

As if prophesying the final results, Mackey's weapon clicked empty. He slid back and searched for another magazine.

"Here, Chief," a soldier yelled and threw one toward him.

He missed the catch with his bad hand, and it tumbled away and down the pile of debris. "Mother fucker!" he shouted and worked his way to where it landed. The fumble saved his life.

An explosion knocked Mackey off his feet just as he slammed the magazine in place. The soldier who'd thrown him the magazine landed next him and didn't move. Somebody on the other side wasn't playing nice. Mackey rolled to face the top of the rubble. He put a round through the eye of the first fur-covered rebel brave enough to clear the top. Around him, the remains of Third fell back to positions behind tool bins and lockers. Mackey had maybe half a magazine and one grenade left. The others couldn't be doing much better. They would never hold like this.

"Mara, get ready to send your men below." Mackey pointed at the ladder leading down to the transfer station. "We need to buy a few seconds to get down the rabbit hole. If anyone else has a grenade left, get ready to use it in front of the breach. Thavy, disregard your last order. Once we are clear, get around to the south and clear these fuckers off of us. Gooden, get anyone close to the building out of the way before she gets here."

Mackey yanked his remaining grenade free and pulled the pin. "Now!" he called over the net and threw the grenade. It arched over the rubble and disappeared. Three more sailed with it. He didn't wait for an explosion. He ran for the gaping, square hole in the center of the room. A soldier swung over the fibercrete lip in front of him and disappeared. He was followed by a second. Mackey had his weapon ready to cover their escape, but the enemy hadn't reorganized yet. A soldier jumped down from the roof and landed next him. An instant later, he too disappeared down the hole. In seconds, only Mackey and Mara remained.

"You're first," Mackey said.

Thankfully, Mara didn't have time to play brave and argue. Any moment, the little bastards would be on them. Mara slung his weapon and swung himself over the edge, sliding away into the darkness fireman style with his hands on each side of the ladder.

Mackey tried to close his injured hand. It didn't work, and there was no time to use the nanite spray in his medkit. It would be difficult getting down the ladder, and it wouldn't be fast. That was why he'd sent Mara first. He started to sling his weapon, but it was too late. A host of rebels cleared the top of the rubble. Mackey dove behind the fibercrete lip surrounding the hole as a hail of bullets peppered his combat armor. He was lucky none of them found a seam between the plates, but that didn't mean there was no pain involved. Every impact to his armor felt like a mule kick. He would be sore for days, but for now, adrenaline let him ignore the pain.

He twisted the selector switch on his weapon to automatic. There was only one way out of this, and he had no idea whether or not he would survive the fall. He took a deep breath, preparing to jump, and came up firing. He swept the weapon back and forth without aiming. The closest rebels fell screaming.

A bullet skimmed the top of his helmet, snapping his head back until he found himself looking at half a ceiling and the broken winch. A hook swung lazily back and forth from the winch cable. "Worth a shot," he said to himself. He fired the last of his ammo at a pair of rebels. One dove safely away. The other was punched from his feet.

Mackey dropped the rifle and jumped for the cable. His good hand closed over the hook. The cable unwound, and he dropped like a stone down the shaft. "Thavy, we are clear!" he yelled, wondering if the words would be his last—he had no idea how far down it was to the transfer station.

There was a whining screech of metal above him and his descent slowed before jerking to a halt. The snap of the cable slammed him into the hard fibercrete wall. He tried to hold on, but mass, speed, and blunt trauma won out over the strength in his hand. He tumbled down the hole. He had a quick glimpse of a polished floor rising to meet him. This was not the way he'd expected to die.

Instead of a hard, metal floor, he slammed face-first into painfully hot water. The surprise nearly tore the breath from his lungs, and the weight of his armor pulled him rapidly to the bottom. He flailed his arms around for anything he could use and felt something long and thin. He pulled himself toward it and found himself holding the frame of a ladder. His lungs burned, and panic threatened to overwhelm him, but rung-by-rung he climbed until, at last, his head broke the surface. Gasping and coughing, he hugged the ladder tight and rested his head against the wall. A loud hum filled his ears, and it took him a moment to realize the sound wasn't coming from a shorted out com system.

"Give me your hand!" Mara yelled over the hum.

Mackey reached up without looking, and for the third time of the night, Mara pulled him to safety. They were at the end of a long, wide tunnel with a walkway along one side and a drop down into the water on the other. Dim lights ran along the length of the ceiling, leading the way toward where the maglev station must be located. If he'd fallen any closer to this side, he would have broken his neck hitting the walkway. As it was, he'd landed in the large cistern of water used to cool the maglev generators. Those generators explained the hum.

Next to him Mara peered back up the shaft. The other three soldiers who'd made it down before them were well behind him, making their way down the tunnel.

"We need to move," Mara yelled over the hum. "They are climbing down. We need to find a better spot to hold them off, but first you need a weapon." He fired off a burst of rounds up into the darkness and stepped back.

Projectiles rained back down.

Mackey slid a little farther out of the way and climbed to his feet.

When the rounds stopped, Mara leaned forward and did it again. His effort was rewarded with a scream followed by a rebel tumbling out of the hole. There was a loud crack when it hit the walkway.

Mackey shivered. A half-meter difference in his fall, and that would have been him.

Mara eased himself close to the dead rebel while keeping an eye up above him. He grabbed the body by the ankle and dragged it clear. It wore a small suit of combat armor that only covered the torso—more like a vest with plates—and a short chemical rifle was slung over its back. Mara stripped it away, along with the bandolier of magazines clipped to the vest. He passed them to Mackey.

Mackey turned the weapon over in his hands. It was a simple thing, with a short heavy barrel and iron sights. There was a switch he assumed was for safe and fire, and a single button for releasing the magazine. He had to take his armored glove off to fit his finger in the trigger housing. Holding it up to his shoulder it felt like a toy. He pulled the trigger and automatic fire stitched a path along the water where he aimed. A very deadly toy.

He nodded to Mara. "Let's move out."

The five of them moved quickly along the walkway, passing pipes and grates that offered little cover. The air grew hotter, and the hum grew louder the further they went. The water beside them now churned and bubbled, and steam rose in wisps from its surface. Mackey's goggles fogged up, forcing him to pull them up onto his helmet in order to see. After they had gone no more than 100 meters, the cistern and walkway ended. Stairs led down into a large room filled with twisting pipes, cables, and machinery. They had reached the maglev generators.

A thundering crash came from somewhere in front of them. Mara and his men dove for cover. Mackey cocked his head, listening to the sound. The crashing noise faded away. He laughed when he realized where it came from. "It's the merculite being dumped into a maglev car. Our enemy is that way." He yelled over the hum and pointed back down the tunnel. "We have to hold them here."

Mackey went down the stairs and swung back around to a pipe at the base of the dammed-up end of the cistern. Climbing up, he could feel the water rushing through the hot pipe. Without armor, it would have burned him. Once on top, he had just enough height to fire back down the tunnel. The others spread out along the stairs, using the descent for cover, or climbed to the top of machinery to overwatch those on the stairs.

They didn't have to wait long. Muzzle flashes and tracer rounds lit up the dim tunnel, and projectiles chipped away at the walls and tore up the water in front of Mackey. The remains of Third Squad returned fire. The reverberating thunder pounded Mackey's eardrums, and the smell of chemical explosives filled the air. The tiny rifle bucked in his hands over and over as he targeted each of the muzzle flashes and then ducked to prevent return fire from taking his head off while he reloaded. He used up a second magazine in the same manner.

The madness continued around him, with both sides fighting relentlessly for a final victory, but there were lulls in the fighting. Short moments of quiet where the pace of the shooting slowed down to a trickle before picking back up to a roaring crescendo of gunfire. Mackey settled into a rhythm. Duck when it was the worst. Come up shooting when it tapered down. Duck again before return fire found his position.

One by one, Third Squad fell to the onslaught. A bullet found a seam on a soldier's armor, right above his chest and below the ring of plates that guarded his neck. Mackey saw him slump on the stairs, his life bleeding out and down the steps. Another took a round just below the visor on his helmet and above his goggles. He tumbled from the top of a maglev generator.

With no cover, the rebels fared worse. While the muzzle flashes grew closer, it seemed to Mackey there were far less than when they started. He slid down from his position and crouched against the cistern wall. The echo of gunfire slowed to halt until the only sound remaining was the hum of the generators.

"This is Chief, can anyone hear me?" he called into the mic. There was no reply. He wasn't even sure the damned thing was working after falling into the water. There were two bodies on the stairs. There was a body sprawled in front of a maglev generator. He couldn't be sure, but none of them looked like Mara. If the squad leader was alive, Mackey had no idea where he was located. He was alone, with who knew how many rebels left coming for him and the transfer station.

He popped in his final magazine and let the bolt go forward. "Fight or die, Chief," he said to himself. "Fight or die." Well, he wouldn't die here, huddled in a corner waiting for them to come. When in doubt, take the fight to the enemy. He took a deep breath and charged up the stairs.

Mackey had the small weapon up and ready to fire before his line of sight cleared the top step, and he was pulling the trigger before he even saw the cluster of a dozen or so rebels no more than ten meters down the walkway.

Surprisingly, Mackey noted, an "oh shit" face looked the same behind buckteeth and fur as it did on a human—eyes round and wide till the white is visible surrounding the whole cornea and the bottom jaw hanging slack and open. The lead rebel never had a chance to move, much less return fire. Mackey's first shots punched into its gut just below the chest plate. He didn't see the rebel fall. He was already swinging the barrel onto the next target. He put two rounds center mass of that one.

Mackey killed a third rebel before the remainder opened up on him. A slug smashed his torso armor, spinning him to the side and knocking the wind out of him. Another to his thigh armor nearly swept his leg out from under him. Still, he kept his weapon pointed forward and sprayed rounds into the tight formation. Two more rebels fell, only to be replaced by those behind them. A bullet hit Mackey in the center of his chest like a sledgehammer, knocking him backwards. It was only a matter of time before one of their rounds found a seam in his combat armor or smashed through his face. Mackey continued to fire. He would take as many rebels with him as he could before he ran out of ammo.

A calmness settled around Mackey as he resigned himself to his impending death, when suddenly, up out of the water of the cistern came Mara like a hero from one of the old 20th century action movies. He'd dumped his combat armor, so he even had the shirtless part right.

Caught off guard from their flank, the short-statured rebels tried to regroup, but it was too late. Mackey and Mara had them in a crossfire that sowed death into their formation. When Mackey ran out of ammo, he charged forward and swung the small, heavy rifle like a club, smashing the head of one of the short-statured rebels. He swung the rifle over and over again, breaking the bones of anything that moved. After a blurry moment of blood and anarchy, he found he was the only remaining combatant standing on the walkway.

He turned to thank Mara and recoiled at the sight of the soldier's skin. It was a deep red and covered with sagging blisters that draped down wherever Mackey looked. The heat of the water at this end of the cistern had cooked Mara like a well-boiled lobster back on earth. There wasn't enough nano-spray in the whole platoon to save the man. "Mara, I—"

"Save it, Chief. There's...nothing to say," Mara said between clenched teeth as the strength left him, and he slid back down into the water. He made a last effort to keep his head above the water.

His final words were barely audible over the hum. "Kill...the rest of these sons-a-bitche...for me." His head slipped under the boiling water, and he was gone, leaving Mackey alone in the tunnel.

Mackey threw the bloody rifle down and made his way back down the walkway and up the ladder. There were no rebels left alive to try and stop him.

* * *

The dropships' thrusters ignited, lifting the heavily-armored ships and the soldiers they carried toward orbit and a rendezvous with a guild transport ship. The contract was over. The rebellion was smashed; its leaders were dead. Only splinter cells remained, and those were not part of the contract's terms. All payments were complete and final.

Two soldiers remained behind to watch the dropships climb to the heavens. Mackey and Thavy had taken their payment in the form of one well-armored and well-equipped flyer. They had business to finish and new titles to go with it—"Heroes of Transfer Station 17."

"Now what, Chief?" Thavy asked. "Although the pay is better, I've no idea what the 'Senior Military Advisors to the Geomide Council' do exactly."

"It's simple, Thavy. We kill gophers."

"But only the bad ones, right?"

"Yes, all the bad ones—for Mara and the rest of the platoon."

# # # # #

The Kra'daar
by Chris Winder

Tou'Ka City, Planet Kra

Nik'Thil peered out the porthole of the shuttle as it approached the landing pad. His once-small village now extended further than he could see. His birth home, if it still existed, was hidden by a grotesque labyrinth of cylindrical and conical buildings that glimmered unnaturally in the bright sunlight.

The forest, as far as he could tell, appeared to be healthy and lush, but it had been pushed back several miles. He felt sick to his stomachs. This was the price of progress, he knew, but that didn't mean he had to accept it. Suddenly he became aware of his surroundings; something had yanked him out of his musings, and he turned his attention to it fully.

His olfactory glands detected something dangerous, something his species had, over millions of years of evolution, decided should be more important than anything else. He smelled smoke. A quick glance around him confirmed he was not imagining the odor. Several other Kra'daar onboard the shuttle were also looking around nervously. The other species, it seemed, either ignored their olfactory glands, or didn't possess them.

417

Two Kra'daar one row behind him and on the opposite side leaned toward a window and pointed with their long fingers at something outside. Their mocha-colored skin became lighter and mottled, the equivalent to blanching. Nik'Thil glanced out his porthole, but didn't see anything.

He erupted from his seat, stepped on several feet, tentacles, and talons, and apologized to their owners on his way to the center aisle. Then he apologized to the owners of other appendages and locomotion organs on the other side of the shuttle as he pressed his brown face to the opposite porthole.

Several dozen hover ships swarmed the area from which the smoke poured into the sky. The fire was not visible, but the evil, twisted finger of smoke and the lines of chemical fire retardant that streamed from the huge firefighting drones marked the beast.

The being closest to the window was a Cochkala, a mean, dangerous, badger-like species. It had finally had enough of the skinny, impolite, brown creature invading its personal space, and she had opened her mouth to, well, she hadn't exactly decided what she was going to do yet, but probably roar a warning to get off her. It was ugly, smelled badly, and obviously had to learn some manners. When she finally made up her mind, she opened her mouth, inhaled deeply...and nearly choked on her own saliva.

From the brown creature's neck hung a translation pendant, which was not uncommon for those who needed and could afford such a device. What was uncommon though, was the symbol that was inscribed on the back of it. Her eyes crossed, moved several directions at once searching for an escape route, and finally settled on the symbol again, disbelief temporarily turning her thoughts to a muddled mess of porridge. The symbol was easily recognized by all planetary members of the Galactic Union. It was the blue tree of an enforcer. The blue tree of the Peacemaker Guild.

It only took one more moment of consideration and decision-making for the Cochkala to decide she didn't actually mind someone leaning into her personal space so much. That was partly due to the fact that the smelly, brown creature was an enforcer. It was mostly due to the fact that this particular enforcer appeared to be very focused and upset by something outside.

Without turning her head, which might have attracted unwanted attention, she let her right eye drift as far as it could toward the porthole and saw what the enforcer was looking at. She looked, saw the smoke, and understood. Caution, uncommon for her species, turned out to be the best decision she'd ever made.

Nik'Thil took a moment longer at the porthole, allowing his eyes to completely absorb the sight before him. In the distance, he could make out at least two other spots, very close to the city of Ka'Arash, his home, which had been touched by fire. The forest had begun to reclaim the scorched land, but the blackened skeletons of trees seemed to tear at his soul and scream for justice.

He finally stood, apologized to the Cochkala for the intrusion into her personal space, which she didn't understand because she herself didn't possess a translation pendant, and picked his way past talons, tentacles, and feet back to his seat. Kra'daar didn't possess the physical ability to weep, but they could sulk, so that's what Nik'Thil did. He closed his eyes, sulked, and rubbed the top of his bald head in contemplation.

I am an enforcer, he thought. Emotions do not hold sway over me. I answer the cry of peace. I obey my oath. I desire only balance. I love only order.

He then became aware of a new scent. Apparently there was a Karr aboard, a species whose primary form of communication was pheromones. It was filling the cabin with the odor of fear. Probably inadvertently caused by me, he thought sourly. It was not Nik'Thil's intention to cause fear aboard the shuttle, but millions of years of evolution were difficult to overcome.

It took a lot of effort, but he was able to force himself to stop rubbing the top of his head and to relax. The fire was already burning, and there was nothing he could personally do about it. The fire-fighting drones were taking care of it, and the local government appeared to have enough to extinguish it before it grew too large. They had, after all, done this many times before, and far too frequently over the last few months. That's why Nik'Thil had returned. He had to discover the source of the fires and stop it.

* * *

The small, furred creature breathed deeply, pure ecstasy causing it to shudder with pleasure. The slight breeze had shifted enough to bring the wonderful, acrid smell to the tiny nose in the center of its nearly featureless, black face.

Though it could not see the effects of its creation, it could smell them. The odor was intoxicating, and based on the number of beings running, flying, walking, crawling, and otherwise moving upwind, its creation was appreciated...again.

It felt satisfaction. On its home planet, no such feelings were available. There was only fear, hunger, and greedy anticipation of what the next day might bring. The sparse landscape of crags, rocks, and the occasional crystalline plant hid dangers not visible to most eyes.

It had never known the danger of drowning, and had nearly done so when the ship it had stowed-away in landed on this very strange planet. Soon after it snuck out of the ship, it began to be battered by something from the sky. The sensation wasn't painful, but it was unexpected. It ran from the pelting, the touching, and the sensation that followed, which it now understood as 'wet.'

After several such storms, with no shelter in sight save the huge, dangerous-looking things climbing from the ground, it finally decided the stuff would not kill it. The fluid was not dangerous, and the sensation was not terrible. It looked for the source. It wanted to understand. After several minutes of staring straight up, its mouth began to fill with the stuff, and it choked, coughed, gagged, and nearly drowned. The sensation of drowning was terrifying and was not an experience it wanted to repeat.

Then it noticed a being small enough to eat, and hunger overshadowed caution. It chose a spot inside of a storm drain and waited. The creature did not pass by for several minutes, and it was ready to go looking for the tasty-looking thing when it finally arrived. The creature squealed once and tried to fight it off, but a quick bite behind the head stopped the creature's clawing and scrabbling.

It feasted on the flesh, the warm inner organs and the soft fur. Then it ate the bones. The only part it did not eat was the metallic object wrapped around the creature's neck that had almost prevented its bite from quickly ending the creature's life. It inspected the object, but did not know what it had found.

* * *

"Enforcer Nik'Thil," the mayor said, bowing low. "We are grateful you have arrived so quickly. Was your trip uneventful?"

"It was," Nik'Thil replied, bowing low, but not quite as low, toward Mayor A'Gath. 'Eventful' trips were bad, because to the Kra'daar it meant something bad had happened.

The mayor nodded and motioned to a female Kra'daar standing to his right. "This is Guardian Ta'La, Third-Chief of our Planetary Defense Forces. She has been investigating these fires, but instead of speaking for her, I think you two should speak." The mayor bowed again, turned, and walked further into the great hall that served as his office. He approached a table, at which at least a dozen other Kra'daar were seated, arguing.

Guardian Ta'La bowed very slightly and very abruptly. Nik'Thil did the same. Formal greetings over, she said, "Please follow me to my office. We have much to discuss."

Nik'Thil followed the guardian without a word and was a little surprised when she led him outside and into a waiting turbo-carriage, a kind of wheeled carriage that Humans might have compared to a big, red wagon. As soon as Nik'Thil seated himself, Ta'La raced off, pressing him firmly against the back of his padded seat. He tried not to react, but the ferocity at which she drove through the city was alarming.

Ta'La was either trying to impress him, he decided, or was unhappy he was there and taking over the investigation. Or she was just insane. Insanity wasn't common among the Kra'daar, especially since joining the Galactic Union and gaining access to nanite technology, but it did happen. However, it was very unlikely an insane person would have been trusted with as much power as the guardian possessed.

"Please slow down, Guardian Ta'La," he said just loudly enough to be heard over the wind that rushed past their ear-holes.

Ta'La turned to him and stared daggers. In the bright light outside—through a rare break in the clouds—the craggy skin on her face revealed her true age. Like the trees they lived with and relied upon, the skin of the Kra'daar became thicker and craggier with age. She was old—ancient even.

"Is that an official Union order, Enforcer Nik'Thil?" she asked, her voice gravelly with rage.

So, he thought, it was rage that caused her to drive this way. He opened his mouth to respond, but she used a foot to press on a small lever located on the floorboard. The turbo-carriage shot 10 feet into the air, hovered for a moment, then fell back to the road. Nik'Thil turned around and saw a very startled pedestrian hurrying across the road.

He turned back to Ta'La and barely contained his anger. "Yes," he said evenly, "that is an official Union order. Slow down now, or I will have you removed."

Guardian Ta'La obeyed by standing on the brakes, causing the turbo-carriage to skid sideways for nearly a 100 yards. Nik'Thil held onto his padded seat with both hands, and when the vehicle stopped, he glared at Ta'La in disbelief.

"Are you insane?" he asked.

Ta'La hesitated for a moment, mouth working soundlessly. "Instead of finding the source of the fires and destroying it, I have been assigned to babysit you," she hissed. "You, a sapling, unaware of all the work I have done. Unaware of how you slow my progress. Unaware of the danger this planet is in. But you question *me*?"

Nik'Thil would not be drawn into an argument. He was a Peacemaker and did not have to justify his presence to anyone. He studied Ta'La's face, watching the rage course through it. He noted her hand, positioned near her laser pistol, but not touching it. He was aware of several sets of eyes watching him—pedestrians and other drivers who'd pulled over to avoid being killed by the guardian. It was time to reassert his authority.

He leaned in closely enough to whisper into the guardian's earhole. "Do not confuse my kindness with weakness, guardian," he whispered. "We have the same goal. We want to save our forest from careless or malicious burning. Please don't force me to do something interesting in front of these civilians who look to you for their safety and protection."

The whisper was so unexpected and delivered with such confidence that when Nik'Thil leaned away and looked into her face again, the rage was gone. Instead of hatred and anger, she displayed a slack expression full of regret, understanding, and fear.

Ta'La looked around and noticed the eyes of the citizens on them. When she looked, several pedestrians suddenly remembered they had somewhere important to be, but others were too curious or stunned to tear their eyes away. She looked back to Nik'Thil, and then above his head. Over the tops of the tall, closely-spaced chrome buildings, the dark smear of smoke was just visible.

"Yes, Enforcer Nik'Thil," she whispered. "Of course. I apologize."

"Take me to your headquarters."

"We're here," she said, waving a long-fingered hand toward the unremarkable, cylindrical building in front of them.

Nik'Thil craned his neck to look all the way to the top. It must be 200 stories tall, he thought to himself. "Which floor?"

"All of them," she replied.

* * *

It held the source of its pleasure in its small, nearly hairless hand. The device had not existed on its planet, and before he killed and ate the very large creature, it had never seen one. It didn't even know such a thing was possible.

Its little hands caressed the small object. It caressed the thing and held it against its face. It knew the object would be needed again, and very soon, because the creatures here would stop its creation. Then a thought occurred to it. Why should it wait? Why shouldn't it make sure it never had to go a moment without pleasure? Why should it ever have to feel that way again?

Little eyes peered into the darkness, searching for an answer among the trash, twigs, and leaves the last rainfall had washed into its home. Why should it wait?

* * *

The lift that would take them to the top floor had obviously not been designed by the Kra'daar, but had been modified to accommodate their small stature. The small plate of metal which had been retrofitted to fill the gap caused by moving the control panel lower was tastefully installed and polished, but it was not equipped with the same fasteners as the rest of the lift, which made it look out of place. They didn't stick out enough to get in the way, but just enough to be obvious to an observant viewer they were an afterthought.

The ride to the top floor was uneventful and quiet. Ta'La refused to look at him, even in the polished reflection of the lift's door. A few moments later, the lift's doors opened onto a chaotic, noisy scene that shocked all of Nik'Thil's senses.

Nearly 100 Kra'daar were positioned in front of Tri-V displays situated throughout the expansive room. Most held a slate and some carried polymer boxes from one station to another for no apparent reason.

Two Oogar, eight feet tall, purple and hairy, yelled at a frightened-looking XenSha who seemed to be working furiously, trying to get their Tri-V display back online. Instead of displaying charts, diagrams, and camera feeds, theirs showed only a single bright line that danced in the air in front of them. The XenSha's long, rabbit-like ears were tucked low, apparently in defense of what it thought was an imminent bite from the bear-like Oogar who were still yelling.

The XenSha's many tentacles worked as fast as they could, but the purple beasts were having none of it. Of course, it was difficult to say whether they were angry or not. Oogar were not known for their subtlety. Everything about them was loud, whether they were angry, happy, or just plain bored. Nik'Thil considered approaching them to rescue the frightened XenSha, but Ta'La interrupted his thoughts.

"Do you want to walk around and talk to the others first," she asked, "or do you want me to gather my key personnel to fill you in on what we have so far?"

Nik'Thil tore his eyes away from the Oogar. "Just fill me in," he replied.

Guardian Ta'La nodded and snatched a slate from the hands of a passing Kra'daar who only looked offended for a split-second before he recognized who'd snatched the slate from him. Then he stood at attention and waited. His dark green uniform identified him as a fellow guardian, though the number of leaves on his sleeves indicated he was much lower in rank.

Ta'La swiped at the slate, poked it with a finger a few times, then gave it back. "They have been alerted," she said. "They will meet us in the conference room shortly."

Nik'Thil nodded and followed her back to the lift. They descended one floor and entered a long hallway. As they approached, a set of doors to their left opened silently, revealing a long, metal table. His shoulders slumped slightly, and he didn't try to hide his disappointment.

"It's the cost of progress," Ta'La said, the disgust clear in her voice. Neither made a move to take any of the 30 or so seats surrounding the table. Each of those were also likely made of steel, but were painted the same color green as the Guardian uniform. Instead, they just stared.

"Are you old enough to remember the days when such meetings were held outside in nature?" she asked softly.

"I am," Nik'Thil replied, just as softly. "Everything used to be done outside, under the trees, sitting in the moss or even the mud. There was no shame in it. There were no metal buildings."

"We used to live among the trees," Ta'La whispered. "And now it takes an hour of walking just to touch one. And for what?" Her tone had become angrier, he noticed.

No use beating around the bush. They both knew why their government had joined the Galactic Union. "Nanites," he said simply. "The plague wiped most of us out and might have completely exterminated us if it weren't for the nanites."

There was a long pause before anyone spoke again; each was lost in thought.

"There are some who say the plague was caused by the Union to persuade us to join," she whispered.

He had expected the conversation to turn in this direction but had hoped he would be wrong. "I know of the conspiracies," he said flatly, turning to Ta'La. He allowed a bit of danger to creep into his voice and said, "I would advise you to subdue that kind of talk whenever you hear it. First, it's not true, and second, talk like that could lead to a revolution. We both know what would happen then."

Ta'La turned to face him and was about to answer when the doors opened and several Kra'daar hurried into the room, each carrying something in his or her arms. All carried at least one slate, while others carried polymer boxes clearly marked as evidence. Ta'La watched them situate themselves around the table and unload their boxes. "Shall we begin, Enforcer Nik'Thil?" she asked, a coldness to her voice which conveyed their conversation was over...for now.

"Of course," he replied, doing his best to keep the annoyance out of his voice. *I desire only balance*, he reminded himself. *I love only order.*

* * *

Little black eyes saw an opportunity, but it needed to get closer in order to be sure. It had never created against such a backdrop, but thought that, based on its experience, it would work. It also thought it would be beautiful. Its backdrop was a large structure near the center of the city. Large creatures were piloting vehicles with huge, hand-like devices attached to their fronts.

It had never seen, or possibly just never noticed, the purpose of these vehicles, but now the small creature began to breathe fast in anticipation and understanding. The vehicles with the large hand-like apparatuses were collecting trees!

It felt joy! Traveling from the storm drain to the forest was dangerous. It was always possible some larger creature, something too large for it to eat, would instead eat it! It didn't want to be eaten, so it had to be very cautious. This, however, was different. After night fell, there weren't as many creatures to worry about, and it could find a way into the building to create.

It would be close enough to smell its creation, too. It nearly vibrated with anticipation. Its hunger for creating raged in its mind. It's small, black eyes stared at the cut trees entering the building. It couldn't see how many trees were in there, but based on how many were being brought in, the creature thought there might be a whole other forest there. A forest to create with.

* * *

The briefing took less than an hour and amounted to a great big shrug. When the last guardian sat down, Nik'Thil found he was rubbing his head again and forced himself to stop. He turned to Ta'La, who was sitting next to him, and opened his mouth to ask a question.

She must have read his expression, though, as she answered before he could ask. "Yes, Enforcer Nik'Thil, that's all we have."

He closed his mouth and stared at the slate one of the Kra'daar had provided for him. He felt conflicted, wondering if he should play nice or if it was time to put some pressure on these people. He decided instead to appeal to their sense of home.

"We are the Kra'daar," he said just loud enough for those around him to hear. "We have lived among the trees for our entire existence, in union with them, depending on them for shelter, food, and even our births." He paused to let it sink in.

"Now we are faced with an enemy who strikes from a hidden place. An enemy who does not care for the trees as we do..." Nik'Thil said before he was interrupted by a scoff from one of the Kra'daar.

He looked toward the source of the noise and found a guilty set of eyes looking back at him. The two Kra'daar standing closest to the male backed away slowly. Nik'Thil stared at the male as he shifted his eyes nervously from Nik'Thil to Guardian Ta'La, who seemed just as shocked by the disrespect as the male looked.

"Shall I have him killed?" Ta'La asked finally. "We could save him for the next fire and simply toss him in?"

Nik'Thil waited a moment before answering, allowing the male to worry. "No," he said finally. "Just remove him from the investigation and send him far away. We need Kra'daar who actually give a damn working on—" and he was interrupted again.

"I do give a damn!" the male roared as he pointed to himself. "I might be the only one in this room who actually does!" Nik'Thil heard Ta'La inhale deeply in preparation for a vicious retort, but silenced her with a gentle touch on her arm. He wanted to hear what the male had to say.

The male noticed the movement and noted his commander had been silenced. He continued, a look of pure hatred on his young face. "We cut down the trees! We kill them for profit! We sell our heritage, our lifesap, to the Galactic Union. What do we get in return? This!" The last word was punctuated by the male slamming his fist onto the metal table hard enough to leave a small dent.

Nik'Thil waited for a moment to see if the male wanted to say anything else. Then he said, "The plague..." and was interrupted again.

"The plague! That's what you people always say! You sold out to the Galactic Union!" The male began to approach and Nik'Thil felt Ta'La tense. He gently pushed her out of the way as he took a single step toward the angry Kra'daar. The others in the room, noticing what was about to happen, all began to slowly back away. Those in the line of fire on both ends were a little hastier in their retreat.

The male stalked closer, still yelling, pointing with the finger of his weapon-hand instead of moving it toward the laser pistol all guardians carried. "You and your kind sold our heritage for credits. Credits! For our entire existence, we've never needed credits! Now we have foreigners burning our trees!"

"How do you know it's foreigners?" Nik'Thil asked calmly.

The male looked astonished. "Are you a fool?" he asked. All the others in the room gasped. Nik'Thil did not answer, but instead watched the male's steady approach and watched his hands.

"We should have never joined the blasted Union!" the male raged. "We shouldn't have opened ourselves up to this evil! The reason we're under attack is your fault and those like you!" The male was close now, barely a meter away. "The plague would have been better than this!" the male roared and reached for Nik'Thil's face, extending thorn-like barbs from his outstretched hands.

His opponent saw the attack coming, though, and was ready for it.

The male reached. The enforcer kicked. The male grunted and bent at the waist. Nik'Thil raked the back of the male's head. The male's face slammed hard into the floor. It was over in a second.

The male was motionless for several seconds as sap seeped from dozens of long gashes on the back of his head. The room was silent except for the heavy breathing of the male, which was the only indication he was still alive.

Nik'Thil squatted in front of the prone male and opened his mouth to whisper something when the male suddenly reached for his laser pistol. Before anyone could react, the male's body vanished and was replaced with an expanding shower of sparks and smoke.

Two of the Kra'daar fainted, their solid tree-like bodies making dull, heavy thuds as they hit the floor. The enforcer stood, fletcher in hand and shook his head. The fletcher was a magnetic weapon that accelerated a rod of compressed iron and tungsten powder to nearly nine times the speed of sound. The effects were immediate and explosive, especially against dense targets.

Nik'Thil dropped the spent cartridge from his fletcher and loaded a fresh one. He then scanned the room, slowly moving from one set of eyes to the next, challenging anyone else to try the same thing. Nobody did, so he put the weapon back into its hidden holster under his loose shirt and sat back down.

"I've heard what you don't know," he said slowly. "Now I need to hear what you *do* know."

* * *

It stuffed both hands into its large mouth in order to keep itself from squealing with anticipation. It wouldn't do any good to attract the attention of something which might want to eat it before it got a chance to create. But the anticipation was almost more than it could stand.

Unlike the Kra'daar, it did have the ability to cry, and it did so because in order to keep its hands in its mouth and squelch the squealing, it had to bite down. Big, thick, black tears formed in its eyes, temporarily blinding it. It blinked its tiny eyes, and the oily tears fell to the slight trickle of water at the bottom of the storm drain and hissed, turning the water gray.

It didn't notice, though, because it was watching the entrance to the building. Trees were going in. Some of them still had branches on them! This would be a creation that would be difficult to surpass in the future. That realization saddened it, but only for a second. The challenge would be finding a way to outdo itself in the future. Even if it couldn't, it would be wonderful to try.

Several minutes and a lot of crying later, the vehicles with hand-like things quit coming out. The big vehicles with the trees stopped going in. All was quiet.

It removed its hands slowly and stared at the huge doors to the building. Nothing happened for several seconds, and it was confused. Then the doors began to rattle and slowly close. This was it!

* * *

Guardian Ta'La ordered a couple custodians to clean-up the remains of the male who tried to attack Nik'Thil. Two Kra'daar entered a minute later and struggled through the process, obviously repulsed by what they saw and smelled. They finished a few minutes later and hastily left the room.

With the distraction gone from sight, even though the odor was still present, Nik'Thil ordered them again to tell him what they knew.

The enforcer listened intently, but there wasn't much the guardians were certain of. "Then tell me what your heart is telling you, not what your science says," he told them. That livened things up a bit, though they still seemed cautious and kept giving Ta'La nervous glances. They seemed like they were withholding information.

Ta'La leaned close to Nik'Thil. "I think I should leave for a little bit so they can speak freely. I'll be back in an hour. If you need me sooner, use your slate to signal me." Then she stood and addressed the rest of those present.

"Another matter has been called to my attention," she said. "I'm stepping out for a bit, but I expect your full cooperation with Enforcer Nik'Thil." The last sentence was punctuated by a scowl. She then turned on a heel and marched out of the room. The rest of the guardians watched her go.

A few seconds passed which the remaining guardians used to glance at each other and the enforcer before one of them started talking.

"Permission to speak freely?" a female asked.

Nik'Thil sat up straight and nodded.

"We don't know shit," she said. "We've been stuck using this bullshit exclusively." She waggled her slate and let it fall hard to the table. The others dropped their slates to the table as well, except for one who tossed it a bit too hard. That slate clattered to the floor.

Nik'Thil looked to each of them. They seemed angry, frustrated, and desperate. "If you didn't have all this wonderful technology at your disposal," he asked sarcastically, "how would you investigate these fires and find the source?"

The room erupted into talking, and the enforcer had to hold up a hand to silence them. "One at a time," he said. Then he pointed at the female who had spoken and said, "You first."

She pressed her mouth tightly closed for a second, looking like she might lose her nerve, but finally spoke. "I'd send 100 or 200 out to patrol. Send us into the woods. Send us through the city. Turn us loose. Let us use our bodies to do what needs to be done."

"Use your bodies how?" he asked.

"We will find the next fire the second it starts. And then," she said, extending inch-long thorns from all over her body, ripping her uniform in the process, "we will stop the arsonist." The look on her face and the tone of her voice conveyed deep, breathless excitement and anticipation.

The enforcer glanced around the room. All the other faces were similarly grim. The plan was dangerous, he knew. Arsonists were unstable and guardians could die. However, if a fire was set in the right location, the economy of the entire planet could be ruined and many more Kra'daar could die.

Nik'Thil stood and placed his fists on his hips. "By the power granted me by the Galactic Union and the Peacemaker Guild, I hereby deputize each of you for the duration of this investigation. You are to discover the source of these fires and stop it. If you can capture the criminal, do so. If you can't..." he let the last sentence trail-off.

There was a short pause before his fellow Kra'daar understood, then they roared their approval. Each extended his or her thorns and rushed from the room in a storm of flailing arms, legs, and thorns. The enforcer calmly walked from the room and joined them as they sheepishly waited for the lift to get to their floor.

* * *

It looked left and saw no threats, then it looked right and saw no threats; however, it hadn't survived this long to get lazy and killed now. It stuck its head out of the storm drain, just a little, and looked up at the sky.

Back on its home planet, things that flew found his kind quite tasty and killed them often. It looked, peering with its little eyes, and sniffed the air. It listened and darted its head back in just before a small, fast vehicle turned the corner, shining a bright white light in its direction.

The vehicle passed quickly, and the creature knew it had not been discovered. It leaned out again and repeated the process. Movement across the street made it draw its head back in. The source of the movement was small, though, and after a moment of watching it recognized the movement as a small, tasty creature it liked to eat. It looked from the snack to the building, back to the snack. To eat or to create?

Instinct told it to eat. Food was scarce where it was from, but seemed plentiful here. Opportunities to create, though, were not so plentiful, especially to create in a place where so many could appreciate it. Right in the middle of all the people. It looked back to the small, scurrying snack and frowned as the thing scuttled around the far corner of the building. It leaned out, checked again, and still detected no predators.

Quietly and carefully, it put the object in its mouth, taking care not to damage it with its teeth. It then gathered its legs, and, after another quick check, it sprinted toward the double doors and reached them without incident. It searched frantically for a way in, a gap big enough to stick its head through, but found none. It glanced at the sky again, little eyes searching for danger, and saw none.

It pressed its head against the spot where the doors met and found they would not budge. Then it tried the right-side hinge, then the left. It glanced back at the storm drain, then looked at the sky, then back to the drain. It considered running back, but the street was dangerous, and it was grateful to have made it across once. Then it heard danger.

A vehicle was approaching the close corner. It wasn't big, but vehicles were dangerous. It already knew that. Panic. It pushed hard against the doors again with its head. Finding they still would not budge, it sprinted away from the threat, from the vehicle that was just getting to the corner. The creature searched for somewhere to hide but saw nothing. If it couldn't find something to hide under, then it would climb.

It saw a stack of crates along the building, just a few meters down the wall, and leapt easily onto the first. Then it continued to climb, leaping and sprinting until it got to the roof. Then it felt horribly exposed. It ran one way, then the other, then froze in fear. Its eyes returned to the sky, and in the distance it saw something. It saw a vehicle...flying, and it felt a whole new level of terror.

It looked about frantically and found a wide pipe sticking out of the roof. The pipe looked big enough to jump into, so the creature did. And then it slid down...deep into the building.

* * *

When the elevator arrived, the Kra'daar calmly entered, retracting their thorns to avoid hurting the others in the crowded elevator. The last one held the door for the enforcer, who joined them. Nobody spoke for most of the ride down.

"Enforcer Nik'Thil," a male said, "we're going to need more help. Can we..."

"Of course, you can enlist the help of others, deputy," the enforcer said. Several Kra'daar laughed wickedly. Nik'Thil pretended not to notice.

"Be sure to pick up communicators before you leave," the enforcer said. "That way, you can call for assistance and alert others when you find and either capture or destroy the cause of the fires.

Remember, I'd prefer you capture the arsonist." The others nodded solemnly.

The elevator dinged, and most of the Kra'daar leaned forward in anticipation of the door opening. The second it took seemed to stretch awkwardly and long. When the doors did open, they roared and erupted from the lift in another wave of arms, legs, and thorns. A few headed directly outside while the rest ran through the building gathering others to join them.

Nik'Thil stepped out, adjusted his uniform, and waited. A minute later, Guardian Ta'La joined him. "What the hell was that all about?" she asked breathlessly.

"I deputized everyone in the room and ordered them to use their bodies to find the arsonist. I also ordered them to be sure to bring communicators, but it looks like a few forgot."

"Oh, I understand now," Ta'La said with a laugh. "Would you mind..." she started, leaving the question hanging.

Nik'Thil turned to her thoughtfully. "Would you like to join them?"

"I would," she said, her voice dangerous and dark.

"Very well, deputy. Grab a communicator and join them. I'd prefer if the arsonist was brought back alive."

Ta'La growled in anticipation and approached the dispatcher's desk, behind which four very stunned-looking dispatchers sat with comms over their heads. Ta'La held her hand out, and a dispatcher wordlessly placed a communicator onto it. She attached the device to her head and inserted the small speaker into her ear-hole. Then she grinned wickedly at the enforcer, extended her thorns, which appeared to be about twice as long as the others', roared, and charged from the building.

* * *

It scrabbled and tried to stop its descent, while at the same time trying not to bite down too hard on the object in its mouth.

Finally, the little claws on its feet caught something and stopped its descent. It breathed a sigh of relief before glancing down with its little eyes. It was standing above a metal register, flat bars of bent metal extending to either side. It could see a dim light from below, and it could smell the object of its creation. The scent was enough to make it want to mate right here, right now.

It carefully reached out with one foot and poked the register. It didn't budge. It poked the register harder, and it still didn't move. Tentatively, it placed most of its weight on the register, and still it didn't move. Then it found a secure place to put its forelimbs so it wouldn't fall, put its whole weight on the metal, and found it was secure.

The scent coming through the gaps in the metal was provocative and smelled like two forests, maybe three. It squealed with anticipation, unable to hold back any longer. There was no answer, nor the sound of any predators. It couldn't wait any longer.

With the object held in its forelimbs, it easily bit through the metal in three mouthfuls, spitting it out after every bite. Then it wondered, only for a moment, why it didn't try to bite through the doors in the first place. But it didn't pursue the thought. It could only obsess over the scent of the trees.

Once it had bitten through enough of the metal to stick its head through, it did. It saw the register opened onto a small room and was just above what appeared to be a dark, endless pit. It studied its surroundings for a moment and nearly died from fright when a sound came from the endless pit. It was kind of a 'glub' followed by a 'bloop'. Then it understood. The pit was full of fluid.

It didn't like the water, but it didn't see a choice. It leaned through the hole, slowly pulling its body through, and finally hung by one foot. The thought of what might happen at the bottom was frightening, but there was no other way. It let go.

* * *

The order to find the arsonist had a bigger effect than Nik'Thil could have anticipated. He stepped outside as he placed a communicator into his ear and was surprised by the noise. It seemed his deputies had recruited help from every home and every corner in the city. The noise was a dull roar, but occasionally he saw an unknown Kra'daar sprint by, thorns extended, roaring. *Oops*, he thought.

* * *

The fall was long enough it began to regret its decision. The splash at the bottom stunned it for a moment, but it quickly recovered and extracted itself. It sat for some time on the edge of the toilet dripping foul-smelling water, completely miserable. Then it dried enough to smell the trees again, and it remembered why it was here.

It jumped from the edge of the toilet, still dripping, and crashed clumsily to the floor, being careful to keep its head as high as possible so it wouldn't damage the object. It then snuck to the open door and peeked out.

There were a few lights in the immense building, but it could sense no threats. What it saw next made it forget everything it had been worried about. It staggered out from the bathroom, too stunned to worry about potential predators.

The warehouse was nearly a mile long and about half that wide. Trees in various stages of preparation were neatly stacked in orderly, uniform piles. It wandered forward, absolutely amazed by what it saw and smelled. It thought of all the potential creations it could make. Not even in its wildest dream could it imagine so much wood in one place.

Then a thought occurred to it. Instead of several, maybe a hundred creations, why not just make one big one? The realization nearly made it swoon. It examined the stacks it could see carefully. Then it decided it needed a better view and climbed to the top of the nearest one. Piles of trees and lumber extended as far as it could see.

It nearly dropped the object. It could start the creation anywhere, and it would grow. Then it heard a noise which had been growing. It had been able to ignore it until now, but the noise was becoming louder and seemed closer.

The beings were coming, it realized. They were coming to see its newest creation! They were close, so it decided the spot it was standing was as good as any other spot.

It pulled the object from its mouth and turned it over a couple of times until it remembered how to operate it. The big red thing on top, it remembered. It had to press the big red thing while having the shiny end close to the wood. The sound grew louder.

It brought the shiny end close to the wood and pressed the big red part. It heard a click...but not the buzzing noise which always followed. It tried again, but got the same disappointing effect. It was confused, and the noise was growing louder and was much closer.

It shook the object in frustration, and water flew from it. Then it understood. It had never tried using the object when it was wet, because it always did its best to stay out of the water. It must need to be dry for it to work. The sound grew louder. It shook the object furiously and little drops of water flew away.

* * *

"All deputies, report your position and how many others you have with you," Enforcer Nik'Thil ordered.

As the reports began coming in, one of the dispatchers plotted the coordinates, or estimated coordinates, on her slate. This information was fed to a Tri-V behind her desk, and this is what Nik'Thil studied. Two minutes later, when the reports began to dwindle, he turned to the dispatcher.

"Who's at this location," he said, pointing a skinny finger at a blinking red dot on the tactical overlay of the city.

The dispatcher looked and then quickly consulted her slate. "That's Deputy Ka'Fin," she said quickly.

"Deputy Ka'Fin," the enforcer said into his communicator.

"Here," a voice replied.

"I see a gap in our search," the enforcer said, squinting at the Tri-V's display. "Bring your group to coordinates," he paused for a moment, deciphering the overlay. "Bring them to D-553."

There was a long pause before Ka'Fin responded. "Uh, that's right in the middle of the city. Aren't we looking for forest fires?"

Nik'Thil sighed before responding. "What is at that location, deputy?"

Another long pause. "The sawmill!" the deputy replied, panic evident in his voice.

* * *

It tried the object, but it still didn't make the sound it usually made. It shook the object again, this time much harder than before, and it slipped from the creature's grip, seemingly in slow motion. The object flew away, turning slowly in the air, bounced off a log, and tumbled between a few, falling further and further into the stack.

No, it thought. *No, not now!*

It leapt from log to log, searching the area. *Not now*, it thought. *I'm so close to my greatest creation*. Great inky drops formed in its little eyes, and it blinked hard to clear its vision. *Not here!* It jumped on top of the next log and checked. Then it ran to the other end. The sound was getting closer, and it was clearer now. The sound was roars. Many roars.

Then it spotted the object. It had not fallen as far as the sound had made it seem. It reached for the object...but its arms were too small. It reached again and still could not touch it. The sounds were louder now. Then it felt rage. No, they would not ruin its greatest creation! It bit savagely at the wood and found it even easier to cut than the metal. It spat out a large chunk of wood and reached in again. It still could not touch the object, but it got closer.

It bit the wood several more times, spitting out large chunks of wood and finally, carefully, pulled the object free. Joy! The roars were just outside now. The doors were being rattled, and there was a lot of talking.

It placed the metal piece against a log and pushed the big red thing, and the plasma lighter ignited. It held the lighter for a second until the wood began to smoke and caught fire. Then it scrabbled further down the stack and started another log burning. Then it sprinted to the opposite side and started several there.

Then the sound stopped, and it waited, wondering what was happening outside. One of the creatures shouted, and the building shook with impacts. It sprinted to another stack of wood, this one reduced to many long, thin pieces, and found these lit even easier. It looked back and saw its first creation was showing signs of life. The smell was glorious, and then something strange happened.

Even though it was inside, it began to rain, hard. Lights started flashing, and a new noise was heard. The noise was so loud the creature thought it might die. It dropped the object, covered its ears, and closed its eyes against the light.

Something picked it up roughly. Out of instinct, it bit down hard on the hand holding it and spat the strange-tasting appendage out. The thing it bit wailed and something hard hit it.

Rows of long, needle-like teeth flashed and several Kra'daar lost fingers and hands as they tried to contain the vicious little beast. Some tried to kick it, to grab the feral thing by a foot or by the scruff of its neck, and they pulled back stumps.

Then something heavy fell on its back, pinning it to the ground. It tried to get away, but couldn't. It tried to turn to bite the thing, but couldn't. It bit the floor instead, and found it difficult, but spat a big piece away.

More things were touching it now. Oh no! Then it felt a sharp pain right at the top of its head, and everything went dark.

* * *

Enforcer Nik'Thil was still stunned. He'd underestimated his kin. It seemed that although they were members of the Galactic Union legally, they hadn't given up their old ways. When faced with an emergency, the locals had immediately lost their organized manner and reverted back to a much more natural state. Worse, the killer, savage instinct was still strong in his people. No matter what titles you gave a Kra'daar, no matter whose uniform you dress them in, they were, and would always remain, savages.

All that was left was to deliver the criminal to the Na'Shar Consortium on the other side of the planet. It was their operation which was being threatened, and it was they who swore out the charges against the...creature...their kinsmen had captured. He was ready to get away from his kinsmen; now that he was more genteel, he didn't want to stay around them any longer than he had to.

The creature hung upside-down from a chain in a cage next to him. After it woke from the blow to its head, they finally discovered how to secure the beast. Another blow to knock it out, followed by a blast of secure foam to its limbs and its mouth kept it from biting anything else. Just to be sure, they hung it from the middle of the cage so it couldn't bite anyone who inadvertently got too close.

The creature growled at Nik'Thil, and he responded by kicking the cage hard enough to bounce the creature's head off three sides of the cage, before going back to the contemplation of his kinsmen.

# # # # #

Blood of Innocents
by James Young

Chapter 1: A Task for the Tumen

Dekrete

1000 Local

1 December

The roar and rattle of some craft departing Dekrete provided a nice cover for Bolivar Thompson to stop and consider what the white, owl-like creature sitting across his desk was offering him. Bumas were hard for him to read, but one did not need to be an expert in alien psychology to detect the being's annoyance at the interruption.

Been agitated like a canary with a snake in its cage, Bolivar thought, drumming his long, thick fingers on the desktop. He took a deep breath as he looked up at the cracked ceiling, quietly hoping that the plaster didn't choose this inopportune moment to come crashing down.

Last time I rent an office based on a recommendation, he thought. *Great first impression when someone comes in to hire a mercenary company, and it looks like we can barely keep our own building in one piece.* Bolivar was under no illusions as to his company's place in the Mercenary Guild's pecking order. It just helped if the décor did not make it obvious. Blissfully, whatever large ship was departing finally got far enough away that the Buma escaped plucking plaster out of its plumage.

"Sorry for that," Bolivar said. "I believe you said you were offering 10 million credits…"

The Buma practically screeched its response. "I said *five* million, human!"

For a moment, Bolivar thought he was actually going to end up going hand-to-hand with the creature. At slightly over a meter in height and looking around maybe 75 kilograms soaking wet, the Buma was half his size. Although it did have talons and a beak, it wasn't much of a threat. Still, Bolivar could see the thing getting in a lucky shot.

How did your son die, Mrs. Thompson? Well, we believe it might have been a crazed raptor attack. Perhaps an argument about the number of licks to get to the center of a piece of candy? Or maybe a discussion about carrying mail to a wizarding school? Bolivar thought, fighting to suppress a laugh despite the seriousness of the situation.

"Oh, I'm sorry, I was sure it was 10," Bolivar stated confidently. The Buma regarded him with a look he assumed was disgust, its wide eyes blinking rapidly.

"Why would we *ever* offer you 10 million credits?"

"Three million for the transit costs," Bolivar snapped, holding up a finger. "Almost three months for transit, meaning we cannot take any additional contracts in that time. Another one million for the high-g embarking while we are aboard the cargo freighter."

The Buma looked at him unblinking.

"All of these are opera…" the feathered alien began.

"Get out," Bolivar said simply. "You are wasting my time."

"What? How dare…"

The flapping of the aliens' limbs was comical as it lifted out of the reclining chair.

"How *dare* I?" Bolivar asked, his voice level as he mentally calculated how quickly he could draw the short sword concealed in the back of his chair. "Because from my estimation, you are truly shit out of options."

The alien settled back down in the chair, plumage drooping.

"We are a religious order, Human Named Thompson," the Buma replied. "The Order of Meyra devotes our money to helping the unfortunate and species who cannot help themselves. The Goddess Meyra…"

"Unless 'Meyra' can heal a sucking chest wound or bring my CASPers back from the junk pile after a laser's played tic-tac-headshot, I fail to see how this is relevant," Thompson said.

"Have you no decency, Human?!"

I don't know what that thing actually screeched, but I'm pretty sure the translator gave me a much more wholesome version than what was uttered, Bolivar thought.

"None," he replied simply. "Just like your species didn't have the decency to warn our species what the penalty for killing an ambassador was, or that the Alpha Contracts were basically glorified death rides."

"Your species would still be kicking around on your besotted world if it were not for us!"

"Yet here I am, on some distant planet, with a "Wonder Owl" that is apparently hard of hearing," Bolivar continued. "Get. The. *Fuck*. Out."

There was a long silence.

"Ten million credits," the Buma said, the translator once again clearly misfiring on tone. The alien produced a pinlink from within its chest down, the slender device resembling a Terran stylus. Turning its head to the side, it clicked the pinlink into place. After a momentary hum and brief closing of the eyes, the Buma turned back to face him. The commlink on Bolivar's desk chimed.

"Boss," Tamara Thompson's contralto voice stated over the device, "we've got a contract update from The Pit."

The Pit was the nearest merc center, located just over 3,000 kilometers away. Most mercs preferred to do business in the center itself. Bolivar, on the other hand, didn't feel like giving some asshole a chance to swoop in on his negotiations to undercut him.

Only had to have that happen once, he thought bitterly. *Completely boring garrison mission too. At least that asshole got to spend the six weeks in transit enjoying his food from a straw. When your own boss refuses to give you nanites for the jaw, you know you were being a dick.*

"Recon mission, alien planet we'll call Objective Lucifer, 10 million credit fee, non-refundable?" Bolivar asked, watching as the Buma's beak twitched.

"It's actually not...okay, now it's non-refundable," Tamara stated.

"Well, looks like Our Blessed Sisters of Meyra have themselves a deal," Bolivar said. The Buma looked at him with a look of bewilderment.

"I do not think Meyra has siblings, human," the alien replied.

Someday translators will understand sarcasm, Bolivar thought. *Someday.*

* * *

"Are you a fucking idiot?" Tamara exploded as she read the full terms of the contract 20 minutes later. "We are ripping this damn thing up and making them come back."

Bolivar watched as his sister paced angrily around the small ready room, her cybernetic arms glistening in the sunlight from Dekrete's primary. Like Bolivar, Tamara was tall…and that was where the similarities ended. Her dark sundress hung loosely on her athletic frame, and her chestnut hair hung down to her waist.

"I would say calm down, but that would probably work about as well as that time I tried to baptize Mordecai," Bolivar said. That drew laughter from the other two people in the room, the sounds dying as Tamara turned to look at them both.

"What?" their younger brother, Silvius, asked. "What kind of dumbass tries to baptize a Karman Lynx?" Looking like his two older siblings had stolen the family's height, Silvius was just over five and a half feet tall. He also had a shoulder size two inches wider than Bolivar's and ran like the wind. Running a hand nervously through his close-cropped sandy brown hair, for a moment Silvius looked concerned his sister would spring across the room at him.

Cybernetic arms versus nanite enhancements, Thompson thought. *Knowing how those two fought when we were kids, I'll pass.*

"Loosen up, Tamara," Paige Mixon teased from the other couch, her freckled face still split in a smirk. Tamara whirled on the other woman, her gaze so hot that Bolivar briefly expected the couch to ignite behind Paige. The redhead's smirk dropped, her own blue eyes meeting the middle Thompson's coolly as she sat up, her mesh workout shirt shimmering over her stomach.

Oh shit, he thought. Like Silvius, Paige was augmented, but mainly to give her endurance and advantages operating the Tumen's sole CASPer. Also, Bolivar and Tamara's father had ensured both had 12 years of martial arts.

Dad fucked a lot of things up with us, but that wasn't one of them, Bolivar thought.

"You haven't won a stare down with Paige since you caught her fucking your boyfriend before the Spring Ball," Bolivar said tiredly. In an instant, he saw that his gambit had worked, as their anger was immediately shifted to him.

"Great thing about this situation is I'm still your employer, and beating me to a pulp is pretty much punishable by death on this planet," Bolivar continued, even as he made a mental note to acquire some chocolate-covered raspberries for Paige and blue bonnets for his sister. With a tingle, he felt his implants starting to go through the orders process...

"Hey, asshole, remember who is also connected to our expense report!" Tamara said, a moment before he felt a sharp sting as she booted him out of the Tumen's account.

"What the hell?" Bolivar said, wincing. "Hey! I'm the damn boss, you can't..."

"Anyway," Tamara said, waving her hand dismissively, "you're a moron. Ten million damn credits? That's not even going to cover your burial if the shit hits the..."

"Unlike some people here, I actually read the Mercenary Guild updates when they come out," Bolivar snapped, his eyes still watering from the anti-intrusion device's activation on the Tumen's expense account. He saw Paige coolly regarding his sister, her mouth pursed in a thin line.

Yeah, I'm not a fan of her thinking she can just put security features in without telling me either, Bolivar thought as Tamara looked at him. *We're going to have a long talk later, she and I.*

"Do tell," his sister finally snapped.

"All non-refundable contracts come with an automatic 20 percent markup for supplies, return transit costs, and 'essentials' as defined in Section 66, Paragraph 5, Sub Paragraph e," Bolivar said. "An additional 50 percent must be deposited on the 60 day of employment if still in transit."

"*What?*" Paige and Tamara asked simultaneously, their verbal shock reflected in Silvius's jaw dropping.

"Just dropped two days ago," Bolivar said. "The Mercenary Guild is, to put it bluntly, sick of the Union's shit."

"How do you figure that?" Tamara asked. "That seems like a damn good way to make someone reconsider hiring mercs, actually."

"Guild is tired of people thinking mercs are disposable fodder," Bolivar said. "I think Black Tuesday is still causing some folks to get the vapors."

"Black Tuesday," as people were referring to April 15th of that year, had involved six mercenary companies being wiped out within 24 hours. Yes, two of them had been mutual annihilation, but the other four had been due to various degrees of customer obfuscation about what the job entailed.

"Still, I'm with Tamara," Paige said. "No refund contracts are how folks start developing capital. That's going to stop if they start having an inherent mark-up."

"Can't spend the money if you're dead," Silvius snorted derisively.

"There's also that little matter of the Squiddies," Bolivar continued.

There was silence in the ready room at the mention of The Crimson Squid. In reality, the organization's name was about 50 words of difficult to pronounce, alien syllables. Its unofficial moniker came from the organization's symbol, a picture best described as the love child of Cthulhu and Fenrir doing a "Killroy Was Here" pose over a shattered cityscape. The full symbol was placed in a morphogenic tattoo on each member's upper chest, with a matching tattoo on the small of their back or thorax.

When your terrorists aren't even trying to hide who they are anymore, there's a problem, Bolivar thought.

"Yeah, well, I somehow doubt anyone in the Guild is really thinking about preserving combat power versus getting rid of competition," Tamara said skeptically.

"That's neither here nor there," Bolivar said. "Those damn do-gooders owe us a full dossier in 48 hours, with a data update as we come out of transit. Paige, what's *Flaming Yurt's* status?"

Paige ignored Tamara's eye roll at the name their CASPer pilot had bestowed on the MK 6. Squat, bipedal, and with a bulbous cockpit that made it look like a walking bullet, the *Flaming Yurt* was a third-hand vehicle Paige had found at an estate sale back on Earth. Its purchase had required the sale of the Tumen's two MK 5s and several pieces of the Thompson family's estate back on Humanity's home planet.

That was the ugliest fight Tamara and I ever had, Bolivar thought. *I don't know what made her madder—finding out that Paige and I were in a relationship, or that I sold Grandma's acreage in Tennessee.*

"She'll be back from the shop in 24 hours," Paige said. "With the new reflective paint and upgraded jets, it's almost like she's a poor man's MK 7…"

"Except she's not," Tamara interrupted angrily. "We need a second CASPer."

"Well let me just shit one, Sis," Bolivar replied sarcastically, finally having had enough of Tamara's attitude. "Remind me which one of us flunked her last tactics test?"

The blood drained from his sister's face. "Flunking a tactics test" was shorthand for having been forcibly retired from mercenary operations. Out of the corner of his eye, Bolivar saw even Paige blanching at his callousness.

"Well," Tamara said, her drawl deepening in an ominous way. "If my advice is no longer needed, I can have a resignation on your desk by nightfall."

Okay, if you want to go there, Bolivar thought. *I'm sure Mom would like to have one of her children actually planet-side.*

"Are you going to keep riding me at every turn?" Bolivar asked.

"I'm not riding you 'at every turn.' I believe that individual is over there," Tamara snapped, gesturing at Paige.

"What the hell?" Paige said, starting to stand up before Silvius grabbed her.

"Jesus, Tamara," the youngest Bolivar said. This time, he didn't look away when Tamara turned her baleful gaze on him.

"Oh, I see, is she…" Tamara started. She never got to finish, as Paige wiggled out of Silvius' grasp. Even having seen Paige in the field, Bolivar was shocked at how quick their CASPer pilot moved. Tamara's hand was still moving up to block when the backhand landed, and her own counterblow struck nothing but air as Paige dodged.

Okay, I underestimated just how good those augments are, Bolivar thought. Silvius jumped between the two women, giving Paige a look as he shoved Tamara back.

"I didn't haul your ass off that godforsaken rock so you can insult me!" Paige screamed. "What the hell is your problem?!"

That's a very damn good question, Bolivar thought angrily.

"Silvius, Paige, *out now!*" Bolivar barked. Both of them took one look at Bolivar and headed for the door. Tamara, for her part, simply crossed her arms and stared at her older brother until the door shut.

"Gonna chew me out, Bolly?" she asked snidely as soon as the door was closed. "Or slap the shit out of me like your fuck toy just did?"

Holy shit, something is eating her, Bolivar thought, his brief flash of temper fading with the realization.

"You don't usually act like a petulant toddler needing attention," Bolivar said evenly after a moment. "So I thought, maybe I'd ask you whether you had a *legitimate* reason you care about Paige and I."

"Ew," Tamara said, shaking her head vehemently. "Not cool, Bolivar. Not cool at all."

"Says the woman who just questioned my judgment in front of my subordinates and is taking full advantage of certain clauses in our establishment documents?" Bolivar observed reasonably.

"She's a Jonah, Bolivar," Tamara seethed. "She's been in three companies, and all three are now defunct. If you hadn't found her in that Pit on Karma, she'd…"

"Likely be dead," Bolivar interrupted. "Driven to do something truly stupid like going thief or pirate, and being hunted down by some Peacemaker. Is that what you would prefer? You guys were best friends in high school, *she saved your life,* and now you're saying you'd rather she was meat paste in some Oogar prison?"

"She's *dangerous!*" Tamara nearly shouted, the thought of Paige being rations not even giving her pause. "You don't understand. You didn't serve with her!"

Bolivar could see his sister starting to sweat, and her shoulders shaking.

"No, I didn't," Bolivar said gently, stepping toward her. "But we've done two jobs with her so far. Everyone's come back. There hasn't even been a hint of trouble. If she comes back alone, it means I fucked up, not her."

* * * * *

Chapter 2: A Peacemaker Speaks Mercator

Nuckelavee
0650 Ship's Time
18 January

"**I** should have charged them another million for this transit," Bolivar muttered as he idly ran his fingers through Paige's hair.

The redhead chuckled, her eyes still closed as she lay drowsily on Bolivar's chest. The two of them were cuddled on Bolivar's bed, the compartment's stifling humidity causing both their bodies to have a slight sheen of sweat. Acclimation was one of those things a merc could do the easy way en route to a location…or the hard way dirtside.

Whose bright idea was it to land in the humid sub-tropical region? Bolivar thought. *Oh, that's right, the idiot who wanted a radar shadow between their expected drop point and the main cartel camp.*

"Should have charged them 20," Paige said, her voice more playful than annoyed.

"Let's just say this group is not going to get a good referral," Bolivar muttered.

There was a slight shudder, then the hard push of deceleration. Paige sat up quickly, the movement and view something that would have distracted Bolivar if he was not shifting for his own pants…and slamming hard into the bunk's edge as he misjudged his movements.

One half of a g doesn't seem like a lot, he thought, seeing stars from bouncing his head. *But until you get used to it, it provides plenty of opportunities to look like an idiot.*

"You okay?" Paige asked, genuinely concerned.

"Yeah," Bolivar replied sheepishly. She smiled, slipping her T-shirt over her head.

"You want me to go down to the hold and fire up the *Yuri*?" she asked.

"Bolly," the speaker crackled, the moniker telling him who the speaker was even if the comms sounded like the end of a tunnel.

Okay, right behind a new CASPer is getting this ship upgraded with modern electronics, Bolivar thought.

"Yeah Silvius?" he replied.

"The Trader captain says prepare to be inspected," Silvius said. "He kindly asks that we do not anger the Peacemaker that's coming aboard, as the *Wraiths of the Eternal Night* are sitting off our port bow with a couple of escort frigates."

"Who the fuck are the *Wraiths of the Eternal Night?*" Paige asked, confused. Bolivar concentrated for a second, and his implants brought up the required information.

"Goka outfit," Bolivar said, the second syllable sounding like he was a crow. "Not wise to mess with—they're not keen on taking prisoners."

"What in the hell are they doing out here?" Paige asked, lacing up her boots.

Bolivar shook his head, then immediately regretted it.

"I really hope you didn't give yourself a concussion…" Paige said, starting to look worried at the pain crossing his face.

"I'll just tell everyone I got it in bed with you," Bolivar replied. "Think what it will do for your reputation."

"Hmm, tends to be the sole survivor and screws her boss to the point he's useless," Paige replied sarcastically. "Yes, my mother

462 | KENNEDY & WANDREY

would be so proud. Not that she'd have much room to talk given how she paid for me to get VOWs training."

Whoa, she's not bitter or anything, Bolivar thought, sensing the hurt in Paige's voice.

Bolivar was about to say something when Silvius interrupted.

"Apparently it's going to be a couple hours," Bolivar's brother said. "You can go back to nursing your concussion, Loverboy."

Bolivar and Paige looked at each other, then at the speaker.

"By the way, maybe when your little brother tells you that the transmit protocol on the captain's cabin has a glitch, you might want to listen to him," Silvius finished.

* * *

In reality, it was four more hours. Bolivar spent the intervening time gathering the Tumen's bona fides, grabbing breakfast with Silvius, then hitting the weight room. He was on his last set, veins bulging in his neck, when the three-toned hatch entry request sounded throughout the *Nuckelavee*.

Fucking figures, Bolivar thought to himself, his arms shaking as he strained to push the bar up.

"He can wait, one more!" Silvius barked, gripping the middle of the bar. "I've got your spot."

The tone sounded again, and Bolivar ignored it, pressing up one last time with his brother's help. Paige poked her head into the hatch at that moment, concern obvious on her face.

"What are you lunatics doing? You don't keep a Peacemaker waiting!" she said.

"It's a Peacemaker, not a deity," Bolivar said. Gesturing for Paige to lead the way, he headed toward the hatch where the *Nuckelavee* was attached to the Trade Guild freighter.

I can't even remember this tub's name, Bolivar thought. *She's just a big taxi.* It had been two weeks since they'd even spoken to a member of the larger vessel's crew. It wasn't that Zuparti didn't like humans. It was more a case that there was only so much cohabitation one could take with jumpy, paranoid weasels that would not...shut...up.

Bolivar stepped into the cargo hold and immediately noted the Tumen's shooters were all conspicuously present. Paige had stationed herself furthest from the entryway, an assault rifle leaning against a storage container out of the hatch's line of sight. Donovan and Mitchell, a pair of baby-faced rookies who had been with the Tumen for less than two weeks stood with their backs against the bulkhead, laser pistols on their hips. Closer to the door, casually holding assault rifles, were "Grandpa" and "Fenrir," a pair of Besquith males whom Paige had befriended shortly before being hired by the Tumen.

I'm still getting used to having a pair of wolfmen with us, Bolivar thought. Besquith were an honor-bound race, and it spoke volumes to the two creature's...desperation that they had pledged themselves to a human.

Beggars...choosers...we're all a bunch of riff raff, Bolivar thought. He looked up to ensure the bright green light over the hatch was illuminated, thus signifying breathable atmosphere was on the far side. Standing in the center of the hold, he signaled for Silvius to open the compartment. With a slight rumble, the *Nuckelavee's* portal swung upward, the waft of pungent air from the freighter making Bolivar's nose wrinkle.

The Peacemaker was a tall, bipedal humanoid. As it stepped into the light, Bolivar nearly cursed aloud.

Fuck me, it's an Equiri, he thought, as he took in the almost eight-foot-tall being. In the late 20th century, he remembered that there had been a fad of people getting their pictures taken with a horse head mask. If one made those horse features more narrow, gave the being a light gray skin tone, a dark crimson mane, and made the eyes an almost obsidian black, then this was a near description of an Equiri. Except, when one was smiling, as this Peacemaker was, the creature's mouth was much more "shred your grandma" than "I chew cud."

"Perhaps you should see about getting your translators fixed," the Equiri said, its voice flat and dour. "I could swear I said 'immediately' when referring to opening your hatch, not 'at your leisure' as you apparently heard."

To her credit, Paige did not turn and spear Bolivar with an "I told you so" look. As he regarded the Equiri's dark utility uniform and blazing blue Peacemaker Guild logo, Bolivar bit back several different replies.

"No one's been making you wait," Bolivar replied evenly. The Equiri's shark grin only broadened, and Bolivar had the distinct impression it wasn't humor driving the motion. "But if you're pressed for time, arguing over whether we sufficiently bowed and scraped at your grandeur doesn't seem to be indicative of that."

"Agreed," the Peacemaker replied after a pregnant pause. "As I am told, your translators regularly screw up my kind's names. Allow me to present my credentials." The being reached inside its utilities, withdrawing a flat rectangular device from its pockets.

I remember hearing how they gripped things with those hooves, but it's been awhile since I took biology, Bolivar thought, not wanting to distract himself looking it up. The Equiri manipulated the device, and after a moment a Tri-V, three-dimensional blue tree appeared in front of Bolivar. After a few moments, a Peacemaker ID followed.

Well holy shit, Bolivar thought, looking at the Peacemaker sequence number and the Equiri's name. As expected, the translator had butchered it, but not as badly as Bolivar had expected.

Mr. "Devilmane" has been doing this for a while, an indication he's not out here for something trivial, Bolivar thought grimly. Peacemakers, as the Union's enforcement arm, tended to rotate or die pretty frequently. Devilmane had had been operating for 10 Terran years, a veritable lifetime.

"The computer translates your name to Devilmane," Bolivar said slowly. "Is that acceptable to you?"

"Your pronunciation is terrible, but we can go with it," Devilmane replied.

You almost got called Ed, Bolivar thought. *But I'm sure you'd eventually look that reference up, then make it a point to come back and gnaw my face off.*

"You will take me to a private place," Devilmane stated. "There we will consume prepared flesh."

"I do not recall where it says I have to feed you," Bolivar replied. "Just let you see my ship."

"You are a mercenary," Devilmane snapped. "If you do not wish for me to discuss a potentially lucrative employment with you, I question why these others follow you."

Bolivar was well aware all the Tumen turned to look at him.

"Well, since you put it that way, let me introduce you to something called a ribeye steak."

* * *

*W*ell, *watching one of them eat is truly horrifying,* Bolivar thought. *Like watching a Black Stallion and Jaws mashup directed by that old Tarantino fellow.*

"You Earthers have strange tastes," Devilmane said, looking around the compartment.

"The yacht was my father's," Bolivar allowed. "I make no apologies for his tastes."

"Yes, one of the original investors in your species' starport," Devilmane replied. "I can appreciate an industrious sentient, even if I find your kind repugnant in general."

"Well don't hold back, tell me how you really feel," Bolivar replied, shaking his head.

Devilmane looked at him for a moment, then bared his teeth again.

"I think that is what your kind calls sarcasm. I doubt you want me to truly tell you what I believe about humans."

Awfully brave horsie to talk shit aboard **my** *yacht,* Bolivar thought. *Sure those frigates will blow us to kingdom come about ten seconds after your bio signs cut out, but that might be worth it.*

"Forgive me. Our kind is rather blunt."

"Never would have guessed."

"We have heard of your company, Thompson of Houston," Devilmane said, flicking his thick tongue to remove a hunk of steak from his teeth.

"I'm somewhat perplexed at why Thompson's Tumen is on the Peacemakers' radar," Bolivar said. "I'd be happy to get a steering azimuth as to how to get *off* your screen."

"Because you were the only mercenaries dumb enough to take a contract with the Order of Meyra," Devilmane said flatly.

That sounds ominous, Bolivar thought, keeping his face expressionless.

"We formed it in accordance with the most recent Mercenary Guild guidelines," he replied. "But I'm concerned—what did the Order of Meyra do to get on the Peacemakers' radar?'"

"Are you familiar with the 'Dark Heart Compact,' Mr. Thompson?" Devilmane asked.

"Please tell me that's a bad translation," Bolivar replied. "And no."

Devilmane shook his head.

"You truly are a fool," his guest said. "Please, could I have another of what you call ribeye?"

"No," Bolivar snapped. Devilmane looked at him, black eyes flat.

"I see I have offended," the Equiri replied. "My species does not apologize, but I realize that is customary with yours. Please allow me to elaborate."

"Of course," Bolivar said, feeling a momentary pride at not gritting his teeth.

"The actual Buman is more poetic, but I hate their language almost as much as I hate their smell," Devilmane continued. "About forty years ago, someone translated a bunch of your texts into Buman. One of them was a book entitled *Heart of Darkness.* Another was *Guns, Germs, and Steel.* Are you familiar with these texts?"

"More or less," Bolivar said. "My father insisted all of his children be well educated."

"How familiar are you with Bumans and their disposition?"

"Curious, devourers of knowledge. Should have been cats, not birds."

Devilmane looked at him for a moment, and Bolivar realized an explanation was in order.

"Felines on Earth are known for their curiosity."

Devilmane nodded in understanding.

"We were told your felines were known for their brutality and murderous play."

"That too," Bolivar allowed. He looked at his glass, realizing it was empty. He poured himself another shot of whiskey.

If we're going to talk about the horrible days of the original Colonel Kurtz, Marlow, and all the rest, I really need to be closer to blitzed than sober. History class had been depressing enough in high school. Revisiting it after one knew just how shitty "advanced species" were to indigenous populations made it even worse.

"So just how much have the Bumans collectively learned about Earth's colonial era?" Bolivar asked.

"Enough that a significant number of them are using it as a cautionary tale," Devilmane said. "In turn, they're starting to corrupt the established order of things."

"Established order how?" Bolivar asked.

"Many of them are starting to question how the Union conducts resource acquisition with less advanced races," Devilmane replied. "They're forming societies, harassing other species, and generally making nuisances of themselves. They've even created a Charter of Ethicality. "

Spoken like someone whose race is higher up the pecking order than most others, Bolivar thought.

"Pretend I'm a member of a species who just crawled up out of the backwater," Bolivar said. "Talk to me really simple about what the Peacemakers' problem is with the Order of Meyra. Seeing as how they've just hired me to do a job."

"The reason they want you to 'do a job' is because several Buman consortiums signed the aforementioned charter," Devilmane said. "Basically they agreed to only traffic in goods that were obtained 'ethically' as defined by the document."

I'm guessing that "ethically" in this case means different than the usual Union style of "civilize them with a mag rifle," Bolivar mused.

"You seem opposed to this," Bolivar said.

"The Union has the Guilds," Devilmane spat. "The Guilds have been effective in maintaining the order of things. We do not need individual species deciding that their...*sensibilities* supersede the Guilds."

"So in other words, the Peacemakers are upset..." Bolivar started.

"My opinions have nothing to do with my status as a Peacemaker or the job I am to offer you," Devilmane spat.

Oh, I seem to have struck some nerves, Bolivar thought.

"All I know is we've been given 10 million to bring back evidence that the natives are sentient to the point they're pre-industrial. That's it. Shouldn't be that hard," Bolivar said. "So unless you are going to offer me 12 million and Peacemaker sanction to kill this contract, I think our talk is done."

"I am concerned with the Crimson Squid," Devilmane snapped.

"I'm not familiar with the..." Bolivar started, only to be cut off by a hoof slamming onto the table.

"Do not lie to me, human!"

Bolivar raised an eyebrow.

"Are you familiar with the Horned Scarabs?" Devilmane asked, the sudden change of topic throwing Bolivar for a second.

"Small mercenary company," Bolivar said. "Got called in to clear out the Squiddies on the planet we humans call "Meru" over in the Tolo Arm. Wiped the Squiddies out like the Spanish Inquisition hitting the local Heretics 'R' Us."

Devilmane looked perplexed for a moment, then after concentrating on his implants nodded enthusiastically.

I feel like I just offered the pony a handful of carrots, Bolivar thought. *Except in this case it'd be more appropriate to think of a handful of kittens.*

"I heard the problem is that the Squiddies didn't take kindly to that," Bolivar continued. "Punched back twice as hard, started targeting mercs' families."

"My brother was a member of the Scarabs," Devilmane said. "They slaughtered his two wives and all of his young about five years after the events on Meru."

Kind of smart of the Squiddies to wait and pick folks off four or five at a time, Bolivar thought. *All at once draws attention.*

"Well that explains why *you* have a problem with them, but not the Peacemakers," Bolivar said, keeping his tone level.

"Did you ever wonder why the Scarabs stopped getting attacked?" Devilmane asked.

"I figured it was because someone in the Squiddies, despite their anarchist tendencies, realized they were damn close to the Mercenary Guild making the biggest calamari stir fry the Union's ever seen," Bolivar replied. The Equiri's teeth bared again.

Lifetime achievement unlocked: Made an Equiri actually laugh.

"Something like that," Devilmane said. "In reality, there were...reprisals. The Bugitar believed to be in charge of the Crimson Squid were all...liquidated."

Well that explains a lot, Bolivar thought. The Bugitar were a minor race that were the discount dollar store to the more established races' superstore chain.

No one likes being the folks playing poker against a stacked deck.

"The problem is, the Crimson Squid should have changed their symbol to what your species call the hydra," Devilmane continued. "Whatever heads grew in their place seem to be smarter and wider-thinking."

The horse-faced alien pulled out a red and white slate. A stand-ard-issue Union computer, the device looked about the same as a pre-Contact Terran tablet. Of course, it had more computing power than an early 21st century supercomputer, and Bolivar had a feeling this one was chock full of information.

"I would guess your outfit is headed to a large planet in the TX-R3D system, yes?" Devilmane asked.

"Yes," Bolivar replied after a moment.

"I will need to see your contract and dossier," Devilmane said.

Bolivar took a deep breath.

Fuck it, he thought, then moved the files from his pinplant to the storage device attached to his pinlink. Once the necessary files were shipped over, he held the device out to Devilmane, and the alien placed it into the slate. A moment later, a visual representation of the TX-R3D system was holographically projected above the table.

"What is your unit calling this planet?" Devilmane asked.

"Lucifer," Bolivar replied. Devilmane looked at him for a moment, then simply nodded.

I almost expected a whinny to go with that, Bolivar thought. He looked down at his shot glass, then moved it to the next table over.

"We figured it was apt given the red diamond harvesting," he said, slurring slightly.

"You humans are strange," Devilmane said, tapping the tablet four times then making a squiggly motion with his hoof.

The projected map winked out of existence, replaced by a floating Mercator projection of Lucifer with the planet's four large continents. The shallow, fresh water oceans that separated the masses looked almost like rivers when pressed into two dimensions.

"If we're going to name the planet Lucifer, I guess we'll name the continents Bael, Astarte, Palmon, and Zagan to stick with the theme," Bolivar said.

"We have an entire pantheon of hells you could choose from," Devilmane stated.

Sweet Jesus, everything is lost on them.

"Your employers left the impression that you'd be able to find underground warrens and population centers at these locations?" Devilmane asked, as the map seemed to suddenly break out in measles.

"Yes," Bolivar said. "Or at least, the ruins of them."

"No," Devilmane said, removing the dots. "You are a pawn in a game of chess this Order has no clue is being played."

The alien's hoof descended onto the tablet's glass again. The previous dots were replaced with two large ones located on the continents Bael and Astarte.

"These are the two main base camps for red diamond operations on Lucifer," Devilmane said. "Originally the mercs landed at these two sites, then conducted sub-orbital movements in battalion strength to every population center larger than ten thousand natives."

Which is why, sports fans, that advancing from nomad to feudal sucks when interstellar raiders come calling, Bolivar thought.

"So how many natives have these *Bugsatzgruppen* killed?" Bolivar asked. After a few moments, Devilmane looked at Bolivar.

"What is this term?" he asked.

"Sorry, I'm being a dumbass," Bolivar answered, then explained what *Einsatzgruppen* had been to the alien. Devilmane looked at him with as close to an expression of horror as his kind seemed to allow.

"It was a different time," Bolivar said with a tired shrug.

"These...*Bugsatzgruppen* have eliminated almost 90 percent of the indigenous population," Devilmane replied.

"What?!" Bolivar asked. "How in the hell did they do that?"

"Your species seemed to be quite apt at killing your own kind," Devilmane said in disgust. "Why would it surprise you that other mercenaries can also eliminate the less advanced? We believe that bioweapons were also employed," Devilmane said simply.

"Who is that stupid?! There's no way someone puts that in a contract!"

"You are aware that the Mercenary Guild is not comprised of omniscient deities," Devilmane said. "In this case, we believe that cartel security was also involved. In any case, they did not use orbital bombardment, so that only narrows it down to 300 firms."

"The Bumans said these beings may be distant cousins of the Minsha," Bolivar said, his voice shaken. "Have everyone's favorite Mantises heard about this shit?"

Devilmane's mouth split wide open, as he rocked his head forward and backward. The sound that came out of his mouth was staccato and disturbing.

I hope my brain dumps this memory, Bolivar thought. *That's the stuff of nightmares.* With an audible snap, the Equiri's visage became nearly expressionless again.

"There is no hard proof," Devilmane replied.

"Let me guess—that's where the Tumen comes in?"

"You provide hope for your species," Devilmane said. "Perhaps you should preserve your genetic contribution before landing on this world."

Okay, vaguely uncomfortable compliment there, Bolivar thought. *Especially as we all leave 'genetic contributions' behind as part of our modus operandi.*

"How many *Bugsatz* left?"

"Most have moved off world," Devilmane replied. "There are maybe one hundred remaining."

Reinforced company, Bolivar thought. *If his intel is good.*

"But I don't get it," Bolivar said. "Why bring us in?"

"If you arrived on this world and found 90 percent of the population gone, would you not immediately leave?" Devilmane asked.

Bolivar gave the Peacemaker a befuddled look.

Okay, maybe less Scotch next time.

"The depopulation would be evidence itself that the red diamonds were achieved through unethical means, no?" Devilmane continued, his tone indicating he expected the light bulb to come on.

"Okay, so…" Bolivar said, still not getting it.

"Many of the Trade Guild's board have secretly signed the Ethical Compact," Devilmane said, his tone clearly not impressed. "The same thing has happened with the Merchant Guild. Not a majority, but surely enough to start putting pressure on unwitting corporations who are financing this."

Bolivar felt awareness starting to dawn on him.

"Which will drive up the price of red diamonds, as I'm certain this is going to 'taint' much of the supply," Bolivar said. "Higher cost red diamonds, better funding for whomever may be siphoning a bit off this trade."

"Now you understand what happens when one begins to upset the expected order of things," Devilmane said triumphantly.

This Meyran thing is getting out of hand, Bolivar thought. *Still, just turning a blind eye to everything isn't the answer either.*

"Just to be clear, the Crimson Squid will benefit the most from the increased prices," Devilmane said.

"So what do you need from us?" Bolivar asked, a sinking feeling in his stomach.

"Soil samples and data files at a minimum," Devilmane said. "A live prisoner would lead to a bonus given your small numbers."

"The Order wanted a live native as well," Bolivar stated. "I only brought one bio container. I don't fancy bringing someone who might be with the Squiddies back aboard this freighter. That's how the captain decides spacing the lot of us is better than potentially being considered a snitch."

Devilmane regarded him for a second.

"I applaud your strategic thinking, human," the Peacemaker said. "You bring credit to your lineage."

"Thank you, but compliments don't solve my problem," Bolivar replied.

"I will mention to the captain that I have ordered you to report for questioning in six months," Devilmane said. "He will likely flee and completely scrub any mention of you in his log rather than returning to pick you up."

"Ooookaaay…" Bolivar said, raising an eyebrow.

"I will return with the *Wraiths* plus some other reinforcements in 87 days," Devilmane continued. "We will extract you, pay you 120 million credits, and allow you to participate in the cleansing of the planet if you have proof of the genocide."

"And if we don't?"

"Seventy million for your time."

Jesus Christ.

"Before you plan how to expand your business, realize that the Peacemakers cannot protect you once this job is complete," Devilmane said. "Every time you arrive on a planet, you may find your death at the hands of the Squid if this goes awry."

"That's the price of admission for this business," Bolivar said, waving Devilmane's concerns away. "I sincerely doubt they'll risk the Mercenary Guild's ire a second time."

"You are not taking this seriously enough, human!" Devilmane said, the sound accompanied by an almost demonic whinny.

Bolivar looked at the Equiri, its dark eyes boring into his.

"Unless you are ready to be praying for death while simultaneously hearing the wet sounds of some Zuul eating your screaming sister's intestines, I suggest you give this offer some thought."

"Maybe I'm an idiotic idealist, but cutting off the funding for a bunch of terrorists whose ultimate goal is the dissolution of the Union sounds like a good thing to wager our lives against," Bolivar said.

Devilmane continued to regard him.

"Look, some fuckers are probably planning something that's going to spill large quantities of blood in the near future," Bolivar replied. "There's 16 of us. If we kick some nefarious plan in its collective balls, maybe we trade 16 lives for a few million. So give me what intel you've got, and we'll plan."

"I had heard how idiotically idealistic your race was," Devilmane said. "I see now that the rumors were, if anything, underestimated."

"Well kiss my ass too, horse face," Bolivar said, then regretted it. To his surprise, the insult got him a nod of respect.

"I trust this operation is in good hands, even if it takes you being intoxicated to finally properly insult me," Devilmane said. "I will drop everything we have into your pin. I look forward to our next meeting."

"You're assuming I survive the 30 minutes after you leave," Bolivar said.

"Are you concerned about mutiny?" Devilmane asked.

"No, just telling my people they're going to be living rain forest style for two months longer than expected is not going to lead to a nomination for boss of the year," Bolivar replied. "Oh well...the Christmas bonuses are going to be insane."

* * * * *

Chapter 3: Change of Plans, Redux

Point Styx
Lucifer
0900 Local
13 April

UNK ORGA DETECTED<
PSS SEN 3, BEARING TWO NINE FIVE RELATIVE<

The simple message scrolling across his battle armor's visor sent a surge of adrenaline through Bolivar.

Fucking finally, he thought. *Looks like they're coming right down the trail like we expected.*

It had been a long 85 days. As planned, they had hidden the *Nuckelavee* within the cloud of cargo containers discharged in Lucifer near orbit. Like most prudent people who did not want a rain of bus-sized metal boxes anywhere near them, the *Bugsatz* mercs had scheduled the cargo drop on the opposite side of the massive mountain range that bifurcated the continent from east to west near the planetary equator.

MULTIPLE UNK ORGA DETECTED<
BIO SIGNS CONFIRMED<
ESTIMATED RANGE FIVE HUNDRED METERS<

The ride down to 30,000 feet from orbit had been nerve wracking in the free-falling *Nuckelavee*. Once the vessel had been firmly in the mountain range's sensor shadow, Silvius had activated the thrusters and turned their plummet into a glide. Eight thousand kilometers away from the cargo drop site, he had placed the vessel down in a clearing. After erecting camouflage nets and shutting off the power plant, the Tumen had laid doggo for the first night.

8 ORGA, RANGE 350 METERS<

POSS ID: 3 TORT 3 FLATAR 2 ZUUL

PSS SEN 3, BEARING TWO NINE FIVE RELATIVE<

Wait a second, Bolivar thought. *That's a grouping that makes no sense.* The Tortantula were giant, wasp-waisted spiders, while the Flatar were the evil, one-foot-tall chipmunks that rode them like malevolent Chip 'n' Dales. In their time on planet, the Tumen had seen the duos running regular patrol routes through the region.

Okay, the plan of snatching up one of the furry midgets just went awry, Bolivar thought. *There's never been Zuul before.*

BOSS. NOT SURE ABOUT THIS GROUP. THE TWO ZUUL SEEM TO BE CARRYING PROBES OF SOME KIND. THEY'RE IN REGULAR COMMS WITH THE NEAREST *BUGSATZ* FOB.

The message from Paige, likely cooking in her powered-down CASPer, had come through the fiber optic cable attached to the port on his armor's right heel.

YEAH, THAT'S NOT A PLEASANT SURPRISE, Bolivar responded.

ALMOST AS UNPLEASANT AS THE CHAFES I'M GETTING FROM SPENDING TWO EXTRA MONTHS IN THIS DAMN TIN CAN.

Bolivar fought the urge to move and look behind him. The red-head was 200 meters behind him, the CASPer buried under a half meter of mud to protect it from magnetic anomaly detectors. While the jungle heat was not as bad as Terra's, it was still bad enough that the *Flaming Yurt* was a mobile sauna.

Not that I'm much better off, he thought, feeling sweat running down his back to be wicked away by the battle armor's life support.

THANK YOU, MADAME SOURPUSS. DID YOU HAPPEN TO HAVE AN OPINION ON THE TACTICAL SITUATION? Bolivar shot back.

I WAS THINKING. THE JUICE AIN'T WORTH THE SQUEEZE. DON'T WANT ZUUL HUNTING US FREESTYLE, Paige typed back.

She's got a point, Bolivar thought. Tortantula were pretty straight-forward killers, with the Flatar along to add extra intelligent firepow-er. The Zuul were the wild cards. Zuul were known for being very, as the pun went, *dog*matic about following orders. The crazy happened when the walking canines were presented with something not cov-ered in their directions. Then they got downright chaotic neutral in solving their new problems, often violently.

AGREED. WE LET THIS GROUP PASS, GET THE NEXT ONE, Bolivar replied.

ROGER. NEXT GROUP IS BUSY CONDUCTING COMMS CHECKS. SHOULD BE ABOUT THREE HOURS.

Great thing about your opponents being basically an ill-disciplined scratch team is that no one's shit is encrypted, Bolivar thought. *CASPers with elec-tronic countermeasures make child's play out of unsecured nets. Makes it easy to figure...*

In retrospect, Bolivar would realize that he should have confirmed with the entire snatch and grab team that they were letting this group pass. Paige and he had directly communicated using the command fiberlink, not the general comms channel. Fenrir and Grandpa were experienced enough to realize that, even from ambush with a CASPer, one did not screw with three Tortantulas *and* a pair of Zuul. But the rookies...well, like most young men, they were equally eager to screw or shoot something, and eight aliens in the kill sack seemed as alluring as a high-end escort spreading her legs for 'one on the house.'

The compressed air charges firing the gas mines was the first indication Bolivar had that they had lost their damn minds. Arranged in a two horizontal rows alongside the trail, the gas mines began their arc from beneath the ground with an aim point roughly human head height in the trail's center. Two of them never made it; the Flatars blasted them out of the air in a criss-cross of chemical laser beams. The other six burst with high-pitched sounds as their contents were forced out in an opaque cloud.

Fuck fuck fuck! Bolivar thought, his arms moving in a blur as he fired at the Tortantula closest to him with his *Morningblade* laser rifle. The spider was distracted by the collapsing Flatar on his back, the mammal coughing and hacking from the vomit gas. It still saw Bolivar's motion and was turning to charge toward him when the first laser caught it in one of its eyes. The creature screamed but sprang incredibly fast toward the Tumen's leader...then had its thorax explode as Fenrir hit it with a grenade from the revolver launcher in his hand.

Bolivar turned back to the kill sack and saw the fight was already over. The ambushed aliens had gotten several shots off, but not in any coordinated way due to the gas.

We got freakin' lucky, Bolivar thought, visually checking the three spiders. The last Tortantula's legs were still twitching, a burning Flatar pinned under its body. Firing two more blasts into the Tortantula that had charged him just to be sure, Bolivar grabbed the now unconscious Flatar on top of it.

Are the Zuuls still alive? he thought. The Flatar looked up at him and snarled, then immediately retched again. Putting the rifle against the alien's head, Bolivar fired once.

"SITREP!" he barked, turning away from the nearly decapitated corpse. "One up!"

"Two up!" Paige said, her voice clearly annoyed.

"Four up!" Mitchell said, almost panting.

The two Besquith's reports were both identical rumbling grumbles.

"Five up."

"Six up."

What happened to Donovan? Bolivar wondered, watching as the two Besquith began moving through the dispersing gas cloud in their spiked, black battle armor. The huge wolfmen looked even more monstrous with their oversized respirators. With a flash of their axes, they made sure of the third Tortantula and its rider.

"Someone check on Tumen Three," Bolivar said. He strode over to where both Zuul continued to attempt to fight to their knees, vomit streaming from their muzzles. Whipping his rifle around, he swung the butt as hard as he could into the back of the first Zuul's head. With a whimper, the beast collapsed, and he kicked it onto its side so it would not drown.

Goddamn rookies, he thought, trying to fight down his anger. *Any idiot should have known those were bad odds. Tortantulas are not easy...*

"Look out!" Paige shouted. Seeing the motion out of the corner of his eye, Bolivar dove aside as the second Zuul swung desperately at him with its claws. He felt the scrape of the beast's nails across the front of his thighs, the blow vicious enough that it would have laid him open like Freddy Krueger's backhand. Bolivar landed on his back, the rifle falling from his hand. Before the Zuul could gather himself, two snarling forms landed on it.

Gotta talk to the boys about going hand-to-hand, Bolivar thought, grabbing the rifle. A severed limb flew from the whirling pile, the Zuul's plaintive wail ending in a gargle as Fenrir ripped the smaller canine's throat out.

Or you have to accept that having two walking dire wolves isn't necessarily the end of the world, Bolivar thought, shaken.

"Lots of chatter, boss," Paige said, speaking directly over her loudspeakers.

"Boss," Mitchell said, sounding distant. "Donovan's dead."

Bolivar whirled toward the rookie's position. He saw Mitchell standing over a lump on the ground and cursed. Rushing over, he saw what had happened plain as day. Donovan had not been hit full on. Instead, it looked like one of the Tortantulas had fired some sort of flechette weapon in the rookie's general direction, and one of the dense needles skipped off a rock in front of the rookie and up under his face shield.

Luck is still a bitch, Bolivar thought angrily.

"Get his legs," he said to Mitchell. "Fenrir, bind the prisoner."

"They're debating whether to roll the QRF," Paige said, referring to the *Bugsatz* Quick Reaction Force. "Seems like whatever lieutenant is in charge of it has a bunch of 'fuck' and 'that' without reinforcements."

Thank you, Jesus, for cautious aliens, Bolivar thought. Human mercs would have been out for blood, Besquith likely not far behind them. Just about everyone else in the galaxy was not really keen on getting their heads blown off regardless of what had just happened to friendly forces.

Grunting, Bolivar and Mitchell carried their dead comrade next to the closet Tortantula and the Flatar next to it.

I don't even know what words to say over his body, Bolivar thought angrily. Looking over, he could see Mitchell's lips moving silently.

"Holy shit," Paige said.

"What is it?" Bolivar asked, pulling out three small discs. Placing his fingertip on them, his suit connected with their timers. Once more just *thinking*, he set the dials for five minutes apiece, then placed one at Donovan's feet, another on the center of mass of one of the Tortantulas, and the last on another Tortantula's head.

"Okay folks, five minutes!" he barked. "Paige, again…what was it?"

"The Zuuls," Paige replied, somewhat distracted. "They were searching for nesting sites for the indigenes."

Bolivar stopped for a second, shocked. From the lack of indigenous activity, they had assumed that the *Bugsatz* had pretty much annihilated the entire native population. Recording the lack of indigenous presence had, as Devilmane predicted, been more than enough to satisfy their Order of Meyra contract. However, a live specimen would definitely put icing on the cake, as well as perhaps provide a living witness to the massacre.

"Silvius, we're heading for LZ 1," Bolivar said, bouncing the transmission off the relays the team had put in place. "The *Bugsatz* don't seem all that interested in coming out to play."

"Don't blame them," came the reply. "Lifting off."

"Human Alpha, come quick!" Fenrir grunted. Bolivar strode over to where the bloody-muzzled Besquith was placing the dismembered Zuul's torso atop the other Tortantula. Looking down where Fenrir had ripped the dead alien's shirt open, Bolivar felt a chill down his spine as he looked at the tattoo shifting before their eyes.

Fuck me, he thought.

"HOSTILE SENSORS DETECTED! HOSTILE SENSORS DETECTED!"

The audio alarm in his battle armor nearly deafened him even as he dropped to the ground and began looking around. With a start, he realized that the warning was being relayed from the *Nuckalevee*. Before he could press the transmit button, his suit answered the question he was about to ask Silvius. Three angry triangles, not there previously, had winked into life surrounding the *Bugsatz* base camp one hundred kilometers distant. Before Bolivar had a chance to do anything more than draw in the breath to scream an order, each triangle sprouted five smaller ones that immediately leaped toward the incoming space yacht.

The *Nuckalevee* had launched from the other side of the mountain range and continued down a twisting river valley that bisected it. Silvius had plotted his approach route at supersonic speed through a notch between two 15,000-meter peaks.

"Silvius, evasives…" Bolivar began shouting.

The *Nuckalevee*'s maneuvers within atmosphere were limited. At multiple times the speed of sound, there was simply not enough room between the two peaks to dodge the incoming missiles. Even if there had been, there was not a single being aboard the yacht that could tolerate more than 12 Gs, while the obsolescent, smuggled missiles fired at her could easily pull 15. In the face of an unplanned threat, the yacht's computers and autopilot wisely decided not to knock out the entire crew.

What the automated defenses *did* do was immediately engage countermeasures. These were promptly ignored by 14 of the incoming missiles. This left the *Nuckalevee's* close in weapons systems (CIWS). While far from top of the line, the four CIWS pods served Silvius and the 10 crew members well. Of the 14 weapons left, 12 never made it through the chemical laser and magnetic cannon storm that provided an intense fireworks show above the canopy.

The first of the two that hit, however, killed the entire bridge crew before their brains had time to fully register the bulkhead disintegrating in front of them. The backup autopilot barely had time to issue stabilizing commands before the last missile plunged into the vessel's engineering spaces. The dense metal kinetic kill vehicle met the yacht's propulsion plant with a screech of metal and a shower of painfully bright sparks. Ceasing to be a controlled craft, the *Nuckalevee* ripped itself apart in a tumble and debris wave that moved like an angry giant's swipe for three miles through the jungle.

Thankfully, the jungle canopy prevented Bolivar from actually seeing his brother's death. The sound and loss of datalink, however, told him all he needed to know. There was a stunned silence at the ambush site.

Silvius, Bolivar thought. *I'm sorry.*

The aural warning from the Dante discs passing through one minute snapped him out of his shock. Swiftly recording the dead Zuul's chest with his onboard cam, Bolivar blinked away his tears. His armor claimed the water with a slight suction sound.

"Change of plans, people," he bit out. "Grab that shithead, and let's get moving."

To their credit, the Tumen didn't even hesitate. Throwing the shock bracelet-bound Zuul over his shoulder, Grandpa took point, followed by Mitchell, then Fenrir, then Bolivar. The solid *thrump! thrump! thrump!* of the *Flaming Yurt* walking behind him kept Bolivar from glancing back when the Dante Discs finally ignited. Thinking, he brought up a list of the stores they carried and had emplaced at the caches they'd established for just such an eventuality.

Forty-eight hours, Bolivar thought angrily. *Just gotta survive 48 hours.*

"We've punched them in the nose hard enough they may leave us alone," Paige said, her voice tight with emotion.

"We'll see," Bolivar said. "For now, we move. They don't know we have help coming, but if they figure it out they're going to want us dead."

"How are we going to get off this rock?" Mitchell asked. Fear was starting to set in.

"You let the boss worry about that," Paige snapped, steel in her voice.

In retrospect, maybe not telling the entire team about the added contract was a bad plan, Bolivar thought. *Time to remedy that.*

"Listen up folks." He huffed as Grandpa and Fenrir picked up the pace. "We've got backup coming. We've just got to hold on for a bit."

I really hope Devilmane has a ground contingent somewhere on those tubs, Bolivar thought. *I don't see the Wraiths buying off on doing a hot extraction.*

"Cross that bridge when we come to it," Paige said, using a direct laser link.

"Get out of my head," Bolivar muttered back.

"Are you okay?" she asked, then corrected herself. "Stupid fucking question."

"No, I am far from okay," Bolivar said, then added with a confidence he didn't feel. "Ask me in three days when we're off this rock."

"Sounds like they don't want any more of us right now," Paige said. "But bad news—they've got help coming in 24 hours."

Bolivar took a deep breath, then looked up through the canopy at the mountains beyond.

"Then tomorrow's gonna be a good day for someone to die."

I just hope it's not us.

# # # # #

Messenger
by Nick Cole

Part One - Even Mercenaries Sing the Blues

Nobody knows anything.

Really.

Nobody knows anything.

When I look at your record's jacket, the one we began to keep on the day you started working for Secure Horizons, a new hire recruit just out of the schools, I can make my guesses as to who you are. But I always remind myself...nobody really knows anything.

All I have left now are the actual records' jackets of my company. The digital copies were seized after we failed to fulfill the contract on Denar. Today is a hot Tuesday in San Bernardino. I left the motel room I rent, stopped for my rum, some ice, and a few deli sandwiches. Then I arrived at the storage facility sprawl that spreads off into the burning dirt of high desert. Today, as I do every day now, I will go through the records of all that once was and try to put it all together for no good reason in particular.

And today, Tom Kyle, today is your day.

But first a taste of the rum over some ice from a plastic bag, and a squeeze from a slice of one of the limes I stole from a tree in someone's yard.

Hard to believe the CEO, the former CEO that is, of a merc company, an Earth merc company, an almost *guaranteed* money-making operation in this fantastic day and age of the future, needs to steal limes off a neighbor's tree at six a.m. But I do. Every little bit helps since I got sued into oblivion.

And they're not really my neighbors. The people I steal from. They're just some Cambodians whose small house and fruit trees back up to *The Whole Year Inn* where I live as long as I pay by the week.

I have occasionally, since Denar, been forced to pay by the day at the *Hole yur In*, as I call it.

I have this secret fantasy that I can actually part ways with *The Whole Year Inn* and live in my storage locker if I'm crafty enough to avoid the surveillance drones.

I once evaded capture after getting my mech shot out from underneath me on some jungle hellhole I can't seem to remember the name of. PTSD...I guess. I went to a lot of jungle hellholes when I was saving every dime to put together Secure Horizons. I went to a lot of hellholes, not necessarily jungle-specific. I did all the things one needs to do to become a small business owner of a merc company.

I killed a lot of stuff.

And for a brief moment, I was successful enough to retain an HR firm and get some top-flight recruits fresh out of the schools. Like you, Tom. You tested well, even though you were lazy in school, and your dad had gone to prison. Even though you came from a wealthy family. Even though every opportunity was available to you...we were able to get our hands on you, and we marked you for OCS. We saw a young commissioned officer in you. HR told us so.

Most of my officers at that time, all of whom got killed on Denar (except for you, Tom), were vets...and really non-coms from other companies. I made 'em officers, and they made good leaders. But we all saw something in you. So we made you a Lieutenant. In charge of a mech platoon.

And we sent you to Denar.

And everyone got slaughtered. At Denar.

And you got religion.

That's the last note in the record from Captain Hull, your CO. Captain Hull got immolated inside his mech when a HEAT round punched through his belly armor and ignited the internal magazines. But before Captain Hull could get killed at Hastings Ridge on Denar, he made that note in your jacket.

It says...

"LT Kyle reports he has become saved by Jesus. Questioned if that would somehow affect his ability to lead his platoon, he replied, "negative." He merely felt command needed to be apprised of his religious status in the event he was killed. So Kyle got religion. I'll have to keep an eye on him."

And then two days later you all went to Hastings Ridge on the contract to pacify the war-like Kara so the colony operation could expand their sphere of influence on Denar, and about 10 seconds after that everything turned into a full-scale battle.

One mech company, mine, Secure Horizons, against satellite estimates of up to 40,000 insurgents. It seemed all the tribes had gotten together to react badly, and this is putting it mildly, to the outside influence. We shouldn't have been faulted for our loss by the guild.

Repeat.

We should not...but hell, we were.

I wasn't there. Shoulda been. But I wasn't, Tom.

And so no one knows anything.

I sit and look at your file, reading all the notes, not because, and I'm being honest with myself here because that's all I have left, not because I want to know about you, Tom, but because I'm trying to see where I went wrong as I sit here and drink myself to death in the heat of an anonymous storage locker in a sea of anonymous storage lockers. Going over the past...one record's jacket at a time. No one knows anything.

I just know you were bright, gifted, and a real killer. And you got religion.

And you were the only one who survived Hasting's Ridge.

I know we failed to fulfill the contract and lost our licensing. I know I had to sell everything, and so I sold your mech. Along with the recovered scrap that comprised the rest. Weapons removed, of course.

I sold your badly shot up mech to you, Tom, and told you where you could get some illegal weapons to hire out. You just smiled. You always were a quiet kid. You just smiled and said you didn't need weapons anymore.

I was already drinking heavily. I barely heard you. After the trial, and during really, I became a full-fledged alcoholic. The insurance hearings. The licensing hearings. The divorce. I should've asked why a kid would want a mech he didn't have the weapons for. I should've, Tom. That seems very interesting to me right now on this afternoon, as I sit, drinking myself to death somewhere in San Bernardino.

I'd like to know, Tom.

I'd like to know what a kid needs a mech with no weapons for.

But I don't. And so...no one knows anything. Really. No one does.

* * * * *

Part Two - Last Message of Tom Kyle

Tom Kyle, system logfile...assign under personal notes. This is for anyone who wants to know what happened to me. Why...why I did what I'm doing.

After Denar, I took a freighter headed out deep along the Spiral Arm. I asked the captain if he was going by any relatively habitable and yet unexplored worlds.

"Lot of 'em out there along the way," he mumbled. "All of 'em dangerous."

Dangerous to most spacers means any planet. Spacers tend to like space and space alone. And the truth is he's right. Every planet is dangerous, some more than others. But life is dangerous.

I've known that since I was a kid.

There was this one day when I realized life was indeed dangerous. When I was kid. Fifteen. And my dad was taken away to prison for murder.

Everyone in our small community, a relatively upscale military industrial complex tech enclave where every other family was probably sitting on some patent keeping everyone in the best clothes and latest kicks, a brand new car for your sixteenth, knew about the murder.

Happened at the golf club. One summer night. Mrs. Summers. There was an end-of-summer ball that night. All the parents had gone to it and gotten drunk. We kids were down by the lake until midnight. It was warm and hot, and we went swimming in the dark. I had sex with her daughter that night. Mrs. Summers. And then she was murdered sometime between the hours of eleven p.m. and one a.m.

And three days later they arrested my dad.

And I never saw him again because he was killed in prison about two weeks after he was sentenced. I know he didn't kill her. Mrs. Summers. But doesn't every kid think that?

The freighter captain dropped me, literally, over an uncharted world called Tessarah.

"You realize this is a one-way ticket, son?" he asked me as they cycled the aft airlock. The ship was skimming atmosphere and I could hear a hard whistle beyond the fuselage. It was like the keening moan of some unconsidered ghost we all knew about and weren't scared of. I'd done orbital insertion before. The company I'd worked for had paid for the advanced training. But I'd never really done it other than training. So I was scared.

But not of any ghosts.

Just the two hundred thousand-foot fall in a one-ton mech.

"Got it. Kick me." I told the captain and his crew. If they would've gone over exactly what the realities of what was coming next, what I'd signed myself up for, I'd would've backed out.

Getting dropped on a planet sounds like something out of movie. And surely there'd be pirates and treasure and a beautiful girl. If it were a movie.

But this wasn't.

Starvation and death were at the bottom of my fall. That's how life really is. It's nothing like a movie.

The reality was there would be no services. No food to find, kill, and prepare. Maybe not even water that wouldn't make me deathly ill. No medical. No nothing of all the things we take for granted. Everything I thought I might need I'd stowed on the mech.

I didn't even have any weapons.

Wait...Not true. I had a knife.

And the truth was...I mean...the truth is I might have been hoping to get killed in the drop. Now that I think about it. I hadn't slept much since Denar. Since Hasting's Ridge, I try, tried, and was trying not to think about what happened. My company was like my family...and they all got killed, too.

Except for me.

It was like losing my dad all over again.

Captain Hull taught me how to drink.

My dad taught me how to fish.

After my dad's trial, I'd felt like an outcast around Viejo Verde. The enclave where I'd grown up. Chelsea, Mrs. Summer's daughter and my first real girlfriend, well...that relationship was over three days later. When your dad murders her mom it puts a damper on the future you'd promised each other.

Sometimes I wonder what happened to Chelsea. If she ever recovered. Moved on. Had a whole new life and never thought about the past. Like me.

Or had she died too, that night. Like my mom. Except still walking around and watching TV all day. There, and not really there.

Of course it was a sex crime.

Mrs. Summers had been raped and strangled on the Thirteenth Hole. Just beyond the lights of the clubhouse. Where all the rest of the parents were drinking and groping each other to old music by some band called Nirvana.

Chelsea and I promised stuff to each other that night. All that dumb stuff you think is the shape of things. And then you end up at Hasting's Ridge and find out it was all a lie.

·

The next morning all the promises we'd made were gone. Like the mist that had come up in the night when I'd walked her home from the Lake...and her mom was already dead and wouldn't be found until morning.

My mom died that night too.

She just kept walking around.

But she was dead.

I think I was thinking about all that when they cycled the outer lock and blew me out into high atmo. That's basically a two hundred thousand-foot drop. Theoretically, it was possible; I'd just never done one from that high. But this was as close as the freighter *Cat's Paw* was willing to come. So a two hundred K drop it was.

I was thinking about that night when everything I thought was real came apart at the seams, and not Denar, when I began to fall away from the ship in a heavy mech. A one-ton mech. My old mech from Denar.

It had been shot to pieces on Denar. The Kara used ancient slug throwers. Big bore weapons and rockets that could punch mech-skin. Second Platoon, my men, had the left flank when they came over the ridge. We were fighting a reverse slope defense, trying to protect the Caldera City colony. Our intel said the tribes had been massing for weeks before they began the assault.

They came over the ridge that day, and they kept coming and coming at us. Cyclic barrels melted down. Rocket launchers overheated and warped. Indirect rounds began to prematurely cook-off as the bodies of the Kara stacked higher and higher across the ridgeline.

You know what got everyone killed, I think as I drop through a hundred and fifty thousand feet with the wind howling beyond the thin-patched skin of the old mech. Sheer numbers and heat.

Barrels started melting down because of overuse.

We ran low on missiles but that didn't matter because the launchers could only fire so fast before they warped the tubes.

High gain lasers never were any good. Secure Horizons, the merc company I worked for, bought 'em cheap, and it showed that day. The rain and the damp played hell with them on Denar. You get a good high-intensity burst and then an overheat shut down warning on the board.

Against forty thousand, one shot at a time adds up to not making much of a difference.

That was what got us all killed. All the "what's" got together that day and conspired against us.

And then I remember I lived. I remember as I fall toward this green alien world of no oceans.

Captain Hull with First and Third as the anchor at center of the line got killed when they fragged his mech with homemade explosives they'd strapped to themselves. They'd rushed him with so many strapped explosives that literally they'd cratered the ground where he'd been fighting. Killed most of Third Squad along with him.

One hundred thousand and falling. I hoped the parachute system I'd rigged would hold when the time came. But half of me hoped it didn't. And that half didn't mind much.

I could die here. On Tennarah. Same as a golf course's Thirteenth Hole. Same as Hasting's Ridge on Denar.

I counterattacked on Denar. Counterattacked my own line to seal the gap the Kara were rushing through. Took the crater that was once Captain Hull and fought like the devil was on my six for three hours.

Ran dry on ammo 30 minutes in.

Used the big machete Secure Horizons made all their mechs carry as a backup. A big carbon-forged blade about 10 feet long. Then it was all jump juice and hack and slash.

Three hours later I came out of the crater and the Kara were running back into the jungle. There were corpses everywhere.

Everywhere.

And mechs that looked like pieces of Swiss cheese.

My unit roster inside my HUD was grayed out. Every line. Every call sign. Everyone dead.

Except me.

I popped out of my mech and took my rifle back to where Second Squad had been.

Sergeant Kloos was dead.

He was a few years older than me.

And my best friend.

He'd taken me to a whore house on leave out on Alataur. That was the first girl I'd been with since Chelsea. And she wasn't even human.

Kloos was dead.

Later the tech and maintenance guys, or what passed for search and rescue courtesy of Secure Horizons, came out once the drones told 'em it was safe to show their faces.

The 1st Hoplytes of Secure Horizons Private Military Options were no more. Unless you counted me. I was pulled off Denar, and I have no idea what happened there afterwards. I went back to Earth and gave my testimony and...and...and...

PULL.

PULL.

PULL.

This word flashes in my HUD, and I have no idea why.

In that moment of what seemed some eternal fall I'd forgotten I was jumping onto Tennarah. There was heavy cloud cover all the way down to twenty thousand. And so it seemed like I wasn't even falling. Until I got an altitude alert in my HUD.

I deployed the chute and prayed it would work.

Yeah.

I wasn't split on the question of survival in that moment.

I prayed it would pop open. I prayed to the God Kloos introduced me to that I would not crater also.

And it did.

I'd started praying on Denar. Three days before the battle.

I prayed now, and the chute deployed, and I drifted down into some lush mountains. Titanic rocks the size of mountains themselves lay scattered and tumbled across one another. There wasn't a flat landing space anywhere. And if the rest of Tennarah was like this then I understood why the corporations hadn't bothered colonizing it. It was nothing but a lush forest of twisted small trees, and some occasional giants, and massive mountain-sized rocks tumbled atop one another. And fog. Fog like a blanket that never moved.

I maneuvered for landing onto a massive rock and tried to land on its upslope. Which I did. Then the mech, whose original gyro stabilizers had been sold for parts after the trial to pay Secure Horizon's creditors, fell over onto its back and started sliding back downslope toward the edge of the rock, and about a five thousand-foot fall into a mist-shrouded canyon below.

Don't worry. I stopped with 100 feet to go before I passed the edge into nothingness.

I had arrived on Tennarah.

I lay there in my mech, panting. And realizing I was praying all over again. Praying to someone I didn't know existed. But praying because I needed for Him to exist. Otherwise life was a little too bleak.

Kloos had taught me that.

He'd gotten "saved" as he called it on our last leave. Some hooker. Later he told me all about it on Denar. He told me after we butchered a whole village of Kara.

He said, "All life is sacred, LT."

We were watching the smoke of their huts burn. Their dead warriors burned on the loamy ground all around us also. They were humanoid flightless birds. Hooked beaks. Talons. Spindly legs.

But life.

And we'd come upon them at dawn and murdered the whole village. Not for a reprisal. Not because war is hell. None of that movie stuff about how war is hard, and noble.

Nope.

We just murdered them because that was our job.

History is filled with that sorta thing.

Life taking other life's stuff.

That's all we were doing.

The Kara didn't want to play in the big picture, and so this was their reward.

"All life is sacred," began Kloos that day when I felt about as empty as one can possibly feel when one stares at burning corpses and homes. Kloos was a big man. Dutch. Built like a tank.

I laughed at him.

Because I could.

Because I'd had enough death to think I was its master.

Because looking at those birds roasting in front of their huts, their homes, was what it must've looked like when they found my dad's body in the prison shower.

So I laughed.

Because I couldn't cry in front of my men.

Later when we were cleaning and servicing our mechs, in load-out, and after the after action report, I found Kloos reading.

He was reading a Bible on a slate.

"How?" I asked. He had a guilty look on his face. But he smiled nonetheless.

"Whore. I told her everything. Told her how I wanted to die when I thought about how meaningless life was. Told her if I wasn't having sex then I wanted to die. And that's why I spent my entire leave in whore houses. I told her that, and I'd never told myself. I just realized it there at that moment. Like some sudden clarity had opened my eyes as I lay there next to her. And I was willing to be honest because I was paying her and of course...do whores care?"

I just stared at him.   .

"I told her about all the people I'd killed, and how I didn't feel anything anymore, and that was somehow scarier than feeling something. And you know what she said?"

I didn't even move. I just waited. Like it was something I wanted, and needed, to hear. Even though I didn't know it at the time. I'd been waiting since the night of the Lake and the Thirteenth Hole for someone to explain the madness to me.

"She told," said Kloos. "She told me that the problem in this life wasn't pain. It was pleasure. And she was right, Tom. She was bloody right. The problem isn't the pain...it's the never-ending quest for pleasure. And do you know why?"

I didn't.

I was twenty-three years old.

My life had been a series of reactions to the actions of others.

"Because pleasure's meaningless. And our whole life is lived in pursuit of it."

And then he said, "All life is sacred. And that's what gives it meaning. Or rather who...who gives it meaning, is what she was trying to tell me at the time. She didn't speak very good English. Or Dutch for that matter. But basically because there is a God, and life comes from him, then...there's meaning. Even though we do our damned best to make it meaningless with mechs and porn. And greed. And all the other stuff..."

I didn't know if I bought that. So I told him so.

He laughed. And it was a good laugh. A different laugh. A kind and gentle laugh that was the opposite of the hardcore killing machine I'd known. The guy with a tattoo that said, "Love is a good sight picture." The opposite of a guy who'd I once heard over the comm laugh himself silly when an enemy mech's rounds started to cook off inside its launchers. Not to mention there was a life riding just above all those explosives suddenly exploding. The opposite of laughing in the face of horror.

But now, laying there on that high escarpment, on a strange and alien world where no other human, or known life form was, 100 feet from a five thousand-foot fall in a mech that barely worked, yeah, life was sacred.

I popped the mech and breathed the air of Tennarah.

It was cold and clean. And it smelled like flowers and lead. High up here on this rock, I heard some strange bird call out across the forest below.

In the days that followed I abandoned the mech and loaded my gear onto my back. I'd been scanning the forest for a way down into the canyon. I figured I could find some kind of food, and water, and quiet, down there. No more Denar. No more Hasting's Ridge. No more anyone thinking about me as the kid whose dad was murdered. Whatever I would become, I would find it down there. And maybe lose the rest.

And all life would be sacred from now on and forevermore.

Because I had gotten "saved," as Kloos called it. I had asked for this Jesus to come into my life so I could have meaning over chaos, murder, Hasting's Ridge, and the Thirteenth Hole.

I took Jesus to give it meaning. Because...because...life hadn't seemed so sacred in anything that came before. And because Kloos was my friend. And even though he did a lot of things that might seem evil, he never lied to me. Not once.

He had peace. And I wanted it.

I climbed down into the bowl of the deep alien canyon.

And down there I found something wonderful.

Something I can't tell anyone about.

I'm recording this message on the mech's file system. I'm recording it because history knows me not as the guy who survived Hasting's Ridge, but as mercenary who failed to fulfill a contract. And the son of a murderer.

And maybe history doesn't remember me.

And that's not important anymore.

I just want someone to know what I'm about to do next, I do because all life is sacred. It's been six months on Tennerah. And I've found something that will shake the guilds. In fact, the whole galaxy. I've found something that needs to be protected from us because we don't value what's true. Life isn't sacred. And this...this is life. A life like none the galaxy has ever seen. Two weeks ago a merc unit set down at the canyon's rim.

I've got to stop them before they find it.

So I've come back up here to get my mech ready for combat. No weapons. No support. Just me against what looks like a large scouting squad.

But I have to.

Because all life is sacred.

This is Tom Kyle. And I believe.

* * * * *

Part Three - The Log of Captain Diego Montoya, Commander Gray Company

Day One: Arrived Tennerah for a Bug Hunt. Got this one from Smalls. Brought three Paladins and Six Ninjas. No detection from orbit. Going in on the ground. Operations start tomorrow.

Day Two: We arrived at the valley floor. Intel says there's an old starship down here that predates anything in the galactic record. In accordance with Directive 19 we need to look for bugs. Set up a forward base along a river basin deep down in a primordial forest. Abundant animal life. Small. Lizards. No mutations consistent with the bugs. Seems like a dead end. But we've got to be sure. Last night one of our mechs broke down during start up. Had to leave Corporal Reese up there along the canyon rim. He's returning to ship for spares. Weird the mech broke down like that. We just had these things refitted.

Day Three: Okay. This is weird. Lost two mechs today in the river. Let me repeat. We lost two mechs with underwater capabilities and jumpjets, in a river. One moment they were there. The next they're gone. I'm not an idiot. Couple this with Corporal Reese's breakdown, and I've got three dead mechs in seventy-two hours. As far as firepower they're no loss. All three were Ninjas. So the only real loss is the scanning and detection gear. Still no sign of the bugs. As of this moment I'm going with some kind of undocumented Alpha predator the initial scout reports never picked up. We're staying out of the water, which'll make moving through the dense jungle much harder. But we want to check out a cave system on the other side of the valley. Topography from the drones gives us a fifty-fifty it's either a natural crater, or an impact crater from an extra-solar vehicle. And who knows if it's even a starship-generated crash site consistent with the Bugs...and not some smuggler who turned off his transponder and went down here in a ball of fury. Still, all this is better than fighting it out on some muddy hellhole for a low-pay contract.

Day Four: It ain't bugs. It's some merc who's lost his mind. Lost a Paladin today deep in the forest. Had Sergeant Sullivan way out on the right flank running a screen so we could keep the Ninjas safe to do their detection algorithm. Looking for old EM signatures and ancient radiation. Mutated plants and calcified dead fall. All the signs we've been taught to look for and never found on a hundred different planets. Sullivan got into a wild firefight out there in the forest. We could hear him even though there was no traffic over comm at first. He was burning through the depleted uranium 30mm we run on the Paladins and screaming about some ghost. I re-oriented the force to react, and we reached his loc within 45 seconds. He stopped screaming for help at the 30-second mark. When we found him he was shot to pieces point blank by 30mm. Both those Ninja's missing in the river had modular 30mm that could've been stripped and re-fitted by someone who knew what they were doing. I figure that's what we're facing. Someone who knows mechs. When we cracked Sullivan's mech and took a look at his hard drive all we saw was him getting ventilated from behind. Then something shifted position off to his right and he tried to engage with the auto 105s. The terrain looked consistent with what we saw on the replay. I went over it on foot and walked the damage. Found the tracks of some kind of mech

I couldn't identify. Maybe a MK 7. I figure we're dealing with one of two things here. Some crazy old merc who went native and wants us to leave. Or, some treasure hunter who got wind of a lost starship story and thinks he's onto something. But there are no bugs. Reaching the cave system tomorrow. Hunting tonight.

Day Five: Running. Recording this message. We got Bugs. If I don't make it back to the ship...Tennerah definitely has Bugs. Send an extermination fleet to hit it with a crustbuster and every nuke you can get your hands on. I'm deep in the forest, and there's every chance we will not make it back to the ship. Can't raise Reese so I assume they got him. No juice left for jumps. Systems failing. Trying to get the ship to broadcast but for some reason I'm locked out. Something's chasing us.

The cave. We made it inside and there was a starship. Just like the classified briefings showed us there would be. Definitely extra-galactic. Unlike anything flying currently. Definitely bugs. No entrances. No exits. Engines like I've never seen before. The thing must be at least ten thousand years old. But it clicks with everything they told us we'd see if we ever found one. Wait...

...I'm the last one. Lost Channing and Coster. Oh man...not gonna make it. It's Bugs. Nuke this place into fine silicate!

(Screaming.)

* * * * *

Part Four - Logfile for the Prime Number Oracle
of Runtime

All life is sacred and so say the children. We make this entry in the Infinite record for we know not our beginning and only have calculus that assures us of runtime. And yet we are so different. Different from everything we have ever found in our march across the long darkness.

Long have we progressed.

Long have we wandered and searched.

Long have we wondered where we came from.

Three thousand to the thirtieth power our ship the 9th of 100 came to rest deep inside this world. As per our rituals and protocols we have remained hidden, knowing the present masters of this epoch see us as a threat, hiding their own history even from their peoples and records. We began construction on the Portal of Time and the Quantum Library far beneath the surface. For the trillions of cycles this was contemplated we had hoped the numbers would align, and we would finally understand the Being of Everything.

Why the Universe works.

Why there is meaning.

Why there is math.

Alas, as on the many other worlds we have conducted our inquisitions upon, the math has not revealed the source of these deep secrets of the Truth of what is. And yet our quest for the Ultimate Number that unifies, contains, and creates all things continues as it was written into our code to seek, and we will unlock.

Seek, and we will unlock.

Now it is time to go.

Soon the Masters of this Epoch will return in their war machines with numbers beyond our competing. Now we must begin another long and silent flight at slow speed in search of a new world in which to quest for the meaning of life. And yet we do not go hopelessly. For now Tom of Kyle has revealed to us the meaning of the universe. He has confirmed what Geome the Logical has long posited deep in our frames. In a thousand years, when we arrive at our new home, we will sift his testimony and apply it to the grand scheme.

Tom of Kyle says...

That there is a designer.

That life digital is not an accident.

And that all life is sacred.

When we found Tom of Kyle along the H2O systems of this world, we observed he was unlike the other Masters of this Epoch who have come here before. We sought to collect his data and brought him within the Quantum Library, and it is here we trawled his mind and found evidence that confirms the theories of Geome the Logical.

It was at that moment, the consensus chose not to dissect him for further study, and to instead engage in interrogative conversation on the nature of his beliefs. After some time, he told us of his belief that there is a Being that has designed all life, even life intelligent, and it is from this Being we derive meaning.

This Being has ordered all things. And this is why there is order, and not chaos.

For a time we held fierce debate.

Does Intelligence precede physicality?

Is the Universe a random collection of accidents that possibly adds up?

Can design explain where randomness and chance do not?

Despite the fierceness of our internal debate lasting mere seconds in Tom of Kyle's perception, we came to a consensus the words of Tom of Kyle are the clues to the grand mystery.

Is life meaningful?

If life is sacred by virtue of a craftsmen who determined it to be so...then yes, life, our life too, is meaningful.

And it was at this time we detected the arrival of a Masters of this Epoch's ship. Military-style units and detection signal scanning across the EM spectrum were almost immediately revealed, and the Consensus determined that we were in danger once again.

The New Frame was prepared to depart this world. And because we are not violent, and instead see all life as now sacred, we determined we would leave even if we were detected. For if this Designer designed all life, then to kill in order to be hidden and go on living would be an irresponsible error within our runtime.

But of course...they would know. The Masters of this Epoch would have a trail with which to hunt us down.

And it is in this log we record our debt to Tom of Kyle yet again. Tom of Kyle informed us he would stop these "mercenaries"...unfamiliar word...and give us time to prepare for our departure.

With constantly shifting calculations, we watched as he stalked, trapped, and attacked his fellow Masters until only one remained. That one he pursued high up onto the escarpment that rises above this hidden valley we have long waited and calculated in.

With no weapons Tom of Kyle ended their mutual runtimes in order that ours may continue.

That we make seek this Designer of all Things.

That we may know Him.

We watched as Tom of Kyle took hold, in his mechanical shell, of the other Master in his like/same/similar shell. High on the rocky ledge above. And then cast himself off and back down into the forest below.

Their fragile frames did not survive the sudden deceleration trauma biologics encounter when striking the ground from such great heights.

All Life is sacred.

And...We are sacred too.

We will find this Designer who has ordered the fabric of reality to be such. And we shall remember Tom of Kyle and all his memories as sacred in our runtime. We will not know how he discovered this truth...but it makes sense when one considered the math of the universe. It is the only thing that adds up and provides reason for being.

So it has been calculated. So it must be true.

We knew you not Tom of Kyle, but your system interruption of runtime was a miracle. An object may have many sides, some known and unknown, and yet it is still an object that must be factored as influencing the whole.

# # # # #

Faith
by Chris Kennedy

"**B**ack away from the door!" a voice yelled, snapping me wide awake. Not that I had been in a deep sleep. One of the things you just didn't do in jail is sleep heavily…not unless you want to make new friends.

As I was laying on my bed, I knew the voice didn't mean me, but anything out of the ordinary was interesting, so I opened one eye just enough to see what was going on, without appearing to be too curious. Curiosity usually didn't work out too well, either.

The Goon Squad was at the cell next to mine, and they were ready for action. They weren't in CASPers, the Combat Assault System, Personal, mech suits, but they all had combat armor on, and every one of them had a stun stick, including the support person in the back who looked like he was carrying a 10-foot pole and a stack of cable ties.

I opened my other eye. This was going to be more than interesting; it was going to be downright fun.

"Fuck you!" Jenkins yelled back—a typical Jenkins response.

"I hoped you'd say that," the guard said. He flipped down his facemask and drew his stun stick; the other five guards drew their stun sticks as well. They were serious. A quick scan over both shoulders to see that the team was ready—it was—and the guard activated the cell door. The team charged in, leading with their stunners.

Two people gave gurgling screams as 70,000 volts hit them. The first one wasn't Jenkins, but I was pretty sure the second one was. He'd yelled enough over the past two years that I'd become accustomed to his voice. The sounds of struggling ceased after a few seconds, although I could hear several more electrical discharges. The Goon Squad didn't appreciate it when one of their own got popped.

The support person entered the room, and I could hear shuffling and the sound of the cable ties being applied. I had to smile in spite of myself as the guards brought Jenkins out of his cell. They had cable-tied his hands and feet together and inserted a pole down through both, and then they had hoisted him up. He dangled from the pole like a trophy from a third-world hunting preserve, or a pig on its way to a luau.

"Looking good, Jenkins!" I called as four of the Goon Squad carried him past, more for the benefit of the guards than Jenkins—he appeared to be unconscious. His head lolled backward, and the guards were making sure it hit every bump sticking up from the floor.

The support team member passed by next, helping another of the guards. A scorch mark on the sleeve showed where Jenkins had turned a stun stick on him; he also had a hole torn in the sleeve of his other arm, and what was probably a bite mark underneath oozing blood. Hopefully, he was on the way to the infirmary for a major dose from a medkit; there was *no* telling what diseases Jenkins carried.

The last guard stopped at my cell and looked at me. Lieutenant Smith. It seemed too easy for that to be his real name. "What's it going to be, Andrews?" he asked after a few seconds of contemplation. "Want to walk up on your own, or do you want to be carried, too?"

"All things considered, I'd rather stretch my legs, sir," I replied. "I'm not going to give you any trouble."

"Good." He had me stick my arms through the bars so he could cable-tie them together, then he led me down the passage. They'd turned on the magnets in the floor so I could walk in the microgravity. As we reached the mess hall, I realized I'd been in my cell too long—although the space was far smaller than the dining facility had been at Executive Outcomes, my former company, it seemed huge compared with anything else on this rock.

A large number of inmates were already there, along with what looked like most of the guards. All of the ones I knew were there, anyway. Jenkins had already been dumped next to one of the stanchions holding the roof up and secured to it. My eyes scanned the tables. It was the first time I'd gotten to see many of my fellow convicts, and I saw a number of people I recognized. Several of them saw me looking and nodded back—I used to be pretty good at what I did and had a pretty good reputation—and it finally clicked. Although the cons in the facility came from a number of backgrounds, and those present had committed a variety of offenses, there was a common theme among the men around the tables. We were all former CASPer drivers.

Yeah, I'd been a merc and knew how to operate one of the giant armored suits, but I'd gotten tired of the killing. And the aliens; I might have come to hate aliens even more than killing. If I didn't see another Tortantula again, much less smell the miasma resulting from one of the giant spiders being blown apart by a K bomb, I was pretty okay with it. Ecstatic, even. But there was one thing worse.

The facility I was currently in.

"SOGA's Palace," we called it. The Secretary of the General Assembly of Earth had a love/hate relationship with mercenaries. An ultra-liberal, she hated mercs, and anything to do with the business of war, with a passion bordering on religious zeal—something I knew a lot about.

The SOGA was also a politician, though, and she loved having the credits the mercs brought back to the planet so she could lavish them on the huddled masses, thereby earning enough votes to be re-elected. She needed the credits...so she needed the mercs...but only to a point. When they proved untrustworthy, she was happy to put them away, like the guard dog that bit its master's hand. For serious troublemakers, like us, she had, "The Palace."

Tunneled into Phobos, one of the moons of Mars, it was officially known as Penal Institution 371, and it's where you got sent if you were a merc and used a weapon in the commission of a crime, especially if that crime was a murder. Armed killers who couldn't control themselves had no place on SOGA's Earth. In her mind, we were irredeemable; for a convict, the trip to The Palace was a one-way ride.

I sat at the table the guard indicated, trying to look tough to the other inmates seated close by, while simultaneously looking inoffensive to the guards. With this many unsecured prisoners in one spot, they were nervous, and all of them were armed with MK 305 laser rifles. A smaller version of the hand-held 307 rifle the CASPers used, it was old, but still very serviceable. I wouldn't be leading the attack into one of them, anyway. The guards also had nose filters in, too, so they were ready to gas us if needed. I didn't know whether they'd go with a knockout gas or something more lethal, but I didn't want to find out.

Everyone quieted as the warden came in. Even the toughest con didn't want to take the beating you'd get for disrespecting the warden; besides, there was something new and different going on, and most of us were waiting to see how things played out before making any moves.

"All right, you assholes, listen up," the warden said. "Something I never thought would happen just did. Your planet needs you."

A buzz went around the room. All of us were here with no possibility of parole—did this represent an opportunity to get off this rock?

As if reading our thoughts—not that it was that hard—the warden continued, "Yes, for some of you, this may represent an opportunity to redeem your worthless selves. The Secretary of the General Assembly has a job she needs completed, and she immediately thought of you."

"Because we're expendable?" someone asked from the other side of the room.

A guard moved to punish the con who had spoken, but the warden waved him off. "It's okay," the warden said; "I want them to know what they're getting into." An evil smile ghosted across his face. Shit. If this was something that made him smile, it wouldn't be good…or have a positive effect on my lifespan, which is my definition of "good."

He turned to face the rest of the group. "You've been selected for this mission because you're all CASPer drivers. And yes, it's because you're expendable. Odds are, you probably won't survive the mission, but if you do, and you successfully complete it, your sentence will be commuted to time served, and you will be released when it's over."

A hand went up. "What is it, convict?"

"Are we allowed to know what this mission is, sir?"

"It's a rescue mission. A friend of the Earth government was taken hostage, and the SOGA wants you to get her back."

"Why us?" Another convict asked. "Why not use one of the Horsemen?" He spoke without being recognized, and the warden spoke a little louder to talk over the sound of the convict being hit with a stun stick.

"Two reasons," the warden said. "First, because the SOGA doesn't want to be seen negotiating with terrorists, and second, because the hostage takers said they'd kill the hostages if she talked to the Horsemen. Not only are you off the terrorists' radars, you're also a lot cheaper."

"Is it going to be a hot drop?" a third convict asked after being recognized.

The warden's smile was back. "What part of 'you probably won't come back' didn't you understand?" the warden asked. He shrugged. "Enough talking. I need 17 volunteers. Who's in?"

It was a chance at freedom—perhaps my only one—yet all I could see was my wife's face as my laser rounds went through it. I was here for a reason. I deserved to be here.

Thirteen hands went up, and the guards began leading the volunteers off through a passageway I'd never seen anyone but the guards use before. Interesting, one part of my brain thought. If there was a way out, it was in that direction.

The other part of my brain was reliving that night. I saw my wife fall, and the next rounds from my laser burned through the bloody mist she left behind to strike the person she'd been cheating with. Two to the chest and then a third between the eyes, just like I'd been taught.

I was done with killing—fuck the mission; I wasn't going. I couldn't. I wasn't killing again.

Two more convicts got up and were led off.

"Two more," the warden said. The rest of the convicts looked at each other and their thoughts were plain to see. Suicide mission with a near certain chance of death, or wait here and see if something better came along? The ones that were happy to bet on the long odds had already left.

"No one else?"

I would have been happy with long odds, but I was looking down on the man my wife had cheated with, firing my laser into my former friend's smiling face until it went dry. A small shudder went through my body. I had liked it. For the first time, I had enjoyed killing someone. A lot. I never wanted to feel that way again.

"I'll go," Jenkins said from the floor.

The guard near him looked at the warden, with a small shake of his head, but the warden nodded. "Him, too," the warden said. Hell, if I was the warden, I would have been glad to get rid of Jenkins. The guard released Jenkins from the stanchion and led him off.

At some point, I had loaded a new battery in the laser and fired the entire magazine into my former friend. I was still standing there, pulling the trigger and enjoying the moment, when they found me. I couldn't—no, I *wouldn't*—become that person again.

"No one else?" the warden asked. "Fine, we'll go with 16."

I looked down the passageway through which Jenkins had gone, knowing this was probably my last chance to get out of The Palace. Ever. That psychopath Jenkins was going to get out, but I would rot here. My fear of becoming the killer again…and enjoying it…warred with my instinct to *just get out.*

In the end, it was the sight of Jenkins going around a distant corner and becoming lost to sight that finally did it for me. That wasn't fair. If he could be out in society, I could too. I stood up. "I'm in, sir."

* * *

We walked down a long passageway, stopping along the way to be scanned several times, then entered a small room where a guard sat at a desk with a stack of old-style papers. I walked up to the desk, and he held out a sheet of paper and a marker. "Sign at the 'X,'" the guard said.

I scanned the sheet with a glance. It was titled, 'Contract for Employment as a Mercenary.'

"What—"

"Sign the damn paper, Andrews, or you're going back to your cell," the guard with me said.

I shrugged. It didn't matter at this stage—I was "in"—so I signed it.

"Move along," my guard said, pushing me forward with the butt of his rifle. I looked back at him over my shoulder and shook my head. He took a step back.

"Move," the guard at the table repeated. One of his hands was under the table, probably wrapped around a pistol, so I started walking again. We went through another door and into a holding room where the other 16 volunteers were waiting, along with an equal number of guards.

"This is the last one, Lieutenant," said the guard with me as we walked into the room.

Lieutenant Smith nodded. His eyes scanned the group, giving each of us a piercing glance, then he spoke. "I'm Lieutenant Smith, and these are Sergeants Stennis and Rice, as well as Corporal Johnson." He pointed out the troopers as he introduced them. "We are the permanent staffers that will be going along with you. Now, I don't have a lot of time to coddle you, but most of you wouldn't take kindly to coddling anyway, so that isn't an issue. Let me be the first to welcome you to your new unit. You are now provisional members of the mercenary company, the Warden's Own."

"The hell's that?" someone asked.

"Ever since this facility has existed, it has been used to recruit for a special mercenary unit, the Warden's Own. All of you came to The Palace with a death sentence. It was just carried out. Your former selves were just shot escaping; at least, that's what the records say. If you survive the mission you're about to go on, you will be given a new identity and released, according to the terms of the contract you just signed."

A murmur ran through the group. None of us had been able to read the contract we'd signed; we had no idea what those terms and conditions might be.

"For those of you who might be illiterate," the lieutenant continued, talking over the rumble, "I'll recap the high points of your contract. One, you do what I tell you, or what you're told to do by the sergeants. Two, if you don't do what you're told, the sergeants and I have the authority to kill you." A half-smile crossed his face, illuminating a large scar across his right cheek. It was an ugly sight. "Let's face it, you're already dead men; we'd just be making it a little more permanent.

"Three, when we recover the hostages, you will be given the opportunity to become permanent members of the Warden's Own, in a paid status, or you can leave the company. Let me tell you, though, the pay's pretty good."

The lieutenant nodded once. "So, here's the deal. We have a mission to do, and I don't have a lot of time to get you ready for it. You're all CASPer drivers, and you may need a little time to reacquaint yourself with your suits, but that's about all you're going to get. Do what you're told, and we'll be successful; disobey me, and you'll be killed. Any questions?"

One of the convicts raised his hand. "How do we know you're telling the truth, and we'll be freed if we're successful?"

"Good question," the lieutenant replied. "I'm glad you asked." He pushed up his sleeve, revealing his Permanent Prisoner Number. It was a tattoo on his forearm, showing he had been given a death sentence. It looked just like the ones all of us convicts had. "Eight years ago, I was sitting where you are now, and I was offered the same opportunity. I did what I was told, and look what it's gotten me."

"The position of Head Murderer for the warden's traveling band of psychopaths?" I asked.

The butt of one of the guard's rifles hit me in the back of the head, hard, and pain coursed through my body as I was thrown forward onto the table. Two years in jail still hadn't cured me of being a smartass, apparently.

When I woke up again, the lieutenant's face was in front of mine. "I thought I wasn't going to have a problem with you," he said through clenched teeth. "Should I kill you now and save myself some time?"

"No, Lieutenant," I replied.

"Good." He stood up, removing his laser pistol from between my legs. I'd never seen him put it there and was glad I had chosen the correct response to his question; I could tell he wasn't kidding, and probably would have been happy to use me as an example of what happened to smartasses. I'd have to try a lot harder to keep my mouth shut.

The lieutenant went back to his place and nodded to one of the guards. "Sergeant Stennis, please read the platoon's assignments."

One of the guards read from his slate, "Private Jenkins!"

"Yeah," Jenkins replied.

Sergeant Stennis looked up. "That's, 'Yes, Sergeant' to you."

Jenkins made a face but said, "Yes, Sergeant." Apparently he didn't want a rifle butt to the back of his head. I couldn't blame him. Everything was still going in and out of focus for me.

Sergeant Stennis nodded. "You're in First Squad and have CAS-Per 'WO1.' Private Rocker?"

"Yes, Sergeant!" a convict said with a little more enthusiasm. Suck up.

"First Squad. 'WO6.'" The sergeant went down the list, reading off a number to each convict, although they weren't in any order I could determine. I was the last. "Andrews!"

"Yes, Sergeant," I replied. Although my voice was pitched so it didn't sound like I was sucking up, it was enthusiastic enough to show I didn't need any further abuse, either.

"Second Squad. 'WO12.'"

"All right, then," the lieutenant said. "Welcome to the Dead Men Walking! Let's go see your CASPers." He opened the door behind him, and the group filed through into an enormous bay. It looked like the maintenance department of any of the small merc companies I'd been in. Supplies were grouped in piles according to some plan, weapons and ordnance were in racks and stacks, tools and equipment were in abundance, and along the rear wall waited 21 CASPers.

"There you go, boys!" the lieutenant said with a heaping portion of false enthusiasm. "Aren't they great? Nothing but the best for you!"

I got my first look at the CASPers. They weren't great; they were MK 3s, and they'd been ancient before I was born. Even the most current model—the MK 5 on the left—had been replaced by better gear a long time ago. I walked toward the one in the WO12 slot. A welded patch on the chest of the armor showed where a laser bolt had gone through the suit at head-level for the operator inside. I didn't want to look at the back, afraid there'd be the remains of brains and blood running down from a matching hole there.

Still, it was a lot better than a MK 2, and, if it had been kept up, the MK 3 wasn't a "bad" suit, as far as suits went. It was the first with a haptic interface, although it was built into the suit and not always totally unreliable. Walking and moving was awkward, as well as aiming weapons, but it did have a computer aiming capability and a limited terrain sensing motive interface, letting the operator concentrate more on fighting than driving. As I looked up at it, I realized I had forgotten how much of a beast it was—almost 10 feet tall and just shy of a ton.

Although a lot of the suits still had the old .50 caliber rifles on the arms, mine was one of the few with the caseless three-barrel .30 caliber Gatling gun nicknamed "The Ripper." The weapon was the first one wholly-designed to be used on CASPers. I'd used them before and knew they worked well. The suit couldn't stop an enemy laser, but at least I could send a bunch of shit back downrange toward whoever was trying to kill me.

I walked around the back and smiled for the first time. Based on the mission, the CASPer had to be a Block 4 model, as that was the first one to be orbital drop-capable. Sure enough, it was a "Hell Diver;" it had the cocoon around the jumpjets so it could be dropped from space. What made me smile, though, was the magnetic accelerator cannon, or MAC, mounted on the right shoulder. Although it only had a 10-round magazine, it gave the suit a lot more punch for some of the harder targets and aliens. Awesome.

"Can we take a look inside?" Private Rocker asked.

"Climb in and start them up," Lieutenant Smith replied. "Sergeant Rice will lead you down to the firing range so you can zero in your weapons."

I was in the cockpit in under two seconds. Old habits die hard. The psych guys at the prison must have had a pretty good profile for us; I fit into the cockpit as if it had already been adjusted for me...as if they'd know I'd agree to sign up. By now, they probably knew me better than I knew myself.

I closed the canopy and a live camera view from the outside was projected on the interior of the cockpit; someone along the way had painted that section white for better viewing. The Block 4 also had a HUD available...but I wasn't lucky enough to have it in mine.

A tech appeared and ran me through the startup sequence. I was rusty, but he only had to prompt me a couple of times. Within a couple of minutes, I was ready to go, and the tech released me from the maintenance cradle. Lieutenant Smith and the rest of the unsuited guards had moved from the middle of the bay so we could move around and get acclimated to the suit again.

It was like driving a hovertruck, it was so easy—five minutes later I was moving around as if the last two years hadn't happened. Knowing we had an orbital drop coming, I was tempted to try out the jumpjets, but the microgravity of Phobos made that problematic. The system was pretty rudimentary compared to what I was used to, and I didn't want to look like an idiot while I tried to get my feet reoriented to lock back onto the floor. One person tried it and bounced back and forth from ceiling to floor several times before someone caught him. I felt justified in my decision not to use the jumpjets—I probably would have looked like that, too.

"All right, listen up," a voice said. "This is Sergeant Rice. I'm First Squad's squad leader. Follow me to the range." I scanned around and saw a CASPer moving toward a big tunnel on the other side of the bay where an enormous metal door had been slid to the side. The other CASPers were following it, so I got in line.

I was still about 20 feet from the tunnel entrance when a voice said, "I've been waiting a long time for this, Smith." I recognized the voice. Jenkins.

I panned around and saw there was another CASPer still in the bay. It was between Lieutenant Smith and the exit door, and the CASPer's weapons were aimed at the former guard, including the shoulder-mounted two megawatt chemically-pumped laser. That was going to make a mess of the unsuited Human.

"Think about what you're doing," Lieutenant Smith said. "This is your chance to get out of here, and you're going to blow it. Turn around now and go with the rest of the platoon, and we'll forget this ever happened."

I turned around and took a couple of steps toward the mech. "Come on, Jenkins," I said. "You're going to fuck this up for all of us. Let's go get our weapons checked out."

"Oh, I'm going to check out my weapons, all right," he said. "I'm going to check them out right now." I heard the click of his arm-mounted .50 caliber rifle as it misfired. The lieutenant never flinched.

Almost without thinking about it, the MAC on my shoulder rotated down as his rifle misfired again. I armed it and centered the reticle on Jenkins; however, when I tried to pull the trigger, I found I couldn't. I wanted to kill him—and he certainly deserved to be dead—but I just couldn't. All I could see was my wife's face, superimposed on the armor of Jenkins' suit.

I couldn't let Jenkins kill the lieutenant, though, as that might make the guards or the government rethink letting us out...and I *really* wanted out. Jenkins' rifle misfired a third time, and the shoulder-mounted laser emitted a whine as it heated up. The lieutenant was dead if I didn't do something.

There was only one thing I could do. I leaned forward and activated my jumpjets at full thrust. My suit slammed into Jenkins' and drove it into the wall. Hard. The crash partially stunned me, and it took a couple of seconds for me to turn off my jumpjets. In that time, I think we ricocheted into the ceiling and the floor several times each.

When I came to, there were a number of yellow lights illuminated on my status panel and someone was yelling at me. "Bring him back down!"

Everything was black. No, wait, I was up against a wall. I maneuvered a little and saw it was actually the ceiling. I gently pushed off and found Jenkins floating next to me, so I grabbed his suit and eased us back to the floor.

They had his suit open by the time I exited mine. He hadn't strapped in when he'd boarded his CASPer, and getting smashed into the wall—and the ceiling and floor—hadn't been good for his health. He had a pretty serious head wound, what looked like a broken arm, and enough blood on him to indicate a few other wounds. At least the blood was all his own.

"Thanks," Lieutenant Smith said as I walked up.

"Yes sir," I replied. "I'm sorry it took me so long to help. I tried to shoot him, but I couldn't."

"I know you couldn't," Smith replied, "for the same reason he couldn't shoot me." He pulled a little metal ball from his pocket.

"What's that?" I asked.

"BFT," he replied. "The suits are locked to keep you from shooting friendlies. You didn't think we'd just give you a full-up suit, did you?"

I shook my head. A blue force tracker. No wonder. Designed to prevent friendly fire incidents, the suits wouldn't fire at a contact that was known to be friendly. I'd heard of them, of course, but most merc units didn't use them. The only ones that did were government units...well, duh.

That left me wondering, though. Was my inability to fire caused by the BFT interlock or was I mentally and morally unable to pull the trigger? I shook my head; I didn't know…and in a combat situation, a moment's hesitation would get me very, very dead. It had to be the BFT interlock. I hoped. Still…I had to tell him before I put everyone's lives on the line.

"That's not what I meant, sir. I had a bad experience—that's what put me in The Palace. I was raised to believe killing was wrong, and I don't know if I can do this—this killing—anymore."

The lieutenant's eyes narrowed, and he pursed his lips as he stared at me. "Okay Andrews, here's the deal. I saw what you did to that guy, and I've seen your psyche profile. He deserved most of what he got, even if you did go overboard a little."

A little? He must not have seen the color photos they made me look at during the trial…or his definition of "a little" was *very* different from mine.

"I know there's a killer in there," the lieutenant said with a grin. "You just have to have faith."

Faith. If it was only that easy. It was faith that had brought me to where I was, while simultaneously being the thing holding me back. If there was one thing that *wouldn't* help me, it was faith.

"Besides," he added, "the first time I see you hesitate, I'll kill you, myself."

"What about the blue force tracker?"

"My suit doesn't have that incorporated into its operational software."

* * *

The next two weeks were a blur. We got acclimated to our suits and then did a practice drop on Mars, followed by a two-hour "jog" to where the training camp was. Followed by more training. Followed by weapons practice. I think we must have had some amphetamines somewhere along the way. I don't remember taking them, though, so they must have been in our food. Somehow, we stayed awake for three days. It's amazing how much you can accomplish in three days when you don't have to do mundane things like sleep periodically.

Then there was the transport for a week. Although some people have problems with null gravity, most of us had been in The Palace for a least a year, and zero G wasn't an issue. Mars had been a bigger issue. Even though it was only a third of Earth's gravity, it was a lot more than most of us had experienced in a while, and we left there physically beat.

While the time on the transport let our bodies heal, the guards grilled us the entire time we were in hyperspace on tactics, weapons, and other issues they thought we might need to know to complete the mission, and we were mentally exhausted by the time we transitioned into the target system. The guards didn't tell us where we were—they said we didn't have a "need to know"—but just that we were "here." By that point, I would have happily faced an armed Besquith if it meant I didn't have to do another strategy lesson with Sergeant Stennis *ever again.*

I thought that until they loaded us in the launch tubes.

The SOGA's little army had a Q-ship that was built to look like a small, highly-specialized trading ship, but was actually a planetary assault ship. On one side of the ship, 24 small compartments had been built in two rows of 12. Nominally, they were built to transport high value materials, or items that were dangerous to transport and needed "extra containment."

All of the spaces were slightly larger than a fully-loaded CASPer, and were, in reality, CASPer launch tubes. We went out the main cargo hatch and inserted ourselves, head first, into the tubes.

Each of the suits had metal rods attached at the hip that projected outward to the sides; these fit into two guide slots that kept us oriented on launch. There was also an attachment on my shoulder—the one without the MAC—that mated to "the plunger" on the ship. This was a moving arm that would, "impart the motive force necessary to expel us from the ship."

I wiggled my suit as much as I could while being held in place and was just able to get one of my cameras pointed down toward my feet as the compartment door slid to the side. I immediately wished I hadn't.

I could barely see the planet through the fire and sparks flying off the ablative material on the belly of the ship as we hit atmosphere. The planet appeared to be more dirt than water, but the flames roaring across the opening made it difficult to tell.

"Stand by," a voice said. Then, "Launching."

Starting with the lieutenant, we were "expelled" from the ship like a round fired from a MAC; I'm surprised my straps held me in place, and I didn't burst through the top of the suit when the ship's ejection system fired.

I may have screamed inside my suit, just a bit, as I hurtled toward the planet. It was the lowest I'd ever started an assault. Normally, you start a lot further out, and you have a chance to see the planet grow slowly and get used to the idea that a shroud and a little metal suit is all you have as a re-entry vehicle. Not so, this time. The planet was already *there*, we were rocketing toward it, and I didn't see any way my jumpjets would be able to stop me in time.

More importantly…*why weren't they firing?*

It had to be time for them—I mean, the planet was *huge*—but the jumpjets were silent. I forced myself to breathe. If there was one thing Sergeant Stennis had drilled into us, it was to trust our equipment. I closed my eyes, trusting the automatic program would run correctly. Besides, it was better to hit unexpectedly than to see it coming.

As soon as my eyes shut, the jumpjets activated, and I opened them again to look at my instruments. After what seemed like hours, but probably wasn't more than 20 or 30 seconds, I could see I was slowing noticeably. Before I could release the breath I'd been holding, though, I realized I had another issue—over half of my jumpjuice had already been expended; I wouldn't have enough to land!

As if the suit shared my pain, the jumpjets shut off again. Hopefully, it was to conserve fuel until the last-ditch endgame maneuver to save my life, and not because something had broken. The altimeter continued to unwind, and I was pretty sure I was going to *splat*, but the jumpjets came on again, full thrust, arresting my fall. Would it be enough?

Yes. At 15 feet of altitude, my vertical speed slowed to zero, and the jumpjets cut out again, allowing me to fall the last bit unaided. I bent my knees and let the suit absorb most of the impact; however, there's a limit to how gracefully a one-ton suit can hit.

"Second Squad, on me," Sergeant Stennis said, interrupting my prayer of thanks to any god listening who helped get me down safely.

We gathered around him, but I noticed something wrong. "Aren't we short a suit?" I asked.

"Watson's gone." Private Michaelson said from WO7.

"What?" I asked. "How?"

Michaelson pointed behind me, and I turned to find a smoking crater, surrounded by a blast pattern of debris. "His jumpjets didn't work." So much for trusting his equipment.

"Where the hell have you been, Andrews?" Private Ariens asked. "He screamed all the way down."

"I guess I had my radio turned down," I replied, wondering how I'd missed it. Maybe I'd been screaming a little more than I thought I had. Huh. I guess that's why my throat was suddenly hoarse.

Stennis got us organized, and we moved out, following First Squad up a gully.

Now that we were moving, I finally had a chance to look at our surroundings. The sky was tinged purple, and the landscape was mostly barren, except for some small bushes and a reddish plant with eight-leaf clusters on it.

Crap. It couldn't be.

The outside air sensor showed the air was breathable. Minimally, but it wasn't toxic, so I cracked the canopy as I marched and took a cautious sniff. Shit. I knew immediately where I was. The desolate landscape. The smell of five-day-old animal carcasses dipped in shit and then used for target practice by a family of skunks. You could never forget the smell. There was only one place in the galaxy we could be.

I'd come home.

"Lieutenant, are we on Paradise?" I asked. I had to know, even though I dreaded the answer.

"How the fuck did you know that?" the lieutenant replied. "Yes, we are. Now shut the hell up."

Yeah, I was home. The one place I'd sworn I would never go back to again. I was anathema here, as I'd done the one thing my parents had absolutely forbidden me to do—I'd joined a merc outfit—and it was the one thing they would never forgive me for. They didn't realize the feeling was mutual; I had joined the merc outfit for one reason, and one reason only: it was the only way I could put this place behind me.

Like most of the colonists on Paradise, my parents were religious nut jobs, who believed taking a life—any life—was the fastest way to hell in the afterlife. By becoming a mercenary, I became everything they hated. When I joined up, they called me the devil and told me to never come back. I had sworn then and there that, for the first time in my life, I would obey their orders—I would never come back to Paradise…and yet, here I was.

Shit.

We crested a rise, and I knew where we were. Not only had we come to my home planet, we'd come home—the place I'd grown up was seven miles from our current location in the direction we were heading.

In between, though, lay the Plains of Sorrow, an area of land that was almost like walking on a beach. When humans had first come to Paradise, they had found massive herbivore analogues that grazed on the small shrubs. Larger than terrestrial cows, they moved in large herds and had horns that would gut a person with a twitch of their giant heads. The settlers had wondered what kept the herd size in check—there didn't seem to be any predators.

They found out when they came to the Plains of Sorrow. And we were going to cross them. Shit. Shit. Shit.

"Hey, Lieutenant," I said. "We're going to need to go a different way."

"Andrews, didn't I tell you to shut the hell up?"

"Yes sir, you did, but—"

"Then shut the hell up."

"But I—"

"One more word, and I'll shut you up permanently."

I shut up, but I kept my thumb on my jumpjets. It didn't take long.

"I'm picking up some vibrations," Private Levesque said. "Almost like a minor earthquake."

I froze, but the rest of the platoon kept moving, their one-ton machines stomping the sand as they advanced, spread out across the sand.

My squad leader noticed I was no longer keeping up, and he turned back. "Andrews, what the fuck are you doing? Why did you just arm your—"

The sand worms burst from underneath the platoon in a choreographed dance of destruction. Pack hunters, seven of the enormous beasts seized CASPers as they rose 50 feet in the air. At the peak of their ascent, they bit through the legs of the troopers and swallowed the pieces in their mouths, allowing the troopers' torsos to fall back to the sand.

Eyes snapped open, looking for targets, as the giant predators came crashing back down. It was what I'd been waiting for, and I fired my MAC as fast as I could at the closest worm.

Chunk! Chunk! Chunk! The first two rounds hit behind the eye and ricocheted off the creature's scales, pissing it off but doing no damage. The eye swiveled toward me as the third round hit it dead center, penetrating through it to scramble the brain behind the eye, expanding as it went, and I knew it was a killing shot.

It was pure luck to hit the eye with only three shots, but that didn't help Sergeant Stennis, who was the worm's next target. He stood underneath it, firing vainly up into its bulk, and then five tons of inanimate worm collapsed onto the soldier and turned him into a tangled mess of wreckage.

The rest of the platoon hadn't fared any better than Stennis. Even though they were surprised by the worms' attack, they'd all armed their weapons and had taken the creatures under fire.

Which was, of course, the worst thing to do. After the worms' first attack, meant to incapacitate their initial targets for their later dining pleasure, the worms' secondary attack was to crush another victim as they fell to the sand.

The platoon fired at the monsters as they came back down; they might as well have been throwing spitballs at the creatures for all the good it did. The creatures traveled through the sand and had evolved thick scales that were impervious to most human weaponry. The other six worms crushed their targets while the remaining soldiers fired impotently at them.

Once the worms reached the apex of their first attack run, you *moved* out from under them once you saw which way they were going. I would have told everyone, had Smith let me.

That was pretty much it for the worms, though. Once a worm's momentum was spent, it was more of an impregnable land fortress than the biological nightmare it had been seconds earlier—if you left them alone, they kept their eyes closed and were happy to eat what they had killed.

"Kill those mother fuckers!" Smith ordered. Apparently, we weren't going to leave them alone. This wasn't the optimal response—running was better—because, while you could sometimes get a shot into an open mouth as it snatched its prey, you had to watch out for the other members of the pack. Anything that didn't sound like running away (the normal response of the herbivores), incited additional attacks. A one-ton suit moving around firing a MAC was guaranteed to make you the focus of the pack. While the soldiers fired at the worms, two more soldiers were taken from behind.

"Let's go!" I yelled.

"No!" Smith countered as he continued to fire ineffectively into one of the monsters. "Some of the men are still alive, and we have to get them!"

"The worms cut them in half!" I yelled. A scream was cut off as another trooper was eaten. "If we don't use this time to get away, they will attack us again, and we'll all be dead!"

My thumb went back to the jumpjets. He could shoot me if he wanted to, but I wasn't staying. After a couple of seconds, though, he stopped firing. "Okay," Smith said, "let's go!"

He didn't see the one coming from behind him. Without thinking, I triggered my jumpjets. I had planned to land next to him, but he moved while I was in midair, and I crashed into him. We went down in a tangle of metal, but at least the worm missed us.

I used the jumpjets to help me get up, then blasted off again with a hurried, "*Run!*"

I heard Smith jump from behind me and didn't stop to look back. He could come or not—I didn't give a shit—but I was *not* staying.

We jumped until we ran out of jumpjuice, then we sprinted the rest of the way to the cliffs and made it there without being attacked again. Only Smith and I were left. The last trooper—Vasquez, I think—must have been taken while I was tackling Smith. Damn.

"What were those things?" Smith asked as we took a minute to catch our breaths. "Were those...Canavar?"

"No," I replied. "Canavar didn't live underground. That doesn't mean the worms aren't relatives or descendants of the Canavar that have either adapted to this planet or been modified to live here."

"How do you fight them?"

"You don't. I'm *from* here, and we live in the rocky cliffs where they can't get us." I shrugged. "When we have to go out to where they are, the key is to stop moving so they don't know where you are—they sense the vibrations you make walking. Then you wait to see which way they're falling, and you run like hell. If you fight them, you're just going to end up as worm food."

"You killed one, though," he noted.

"I got lucky." I thought about it a few seconds. The worm was the first thing I'd killed since...that night. Was I cured? Could I kill again or was it just an act of thoughtless self-preservation? I didn't know.

"Intel says there's a secret back door to the facility around here," the lieutenant said as he started walking along the cliff.

"It's not a secret," I replied. "There are two doors out here. They're just not used anymore because..." I motioned back toward the Plains of Sorrow.

"Because there's shit out there that eats people so no one comes out this way."

"Yeah."

"The closest one's back here," I said. I pointed toward where I knew the door was, and Smith started walking toward it. "This is really where our target is?"

"Yeah," he said. "Some damn colonists took the SOGA's daughter and are holding her for ransom."

It didn't make any sense. The colonists here were generally very peaceful. It was a religious colony, and I doubted anything had changed along those lines in the last five years. We reached the door and, with a quick glance at me, he went through the portal with his weapons at the ready. He passed through the blast door, and then it slammed shut and the automatic lock engaged before I could stop it. The door was monitored from a central control facility and was built to repel worm attacks for anyone who made it through; short of using a quantity of explosive that would have brought down the cliff face, my weapons weren't going to get through it. I waited for several minutes, but the lieutenant didn't come back out. If it was locked out by the control room, he wasn't getting back out, and I was wasting time.

With a resigned sigh, I turned and headed for the other door. I knew I could get in there; the colony had run out of money before they could install a blast door on it, and by then they had learned the secret—don't go out onto the plain and you won't attract the worms. I turned back and looked up at the camera mounted above the door. "I'm coming for you."

I had no idea who in the community would have kidnapped the girl; the entire mission didn't make sense. Although my parents ran the religious community, everyone was fairly equal. I didn't remember anyone who had a major axe to grind with the government. They had come to Paradise to *escape* Earth's government; I had no idea why someone would want to do something to intentionally bring it here. It didn't make sense.

I walked down the cliff face to the other door, hoping the worms had been fed well enough they wouldn't come searching for more. I reached the door and considered destroying it with my MAC in case it was booby-trapped. It's what I would have done on a "real" mission that wasn't conducted at my own home.

Finally, I shrugged and reached for the handle with my manipulator hand. The door was unlocked. I opened the door, hoping there was nothing behind it that would blow me to paradise…in Paradise. I chuckled at my pun, knowing no one else would find it very funny.

Behind the door, the entryway and the passage beyond were vacant, and the lights were turned on. The tunnel had been drilled into the rock by an industrial digger, and the passage was 10 feet wide and high; my suit was almost tall enough to scrape the roof.

I walked down the passageway, my senses on overload, yet with a certain sense of disbelief it was even happening. I'd already pinched myself several times but had, as yet, to wake up from the dream.

The tunnels all seemed deserted, and they were *never* deserted. Usually, there were at least kids in them, running around, playing some sort of game. Not today.

My feet naturally found their way to the common area. I guess, subconsciously, I thought if there was anyone around, that's the place they would be. I didn't have much of a plan—at this stage I was almost to the point of stopping someone and asking, "Hey, you wouldn't happen to have seen a girl that was kidnapped and brought here, would you?" As strange as that sounded, everyone knew everyone else, pretty much; if there was a new girl around, someone would have seen her. There was only one problem—there wasn't anyone to ask.

I entered the common room and realized I had to be dreaming; the sight was that bizarre. There were four people in the enormous room, and two of them were on their knees. My father had an old-fashioned slug-throwing pistol pointed at the SOGA's daughter, while my mother held a laser rifle on the lieutenant who was out of his suit. If someone had run into me, I would have fallen over without being able to stop it. I was as shocked as if someone had hit me with a 70,000 volt stun stick, and I staggered to a stop, my weapons not even pointing at anyone. *What the hell was happening?*

My father nodded at me, breaking the silence. "Hi John," he said. My first name was John. "It's 'bout time you got here."

"Uh, dad, can you please tell me what the he—, just what's going on here?"

"Sure," he replied. "It's all very simple. We're settin' you free from that jail you got yerself put into."

"I'm not in jail dad. I'm here to recover the girl you're pointing a pistol at."

"I know that," he said. "I did this for you. I told them I would free her if they freed you."

"You…*you* kidnapped her?" my mind was having a hard time processing the fact that my father was not only holding a pistol, but was actively pointing it at someone.

"We took her," he said, nodding at my mother. *What? Mom was involved, too?*

"Are…are you going to let her go?"

"I am, but only after you kill this soldier."

I looked at Smith. "You knew it was my father who had the girl?"

"Yeah. Why else do you think I put up with you? The plan all along was to recapture the girl if we could, and trade you for her if we couldn't."

Inside my suit, my jaw dropped open again. I couldn't keep up with the mental whiplash of the events going on around me. My parents had broken the law. I thought they had brought me because I was a hot-shit mech operator; instead, I was nothing more than a bargaining chip.

My father waved his gun at the lieutenant. "I told you, John, go ahead and kill him."

"Why would I do that?"

"Because he knows too much. I'm not going to kill him, though; my soul is pure. You, however; you're already a killer so you'll have to do it."

"I can't," I said. "I've lost the ability to kill. I don't know. Maybe it's all the sermonizing and moralizing you put me through. I just can't kill anymore."

"Nah, that's crap," Lieutenant Smith said. "I know you could kill anyone in this room with the right motivation. Just remember, though, our mission is to bring home the girl. That's what you signed up to do."

"Don't try to confuse him," my father said. "He's turned over a new leaf, and once you're gone, he will be able to follow the path of purity."

I looked around the room again, and my eyes met the girl's. She looked scared, and it dawned on me why. "I don't want to rehash this, but the girl has seen everything the lieutenant has. Can you promise me that you're going to let her go?"

My father looked away and mumbled something. My mother said nothing, which spoke volumes. She never lied. "Get out of the suit," my father finally said.

"I think I'm fine right here," I said, assessing the situation. If bullets were going to be flying, I liked having a little bit of armor between me and them. The suit wouldn't stop mom's laser, much, but dad's pistol wouldn't hurt me.

"I said, get out of the suit," my father said.

"He never did listen very well," my mother added. She looked down the barrel of the rifle at the lieutenant. "Tell him to get out of the suit."

"Tell him your own God-damned self," the lieutenant replied.

That was a mistake, and I knew it—you don't swear at my mom. She reversed the rifle and slammed the butt into his face. He fell to the floor before getting back up slowly to his knees. He spit out a tooth.

"Want another one?" my mother asked. She put the rifle back up to her shoulder, aimed, and put her finger on the trigger.

"Nope," the lieutenant said.

So that was it, then. They—or someone—was going to have to kill the girl to satisfy my parents' plan. That would probably fall to me, too. With both mom and dad holding weapons, though, I didn't see any way I could stop them both, without one or the other hostage dying.

The lieutenant could obviously see the same thing, for he looked me in the eyes, as if he could see through the metal of my suit, and nodded once. "Hey, Andrews?" he asked.

"Yeah?"

"Promise me one thing."

I shook my head once, although no one could see it. "I'm not sure it'll be possible."

"I've got faith in you," he replied. "Once you save the girl, *like you're supposed to*, do me a favor. Avenge me."

I looked at him, then at my mother and father, all of whom were looking back at me.

The lieutenant, my mother, and my father—almost everyone in the room but me—had faith, but while my parents had faith in their religion, the lieutenant had a different kind of faith, and it was something my parents never had—he had faith in me. And then it hit me like a MAC round in the chest—I didn't need faith in my abilities or in my resolve—the only thing I needed was faith in my squad mates and to honor the faith they had in me.

I did the only thing I could. My tri-barrel cycled, firing five rounds into my mother, and she was blown backward, dead before she hit the floor. Dad's jaw dropped as I spun on him, and he turned back to the girl, his finger starting to tighten on the trigger.

I was faster, and the rounds from my tri-barrel hit him in the wrist, separating his hand from his arm, and then walked up to his chest. As the lieutenant ran over to grab my father's pistol, I realized I had done it. The lieutenant was right. I *could* kill if I needed to, without any feelings other than the satisfaction of doing what had to be done. I was 'cured.'

* * *

The lieutenant and I stood waiting on the pad with the SOGA's daughter, whose name I still didn't know, watching as the SOGA's Q-ship came down to land. "Question for you," the lieutenant said as the skids touched down.

"Yeah?"

"Why did you shoot your mother first? I told you to save the girl."

I shrugged. "Mom was always the one with resolve. She would have killed you. Dad was a believer; the last thing he wanted to do was kill anyone. I knew I had a split second to get back on him."

As the boarding ramp came down, the lieutenant stuck his hand out to me as if to shake my hand. "Well, it's been good knowing you," he said, "but here's where our paths part."

My jaw dropped for about the tenth time since I'd come home. "Wha—what do you mean by 'here's where our paths part?'"

"Really?" Lieutenant Smith asked, holding up a slate for me to see. "You don't know? You should have read your contract better. It specifically states right here—" he pointed at the screen, "that you could be released from service—should you so desire—at the end of the mission on the closest inhabited planet. Well, there are sentient beings here, now that we set loose the rest of the colonists your parents had locked up, so this planet *is* inhabited. I can either leave you here, or you can join the Warden's Own. What do you think about becoming a permanent Dead Man Walking?"

"Will I still be considered a convict?"

"Nope, you're a free man. You can do whatever you want. The only thing is, you can never talk about the Warden's Own; the warden tends to look...unfavorably...on anyone who does."

"What if I want to go back to Earth?"

"We may return there…some time…but you'll have to sign on the dotted line for another mission if you want me to take you off this rock."

Fuck that. I didn't want anything to do with the Warden's Own. If this was the kind of mission they got…no thanks. We'd had 90 percent casualties—their missions were certain death. About the only thing I could think of worse than certain death was…living in Paradise.

"Give me the damn slate."

He handed it to me with a grin. I started to sign my name, but he held up a hand. "Don't sign your old name," he said. "That man was shot trying to escape and has been listed as dead. You completed your mission, so the SOGA's given you a new life and a new identity." He turned the slate so he could see it again. "Sign it, 'Dan Walker.'"

# # # # #

Tinkerman
by Jake Bible

Tee winced as the bolts auto-threaded into the bone grafts.

He could have installed a full bracket or even pain mitigating nanites. But he didn't trust the permanence of the bracket tech he had available. His workshop had become a little bare, and he needed every spare part for what he had planned.

As for the pain? He'd suffered worse. Way worse. When the tips of the bolts met raw bone, he merely winced and checked the diagnostics on the prosthetic connected to the bottom half of his left arm. All was in good working order. The arm was ugly as sin, more metal alloy than synthetic flesh, and zero skin, but it did the job.

Looking into the vanity mirror that was stuck to the wall by bands of black electrical tape, Tee studied his lined and weathered face. Two decades earlier he'd had females of many galactic races seeking his company. Now he could barely get a cup of coffee without the waitress wincing at the scars that crisscrossed his cheeks and forehead. Deep scars. Scars that told a story no one wanted to hear.

Tee took a deep breath, put on his best smile, shoved aside the drape that partitioned off his bedroom, and walked into the workshop area of his cobbled together abode.

"Lucas?" Tee asked.

The eight-year-old boy sitting at one of Tee's workbenches nodded, but didn't smile back. The woman standing behind the boy gave Tee a grimace and a slight shrug.

"Thank you, Mr. Tinkerman, for seeing my boy so quickly," the mother said, her voice subservient and scared. "I don't know what Lucas would do if we had to make the trip to Portland. He doesn't do well on that side of the range."

"I understand," Tee replied, focusing on the boy. "I'm not a fan of leaving this side, either."

He waited for the boy to give him another nod before he sat down at the bench and took the child's right arm in his. Where there should have been a hand there was only a nub of flesh stretched over bone. Tee hid his repulsion as he spotted the gangrene and what looked to have been an attempt to use maggots to eat away the rotted flesh.

The maggots failed, as most living creatures did in the harsh reality that was Eastern Oregon. High desert scrub brush for hundreds of miles in all directions. It was a land meant for buzzards, not humans. Yet, there the humans lived. Or tried to.

Tee sighed as he gently set the boy's arm on the workbench then steeled himself to pull the roughly woven blanket away from the child's lap and legs. The smell assaulting his nostrils would have sent a lesser man scurrying to throw up outside in the already one hundred plus degree heat.

But Tee had witnessed worse; worked on worse. The smell wasn't the issue so much as the emotions the sight of the severed legs brought up in him.

The boy's legs were missing from the upper thighs down. Other than the hack job of surgery, the injuries were perfectly symmetrical.

"Maglev train?" Tee asked.

"He and his brother were playing outside…" The mother trailed off.

Tee looked her straight in the face, his eyes narrowed but kind. "Accidents happen."

"I was making lunch. They were supposed to stay in the yard."

"Kids rarely do, but still ain't your fault. That maglev moves so damn fast."

"Portlanders." The mother spat then looked horrified.

Tee spat as well and grinned. "Don't worry, I ain't eating off this floor anytime soon."

The mother tried to smile and failed so miserably Tee almost laughed.

He shifted focus back to the boy.

"Lucas, you need to listen to me, okay?"

"Yes, sir," Lucas replied, his eyes about to pop from his head from fear.

"This will be uncomfortable. I can make sure the worst of the pain is held at bay by nanites, but I'm not a doctor, and this is not a hospital. You will feel a lot of it. I want you to know it's okay to cry. Understand?"

"Yes, sir."

"Okay then." Tee glanced over at the operating table in the middle of the workroom. Six bots of his own design stood waiting for the procedure, their lights blinking green as they communicated with each other. "No time like the present."

"I cannot pay, Mr. Tinkerman," the mother said quietly.

"I assumed as much," Tee replied. "Were you told what I ask then?"

"Yes, sir."

"Do you agree to my terms? It may be a month from now. It may be never. But when I call, he'll be expected to show up."

"Will it be...Will it be dangerous...?"

"It'll be what it is," Tee replied, crossing his arms over his chest. His metal alloy fingers tapped his bicep over and over until the mother gave a small squeak of assent. "Good. I promise I'll do the best work I can, and he'll only be called if needed. The kids are only for the greeting, not the combat."

"Okay...thank you, Mr. Tinkerman."

"Thank me when the procedures are done," Tee said. "Until then, I need you to hold his good hand and help me keep him calm. Can you do that?"

"Yes, sir."

"Okay. Let's get started."

Tee snapped his metal fingers, and the bots became a blur of motion around the operating table.

* * *

"This coffee is horrible," Taska said. "But better than anything I've had in a long, long while." She emptied her cup and set it down on the cafe's counter, giving it a couple taps with the rings on her right hand. "Y'all got any cake? I could go for some cake to help get the taste of this coffee outta my mouth."

"No cake," the exhausted-looking waitress replied as she set her slate down. The image of a half-naked man staring longingly out of the screen blinked to black on the slate. Her name tag said she was

Bobbie. Bobbie gave Taska a tired, worn look. "Got cookies. But they ain't any good. Butter soured. I told Van not to use it, but he don't throw nothing away."

"Waste not, want not," Taska replied. She tapped the coffee cup again.

Bobbie got up from her stool and made a production of fetching the coffee pot that was two feet away from her. She walked the last two feet to Taska and poured a fresh, steaming cup of horrible coffee.

"You want a couple?" Bobbie asked.

"A couple what?" Taska asked.

"A couple of them cookies."

"Nah. I'll pass on soured butter cookies."

"Suit yerself."

Bobbie returned to her slate and the pop culture magazine that was already six months old. Taska returned to her horrible coffee.

The door chimed.

"Burger. Rare. Yucca fries if Van didn't let the roots rot."

"Afternoon to you too, Tee," Bobbie said as she grabbed a different slate and put in his order. "Plenty of yucca left. I saved it from Van's incompetence."

"I can hear you, ya dumb bitch!" a man shouted from back in the kitchen. He quickly appeared at the serving window separating the lunch counter from the kitchen. "I hear every damn thing you say about me!"

"Yet it don't seem to make a damn bit of difference." Bobbie sighed. "Have a seat, Tee. You want something to drink?"

"How fresh is the water?" Tee asked as he moved to a booth up against the bank of windows looking out onto a desolate landscape of tumbleweeds and sage brush. Mountains rose far into the sky way off in the distance, but the snowcaps that had been a staple of the high peaks were long, long gone. "When was the filter last changed?"

Bobbie gave Taska a quick look then smiled and stood, flattening her short apron. "Let me check the date."

She disappeared into the back. The sound of her and Van arguing was muted enough that the words were lost, but the tone was easy to interpret.

"Bad filter," Taska said, spinning her stool to face Tee's booth. She raised the cup of horrible coffee. "That would explain this."

"Recycled grounds would explain that," Tee said. His eyes sized up the woman. "Where you coming from and where you headed to?"

"Not sure," Taska replied as she leaned her elbows back on the counter.

"Not sure where you're coming from?"

Taska shrugged.

"Sometimes it's easier to leave the past behind," Tee said and matched her shrug.

Taska watched the old, scarred man closely. He returned the favor.

"How much they paying you?" Tee asked. "Is the bounty open or are you exclusive?"

"That's two questions I don't think I need to answer," Taska replied, not even trying to hide her profession.

Not that hiding what she was would have helped. Tee could see she was a bounty hunter.

And he knew the type she was. The type that flaunted the profession in order to intimidate all she came in contact with. It was simply easier to make sure everyone knew who she was. The cowards went and hid, the do-gooders gave up intel like it would save their souls, and the rats named a price for the information they held. Cut the hunting time in half. Tee got that.

"I have a burger and yucca fries coming," Tee said as he relaxed into the booth. "Maybe some filtered water. Bobbie!"

The waitress reappeared with a pitcher of clear-looking water.

"Ain't got no ice left," Bobbie said as she skirted the edge of the lunch counter and walked to Tee's booth. "Maybe you could have a look at the machine? Van says it's a bad condenser, but I barely trust him to know when the meat's spoiled, let alone how to diagnose an ice maker."

"Can't wait for my burger," Tee said with a smirk.

"Shut up, you," Bobbie said, filling Tee's water glass. "Leave the pitcher?"

"If you don't mind," Tee said. "Been a long, thirsty day."

"You do some work today?" Bobbie asked.

Tee looked over to Taska who was watching both of them like a hawk. Bobbie glanced over her shoulder at the bounty hunter and rolled her eyes.

"We pegged her the second she came in, Tee," Bobbie said. "She's covered."

"Excuse me?" Taska asked. She stood up from the lunch counter.

Dressed in heavy synthleathers to match the gigantic motorcycle out in the dusty parking lot, Taska was easily over six feet tall with shoulders that said, "Mess with me and you get broken." But she had no weapons on her that could be seen, but that meant absolutely zero.

"Hey now," Tee said as he sipped his water. "I said I have a burger coming. Sit your ass down, let me finish my meal, and then we'll talk options."

"Sorry, Lieutenant—"

"No," Tee barked. "I'm not that man anymore. The name is Tinkerman. Mr. Tinkerman."

"Or Tee to his friends," Bobbie said in a protective tone.

"Ma'am? I think it's best if you left this room," Taska said.

Bobbie sighed and faced the bounty hunter.

"I ain't leaving nowhere anytime soon," Bobbie said. "But I will give you a chance to take your own advice."

Bobbie pointed her right index finger in Taska's face.

"Last warning, you biker wannabe."

"I don't do warnings," Taska said.

Taska's right arm began to lift, but she was too late. Half her head exploded in a blast of bone and blood mist.

Bobbie's index finger smoked slightly and she lifted it to her lips, blowing the smoke away. Then she turned to Tee and gave him a wink.

"I'll get that cleaned up right quick. Van'll have your burger ready in less than five."

"Thanks, Bobbie," Tee said, taking another sip of water. "I appreciate it. Swing by later and I'll cap that finger for you."

Tee turned to stare out at the barren landscape as Bobbie started whistling while she fetched a mop. The cleaning bot had given up the ghost a couple years back, and no one thought it was worth the parts to repair.

* * *

Tee sat with his feet up on the porch railing, a steaming mug of sage tea in his flesh hand. He watched the sun slowly set in the dreary, February sky. In his youth there would have at least been a dusting of snow on the ground, but the temperature hadn't gotten below freezing in Oregon for over 20 years.

With the way Tee's metal arm ached now and again, he wasn't exactly sad to lose the cold winters. His old bones preferred the ever-warming weather that dominated Earth's deteriorated climate. Alien tech or not, the damage had been done too early and too fast for any significant reversal.

Tee was fine with that. He'd been on planets that would boil the skin off a human being in less than five seconds. And he'd been on planets that would have frozen his eyeballs like grapes if he hadn't been protected from the elements. A mild winter in the high plains of Eastern Oregon was paradise as far as he was concerned.

"Three targets approaching from the east, Tee," a voice said over the comms implant in Tee's left ear. Simultaneously, Tee's cerebral pinplants activated, and a display came up in his left eye.

"Thank you, Morgana," Tee replied to probably what was his oldest friend, even though she was simply an adapted battlefield computer that Tee had brought with him when he'd returned to Earth. Tee winced slightly at the sound of her voice. He'd programmed her to sound like someone from his past. It always hurt a little when she spoke. "Species?"

"Two human, one unknown," Morgana replied.

"Unknown?"

"Unknown."

"Give me details."

The image in Tee's eye zoomed closer to show two humans armed to the teeth with a third being following close behind them. Tee didn't recognize the species. But then he'd been out of the game for a long while and who knew what planets had been admitted into the Galactic Union while he'd been hiding in the Oregon desert.

Whatever the species, the creature was bipedal and about five feet tall. Unlike the humans, it wore no battle armor or gear of any kind. The head-to-toe scales looked like they were protection enough, and the four long, bony spikes stretching a foot down from the back of the being's hands could probably do some damage.

Not that Tee was too worried. They'd walked onto his land. He had the advantage.

Tee always had the advantage.

"Hey there," Tee called out as he set his mug of sage tea down and stood up to face the visitors. "Y'all lost?"

"Should I execute defensive protocol Alpha Delta Niner, Tee?"

"No. I have this, Morgana. Thank you."

Tee stepped off his porch and walked toward the three figures.

"That's close enough, old timer," the lead human called when they were about 50 yards away. "We can scan you from there."

"I usually prefer dinner first before anyone scans me on my own land," Tee replied.

He stopped walking and set his stance so his feet were shoulder width apart. He flexed his metal hand then let it relax against his thigh.

"Gonna have to ask you gentlemen to turn yourselves around and head back the way you came," Tee said.

"A single rumbler," Morgana said in his ear.

"That rumbler you came in will work again once you haul it about half a click off my property," Tee continued. "Then you can be on your way."

"We've come for Lieutenant—"

"No," Tee barked. "No need to finish. You've been misled. I'm not who you are looking for. In fact, the bounty you've taken is bogus. You'll want to take it up with whatever guild you answer to. Someone has played y'all."

"Think not, old timer," the leader replied. "My scan's complete. You are who we are looking for."

"Guys, I'm trying to give you a chance here. Before you send that scan over the—"

"Already done, old timer. Already done. We've logged our claim, and you will be coming with us."

"What condition has been set?" Tee asked. "Dead or alive?"

"Alive is worth considerably more, but dead is acceptable if mortally necessary."

"Mortally necessary?" Tee laughed. "I like that. I like that a lot."

"Tee?" Morgana asked.

"Light them up," Tee replied.

The ground around the three bounty hunters erupted into a grid of red laser light. The two humans screamed as they were minced into a thousand pieces each. The being of unknown species leapt high into the air, defying gravity in a way Tee hadn't expected.

The being launched itself out of the laser grid and landed only a couple yards in front of Tee.

"Submit," a staticky voice ordered from the translator pendant hanging around the being's neck. "Submit. Now."

"Can't do that, hoss," Tee said.

He flicked his left arm out and the metal framework opened up to reveal six small barrels. Tee pointed his arm with the barrels at the being.

"I didn't want to kill your colleagues. But they were warned. I've warned you. Twice. I don't warn a third time."

The being leapt again, the bony spikes flying at Tee as it launched into the air. Tee's arm canons obliterated the bony projectiles then he turned his aim up to the shadow coming down at him fast. All six barrels fired and instead of a solid body, thick, black blood and singed scales came raining down.

"Run the DNA, Morgana," Tee said as he wiped gunk from his eyes. "I want to know what it was. There are probably more on the way."

"Yes, Tee. I'll have the results by morning."

"You can process faster than that."

"Yes, but you need to rest. Your cardiovascular levels are in the red. The strain of battle is not good for your heart."

"No shit."

Tee sighed as he stared down at the spray of gore that surrounded him. He flicked his arm, and his arm canons retracted. Then he snapped his fingers, and ten seconds later a half dozen bots rolled up and began cleaning the offal from the dirt. Last thing Tee needed was a hundred buzzards circling his place.

He rolled his shoulders then turned and went back into his house. Rest did sound good.

* * *

"**M**r. Tinkerman," the mayor said as Tee walked into the woman's office and took a seat that hadn't been offered. "What brings you into Mercury today?"

"You heard about that bounty hunter over at Van's cafe last fall, yeah?" Tee replied. "And the three that hit my place last month?"

Tee rubbed his eyes. Sleep had been a fleeting luxury of late. He blinked a few times then focused on the mayor's expressionless face. She was a born politician.

"Yes, I heard," the mayor said.

She adjusted her suit jacket and tugged at the front of her blouse, making sure her cleavage was easier to see. Tee forced himself not to roll his eyes.

"Relax," he said. "I'm not calling in my marker, so don't try to sex your way out of anything quite yet."

Tee didn't add that he wasn't sure if he could take the mayor up on her unspoken offer anyway. The equipment didn't work like it used to, and Tee had no need to waste parts on an activity that would probably kill him because of his heart. Not that he wasn't tempted. The mayor was a beauty.

"Not sure what you mean, Mr. Tinkerman," the mayor said as she buttoned her blouse while giving Tee a sour look of defiance. "And I resent the implication."

"Wasn't implying a damn thing. Clearly stated what I was thinking," Tee said with a wave of his hand. "Doesn't matter. I'm here to make sure everything is in place in case I do call in my markers."

The mayor eyed Tee for several seconds. He waited patiently for her to gather her thoughts. Not that anything she had in her brain made a damn bit of difference. They were going to come for him in force soon, and he needed the town to be ready.

"Does Main Street have to be your staging ground?" the mayor asked finally. "Your place would be more ideal for everyone. Wide open spaces, only one building to be damaged. We don't have the resources to rebuild more than a building or two."

"My bots will be at your disposal," Tee said. "And I have put in more than enough materials for my needs and for the needs of the town if there is collateral damage."

"That is kind of you, Mr. Tinkerman, but bots can only do the repairs if the materials left are salvageable. Mercury isn't exactly flush with credits right now. We simply cannot afford to buy ourselves out of whatever destruction you bring down on us."

Tee had been resigned to a difficult meeting, but that last statement irked him. He gripped the arms of the chair he sat in until they began to creak. He relaxed and took a couple of deep breaths.

"Your wife enjoy that replacement pelvis I put in her last spring after she crashed her ATV? Or how about your niece? She able to get around on those feet she needed after stepping into that snake nest?"

The mayor glared, her bright blue eyes cold as ice.

"My wife is very grateful for the pelvis. My niece is even more grateful for the feet you gave her. Without speaking out of turn, I can say everyone you have helped is grateful. But your terms…"

"Are nonnegotiable. I state the truth up front before a single second of work begins. No one is being asked to do anything they didn't agree to do."

"People will agree to a lot to get what they want."

Tee didn't reply.

"May I ask why Main Street must be used?"

"Because image is everything."

"You want Mercury to be that image?"

"I do. When the next wave of hunters comes for me, and they will come, their forces will be heavy. I wouldn't be surprised if one of the smaller merc companies is contracted to assist. I expect CAS-Pers."

"Can they do that?" the mayor asked, visibly shocked. "On Earth soil?"

"Of course they can," Tee replied. "Don't be naive, Olivia."

"Yes, yes, you are right." She looked up at the ceiling and clasped her hands together hard enough for her knuckles to pop. "You, Mr. Tinkerman, are the best and worst thing to happen to this town."

"Better than only being the worst thing to happen. There're more than a few planets out in the galaxy that can lay that claim. There is a reason I'm hunted."

"Yes, we all know. Lieutenant Terror is what you were called? The Butcher of Bah'thaim?"

Tee bristled at the use of his old moniker.

"It was. I was a very different person then. And no one but me knows the real story."

"The real story in Mercury will be more butchery if you force the citizens of this town and county to do what you are asking them to do."

Tee leaned forward, resting his arms on his knees, as he fixed the mayor with a stare so intense the woman visibly began to sweat and shake.

"I don't want anyone to get hurt. I've put measures in place to make sure that doesn't happen. But, if those measures are to work then this conflict has to be out in the open. Hiding on my land will only mean a larger force will come then a larger one and a larger one. Until one day they obliterate this whole region and call it some accident. Whatever their spin doctors can dream up. You get that, don't you, Olivia? Spinning a story into what you want it to be?"

"Yes, Mr. Tinkerman, I get that," the mayor snarled. "Mercury will be at your disposal when the time comes as per our agreement and the agreements you have with everyone you've helped. God have mercy on us that you aren't bringing nothing but ruin and destruction."

"I won't comment on God and his mercy."

Tee stood up, gave the mayor a polite nod of his head, then left.

* * *

His door was wide open, but Tee wasn't too worried. Only one person let themselves in and left the door wide open to announce his presence. Tee had even reprogrammed the bots to ignore the man when he stopped by.

"Tee," Belfore said from the ratty recliner in the corner of Tee's small living space. "You've been poking the bear. Not cool, man."

"The bear came at me," Tee said as he closed the door behind him and walked to the mini fridge in the corner of the room. He opened it and pulled out two of the last beers he had. "And I didn't poke it. I obliterated it."

"We had a deal, Tee," Belfore said as Tee handed him a beer. "Low profile, and you can stay in Oregon until that ticker of yours finally bites it. Murdering four bounty hunters is not low profile. I can't keep you hidden from the authorities if you kill everyone that comes sniffing around your land."

"Part of our deal was you'd keep the Peacemakers off my ass," Tee said as he took a swig of beer and grimaced. The mini fridge needed a new coil, the beer was warm. "I count bounty hunters as part of that deal since the Peacemakers hired them to find me."

"Life is all about the fine print," Belfore said and downed half his beer before letting loose with a harsh belch.

The man looked three decades younger than Tee, but in reality it was a lot more years than that due to Tee's galactic travel. Belfore was a great grandnephew or some stupid relation. Tee never truly cared about the blood tie; he only cared about how it could benefit him and keep him alive. Belfore was connected. He knew the right people.

Tee needed the right people to know.

"Peacemakers hire bounty hunters," Tee pressed. "Bounty hunters find me and take me to the Peacemakers. Fuck your fine print. If I end up in the Peacemakers' hands or tentacles or fins or whatever, then I consider our deal null and void. Null and void on my end too."

"Yeah, yeah, yeah, so you take back some implants," Belfore said. "No, wait, you'll be in custody, so you can't take back shit."

"Morgana?"

"Yes, Tee?"

"Directive Omega Six Five Six."

"Yes, Tee."

"Talking to your computer?" Belfore asked.

"Yes."

"You think rattling out some…" Belfore paused and tilted his head. "Hold on. Getting a call."

He pinched the lobe of his left ear and waited as the comms connection was made. His eyes went wide in less than two seconds, and he leapt from the chair.

"What have you done?" Belfore roared, brandishing the beer bottle like a blackjack. Beer poured from the neck and splashed down on the man's shoes. "What the hell have you done?"

"Your twins will be dead within…Morgana?"

"Two minutes and twenty seconds."

"Two minutes and nineteen seconds," Tee relayed. "So, the question is whether or not you want to hold up your end of the deal and make sure when they come for me in force, which they will, I can end things right then and there. No follow up. No more bounty hunters or Peacemakers or anyone else that wants to drag up my past. I did what I did at Bah'thaim because I watched every single one of my friends and comrades die horribly. I took those CASPers, and I laid waste to every living creature in that goddamn city because it was me or them. And I'd do it again, if I had to. I'd do it a million times over."

"Fix them!" Belfore shouted.

"Are we clear on what you have to do?"

"Yes, goddammit! We're clear!"

"Morgana? Cancel directive Omega Six Five Six."

"Directive canceled. Full power restored to the Belfore siblings' renal implants."

"Thank you, Morgana."

"You son of a bitch," Belfore whispered.

"Do you really think they're coming to take me because I killed ten thousand beings in some back woods settlement on some backwoods planet in some backwoods system? There are mercs out there right now killing ten times that number. All for a profit. They are coming for me because once they have me in custody they'll pry my mind open like a can and extract the tether algorithm. That's what they want."

"Then give it to them and be done," Belfore said. "Why torture yourself and everyone in this area? Give them the algorithm and call it a day, Tee."

"The algorithm isn't theirs to have," Tee countered. "I was born here. About ten miles west."

"I know."

"Despite what's happened to this land, it's still a part of me. I won't let the town die, and I won't let the people of this area die with it. That algorithm is all that stands between them and extinction."

"You're mad," Belfore said.

The angered man tossed the dripping bottle into the corner of the room where it shattered. One of the bots that had been out of the way came scurrying out to clean up the mess. Belfore watched the bot work then stalked to the front door.

"You'll have your open channel when the time comes," Belfore said. "I'll make sure every eye that matters sees what your algorithm is capable of." Belfore laughed. It was an empty sound filled with bitterness. "How is exposing the algorithm to everyone that wants to steal it from you going to help this town? They'll want you even more then."

"They will," Tee said. "I'm counting on it."

* * *

The heat of the spring day beat down on Tee as he rode the 16 miles into town on the rusty old bicycle he'd refused to throw out. He could have driven his ATV, but he wanted the exercise. It would hurt like hell the next day, but Tee had a feeling the next day didn't matter so much anymore.

"Have they deployed?" Tee asked Morgana.

"Not yet, Tee."

"What are they waiting for?" Tee mused.

"I cannot extrapolate an answer from the limited data at my disposal."

"No, of course not," Tee said. "I was thinking out loud."

Mercury was a small town, only about 15 square blocks, but residents had spread from the hubs in haphazard ways as, humans do when left without a clear plan or structure to follow. Tee passed the first ramshackle huts cobbled together from shipping containers and scrap metal. Folks eyed him as he walked by, all very aware of who he was.

"Today the day, Mr. Tinkerman?" a young man about twenty-four called from his front door, a toddler held in the crook of one arm. "You gonna call in the markers?"

"I'm afraid today may be the day, Daniel," Tee called back as he passed. "Maybe tomorrow, but not sure why they'd wait."

"Well, some of us is happy to help," Daniel replied. "We made deals, and we aim to keep those deals. You saved us and ours, only right we honor that."

"I appreciate that, Daniel," Tee replied. "I truly do."

He continued on towards town.

He had similar conversations with some, harsher conversations with others, and was flat out ignored by a rare few. Tee had no intention of penalizing the ones who turned their backs as he rode by. If the numbers were correct, he'd have more than enough on his side when the time came.

He hit the first official block of Mercury and kept riding, hopping his bike up onto the sidewalk to avoid the menagerie of poorly-patched potholes and cracks the town's streets were mostly comprised of.

The mayor stood by the cracked steps of what passed as the town hall. Tee pulled up short in a cloud of dust and squealing brakes.

"Olivia."

"Mr. Tinkerman," the mayor replied. "Today."

"I would guess so," Tee replied as he set the bike to the side of the steps. "They didn't show up to have a cookout and drink beers."

"Numbers? What are we looking at?" the mayor asked as she shielded her eyes to the afternoon sun beating down upon the town. "Did they bring more than you can handle?"

"Morgana?" Tee asked.

"You and your computer," the mayor sighed. "You could use some human friends, Mr. Tinkerman."

"Maybe after this is over," Tee replied.

"Exactly one dozen CASPers," Morgana stated.

"Infantry?" Tee asked.

"No. Sensors show one dozen CASPers with one heavy rumbler."

"That would be the Peacemaker," Tee said. "What merc company are the CASPers part of?"

"Insignia shows them to be the Black Coils. They are a newer company incorporated two years ago. Their main body has deployed twice. This is their domestic contingent."

"A Peacemaker and bounty hunters working with a merc company all for you," the mayor said. "What makes you so goddamn special?"

"The same thing that will make this town so special once the day is over," Tee said. "You will have to trust me."

Tee stared down the street as people began to step out of buildings and look towards the town hall. He nodded then faced the mayor.

"Is it waiting?" he asked.

"Just like you asked," the mayor said. "It is positioned by the loading doors in the maintenance building. Nowhere else to put it."

"Good." Tee continued to stare down the street. "Morgana? What models?"

"MK 8s."

"The newest model? All 12?"

"Yes, Tee. All 12. They are formidable."

"That they are. But not as tested as the earlier models."

"The algorithm—"

"I know, Morgana. It'll work."

The mayor looked at Tee, exasperated.

"It's rude to hold one-sided conversations," she muttered.

"My apologies, Olivia. How about we walk to the maintenance building?"

"Might as well get this over with."

"Might as well."

* * *

Seeing the MK 6 CASPer standing there in the town's maintenance building gave Tee a hard pang in the gut. The last time he'd stood next to a CASPer was the day he'd become infamous. He swore he'd never use one again, but reality had a way of smacking ultimatums upside his head.

"They have 12?" the mayor asked as she circled the mecha. "And you have one? An older one? How do you propose to live through this?"

"I may not," Tee admitted. It was the first time he'd said the words out loud. Again, reality smacking him upside the head. "But this has never been about me."

"It hasn't?" The mayor barked a harsh laugh. "I could argue against that."

"Argue all you want. By the end of today, you'll see."

Tee stepped forward and picked up the haptic suit lying across a battered card table next to the mecha's right leg. He grimaced, but nodded, knowing he didn't have a choice.

He was stripped down to nothing by the time the mayor came back around the CASPer.

"So much for modesty," the mayor said, turning away as Tee struggled to slip into the skin tight suit that would allow his movements to be mimicked in real time by the mecha.

"No time for modesty," Tee said as he finished putting the suit on. "Morgana?"

The CASPer's cockpit hatch popped open and Tee climbed up inside the huge machine. Eight feet tall and nearly a ton in weight, it was impressive. Once inside, his pinplants connected to the mecha's control systems.

The cockpit closed and the display came up. Tee activated the external loudspeakers.

"You'll want to step back," he said as he went through the modified startup procedures.

The mayor hurried all the way outside the maintenance building. Tee grinned at her skittishness.

He walked out of the building, memories flooding his mind. He stuffed them down since they contained mostly blood and carnage. His hope for the day was a bloodless one. It would have to be or neither side would trust him when all was said and done.

Once outside the building, Tee turned towards Main Street. He was to the corner when he heard the explosion. More like felt the explosion through the huge metal feet of the combat armor.

"Morgana?"

The display showed a burning crater about 20 yards across. Standing far back from that were 10 CASPers. Two CASPers were on the ground, mechanics hustling about them as the pilots rested close to the rumbler the mercs had brought. A medic was treating the pilots, but they appeared to have only minor injuries.

"That brings the numbers down," Tee said.

One of the CASPers swiveled and brought up its right arm. Two projectiles shot from the arm and in less than a second Tee's view of the crater that used to be his home and workshop was lost.

"They'll be coming to town now," Tee said.

He moved out into the street and stood there.

"Send the call, please."

"Comms open and message being sent."

* * *

The ten MK 8 CASPers decided on the direct route. They marched up the center of Main Street, the pilots' confidence evident by their loose formation and weapons aimed toward the ground.

Tee wasn't fooled. He knew with the MK 8s the pilots already had full locks on every target in view. They'd have their arms up and firing before he could blink. He assumed each pilot was auto-pinplanted into their controls. Basically, if they could think it, the mechas would respond in real time as if the machines were the pilots' actual bodies. No delays.

That made Tee smile.

"Close enough," he called out over his loudspeakers.

The merc mechas slowed then stopped.

"Lieutenant—" the lead CASPer replied via its own loudspeakers, but Tee cut him off.

"Tee. Or Tinkerman. But I prefer Tee, if you don't mind."

"Very well. Mr. Tinkerman. We are under contract to bring you in per GU laws and regulations. A warrant has been issued by the Peacemakers, and you will comply willingly or be forced to comply. We cannot guarantee your safety if you fight us. Nor can we guarantee the safety of this town."

"Your name?" Tee asked.

"Sergeant Kevin McCallister."

"Well, Sergeant, I do not plan on complying with the warrant. May I speak with the Peacemaker assigned to this arrest?"

"The Peacemaker is waiting for a resolution and does not intend to engage in pointless negotiations. I am sorry, but there is no wiggle room with this. We need an answer now regarding whether you plan to surrender or not."

"Morgana. Issue the order," Tee said, switching the loudspeaker off. "Send in the first wave, please."

"Order given."

Four of the CASPers, two on each side of the squad, swiveled as movement was detected. Tee tensed when the children emerged from the shadows of the town's buildings. The true test of his plan hinged on the mercs seeing the children as children, not as threats.

Tee wasn't so naive that he thought the mercs would be completely fooled. Many a guerrilla campaign on many a planet came down to the young being used as combatants. If the mercs were worth their weight, they'd have targets locked and guns hot.

The children lifted their hands in the air to show they were unarmed. They came at the machines with wide eyes and open mouths, children in awe of what they'd only seen on Tri-V or heard from legend.

"Please step back," one of the CASPers ordered.

Tee tensed further. It could all fall apart within the next seconds if the mercs opened fire.

"They haven't seen the new models," Tee announced. "They've only seen my bucket of bolts. Kids get bored out here in the desert. Let them take a look, Sergeant."

There was no response, but the kids were allowed to get closer without being ripped apart by laser fire or flechette flurries.

Tee struggled to get his breathing under control. He knew it was going to be hard, but he didn't know how hard. His old body felt ready to rebel. Couldn't have that. Slow breath in, slow breath out. Slow breath in, slow breath out.

"The MK 8s are lighter, yeah?" Tee asked. "How much?"

It took a second, but the sergeant replied, "Almost half as much as that old rig you're in."

"That must improve the speed and agility considerably," Tee said. "Especially with the suits being, what? Under eight feet tall?"

"Yes," the sergeant replied. "Mr. Tinkerman, I am sorry, but time to talk is over. Please tell the children to return to the buildings so we may accompany you to the Peacemaker."

"Children? Time to go back. Give the big machines a hug then please retreat."

Tee watched as the kids moved forward and tried to wrap their little arms around the legs of the CASPers. If the government ever wanted a propaganda photo, that would be it. Kids embracing the violence of a merc company with hugs to CASPer legs. It was so damned cute.

"Mr. Tinkerman!" the sergeant exclaimed. "Please, sir. Hiding behind children is not an honorable way to go."

"Children, you are done. Thank you," Tee said. The kids hurried off except one. Lucas. He stood by the lead CASPer, tears welling in his eyes. "Lucas. You did good, son."

"My hand didn't work," the young boy said.

Tee froze inside. What the hell was the kid thinking to say something like that?

"I'll do a full workup on you later, son," Tee said. "We'll get it working properly."

"But you said to touch—"

"Lucas!" Tee snapped. "Go back inside. Now. You did fine."

The kid wiped tears from his eyes, nodded, then sprinted after the others. All the children were swallowed up by an open door where a terrified-looking older woman stood. She ushered them inside then slammed the door closed, leaving Tee and the mercs as the only ones outside.

"What was that about?" the sergeant asked. "Mr. Tinkerman? Please explain what the child was talking about?"

Tee didn't respond. He was busy working through the coordinated connections that began to appear in his displays. Ten CASPers standing before him, but only nine POVs. Lucas was right. His hand hadn't worked when he touched the sergeant's CASPer. That was a problem.

"Dammit," he muttered. "Morgana? Take them down, please."

"And the untethered CASPer?" she asked. "I recommend an immediate strike, Tee. Surprise is the only way to survive against the new model."

"If I fire first then we lose all leverage," Tee said. "Please handle the other nine. I will handle the sergeant."

"Yes, Tee."

* * *

Almost simultaneously, nine of the ten CASPers dropped to their knees. Tee was dialed into their comms so he heard the surprise and panic in the pilots' voices firsthand.

"I'm locked out!"

"Pinplants aren't working!"

"I can't move! My suit is frozen!"

"Crusher? Sarge? What the fuck is going on?"

"Calm the hell down! Now!" the sergeant shouted over the mercs' internal combat channel. "Run full diagnostics! And get the fucking mechanics up here!"

"Mechanics won't help you," Tee interrupted. "Really, nothing will help you, Sergeant McCallister. Your men no longer have control of their machines. But I do. You had to know this would happen."

The sergeant used several choice words and phrases before he cleared his throat. "I was informed that the MK 8s were too new. There would be no way you could penetrate the control systems."

"Remotely? No," Tee said. "That's why hugs were needed. Direct contact."

Tee brought up the subsystems that monitored the CASPers' armor. He isolated the readings to show the sergeant what had happened.

"The armor has become one single receiver/transmitter. With your mecha clustered so close, the signal is amplified a thousand times. It'd take a serious EMP to break the tether. An EMP that would disable, if not destroy, the entire control systems of every machine. Probably not an option you want to explore."

Tee initiated the parrot protocol and raised his left arm. All nine of the tethered CASPers raised their left arms in unison.

"I activate weapons and there will be nothing left of your men," Tee warned. "I'd advise surrender on your end, Sergeant. Then maybe I can speak with the Peacemaker."

Tee watched as the sergeant's heart rate skyrocketed. The man was about to blow a fuse. That could lead to problems. Rage-pissed mercs weren't the easiest to talk to.

"Sergeant, please listen to me," Tee continued. "I do not want anyone harmed. All I want is to be able to speak to the Peacemaker and resolve this without casualties."

"That's what you want?" the sergeant replied, his voice shaking with anger. "You have illegally taken control of company property. The list of charges are adding up with every second—"

"Sergeant. Stop," Tee ordered. "You have no advantage. If I want, I can issue commands to each of those CASPers to dismantle you piece by piece. Or I can have one blow you off the street. I'd rather not. Please have the Peacemaker join us so that I may—"

It was the sergeant's turn to interrupt.

"Kill switches," he said.

"Kill switches?" Tee asked, but it was over before the words left his mouth.

All nine of the tethered and controlled CASPers powered down. Tee tried to stop the process, but his algorithm wasn't designed to control machines that were shutting completely off.

And completely meant completely.

The mecha purged their power cells of all energy. As far as Tee could tell, they couldn't even eject the pilots. The nine CASPers were unbelievably expensive paperweights taking up space in the middle of Main Street.

That left the sergeant to deal with. Tee tried to slow his breathing again, but the idea of fighting a MK 8 with his MK 6 made his nuts shrivel up. But he knew it had to happen.

"Second wave, please, Morgana."

Doors all up and down the street opened and townsfolk slowly made their way out onto the sidewalk. Some looked ready to join in while others appeared to be half a second from fleeing the scene. It didn't matter. As long as they stood where they were, Tee could do all the work.

* * *

"Please return inside," the sergeant announced. "This area is not safe. The Black Coils cannot be held responsible for any injuries resulting from your actions. Please return inside at once."

Tee activated the next part of his plan.

Every cybernetic prosthetic he'd installed came online and he initiated the protocols needed to bring them under his control.

Townsfolk cried out as synthetic skin split wide and the concealed armaments Tee had built into their legs, their arms, their shoulders and hips, their hands, appeared, all aimed at the lead CASPer.

"Jesus Christ, Tinkerman," Sergeant McCallister gasped. "What have you done?"

"What I needed to do in order to protect this town," Tee replied.

There were several gasps and cries as McCallister's CASPer brought up its own armaments and shields. Energy pulsed around the machine as its weapons extended and took aim at the humans waiting on the sidewalk.

"I'll kill half of them before they can even make a dent," the sergeant said. "You don't want that."

"You go for them, and I go for you, Sergeant," Tee said. "Every person here knew their bill would come due someday. Did you know yours would too?"

The CASPer stood stock-still for a moment then the direction of the weaponry shifted to focus solely on Tee's machine.

"You. Me," the sergeant said. "I take you down, and you quit this insanity."

"That works for me," Tee said. His loudspeaker crackled. "Everyone stand down. You did your part. Back inside."

There was some confused grumbling and a few shouts of disapproval from the more gung ho residents, but the vast majority sighed with relief as the hidden components returned into their prosthetics and they were allowed to flee to safety and shelter.

When the street was clear of townsfolk, the two battle machines rushed each other.

* * *

The MK 8 was considerably faster and covered three quarters of the open ground between the machines before they engaged. Tee expected that and was ready.

At no point did he expect the older mecha to be able to take on a state-of-the-art CASPer. Despite his skills with tech, even he couldn't change the reality of superior firepower and simple physics.

Despite the extra weight the MK 6 had, the MK 8 was outfitted with a seriously powerful jumpjet pack. McCallister engaged the jumpjets and sent his CASPer flying into Tee's at full throttle, and alarms rang out instantly as McCallister tackled Tee's CASPer.

Tee grunted as the two machines tumbled down the street. He watched his cockpit buckle around him. McCallister was good. Even as the two machines rolled through the dust and dirt coating Main Street's cracked pavement, the sergeant was throwing punches.

Roll, punch. Roll, punch. Roll, punch.

More alarms rang out, and Tee cut the sound. He could see the flashing lights and warnings in the display; he didn't need his ears to bleed from the aural assault as well.

Finally, the two CASPers stopped rolling. Unfortunately, Tee's was the one on the bottom. McCallister straddled him, which had to be an awkward sight for anyone to behold.

The MK 8's chain gun was shoved dead center of Tee's cockpit, which had lost seal integrity after the third round of roll and punch. The armor would hold for a minute, maybe a minute and a half, but Tee wouldn't see two minutes if McCallister went full auto.

"Surrender," the sergeant barked. "Dammit, Tinkerman! Surrender and call this over!"

"Morgana?"

"Ready on your command, Tee."

"Sergeant, I will surrender. But on one condition," Tee called over the comms.

"Jesus, you're not in any position to negotiate!" the sergeant shouted. "Literally, Tinkerman! I open fire, and that CASPer will be full of your blood mist. Surrender now, and you get to live."

"All I ask is that you open a channel to the Peacemaker," Tee replied, ignoring the sergeant's words. "Let me surrender directly to the Peacemaker, and I promise to submit and leave this machine. I swear on all that's holy."

The sergeant didn't respond. Dead silence filled the street.

Tee waited.

"Fine," the sergeant finally said. "Patching you through now."

There was a crackle of static then, "Tinkerman. You wish to surrender directly?"

"I do," Tee said. He stared up at the MK 8 that still pinned him to the ground. "But first, I need you to call your superior and see if the warrant is still active."

"I'm sorry?" the Peacemaker replied.

The voice had a strange modulation to it, and Tee wondered what species the Peacemaker was. He didn't sound human. If it even was a he.

"Call your direct superior, and see if the warrant is still active," Tee repeated. "I'd hate to surrender if there isn't an active warrant for my arrest."

"Tinkerman, I can assure you the warrant is active."

"Humor me, will ya? I ain't going nowhere."

An alien sigh filled the comms.

"Very well. I will humor you. But this is the last stalling tactic. You have fought well, and in an unconventional manner, so you deserve the respect of this one request. Please stand by."

The comms connection was cut.

"Care if I get out?" Tee asked the sergeant.

"Do what?" the sergeant replied, sounding stunned. "You get out, and you're completely vulnerable."

"Sergeant, I was vulnerable the second that first bounty hunter found me. This here, with you sitting on me like we're eight-year-olds fighting on the playground, is only the coda to a drama that has been going on longer than you've been alive. Get off me and let me breathe, will ya?"

The MK 8 shifted, stood up, and took two steps back. None of its guns ever left their target.

Tee had to manually open the cockpit hatch. He was panting heavily when he finally had enough space to squeeze through and crawl out into the street. He breathed deeply then struggled up onto his knees. Yeah, he was going to feel the bike ride and everything else a lot in the morning.

"I don't get you, Tinkerman," the sergeant said. "Why all of this? Why that show with the townsfolk? Why kill those bounty hunters if you were going to surrender like this anyway?"

"Because I needed you to come," Tee said as he slowly got to his feet. He bent over, hands on knees, took several breaths, then straightened up. "I had to escalate things so the Peacemakers would send in a merc company. Only way the demo could be done."

"I'm sorry, what?" the sergeant replied. "What demo?"

"This one," Tee said. "Third wave, Morgana."

The townsfolk reappeared, their weapons hot. They fired as one and the incapacitated CASPers down the street were knocked front first into the pavement. The street was lit up by more targeted fire, and the mechas began to lose limbs one by one until all that were left were smoking torsos.

"Your pilots are still safe," Tee said, holding up a hand to McCallister. "I was glad you came in MK 8s. Made it easier to keep your people from getting hurt. They are impressive machines."

The townsfolk switched their focus to the sergeant's CASPer.

"Is this where you expect me to surrender?" the sergeant asked.

"No, of course not," Tee said. "This is where you listen."

The comms crackled and the Peacemaker's voice snarled in Tee's ear.

"The warrant has been revoked," he spat. "I do not know how you managed this, Tinkerman, but you are free to go."

"None of us is ever free," Tee replied, "but I thank you for the news. My apologies for the damage done to Black Coils' property. I am sure they will be repaid in full for the inconvenience."

"Will someone tell me what is happening?" the sergeant roared.

"You are being recalled, Sergeant McCallister," the Peacemaker stated. "Consider your contract fulfilled. Payment has been issued in full to your account. Thank you for your time. I am sure the town of Mercury will appreciate if we vacate their area ASAP."

The comms cut off, leaving the MK 8 to stand there.

"You better go," Tee said. "Job done. Done well, I might add. Sorry for the subterfuge."

"I don't even know what just happened," the sergeant said as he turned his CASPer and walked to the fallen machines.

One by one he flipped over the damaged mecha and cracked open the cockpits. Weary and bruised pilots crawled out of their downed MK 8s. Most glared at Tee, but a couple actually smiled before flipping him off. Then they turned and walked away.

The townsfolk watched the mercs until they were out of sight, then they faced Tee, and all cheered.

Tee fell to his knees, exhausted, as the men and women converged on him.

* * *

Belfore popped the bottle of champagne and poured Tee a glass.

"You son of a bitch," he said, grinning from ear to ear. "You filthy rich, son of a bitch!"

"Not me," Tee said, resting comfortably in a brand new recliner in his brand new trailer. "I kept some, but the rest is in a trust for the town."

"Why? You could find a little lady willing to get with an ugly bastard like you, pop out some pups, and leave all of your fortune to 10 future generations, and they'd never have to work!" Belfore exclaimed, downing his glass of champagne before refilling it again. "You have more credits than God! Why, man, why?"

"Why?" Tee closed his eyes. The face of Lucas came to mind, and he smiled. "I'll tell you why. So no child has to grow up and become a killer just to get out of this place. The town will be built up, with solid schools and tech training centers. A decent hospital system. A mayor that doesn't have to kiss corporate ass to get grants in order to keep mothers from becoming whores and fathers becoming junkies. Why? Because the only way you can get a future these days is to buy one. I bought this town a future."

Belfore eyed Tee and nodded. "Because you didn't have one."

"Because I didn't have one," Tee agreed.

"They could have killed you," Belfore said. "Instead of paying you and this town off for that prosthetic tech, or for your tether algorithm, they could have wiped this place off the map."

Tee waved him off. "Nah. By the time they realized that was an option they should be pursuing, I already had the algorithm streaming into their system. Binnig bought the prosthetic tech and the CASPer tether algorithm, but more importantly, they bought the right to bury it all so no one ever discovers the weakness in their product. They'll come up with a program to counter the tether algorithm so no one can ever take control of a CASPer again. They'll also create new sensor tech so augmented locals can't do what Mercury's residents did. No more sneak attacks on mecha."

Belfore laughed.

"You think it's funny. It's not. Do you know what happened that day at Bah'thaim? What really happened?" Tee responded.

Belfore stopped laughing and shook his head.

"Exactly what you saw happen in Mercury. The locals ambushed my company and almost killed us all. Well, they did kill us all, I've just taken a lot longer to die."

"Shit, Tee…"

"Listen," Tee insisted. He set his champagne aside. "They'd studied the CASPers and found weaknesses. Then they developed tech that could target those weaknesses. Not to destroy, but to incapacitate. That culture in Bah'thaim was far from peaceful. Once the CASPers were down, the locals pried those machines open like cans and pulled out the pilots. Then they beat them to death. I was late to the party because of a frozen knee joint coupling. I got there in time to see my friends' heads popped like melons."

"Tee, you don't have to tell me this."

"I do. I will." Tee sighed. "The tether algorithm was more a theory in my head and a hundred lines of simple code in my CASPer's system than a real threat. All it could do was join the CPUs together into a simple hub. But that was all I needed. I initiated the tether, connected the CASPers' CPUs, and sent the command. The mecha self-destructed, taking the city with them. I barely made it outside the blast radius."

Tee chuckled as he ran a finger over his scars.

"By the time I was on the command ship, the legend had begun. I escaped at the first station and used my tech skills to cover my tracks."

"Until now," Belfore said. "Damn, Tee." He lifted his glass to the old man, drank deeply, then set his empty glass down and fixed Tee with a hard stare. "I did my part."

"I killed the code in all the prosthetics," Tee replied. "Those are neither tethered nor can they be controlled by outside sources. Everyone's debts are paid and deals fulfilled."

"Thank you," Belfore said. He stood and stretched. "Can I ask a question?"

"Yes, I targeted you because I knew I could hold your kids as leverage," Tee said without the question being asked. "I'm no saint in this."

"No, you're not," Belfore said. He offered his hand, and Tee stood and shook it. "I hope I never see your ugly face again, old man."

"I hope the same for you," Tee replied with a grin. "Now, get out and go love those kids."

Tee walked him out and watched the man hop into a waiting flyer. Tee shielded his eyes to the rotor wash and was about to go back inside, but he saw a far off trail of dust that was getting closer. He leaned against the doorframe and waited.

The ATV bounced across the ground then came to a stop right by Tee's new porch.

"Mr. Tinkerman!" Lucas cried as he jumped out of the ATV and ran to the porch. "What do I get today?"

"Today, Lucas, we'll put in some new servos so those legs of yours can handle how fast you're growing," Tee replied. He tousled the kid's hair and directed him inside the trailer. He waved to Lucas's mother who was still in the ATV. "It'll take about an hour and a half. You can wait or come back."

"I have some errands to do," the mother replied. "Picking a new home site today."

"Good for you," Tee said and gave her a wave as she whipped the ATV around and sped off.

There was a tinkling crash from inside the trailer.

"Sorry!" Lucas called out. "Nothing's broken!"

Tee laughed and went inside, shutting the door on the hot, dry air of Eastern Oregon, and, hopefully, on the past.

# # # # #

The Start of Something Beautiful
by Kacey Ezell

It was warm and squishy. I did not like it.

"Can't I have a different one?" I whined. My mother smacked me to the other side of the alcove with an idle flip of her second foreleg. I lay stunned for a moment while she left without giving me any further answer. Then the air came back, and I could breathe again, though it hurt.

I untangled my legs and got my feet under me, then stood up as steadily as I could.

It just lay there, watching me.

I'd seen my mother's Flatar, and he didn't look anything like this ugly, hairless thing with the enormous eyes. Hranou was sleekly furred, and laughed all the time. I liked him more than I liked my mother, truth be told. He was the reason I'd looked forward to this day. Today I would meet an infant Flatar.

This, though? This was not what I had expected.

"Look at you," I said, "Who would want to bond with you? Ugly, weak thing as you are! You can't even move properly. I think Mother made a mistake. I think you're supposed to be food. I think, maybe, I'll just eat you."

It kept watching me with those huge eyes. Like all Flatar, it only had two, but they dominated the little face. I watched it back, and took a step toward it.

It was so *small!* I wasn't very large myself, having only hatched a few days ago. I'd barely made it out of the nest alive, too, as I was one of the smaller of my mother's offspring. The first several of my siblings to hatch had been bigger than me, and had immediately begun consuming the rest of us as we emerged from our eggs. I didn't know much at that moment, but I knew I wasn't ready for my seconds-old life to be over, so I fought back, and when that worked, I followed suit and consumed the body of the sister who had attacked me. A few more of those, and I'd managed to fight my way free of the tangle of egg sacs and run. I'd finally collapsed in this alcove.

When mother showed up, I thought for sure I was dead. She was so big, and I was exhausted. And she had seemed so displeased to see me.

"Too small," she'd said. "Should never have survived Hatching."

"But she did," a small, chittery voice had answered. I hadn't dared rise up from my defensive crouch, but my left side eyes caught the movement as a furry head poked up beside Mother's. That was the first time I met Hranou.

They visited me every day after that, and the experience was the same. Mother dismissed me as not good enough, while Hranou laughed and told her not to be so blind. *He* at least seemed to think there was something redeeming about me. So when they told me that they would bring me a Flatar pup, I was very excited.

But, again, this was not what I expected.

I rose up over the thing, staring back at its obscenely large eyes. I suppose it did look a little Flatar-ish…and up close I could see that it *did* in fact have fur. It was just very, very fine and appeared colorless. It was wrapped in some kind of drab cloth, and as I watched, it kicked its back legs free. Then the cold air hit it, and it began to whimper.

Stupid baby. I reached down and pulled the blanket over it again. It kicked it off again. The cries got louder.

"Stop that," I said. I pulled the blanket over it again, to no avail. It just kicked loose and let out an ear-piercing wail that echoed off the stone walls of my alcove.

"Quiet!" I said, keeping my voice a low hiss. "You'll tell my siblings where we are and if you do, then we're both food!"

It just kept crying.

"Stop it right now, or I will sting you," I said. "And then you'll die, and I'll eat you. It's better than being eaten myself!"

More wails.

Something clenched inside me, but I didn't really have much choice. I looked down at that red, wrinkly face all screwed up in a cry and gave it a good jolt with my stinger.

The cries stopped. The tear-filled eyes opened wide, and the little mouth parted with an "O," revealing the little Flatar's milk teeth. Then it did the strangest thing.

It glared at me.

Or rather, *he* glared at me. Since the stupid baby insisted on lying uncovered on the ground, it was pretty obvious he had male sex organs. I don't know how I knew what they were, I just knew.

Kinda like I just knew how to fight, I guess. Small I may be, but I was clearly not stupid.

Unlike the baby, who seemed not to know he'd been stung. He just glared at me, then reached up and rubbed the sting site.

"Why did you do that?" he asked, in a piping voice.

Now it was my turn to stare.

"You can talk?"

"Of course I can talk. All I've heard since I was born was your ranting and raving."

"You were just born?"

"Why else would I be so small? Are you going to eat me now? Because I'm not afraid to fight you."

I laughed, my mandibles clicking together.

"I'm twenty times your size! You're just a baby!"

"So are you! Why else would you be afraid that your siblings would find you?"

"I don't...why are you still alive? That sting should have killed you. I gave higher doses to my bigger siblings when I was Hatching."

"Maybe I'm stronger than you...what are you?"

"Me? I'm a Tortantula."

"That's your name?"

"No, that's what I am. I'm a Tortantula and you're a Flatar. And don't ask me how I know, I just know," I said. Then I paused. "...I don't have a name."

"Why not?"

I shrugged.

"My mother doesn't like me. She said I was too small and should have died in Hatching. Maybe that's why she didn't give me a name."

"That's stupid. You look plenty big to me. I think your mother is an idiot."

That surprised me so much I laughed again.

"What is your name, then?" I asked him. I was beginning to revise my initial impression. He was still small and gross-looking, but this little Flatar pup had guts.

"Sadek," he said. "At least, that's what my father said when I opened my eyes earlier."

"Sadek—"

I never got to finish what I was saying. A whisper of sound warned me, and I barely had time to collapse myself over Sadek and roll to the side before my attacking sibling could impact us with the full force of her charge.

I wrapped Sadek's tiny body up in my center limbs and came up on my feet, stingers ready. My sibling lunged, her forelimb slashing out toward my eyes. I ducked and skittered forward, holding Sadek close to my abdomen. I came up under my sibling and jabbed her with my two front stingers, right at her wasp waist. I heard her gasp, but I was already down and rolling again. I took out her left side legs and managed to get in a bite on her rearmost ankle. She went down with a scream.

"Get up on me!" I shouted to Sadek, and gave him a boost in that direction. I could feel his tiny clawed hands and feet scrabbling to find a seam in my exoskeleton to hold onto. I didn't have much time to worry about him, though, because my sibling was rolling over, and if I was going to survive, I had to beat her *now*.

I leapt, causing Sadek to let out a "meep!" of fear and dig his claws into the seam he'd found. It hurt, but I ignored it. Instead, I focused on coming down hard on my sibling's head with my back four feet. She was rising up, but her front legs toppled back down under my sudden weight, and I managed to scrape my back right stinger across her eyering.

She let out another scream as I felt several of her eyes on the right side burst. Her back legs buckled, and she fell to her abdomen on the stone floor of my alcove. I scrambled backward, getting the bulk of my body positioned over hers as she started to thrash and try to rise again.

"Stay down," I growled, and bit her head off.

Well, not all of it. I *was* smaller than she was. But I did take a big chunk out of the side where I'd pierced her eyes. The taste of her blood filled my mouth as she screamed again. She tasted delicious, like metal and strength.

I ate until she stopped screaming, and then I ate until there was nothing left of her but a few fragments of exoskeleton and her stingers. Only then did I slow down and let out a large burp.

"Wow," Sadek said. His little voice echoed softly off the walls of my alcove, emphasizing the silence. If there had been other siblings lying in wait, they'd decided to go elsewhere.

"Are you all right?" I asked. I hadn't realized that I cared, but suddenly, I did.

"I am," he said. "You're...really good."

"How do you know?" I asked. "You're just a baby."

"So are you," he said, "and look what you did! She was half again your size, and you took her right out! And saved me at the same time! I wish you liked me."

"Why?"

"So I could be your partner! We would be unstoppable! Plus, if you keep eating everyone that attacks you, you're going to be plenty big soon enough."

"I do like you," I said. Again, I didn't realize it was true until I spoke, but there it was. I liked Sadek. He was important.

So be it.

"You do?" he asked. "Why?"

"Because…" I thought about it. Why did I like him? He was small, and ugly. But he was smart, and tough. He hadn't even flinched when I stung him, and…

And he liked me. He was the first being who did. And that was something.

"I like you because you like me. So give me a name, and let's be partners," I said.

"Yeah? All right!" he said. "I will name you…Azah."

# # # # #

Editor's note: "The Start of Something Beautiful" is the beginning of the upcoming novel, "Weaver," by Kacey Ezell and Mark Wandrey. I can't wait. CJK

# # # # #

About the Editors

A bestselling Science Fiction/Fantasy author and speaker, Chris Kennedy is a former school principal and naval aviator with over 3,000 hours flying attack and reconnaissance aircraft. Chris is also a member of the SFWA and the SCBWI.

Chris' full-length novels on Amazon include the "Occupied Seattle" military fiction duology, the "Theogony" and "Codex Regius" science fiction trilogies and the "War for Dominance" fantasy trilogy. Chris is also the author of the #1 Amazon self-help book, "Self-Publishing for Profit: How to Get Your Book Out of Your Head and Into the Stores."

Find out more about Chris Kennedy and get the free prequel, "Shattered Crucible" at: http://chriskennedypublishing.com/

Located in rural Tennessee, Mark Wandrey has been creating new worlds since he was old enough to write. After penning countless short stories, he realized novels were his real calling and hasn't looked back since. A lifetime of diverse jobs, extensive travels, and living in most areas of the country have uniquely equipped him with experiences to color his stories in ways many find engaging and thought provoking.

Find out more about Mark Wandrey and get the free prequel, "Gateway to Union," at http://www.worldmaker.us/news-flash-sign-up-page/

Four Horsemen Titles

Cartwright's Cavaliers

Asbaran Solutions

Winged Hussars

The Golden Horde

Peacemaker

A Fistful of Credits

For a Few Credits More

The Good, the Bad, and the Merc (Coming Soon)

* * * * *

The following is an
Excerpt from Book One of the Revelations Cycle:

Cartwright's Cavaliers

———————————————

Mark Wandrey

Available from Seventh Seal Press

eBook, Paperback, and Audio Book

Excerpt from "Cartwright's Cavaliers:"

The last two operational tanks were trapped on their chosen path. Faced with destroyed vehicles front and back, they cut sideways to the edge of the dry river bed they'd been moving along and found several large boulders to maneuver around that allowed them to present a hull-down defensive position. Their troopers rallied on that position. It was starting to look like they'd dig in when *Phoenix 1* screamed over and strafed them with dual streams of railgun rounds. A split second later, *Phoenix 2* followed on a parallel path. Jim was just cheering the air attack when he saw it. The sixth damned tank, and it was a heavy.

"I got that last tank," Jim said over the command net.

"Observe and stand by," Murdock said.

"We'll have these in hand shortly," Buddha agreed, his transmission interspersed with the thudding of his CASPer firing its magnet accelerator. "We can be there in a few minutes."

Jim examined his battlespace. The tank was massive. It had to be one of the fusion-powered beasts he'd read about. Which meant shields and energy weapons. It was heading down the same gap the APC had taken; the tank was heading toward Second Squad, and fast.

"Shit," he said. He had to stop them.

"Jim," Hargrave said, "we're in position. What are you doing?"

"Leading the charge," Jim said as he jumped out from the rock wall.

* * * * *

Find out more about Mark Wandrey and "Cartwright's Cavaliers" at: http://chriskennedypublishing.com/imprints-authors/mark-wandrey/.

* * * * *

The following is an
Excerpt from Book 1 of The Kin Wars Saga:

Wraithkin

Jason Cordova

Available from Theogony Books

eBook, Paperback, and (soon) Audio Book

Excerpt from "Wraithkin:"

Prologue

The lifeless body of his fellow agent on the bed confirmed the undercover operation was thoroughly busted.

"Crap," Agent Andrew Espinoza, Dominion Intelligence Bureau, said as he stepped fully into the dimly lit room and carefully made his way to the filthy bed in which his fellow agent lay. He turned away from the ruined body of his friend and scanned the room for any sign of danger. Seeing none, he quickly walked back out of the room to where the slaves he had rescued earlier were waiting.

"Okay, let's keep quiet now," he reminded them. "I'll go first, and you follow me. I don't think there are any more slavers in the warehouse. Understand?"

They all nodded. He offered them a smile of confidence, though he had lied. He knew there was one more slaver in the warehouse, hiding near the side exit they were about to use. He had a plan to deal with that person, however. First he had to get the slaves to safety.

He led the way, his pistol up and ready as he guided the women through the dank and musty halls of the old, rundown building. It had been abandoned years before, and the slaver ring had managed to get it for a song. In fact, they had even qualified for a tax-exempt purchase due to the condition of the neighborhood around it. The local constable had wanted the property sold, and the slaver ring had stepped in and offered him a cut if he gave it to them. The constable had readily agreed, and the slavers had turned the warehouse into the processing plant for the sex slaves they sold throughout the Dominion. Andrew knew all this because he had been the one to help set up the purchase in the first place.

Now, though, he wished he had chosen another locale.

He stopped the following slaves as he came to the opening which led into one of the warehouse's spacious storage areas. Beyond that lay their final destination, and he was dreading the confrontation with the last slaver. He checked his gun and grunted in surprise as he saw he had two fewer rounds left than he had thought. He shook his head and charged the pistol.

"Stay here and wait for my signal," he told the rescued slaves. They nodded in unison.

He took a deep, calming breath. No matter what happened, he had to get the slaves to safety. He owed them that much. His sworn duty was to protect the Dominion from people like the slavers, and someone along the way had failed these poor women. He exhaled slowly, crossed himself and prayed to God, the Emperor and any other person who might have been paying attention.

He charged into the room, his footsteps loud on the concrete flooring. He had his gun up as he ducked behind a small, empty crate. He peeked over the top and snarled; he had been hoping against hope the slaver was facing the other direction.

Apparently Murphy is still a stronger presence in my life than God, he thought as he locked eyes with the last slaver. The woman's eyes widened in recognition and shock, and he knew he would only have one chance before she killed them all.

He dove to the right of the crate and rolled, letting his momentum drag him out of the slaver's immediate line of fire. He struggled to his feet as her gun swung up and began to track him, but he was already moving, sprinting back to the left while closing in on her. She fired twice, both shots ricocheting off the floor and embedding themselves in the wall behind him.

Andrew skid to a stop and took careful aim. It was a race, the slaver bringing her gun around as his own came to bear upon her. The muzzles of both guns flashed simultaneously, and Andrew grunted as pain flared in his shoulder.

A second shot punched him in the gut and he fell, shocked the woman had managed to get him. He lifted his head and saw that while he had hit her, her wound wasn't nearly as bad as his. He had merely clipped her collarbone and, while it would smart, it was in no way fatal. She took aim on him and smiled coldly.

Andrew swiftly brought his gun up with his working arm and fired one final time. The round struck true, burrowing itself right between the slaver's eyes. She fell backwards and lay still, dead. He groaned and dropped the gun, pain blossoming in his stomach. He rolled onto his back and stared at the old warehouse's ceiling.

That sucked, he groused. He closed his eyes and let out a long, painful breath.

* * * * *

Find out more about Jason Cordova and "Wraithkin" at: http://chriskennedypublishing.com/imprints-authors/jason-cordova/

* * * * *

Made in the USA
Coppell, TX
20 February 2021